# SPARROWHAWK

## Book Six
## WAR

A novel by

# EDWARD CLINE

*For Paul and*
*On to Hyperborea!*
*Ed Cline*
*20 Dec 2006*

MacAdam/Cage
155 Sansome Street, Suite 550
San Francisco, CA 94104
www.macadamcage.com

Library of Congress Cataloging-in-Publication Data

Cline, Edward.
Sparrowhawk–war / by Edward Cline.
     p. cm. – (Sparrowhawk ; bk. 6)
ISBN-13: 978-1-59692-198-6 (alk. paper)
ISBN-10: 1-59692-198-6 (alk. paper)
1. United States–History–Colonial period, ca. 1600-1775–Fiction.
2. United States–History–Revolution, 1775-1783–Fiction.  I. Title.
II. Title: War.
PS3553.L544S6275 2006
813'.54--dc22

                              2006019869


Manufactured in the United States of America.

10 9 8 7 6 5 4 3 2 1

Book and jacket design by Dorothy Carico Smith

Cover painting: John Paul Jones on The Bonhomme Richard during its
battle with the Serapis, September 23, 1779. (Artist unknown).
Courtesy of The New York Public Library / Art Resource, NY

# SPARROWHAWK

## Book Six
## WAR

A novel by
# EDWARD CLINE

MacAdam/Cage

"To hold an unchanging youth is to reach, at the end, the vision with which one started."

Ayn Rand, in *Atlas Shrugged* (1957)

# CONTENTS

# Foreword

The engine of tyranny is a blind, indifferent juggernaut, insensible to reason, justice and equity, and so necessarily inimical to them. It matters not the good intentions of the hand that launches it into the affairs of men. Once started, it moves almost of its own volition, corrupting, consuming and destroying everything in its path. It is a fundamentally nihilistic phenomenon. Its power is both centripetal and centrifugal, on one hand drawing its potency from that which it can corrupt; on the other, crushing or flinging aside the incorruptible.

The juggernaut of Parliamentary supremacy collided with the American colonies' incorruptible sense of liberty, which could be neither crushed nor flung aside. The result was a spectacular explosion: the American Revolution. That explosion was neither necessary nor foreordained. The colonies could have submitted to that supremacy, and existed for a time in a haze of semi-legality, occasional concession, and dependent prosperity. But British-Americans valued their liberty and were willing to claim it whole, come what may. Therefore, the clash between them and the legislative authority of Parliament could be postponed but never resolved. The colonials would not allow their claim to unabridged liberty to be corrupted. In the course of that political transfiguration, they became Americans.

Their original complaint was two-fold: against Parliament, which legislated their shackles; and against King George the Third, who by colonial charter had been empowered to protect them from Parliamentary avarice, caprice and the shackles of economic incarceration. The "patriot king" failed to protect them. He did not suggest, originate, or author any of the legislation subsequent to the Declaratory Act meant to bind and pillage the colonies without limit; it was merely his royal pleasure to sign it, although it was within his power to veto it. But, he would be a king, and so he surrendered that executive power to the exigencies of an empire of which he wished to be sovereign, but which, in fact, was Parliament.

This was the nature of the events that followed repeal of the Stamp Act and passage by Parliament of the Declaratory Act in 1766. By 1774, many of the men who had lent their hands to the imposition of an imperial design had come and gone since that repeal and passage. George Grenville. Gone.

Thomas Whateley, his protégé in power. Gone. Charles Townshend, author of the notorious Townshend duties. Dead and gone. And so many more enemies of liberty, as well.

As good as gone had been William Pitt, Lord Privy Seal, whose ministry followed Rockingham's in 1766, but whose maladies and unpredictable temperament so debilitated him that Augustus Henry Fitzroy, third Duke of Grafton, and First Lord of the Treasury, became its effective head instead. Grafton, not by his own temperament hostile to the colonies or particularly ambitious, by ineptitude let his party and ministers establish colonial policy and enact legislation that increasingly worsened tensions between the colonies and Britain. His ministry was the epitome of malign neglect.

Uneasy with his political impotence, Grafton resigned, and went into opposition against the next ministry. Later, in Lords, he consistently voted against stringent measures against the colonies. He opposed the ministry he had sworn to support.

This was that of Frederick Lord North, a childhood friend of George the Third, who had succeeded Charles Townshend as Chancellor of the Exchequer, or prime minister, on the latter's death in 1767, and was now First Lord of the Treasury. He was a nondescript, pliant, unimaginative man content to be merely a member of a cabinet, not its head. Frequently, over his twelve-year tenure as prime minister, he begged his royal patron for permission to resign from the onerous post. George would not grant him that relief. Out-maneuvered by both king and party in their quest for conquest of the colonies, his ministry would oversee their loss, and be blamed for it.

In Virginia, gone also were Lieutenant-Governor Francis Fauquier, and his short-reigned successor, Norborne Berkeley, Baron de Botetourt. Both had died here, Fauquier in 1768, after ten years in the Palace, Botetourt, in 1770, after only two.

They in turn were followed by the epitome of royal ambition, hauteur, and insolence: John Murray, fourth Earl of Dunmore, Viscount Fincastle, Baron of Blair, of Moulin, and of Tillymount. He arrived in Virginia in September of 1771, after a brief but notorious reign as governor of New York. That man, suspected many Virginians, planned to remain and create his own empire. Liberty-minded burgesses noted the Governor's appetite for land, particularly in the Ohio Valley and the lands west of it, notwithstanding the Proclamation of 1763. They also noted his arrogance, bad temper and royally colored presumptions, which were of an abrasive character heretofore unknown to the Virginians in their governors. His wife, Lady Dunmore, and their three daughters and three sons arrived on the *Duchess of Gordon* at Capitol Landing on the York River in February of 1774, and settled themselves in the Palace in Williamsburg with every intention of becoming a royal family by proxy.

It was to be a brief residence.

By the time the Earl's family arrived in Virginia, and since repeal of the Stamp Act and passage of the Declaratory Act in 1766, Parliament had enacted nearly twenty acts specifically designed to harness the North American colonies, only one of which was repeal of the Townshend duties on all imported British manufactures, except on tea. These were supplemented by Orders in Council approved by the king, to the same end.

The Revenue Act of 1766 followed the Declaratory Act, and disguised new controls with paltry concessions on imported cloth and molasses. The Revenue Act of 1767 imposed the Townshend duties on paint, lead, paper, tea and other imports, and legalized writs of assistance for indemnified customs officers. Accompanying it was an act for creating an American Board of Customs Commissioners, whose purpose was to make customs collection more efficient.

In the same year, Parliament passed an act that suspended the New York Assembly for refusing to vote funds to supply occupying British troops. The Assembly eventually capitulated and voted £2,000. Alexander McDougall, of the Sons of Liberty, was imprisoned for contempt of the Assembly for having called the action a betrayal. In 1768, an Order in Council established four vice-admiralty courts to deal with smuggling and violations of the Revenue Acts and Navigation Laws.

General Thomas Gage garrisoned Boston in October 1768, with two regiments and artillery. Later he moved his headquarters there from New York, replacing Thomas Hutchinson as governor. In 1769, in response to the rebellious behavior of colonials, especially in Massachusetts, Parliament passed resolves that basically treated resistance to its authority as treason, such treason to be determined by trials in Britain. The next year, Parliament repealed the Townshend duties, except on tea.

In Boston, one March night in 1770, a mob of men and boys spoiling for a fight taunted British soldiers sent to protect a sentry and abused them with snowballs, sticks and insults. Someone in the mob yelled, "Why don't you fire, damn your eyes!" This the soldiers did, mistaking the taunt in the noisy chaos for an order from their commanding officer. Three of the mob were killed, and two mortally wounded. In late October John Adams defended the commanding officer, Captain Preston and six soldiers, securing acquittal for Preston and four of his men, while two soldiers were branded on their hands and released.

More efficient revenue collection, aided by the navy, only precipitated more resistance. In March of 1772, the Customs schooner *Gaspee* ran aground in Narragansett Bay, was boarded by Rhode Islanders, its crew roughed up and set ashore, and the vessel burned. Its captain was arrested by a local sheriff. It was the third cutter to be destroyed by rebellious colonials. A royal commission of inquiry was named with the power to send those responsible to Britain for trial. The commission adjourned in 1773 for lack of evidence and a paucity of willing witnesses.

News of the commission and its powers caused the creation of permanent intercolonial committees of correspondence among the various colonial legislatures and patriotic organizations to share intelligence of colonial and British actions. In that year all colonial legislatures but those of North Carolina and Pennsylvania voted to establish such committees. In Virginia, Patrick Henry, Thomas Jefferson, and Richard Henry Lee in March were named by the House of Burgesses to its committee.

In the meantime, the Tea Act, passed in April of that year, which gave the East India Company a monopoly on the sale of the beverage to the colonies, was having predictable consequences. Company stock, in which the government had considerable shares, had fallen in value because of a surplus of tea created by the smuggling of Dutch tea by colonials to bypass the duty on it. The Act gave the Company the ability to undersell even smuggled tea and the power to appoint its own consignees in the colonies. The Company contracted merchantmen to deliver half a million pounds of tea to a select group of merchants in New York, Philadelphia, Boston and Charleston.

On the night of December 16th, Samuel Adams signaled a party of men disguised as Mohawk Indians to board the *Dartmouth* and two other merchantmen docked in Boston, and dispose of the tea in their holds. Three hundred and forty-two chests of it were dumped into the harbor, worth over £10,000. The raiders took care not to damage any other goods or property on the vessels. As with the appointed stamp collectors nearly a decade before, most consignees up and down the seaboard were compelled to resign their commissions. "Tea parties" were thrown in many other ports, and tea that was not destroyed was stored in government warehouses, later to be sold to raise funds for the Revolution.

In late January 1774, Benjamin Franklin, agent for Massachusetts and still working to avert a war between the colonies and the mother country, was summoned before the Privy Council and called a man without honor and a thief by Solicitor-General Alexander Wedderburn.

The occasion was the publication in the colonies of ten letters by Thomas Hutchinson, then chief justice of Massachusetts, and Andrew Oliver, the colony's secretary, to Thomas Whateley, the late George Grenville's protégé, between 1767 and 1769, giving advice on how to deal with the contentious colonies. Franklin had obtained the letters from John Temple, former surveyor-general of customs for North America and now a member of the Board of Customs for America. Franklin sent the letters to Speaker Thomas Cushing in Massachusetts with the proviso that they not be published. Samuel Adams nevertheless published them, resulting in the House petitioning the king for Hutchinson's and Oliver's removal from office.

The petition arrived in London about the same time as news of the Boston Tea Party. To avoid a second and perhaps fatal duel between Temple, who was originally suspected of having sent the letters, and Thomas Whateley's brother, Franklin admitted that he had sent the letters to Boston. After his verbal reprimand by Wedderburn, Franklin was dismissed from his office of deputy postmaster general for America. His treatment by the government convinced him that no reconciliation was possible between the Crown and the American colonies. In March, he left his comfortable rooms on Craven Street near Westminster, never to return.

John Wilkes, however, had returned from his exile and was still contesting against a stubborn Parliament for the seat for Middlesex. He was £4,000 richer from a successful suit against Lord Halifax, who signed the general warrant against him over the *North Briton* affair years before. He was then elected alderman, sheriff and now was lord mayor of London. He was incurring fresh Tory wrath by speaking in defense of the American colonies. John Horne Tooke, an ex-clergyman and founder of the Society for Support of the Bill of Rights, broke with Wilkes in 1771 and founded the Constitutional Society. He, too, championed the American cause from beginning to end.

Ironically, William Murray, Earl of Mansfield, chief justice of the King's Bench, who advocated the most stringent measures against the rebellious American colonies, in 1772 found for the freedom of a slave, James Somerset, not to be returned by his owner to Virginia for punishment. Somerset had run away from his visiting master in the metropolis. Mansfield's decision was misinterpreted by slaves in the colonies as an endorsement of abolition, and moved countless numbers of them to enlist in British ranks at the outset of hostilities years later.

England was host to other ironies, as well. In 1769, James Watt patented a steam engine, using a separate cylinder to condense steam, producing rotary motion for the first time. Henry Cavendish discovered hydrogen in 1766, Daniel Rutherford nitrogen in 1772, and Priestley oxygen in 1774. Richard Arkwright patented the water frame to spin cotton in 1768. The Royal Society was abuzz over the experiments of Luigi Galvini, who in 1771 produced an electric current in frogs' legs.

Thomas Arne was still laboring to digest composer Christoph Gluck's preface to his 1766 opera "Alceste," in which the German expressed a philosophy of musical and dramatic elements. Portraitist Joshua Reynolds, president of the Royal Academy of Art, in 1774 would soon be challenged by Thomas Gainsborough. Phyllis Wheatley, a young black poetess from Boston, conversant in geography, history, classical literature, and astronomy, traveled to London in 1773 with her master and was a sensation as the "sable muse." A collection of her verse, *Poems on Various Subjects, Religious and Moral*, was published the same year. Her work was praised by Washington, Franklin, and Voltaire, and by critics in London and America.

Samuel Johnson, still basking in the glory and proceeds of his *Dictionary* and royal pension, in 1774 published a pamphlet, *The Patriot*, as election publicity for his friend Henry Thrale, member for Southwark and a staunch Grenvillite who wished to retain his seat in the new Parliamentary elections. Johnson, a Tory and no friend of America, would pronounce in his screed:

"He that wishes to see his country robbed of its rights, cannot be a Patriot. That man therefore is no Patriot, who justifies the ridiculous claims of American usurpation…We have always protected the Americans; we may therefore subject them to government….That power which can take away life, may seize upon property…it may therefore establish a mode and proportion of taxation…."

It was beyond his grasp that it was already another country whose inhabitants' rights were being usurped, and that the Boston Port Act, together with its accompanying Coercive Acts, passed by Parliament earlier that year, was fundamentally an act of war against it.

Meanwhile, in that other country.....

# Chapter 1: The Moment

The fog had cleared, and the moon and stars were brilliant, and the white sails of faraway ships on an invisible horizon were sharp and almost luminescent as they glided past on their grand, unknown errands. In time, there was a hint of a horizon in the east, and the stars began to fade in deference to a sun still unseen. It was a quiet, precious time, when he knew that the world was not so much focused on him, as he was on the world, through a special lens in his soul. It did not strike him without warning; he had experienced this moment often before. At times, however, the clarity was stressed by an ineluctable intransigency. This was such a time.

Jack Frake stood in a space on the side of the bluff that overlooked the York River on a far edge of his property, a rough length of bare rock hewed by rain and wind ages ago and sheltered beneath a cluster of black locust trees above. He had discovered it shortly after his arrival at Morland as an indentured felon. He claimed it as a kind of sanctuary, a place to pause and think and reflect in the necessary closure of solitude. He came here after long periods of living and dealing with other men. It served the same purpose as the cubbyhole on the cliff of Cornwall he once repaired to as a boy.

He was thinking of the words he had written about the colonies and England last night in his study:

"What cleaves us is as wide as the ocean that separates us. It is a distance between souls, between minds, between ways of looking at things. That ocean helped to create that cleavage. It removed our ancestors for a time, as it once removed us, from the immediate concerns and power of kings and the ambitions of men who would be kings, and allowed us to see what could be accomplished without them. It allowed us to see clearly — those of us who bothered to see — what was necessary for men to live their lives unfettered by allegiances to the arbitrary and superfluous. For it not only obliged us to rely on our minds to master nature here, but to look at ourselves in a cleaner, more radical light, and to see what was possible within ourselves and without. And, once we had done that, that other cleavage in soul and mind between the nations became as much a fact as the ocean, and there was no returning to an ignorance of it. Once that was done, we could bow no more, neither to nature nor to kings nor to men who would be kings...."

There was one word, or one brief expression, that would identify one side of that cleavage and explain why no reconciliation with the other was possible. The answer still eluded him, after all these years. The problem did not distress Jack Frake. He knew that the answer would come to him, in time. His soul, or his being, shone with a certitude as bright as the rising sun.

Etáin's constant reminder to him over the years had been that so many men had yet to catch up with him. The years had passed, and now it was no longer a matter of so many men. Nor was it a matter of the colonies catching up. Rather, it was a country that was beginning to catch up with him, a country that was beginning to see itself as such, and not as a collection of deferential dependents. A series of crises and protests, intervals of escalating violence and retaliation, were convincing his fellow Americans that no reconciliation was possible with men who intended to rule. He had known it for years. No, he thought. For decades.

Such certitude does not breed vanity in a man. Pride, yes. Impatience, yes. Even a persuasive, unanswerable arrogance. But, never vanity.

He reflected now on the years that had passed, on all the events that had populated them, the events that had impelled his fellow Americans closer to his state of certitude. Closer, but not quite there. Not quite able to grasp the sense that, regardless of the wisdom or ignorance of the men in power, regardless of their intentions or benevolence, those men were either the blind or willing pawns of an idea that would not die until it had been challenged and refuted.

Gone were many of the men in power who had contributed to the widening cleavage. George Grenville. Gone. Thomas Whateley, his protégé. Gone. Charles Townshend, who wished to relieve England of the burden of taxes by imposing them on America. He had read that Townshend, when he proposed his duties in the Commons, laughed at the idea of a distinction between internal and external taxation, and had sneered at the gallery that as a consequence he did not expect a statue to be erected in his memory in America. He was gone, too, as well as most of his taxes, except the one on tea. And it was that remaining tax that was going to undo the empire.

Gone, too, were many of liberty's friends. Wendel Barret, who died with his *Courier*. Dogmael Jones. Murdered in London. Thomas Reisdale, who three years ago succumbed to his exertions during a Herculean effort to produce pamphlets excoriating the establishment of three more vice-admiralty courts and a Parliamentary assertion that resistance to authority constituted treason.

Reisdale had already received a polite reprimand from Lieutenant-Governor Fauquier for being the author of a Maryland-printed pamphlet attacking not only the Townshend duties, but the article appended to it that empowered the establishment of a civil list. "Liberty can be rebuffed by the cowardly and the meek and the indifferent," he had written in his last pamphlet, "and even suffer attrition among its champions, but its value can never be refuted. It can be denied men, but never erased from their minds once they have tasted it. We have indeed tasted it, but now must find the courage to keep it."

Jack remembered his last words to Reisdale after reading the pamphlet one evening in the lawyer's home. "What you are saying is that we will not suffer being branded transported felons of another kind, and taken back across the ocean to certain death."

Reisdale had laughed and slapped his head. "God, man! I wish I had thought of that!"

The next morning a servant found him dead in his library. In the course of the mourning for the passing of its resident "antiquarian," Caxton was astounded when Edgar Cullis, also a lawyer, read Reisdale's will, and revealed that the late scholar had left his entire property to John Proudlocks, his student in law. By Virginia law, Proudlocks, as an Indian, could not own such property. But no one contested the will, not even Reisdale's distant relations. As a tribute to his mentor, Proudlocks renamed the property "Sachem Hall."

Proudlocks had then chosen to accept Jack Frake's offer to underwrite a journey to London to study law at the Middle Temple. "If I am to understand the coming troubles," he told his friend and employer, "I must see their source myself. I cannot be satisfied with my book-learning. I must observe the enemy on his ground, before I engage him on my own."

Jack Frake agreed with his purpose and reasoning. Through a transaction with Hugh Kenrick and his father, he wrote a draft on Swire's Bank in London to sustain Proudlocks during his sabbatical. He also agreed to oversee Sachem Hall during Proudlocks's absence. Garnet Kenrick even found him rooms in London near the Middle Temple, and he was a frequent guest of the Kenricks in Chelsea. Proudlocks was due to return any day now, most likely on the *Sparrowhawk*. Jack Frake had received a letter from him three months ago, reporting that his studies were completed.

Four years ago John Ramshaw had sold his interest in the *Sparrowhawk* and retired to Yarmouth, Norfolk. "I have sold my place in Norfolk on the Roads," he wrote Jack Frake, "and have consented to advise the ship-builders here for a consideration. Parliament has taken the joy out of the business, and I confess I am at sixes and sevens about how to confound its repeated imprecations." He corresponded regularly with Jack Frake about commerce and politics. The *Sparrowhawk* itself had been careened and refitted twice since repeal of the Stamp Act and the merchantman was now commanded by Elyot Geary, the son of one of Ramshaw's ship husbands in London. The new captain and master had retained the secret compartment in the vessel that churned out counterfeit Crown forms, allowing Jack and Ramshaw and other York River planters to keep their heads above the waters of an indebtedness desired and imposed by the Crown.

Jack was almost envious of the northern colonies, for they had picked up Patrick Henry's torch of 1765 and with it singed the Crown at every opportunity. He had been kept apprised of events up north by Hugh, whose network of correspondents there sent him regular letters about the tumult and rebellion among the citizens and in the various legislatures. Otis Talbot and Novus Easley in Philadelphia, and other friends and acquaintances of Hugh sent him a constant stream of letters. And now there were two Virginia *Gazettes,* competing with each other to see which would broadcast the latest news first.

And, as nominal head of the Queen Anne Sons of Liberty, Jack Frake received many letters himself from the heads and secretaries of similar organizations throughout the colonies.

The events recurred with ever-growing force, like the waves that first lapped, then scoured, and finally swept over the sandy banks of the York as a prelude to an approaching storm, working with the moon and tides. The moon in this instance was the idea of liberty; the tides, the tumult.

It was coming to a climax. Soon the storm would burst.

\*   \*   \*

On that same morning, the 24th of May, a lone figure paced back and forth in the piazza of the Capitol in Williamsburg. Another figure, a statue, seemed to watch the figure below with benign unconcern.

The life-size statue was of white marble, poised atop an ornate white marble pedestal nearly the height of the statue, enclosed by an iron balustrade. It stood in the middle of the covered walkway that connected the House of Burgesses with the General Court and Council chambers. Its back was to the doors to the Council, and faced the doors to the House, as though to remind emerging members of the House of the Crown's authority. The figure could have been mistaken for that of George the Third; it was actually that of a lowly peer, the late Norborne Berkeley, Baron de Botetourt, Governor of Virginia.

The figure struck a regal pose without being imperious, the left arm akimbo, its hand clutching the cap of Liberty; the right arm extended, its hand holding a roll of parchment, a symbol of Virginia's original charter. It was the classic stance of a contemporary orator. The head was pudgy, from cheek to nose, but seemed to be grafted to the torso of a thinner man who happened to have a prominent paunch. Its expression was fatherly, untroubled, and serenely stern at the same time. It sported a court wig, and meticulously detailed court robes whose fur-lined hem was bunched near the figure's heels and calves.

The pedestal had required perhaps nearly as much labor to sculpt as the statue itself. It was lavishly ornamented with intricate decorative orders and motifs of acanthus leaves, papyrus, garlands and shells. On one side of the pedestal was inscribed a florid dedication to Botetourt, with the date the General Assembly had voted to "transmit his illustrious character to posterity," in July 1771. Beneath it were the words: "Let wisdom and justice preside in any country, the people will rejoice and must be happy." On the back of the pedestal were the carved figures of Britannia with her shield and spear, and America with her bow and quiver, each holding an olive branch over an altar marked "Concordia."

The statue had been the commission of Richard Hayward, a prominent London sculptor, and was erected in the piazza exactly a year ago. It had cost £950, exclusive of shipping, insurance, and other charges, plus the pay of the mason who had accompanied it from London to supervise its installation.

The burgesses had commissioned the statue of Botetourt as a measure of their lingering esteem for a gentle, royal master. But, many had thought, it was curious that a lord known to be hostile to the colonies' assertions of right would be honored as an ideal governor, and not Francis Fauquier, his predecessor, who had occupied the Palace for ten years and had been nominally sympathetic to Virginia's straits.

Botetourt had been a practiced, effective courtier, devoted to the Crown. When he spoke, burgesses imagined themselves being swaddled in rich, warm, comforting velvet. Few burgesses and Council members could resist his smoothly imperial though cordial manner. He dissolved the Assembly after the House had passed three resolutions in protest of the Townshend Acts, but was forgiven with the understanding that he was merely doing his duty. His smile had assured even his committed foes in the House that he meant no harm and bore them no malice, and that he would work to reach rapprochement between the colony and the mother country.

Botetourt had been precisely the kind of governor that Hugh Kenrick and a few other burgesses believed every man should fear. Instead of being a courtier to the king, he had played courtier to the Council and House. Botetourt, said Hugh occasionally during the Governor's tenure, represented a delusion, a false alternative. Hugh's dislike of him was buttressed by information that his father had sent him, that Botetourt had voted for the Stamp Act and against its repeal, and had spoken effectively in Lords on those subjects.

Botetourt had been accommodating and pleasant company, yet "royal" in every sense. He had such an effect on Virginians that he distracted them from the contentions between the colonies and the mother country, convincing Virginians that reconciliation was not only possible but a pleasant state of affairs to achieve, as well. But, he was just as capable of dissolving the General Assembly as was Fauquier. Botetourt had dissolved the Assembly of 1770 over resolutions adopted by the House in protest of resolves adopted by Parliament, which asserted Parliamentary authority to the extent that it would tax the colonies in any case whatsoever and take to London for trial any colonial charged with treason.

The sets of resolutions contradicted each other. Botetourt resolved the contradiction by dismissing the House. It was common action taken by most royally appointed governors in the colonies.

Many had been seduced by Botetourt's easy civility. But, now they were burdened with what Hugh Kenrick had also warned the House about years ago, a veritable lord-lieutenant answerable to no legislature and scornful of colonial presumptions of self-governance, Lord Dunmore, Botetourt's successor and the second royal appointee who literally began to govern. This man had dissolved the Assembly twice so far, and prorogued it as often as it pleased him. It was likely he would dissolve it again, perhaps today, perhaps tomorrow.

It had taken most colonials nearly a half score years to grasp that it was fruitless to attempt compromise or reconciliation with a wolf. A wolf, after all, sustained itself on prey. The colonials did not believe themselves prey, but neither did they believe that the Crown was closed to compromise, nor did they believe that it would deny them their rights as Englishmen. They expected reciprocity. What they got over the years were growls and gestures of bellicosity and repeated attempts to clap them in regulatory and economic irons.

Hugh Kenrick paused in his pacing now and then to glance up at the statue. He had voted against the resolution honoring Botetourt and against the "unanimous" resolution to erect the statue at "public expense." He was not by nature a cynic, but he could not decide if the expensive gesture was an expression of sincere affection on the part of his fellow burgesses, or a sly act of mollification. Then he stopped and faced the statue. He thought to himself: Wendel Barret deserved a statue. And Dogmael Jones. Thomas Reisdale had earned at least a medallion. But this man? He still felt a touch of disgust with the House for having decided to honor the memory of Botetourt. "People who are not happy, certainly do not rejoice," he muttered thoughtfully to himself.

"That is not an answer the Crown our Sphinx would wish to hear, Sir Oedipus," said a voice from over his shoulder. "Prepare to be eaten."

Hugh turned to see the smiling, freckled face and green eyes of Thomas Jefferson, burgess for Albemarle.

"And what answer to the riddle of Crown purpose would you give, Mr. Jefferson?" asked Hugh. "One that would cause it to sheathe its claws and teeth?"

"I am tempted to say no answer but a sincere and prolonged curtsy of gratitude. Clearly, it does not like the sound of our voices. And then, instead of ending itself, as it did when Oedipus gave it the correct answer, ours would grow in magnitude and consume us all."

"Well, perhaps it is not truly a sphinx, but a lion in disguise."

Jefferson laughed. "Now, there are some claws and teeth!"

The piazza was becoming busy with arriving burgesses and Council members, and the pair descended the steps in the bright late-morning sun to talk in private on the clipped lawn nearby. Hugh had corresponded with Jefferson over the years since repeal of the Stamp Act, and with other burgesses who fought for Patrick Henry's resolves nearly ten years ago. Their letters dwelt not only on politics — their exchanges on the "Farmer's Letters" pamphlets of John Dickinson revealed some disagreement on a few issues, and on the letters of "Junius" in the London *Public Advertiser*, they both agreed their author was someone in the War Office — but were mutually informative and served as opportunities to address and articulate ideas that demanded more and more of their intellectual labor. They agreed that a British-American empire was feasible, and took heartened interest in an idea circulated by Joseph Galloway of Pennsylvania, that of a "Plan of Union" of Britain and the colonies.

"Today's sitting promises to be very interesting," said Hugh. It was ten-thirty. He had encountered Jefferson earlier at breakfast in Marot's Coffee-house, where the tall red-head had confided that he, Patrick Henry, Richard Henry Lee, Francis Lightfoot Lee, and George Mason planned to persuade Robert Carter Nicholas, the treasurer, to introduce a resolution calling for "a day of prayer, fasting, and humiliation" on the first of June in support of Boston, closed by Parliament by the Boston Port Act until the destroyed tea had been paid for. Hugh promised to vote for the resolution, although, he said, "I do not believe that fasting, prayer, and humiliation are proper substitutes for action."

Jefferson now answered, as they strolled leisurely on the grass, "Interesting, and necessary. Colonel Washington will distract the Governor and travel with him tomorrow to the Porto Bello lodge to talk land and inspect the place. He will not mention the resolution. You know that land is a favorite subject of His Excellency, and whets his appetite at the expense of his caution. This will allow Mr. Nicholas to introduce our resolution without interference, and allow the *Gazettes* to print it and broadsides for distribution."

"You realize what are the likely consequences of that resolution," said Hugh.

"Very likely Lord Dunmore will want to demolish the House with his own hands, once he has heard of it. But more likely he will simply dissolve the Assembly."

"One cannot much exaggerate His Excellency's temper. I can picture him now, taking our chamber apart, brick by brick. He has the strength, constitution, and temper of a bull. A Scotch bull, no less."

"This is true. He may also be intemperate enough to cancel the ball that Mr. Randolph offered in Lady Dunmore's honor. That would be a shame."

"And a slight," Hugh added. He sighed. "Now we are blessed with two Charlottes, at public expense," he remarked, referring to the Governor's wife and the wife of George the Third. He had nothing to say on the subject of the ball that was scheduled to be held at the Capitol in a few days.

Instead, he observed, "It is curious how things come in pairs. A week before Lady Dunmore's arrival, there arrived in Yorktown some five tons of copper half-pence from the Royal Mint for circulation here. After years of pleading for specie, it is too little, too late."

Jefferson shook his head and laughed in irony. "They rob us of pounds, and reward us a vail of pennies! They nullify our rights, but begrudge us a few privileges! There's no irony in that, sir. That is the way of our particular sphinx."

"Mr. Henry began his career with a penny," mused Hugh, referring to the Parson's Cause of 1763. "At times, liberty can be had very cheaply. Think of what he purchased us for that penny."

"What?" asked Jefferson.

"Virginia's name at the top of the roster of moral courage. Like a modern Prometheus, he brought the fire of liberty to the continent."

"I cannot dispute that fact," Jefferson answered.

They turned to other matters, such as Hugh's recent visit home and his trip to France, Holland, and Prussia. But conversations these times, even on the most mundane matters, always returned to politics, as it did now. Hugh described his one-month visit to the Continent. Jefferson asked him about conditions there. "Are they as bad as I've heard?"

"Yes," Hugh said. "The poverty and misery in France are unimaginable. One must wear blinders to avoid being made ill by the sight of the low state of the people there. They exist under the crushing weight of an iron monarchy, legalized corruption, an indifferent aristocracy, and a rapacious clergy."

"Everything we protest now," mused Jefferson. "I understand that their *parlement* is a mere ormolu, and absolutely useless."

"If revolution ever occurs there, sir," warned Hugh, "the people will behave like a maddened beast, and destroy good as well as evil, innocent as well as guilty lives. Our sense of *right* is alien to them. The philosophers and educated men there exist in a society effectively separate from the people, and so very little of their wisdom is communicated to the populace. Instead, I believe they will strike out at anything or anyone who reminds them of privilege, or who does not appear downtrodden."

Jefferson chuckled. "Well, in that event, if one were present to audit such a revolution, one would be wise to sport ragged clothes and a soiled face, and feign a natural ignorance of books."

"Speaking of parliaments and ignorance," Hugh said, "my father writes me that, beginning with the new Parliament in November, its business will now be allowed to be reported in the press without penalty. The public there will now become informed of that body's machinations. A fellow by the name of Luke Hansard has secured that post in the Commons. Lords, however, is still claiming private privilege."

"That is progress of some kind," said Jefferson. "It tempts one's hope that our differences can be settled amicably." After a moment, he said, "I have been reflecting on your reservation concerning our resolution, that you do not believe fasting, prayer and humiliation are proper substitutes for action. I must reply that any other action would mean rebellion, and we are not ready for...civil war."

Hugh merely smiled, and hoped he disguised the sadness in the smile. "I know."

They stopped to watch the arrival of other burgesses, and nodded in greeting to many as they trooped singly or in pairs into the House. Then the grave, rotund figure of Robert Carter Nicholas emerged from a carriage and walked briskly past them into the House. Jefferson glanced around and spotted Henry and the two Lees with whom he had discussed and drafted the resolution. He nodded to them, then turned to Hugh. "You will please excuse me, sir. Our 'monk' has arrived." He turned and joined the other men and followed Nicholas into the Capitol.

Hugh glanced at his pocket watch. In fifteen minutes, a House servant would ring a bell, calling the other burgesses inside to begin the day's business.

He had watched Jefferson mature over the years, from a law student to burgess, from a youth finding his way and his career, to one of the leading spokesmen against Crown power. He observed the older burgesses who fought the younger burgesses for the leadership of the House. But, it was a losing battle for what Patrick Henry had called the "Tidewater grandees." Events precipitated by Crown actions had overtaken them, and they had no choice but to agree with the younger burgesses, or be branded timid fools. Some of them were being impelled, quite against their will, to recognize the perils. Most of the younger burgesses, including Hugh, strode boldly in that direction, heedless of the strife and war that were sure to accompany any move to independence. The older burgesses crept inexorably to the same conclusions, and joined in the same protests and gestures of defiance. Richard Bland, George Wythe, even the Randolphs were inching painfully and reluctantly along an irresistible path of logic.

Governor Dunmore had given the timid and bold alike a warning, when he addressed the burgesses in the Council chambers early in May, after the House had reported to him the election of the Speaker, Peyton Randolph. "I hope that your resolutions on the various matters," he had said that morning, "may be influenced by prudence and moderation." It was a veiled threat to dissolve the Assembly at the least hint of rebelliousness over the Boston Port Act. The House in turn, in its courtesy address to the Governor, promised that "every resolution we may be pleased to adopt, will be marked with that prudence and moderation, which you are pleased to recommend."

Prudence and moderation! mused Hugh. The very virtues he assailed the first time he had spoken in the House years ago! But, the colonies behaved like a collection of separate nations. He could not see them uniting without dissolving shortly thereafter in an embittered fanfaronade. Any unity among any number of them, or even among all of them, could not last, because they would then begin to view each other with suspicion and even rancor, just as the nations in Europe did. He did not fault them for that likely contention; each was a unique entity with its own history and special future.

But, Virginia had shown the way, some ten years ago. Now Massachusetts was the leader; Georgia, the laggard. And in all the continental colonies between them, except the Floridas and Quebec, rebellious incidents had recurred as often as bubbles in boiling water.

A clerk appeared in the piazza and rang the bell to call the loitering burgesses into the House. Hugh joined the file of representatives and found a seat on the top tier, on the opposite end from Edgar Cullis, the other burgess for Queen Anne County. There were nearly a hundred burgesses present today; only fifty had arrived on May 5th at the opening of this sitting.

With the mace on the clerk's table, the House proceeded to deal with a number of prosaic petitions — from both *Gazettes* to be appointed the official public printer by ballot, from the minister of Shelburne Parish in Loudoun County to receive the same salary as a minister in a neighboring parish, from residents of King William County to settle a land dispute — and recommend them to the appropriate committees to work into bills or resolves. Time was taken to hear Robert Carter Nicholas read an order committing the House to a day of prayer, fasting and humiliation on the first of June, "devoutly to implore the divine interposition," and for the House to attend a service at Bruton Church that day to hear a sermon on the subject. The order received near unanimous approval, and arrangements were made to have it broadcast to the public.

The day ended with a petition from farmers in Dinwiddie County to prohibit the importation of distempered cattle from North and South Carolina, which were infecting Virginia cattle. The petition was referred to the Committee of Propositions and Grievances to work into a bill. With that concluding business, the House adjourned until the next morning at eleven o'clock.

On the night of the next day, a Wednesday, a footman found tacked to a gate to the Palace a broadside of the resolution. He took it down and gave it to Captain Edward Foy, Dunmore's private secretary, who in turn presented it to His Excellency the next morning at breakfast.

That very day, as the House voted on amendments to the bill prepared by the Committee of Propositions and Grievances to increase the salary of the minister of Shelburne Parish, the burgesses received an abrupt though not unexpected summons from Lord Dunmore to present themselves in the Council chamber. Peyton Randolph led a group of burgesses outside past the statue of Botetourt, and into the Council chambers to climb the stairs to the Council's meeting room.

There Lord Dunmore scowled at the group as it assembled around the great table, at whose head he sat, the fingers of his stubby but strong hands tattooing on the cloth to mark the time and his patience. His Councilors, bracing for an outburst by either the Governor or the burgesses, looked at anything else in the sumptuously appointed room but at His Excellency or the burgesses.

On the table before the Governor was a copy of the broadside. It appeared to have been crumpled up in anger, then smoothed out. When the burgesses removed their hats and looked attentive, the Governor picked it up and waved it once in the air.

"Mr. Speaker and gentlemen of the House of Burgesses," he said in a thick Scottish burr, "I have in my hand a paper published by order of your House, conceived in such terms as reflect highly upon His Majesty and the Parliament of Great Britain, which makes it necessary for me to dissolve you. And you are accordingly dissolved." With a brief but accusing glance at Washington, who stood behind Randolph, he sat back in the great chair to await a reply.

Peyton Randolph nodded once. "Your pleasure, your excellency."

At his silent signal, the burgesses parted to make way for the Speaker, then turned to file out of the chamber behind him and back down the stairs into the late afternoon sun.

# Chapter 2: The Governor

An impromptu meeting of the House leaders beneath the statue of Botetourt resulted in a decision to reconvene the body in the Apollo Room of Raleigh Tavern further down the boulevard to discuss immediate action, and to troop en masse to that place once George Wythe, Clerk of the House, and his charges had finished their journal entries and saw to other formalities for ending the session.

Hugh Kenrick, who had had to settle for standing with other burgesses on the stairs that led up to the Council chamber to hear the Governor dissolve the House, stood apart from groups of them on the Capitol grounds and observed the predictable division of the representatives: the foot-dragging conservatives in several knots to one side, dominated by Peyton Randolph, Richard Bland, and George Wythe, while the "radicals" and "hot heads," dominated vocally by Patrick Henry, and physically by Colonel Washington, gathered in clusters on the other. He smiled in sad amusement at the predicament of the blondish Edmund Pendleton, who seemed to hover between both groups, wanting to be associated with both. The man was still settling the estate of John Robinson, who died in 1766 leaving the colony in debt; Pendleton seemed more conscientious about that onerous task than about his political principles.

Edgar Cullis emerged from the Capitol and approached him. "I am departing for Caxton," he said with petulance. "I will not participate in the outlawry I have heard proposed here."

Hugh shook his head. "That is unfortunate, sir," he replied coldly. Cullis was the sole burgess to speak in the House against Nicholas's resolution, claiming that it would "damage the natural affection between the colonies and the mother country." It was rumored that Cullis or John Randolph, the Attorney-General and the Speaker's brother, had personally informed Lord Dunmore of the resolution, either verbally or with a copy of the broadside. "You will miss the chance to note what will be said by this band of outlaws, and to report that to the Governor, as well."

Cullis bristled at the insinuation. "That is a lie! I know for a fact that it was — " Then he stopped, realizing that Hugh had not actually accused him of being an informer. Instead, he remarked, "I am surprised that you voted for the resolution, Mr. Kenrick. You are not known to much fast or pray, and humiliation is not to be found in your catalogue of virtues."

"Thank you, sir," Hugh replied, by way of agreement. "Short of storming the Palace and demanding an apology from His Excellency, it is the only action open to us, for the moment. But, you are right. I shall not do much fasting or praying, and I do not believe in the efficacy of humiliation in any circumstance. Least of all, this one."

Edgar Cullis merely smirked.

Hugh then asked, "Do you recall the awful poem that appeared in one of the *Gazettes* celebrating Lady Dunmore's safe arrival with her three sons and three daughters?"

"Vaguely," said Cullis, wondering what his fellow burgess was leading up to. He relented in his hostility to Hugh to add, "If I correctly recall, there were several odious eclogues dedicated to her and her children. I confess I blushed in shame, knowing they were penned by Virginians."

"No more than I, Mr. Cullis. Well, allow me to appropriate some lines from the most offensive one. 'Your lovely offspring crowd to his embrace, while he with joy their growing beauties trace. The tears of pleasure from each cherub flows, all eager pressing round about his knees.'"

Cullis sniffed in amazement. "I am surprised that you remember such bad verse."

"Remarkably bad and exceptionally good lines etch themselves permanently in my mind. However, many in the House remind me of tearfully pleased cherubs pressing against the Governor's knees, though I can't imagine a less appropriate description of Lord Dunmore. He can hardly tolerate knee-embracing burgesses, never mind children."

"You insult his character, Mr. Kenrick, and impugn the loyalty of so many of your colleagues."

"I have neither insulted his character, nor impugned the loyalty of my colleagues." Hugh grinned in mischief. "What do you think, Mr. Cullis? I'm willing to believe it was Mr. Randolph who informed the Governor. After all, his and the Speaker's father was the only knighted Virginian on the whole continent. Perhaps his son yearns for the same distinction. I'm certain His Excellency could arrange it."

"That is a slur on his character, as well, sir."

"No, that is mere speculation on the man's base motive, for base it must be." Hugh shook his head. "After all these years, Mr. Cullis, you have yet to learn this about me, that I do not voice opinions. I make observations."

Cullis sighed in impatient defeat. "Then you will observe my departure. Good day to you, sir." He turned and strode across the Capitol lawn in the direction of a tenement house he was staying in for the duration of the session.

Hugh shrugged. "Departure observed, sir," he said to himself.

Later he joined the parade of burgesses — eighty-nine of them out of the one hundred and three who eventually attended the dissolved Assembly — down Duke of Gloucester Street to the Raleigh Tavern. No Council members were among them. Hugh was joined by Patrick Henry and Colonel Robert Munford, burgess for Mecklenburg. Together they had worked in 1765 to have the Stamp Act Resolves adopted and broadcast throughout the colonies. "Well, Mr. Kenrick," queried the burgess from Hanover, "what do you think His Excellency will do now? I am sure that he waited for the least excuse to be rid of the Assembly for the year."

"Perhaps he will retire to Porto Bello again to pick peaches," quipped Hugh with contempt.

Munford laughed. "It has a fine orchard, and good pasture land. I'm sure His Excellency beat poor Mrs. Drummond down on her asking price for the place."

"Doubtless he will dun the colony for the construction of the stone bridge he threw over Queens Creek to Capitol Landing," speculated Henry. "I heard talk that he has filed an action in the York County Court to collect reimbursement for the cost."

"He is a descendent of the Stuarts," Hugh said by way of explanation, "and, like them, believes absolutely in the range and permanence of his privileges."

"And the rightness of his power."

"I have heard that he plans to confront the Shawnees and Ottawas if they rise up, which will likely happen this summer."

"Who would answer his call to arms? And how could the Assembly now approve an appropriation for an expedition against them, unless he called a new Assembly?"

"The western militia would answer," answered Munford, "without even the promise of pay. They would be in the direst jeopardy, and would not need coaxing."

As Hugh talked with his colleagues, he did not observe two horsemen who had stopped to watch with astonishment the long string of burgesses as it threaded down the boulevard. He joined the other burgesses in the spacious Apollo Room at the Raleigh, where, under Peyton Randolph's moderation, debates ensued about what the proposed association should advocate, whether or not a regular general congress of the colonies was feasible, and whether or not to call for a convention of Virginia burgesses to choose delegates to such a congress, should one be agreed to by other colonies.

The General Court was also in session, and so the town was more crowded than usual with visitors. The two horsemen, one of whom held the reins of a third mount that carried their baggage, were not the only spectators of the parade. Merchants, farmers, planters, lawyers, and families who had come to Williamsburg on business for the "public times" and market days, also lined the boulevard to watch the irregular procession and to speculate or comment on its cause.

One of the horsemen remarked to his companion, "It may be difficult to find lodging here, Mr. Manners. This place is nearly as busy as Charleston." He glanced up Duke of Gloucester Street, and nodded. "That must be the legislature, up there." Even as he watched, the Great Union flag was yanked down from its pole atop the cupola and belfry. The stranger frowned, and thought there must be some connection between that event and the procession to the large, white-painted tavern in front of them. "I say, sir," he hailed one of the spectators, who looked like a merchant, and pointed to the Raleigh with his riding crop. "That place seems to be very popular. What is happening here?"

The gentleman looked up at the stranger. "Well, sir, you could say that the Raleigh there is the other Capitol chamber for our burgesses. You see, the Governor dissolved the House not an hour ago over some matter that displeased him, and that's where those fellows usually go to meet again when they're in a funk. Third time in as many years, I believe."

"I see. Thank you, sir." The stranger abruptly smiled when he recognized one of the faces among the burgesses. He suppressed a compulsion to hail that man, permitting himself only a chuckle. He turned to his companion. "Well, let us find lodging, Lieutenant. The day grows old, and we must see some of this town, and rest before we present ourselves to Lord Dunmore tomorrow."

Captain Roger Tallmadge and Lieutenant William Manners reined their mounts around and rode back down the boulevard. After several inquiries, they eventually found lodging in the establishment of Gabriel Maupin, a tavern and hostelry on the corner of Market Square. Two burgesses who elected not to join their colleagues at the Raleigh Tavern had claimed their riding chairs and mounts and departed for home. No one who observed the newcomers knew that they were serving officers in His Majesty's forces, for they wore civilian clothes and did not identify themselves or state their business in town.

In the course of the debates in the Apollo Room, Hugh asserted, and many former burgesses nodded in agreement with him, that "the colonies may exist in harmony as separate nations, if you will allow it, and perhaps combat Parliament's encroachments on our liberty with the general congress under consideration here, united temporarily under one *ad hoc* political affiliation." A boycott of East India tea was also debated, as well as what other British goods should be banned from importation and use until the Boston Port Act and other abuses had been repealed.

During a break in the debates, Hugh and Jefferson again talked privately outside, in the rear of the tavern, both wanting to escape for a while the stifling atmosphere inside and breathe the fresh spring air. Jefferson shared his thoughts on a paper he was planning to write on the complaints of the colonies addressed to the mother country, "absent our usual expressions of servility — I know you will appreciate that aspect of it — in the event a convention is decided on. A summary view of matters that outlines the salients of our arguments and explains our resistance to Crown depredations."

Hugh also confessed a plan to pen another pamphlet. "When one thinks hard on it, the requirement by the Board of Trade and Privy Council of a suspending clause in all our legislation was not so niggling a matter as we were want to think. It was simply an overture, if you will, a precursor to a summary suspension of all our rights. It is no surprise to me that the Crown has never relinquished or relaxed the requirement. Its refusal to surrender that rule should have been a warning."

Jefferson nodded in agreement, then sighed. "So many things are clearer in hindsight."

"Yes. And now we must acquire the strict habit of foresight."

"Are so many men capable of that habit?" wondered Jefferson.

"I know of one or two," Hugh answered. He was thinking of his friend, Jack Frake.

*     *     *

The next morning, in the Palace, Captain Tallmadge and Lieutenant Manners were made to wait before being granted an audience with the Governor. The captain eventually presented his commission to Captain Edward Foy, Dunmore's personal secretary, who appeared about an hour after they announced themselves to the footman who admitted them. He queried Foy about yesterday's parade of burgesses. Foy replied brusquely and unconvincingly that he was ignorant of the cause, and left to report the presence of the visitors to His Excellency.

The two officers resigned themselves to another hour of inactivity, and decided to amuse themselves by identifying the many kinds of muskets that decorated the ceiling and walls of the marble-floored foyer, and so were startled when Foy returned almost immediately and escorted them from the Palace to the Governor's offices in the annex next door. Foy asked the lieutenant to wait in another room while he escorted Tallmadge upstairs to the Governor's office.

"From the War Office?" blurted Dunmore contemptuously after the introductions had been made and drinks poured. "Rather premature of the *member for Plymouth*, I would say, to begin assessing native strengths! And, pessimistic, I might add!" His rancor was reserved for William Wildman, Irish Viscount Barrington, Secretary-at-War since 1765. Irish peers could not sit in the House of Lords, but could hold seats in the Commons. He handed back over his desk Tallmadge's commission, which was signed by the Earl of Rochford, Secretary of State for the Southern Department, and Lord Barrington.

Taking it and resuming his seat before the Governor's desk, Tallmadge replied, "General Gage's reports to His Majesty, the Privy Council and the Board of Trade have moved the ministry to seek a better grasp of the situation here, and to better appreciate the strengths and weaknesses of the militia. I understand that on Lord Barrington's recommendation, the government are preparing for worst contingencies, your lordship." After a pause, he added, "I will submit my report to General Gage in Boston, and a copy to Lord Barrington, as well."

"Well, better they all worried about those devils the Shawnees and Ottawas, and I would commend them for the foresight if they had! The filthy beasts are about to burst upon the settlers in the west! I felt obliged to take action on my own initiative." He paused to smile in confidence. "I have taken steps to claim that western part of Pennsylvania occupied by the proprietors of that sorry colony to the north. I have even arranged to appoint a governor of it. Of course, the Shawnees and Ottawas will dispute the annexation, and no doubt the Pennsylvanians." He chuckled. "Well, if His Majesty and the Council can redraw the boundaries of Quebec clear down the Mississippi, they can settle our differences with Pennsylvania by ceding Virginia what it lawfully claims, and redraw those lines, as well!"

Tallmadge shifted in his chair and replied as tactfully as he could, "But, your lordship, I had thought that the Proclamation of ten years ago ordered that part of the continent closed to settlement."

Dunmore shrugged. "To private settlement by these land companies, yes. However, it does not bar the Crown from formulating its own designs on the region." He sighed. "But, private settlers aplenty there are there, and scruffy shirtmen and other English barbarians by the score. They range over the area at will, poaching as they like and clearing land for farms and provoking the savages. But, the region is ripe with possibilities in land and trade. Why, George Washington and I discussed the idea of a joint venture there just the other day, while his fellows in the House were plotting the offense for which I dissolved them. Mr. Washington — a likeable fellow, but at times too full of himself, I would say — likes to be called 'colonel,' a grave disappointment to me. Seems his task was to keep me away from the Capitol while they did their dirty work." He snorted once in the lingering humiliation of having been duped.

Tallmadge kept his thoughts to himself. He had heard of the Earl's appetite for land. It was in conflict with the Crown's. He doubted that the ministry would approve of the "initiative."

Dunmore's brow furled in curiosity. "What is your regiment, Captain Tallmadge?"

"None at present, your lordship," replied Tallmadge. "I am on detached service. However, I was ensign with the 20th Regiment of Foot under Major General William Kingsley at Minden, and brevetted lieutenant at that action. Since the war, I have served in a number of diplomatic posts, and taught artillery at Woolwich. Also, I have sat for Bromhead in the Commons for eight years." He took a sip of the wine that a servant had poured him, then added, "Lord Barrington himself interviewed me for my present mission, and pressed upon me its importance."

"And why do you and your aide present yourselves to me out of uniform?"

Tallmadge, sensing that Dunmore was a little vexed by this fact, attempted some humor. "Because we do not have a regiment behind us, your lordship." Dunmore simply stared at him, unamused. "We judged discretion the better part of valor, in this instance, given the troubles here, and chose to make our inquiries in gentlemen's garb. In the course of our journey from South Carolina, we learned that in many venues, His Majesty's scarlet was most assuredly not welcome. We could not have gathered as much information as we have, had we flaunted our presence and purpose."

Dunmore hummed in concession to his guest's reasoning, but still did not like it. "Well, Captain Tallmadge, what *have* you learned?"

Tallmadge sighed. "I can offer you an assessment, your lordship, in lieu of an incomplete report from my journal notes. It is that if there is trouble, the army will have a difficult time reestablishing authority and order."

"Why do you think so?"

"I would say that fully one-third of the armed populace here would be enough to tax the army's abilities, and that this one-third would outnumber our forces by five to one. And, it would not adopt regular methods of fighting. One-third of the populace seem to be loyal, and the remaining third indifferent." Tallmadge felt obliged to qualify his assessment. "What the militia lack in discipline and order, they would make up in numbers and tenacity. In any military action, our army might prevail and carry the field, but it would be at obscene cost."

Dunmore waved the assessment away with a hand. "You over-worry the situation, Captain. I see the solution immediately. The loyal third could be treated as allies of our forces, and the navy could blockade the ports here to prevent arms or munitions from reaching any rebels."

"If they are merely rebels, your lordship. The Americans here would fight on, no matter what steps were taken to debilitate them. And, they are quite adept at smuggling, as you doubtless know." After a pause, Tallmadge ventured, "I believe it would be a fatal error to regard them as mere rebels."

"Why do you say that, sir?"

"They would be fighting for their liberty. That one word has rung in our ears all the way from Savannah."

Dunmore snorted again and shook his head emphatically. "All this talk of liberty and such, it's just a moonraker for the merchants and planters here! Makes 'em feel good about their treason and grasping ways, and lets 'em bedazzle the noodles of the common folk! High talk by and for low men, that is all it is! Don't let it scruple your assessment, Captain."

"No, your lordship. Of course, not." Tallmadge exercised the discretion he had boasted of, and refrained from reminding His Excellency that it was not a London mob that the army could be faced with, rioters who could be dispersed with a single volley from grenadiers and a charge by sword-wielding cavalry, but an army largely and ably officered by men who had seen service in the late war.

Dunmore continued briskly, "If there is trouble, Captain, it will be easily dealt with. No doubt, when you passed through North Carolina, you learned how Governor Tryon dealt with the Regulators there some years ago, when they stirred up disaffection in the hills and challenged Crown authority. He marched out and thrashed them in battle, then executed many of their leaders even as the smoke cleared. Mr. Tryon now governs New York, and I daresay he will act with like verve if there is trouble there. I will act with no less authority, at the first sign of rebellion."

After another gulp of wine, the Governor continued. "It's intolerable, the way these people behave and talk! To listen to them, you would think they resided in France, or Prussia, or Spain and were pauperish wretches who never had two coins to rub together! And, the seditious literature they pass around among themselves! Outrageous, libelous twaddle! But the London papers republish it as though it were amateur poetry!" The Governor paused to lean forward over his desk and shake a finger at his guest. "Mark my words, Captain, when the Crown moves to settle scores, English as well as colonial necks will snap by the dozen, there won't be enough hemp for all the hangings, and there will be weeping and wailing and the gnashing of teeth in many a house on both sides of the Atlantic!"

"Yes, your lordship." After a moment, Tallmadge recovered from this tirade and replied, "We did hear of the Regulator episode." He did not add that he had also heard that the Regulators' chief complaint was that they were not represented in that colony's legislature, and as a consequence were taxed and harassed without any legal means of redress.

Dunmore looked mischievous. "You know, I was Governor of New York for a while, as well, but received instructions to occupy this Palace after less than a year there, while Governor Tryon was reappointed to New York. I offered to trade posts with him, but he turned me down. I think I got the better part of the bargain!" When he saw the courteous but blank smile on his guest's face, he said, "Well, you have journeyed through one-half of Virginia, Captain. What is your assessment of trouble here?"

"Again, your lordship, I judge the populace here to be divided in thirds. I do not expect that assessment to much change as we go on. If your lordship could provide me with whatever numbers he might have on the militia he commands, it would greatly aid my purpose."

"I see. Well, my secretary, Captain Foy, can oblige you with those. See him about it. What are your immediate plans?"

"Lieutenant Manners and I will tarry here for a few days, collecting what information we can, then continue our journey northward, through Maryland, Pennsylvania, New Jersey and New York. We will end our survey in Boston, where we will report to General Gage."

"Is he expecting you?"

"Doubtless he has been apprised of our presence and mission and expects our arrival."

"How did you come here? By way of Norfolk? There's a loyal town!"

"True, your lordship," Tallmadge replied, remembering all the Scottish merchants in that city, which was far larger than Williamsburg. "We passed through it, and Portsmouth, as well. We took a ferry from Surrey to Jamestown and arrived yesterday afternoon, and found lodging. We came into town just as the burgesses were reassembling at a tavern here."

"Recalcitrant beggars, those men!" exploded the Governor, hammering a pile of papers before him with a closed fist. "Why, do you know that I tried to get them to pass a bill that would pay Captain Foy a salary from public funds, as was a proper arrangement? They dug in their heels and refused to! Now I must pay him from my own chest! Well, that will change! Many things will change! The government, I hear, are getting up enough bottom to rewrite all these bothersome charters. Massachusetts is just the beginning! There comes a time when a parent must cease coddling his bairns. I told my oldest son that, just the other day, as a warning."

Tallmadge let the Governor rant on again about the ingratitude of the colonies and the treason of the agitators, and nodded mechanical agreement at the appropriate times. He thought he could sympathize with the legislature that defied such an abrasive person. Abruptly, Dunmore's features softened. "Well, Captain! Enough business for now! Would you and your lieutenant be my guests at supper tonight? I am certain, that after so much time in the saddle, you must be starved for decent fare and civil company."

Tallmadge had planned to frequent several of the town's taverns and coffeehouses over the next two days to pick up intelligence, beginning today, and knew that the sooner he and his aide saw to it, the sooner he could make his way to Caxton to see his friend and brother-in-law, Hugh Kenrick. But, he could not decline an invitation from the Governor, for whom he was developing a marked dislike. He said, repressing a sigh, "We would be honored, your lordship. Thank you."

# Chapter 3: The Intriguers

Notwithstanding the renewed ill-feeling between the Governor and the burgesses, the ball held in the Capitol in honor of Lady Dunmore the evening of the next day was a grand, well-attended affair, enjoyed by all. The burgesses' chamber was filled to capacity, overflowing into the adjoining hallway and even to the piazza. Many burgesses still in town had brought their wives with them in anticipation of the event. Minuets, court dances, country-dances, reels and jigs were performed. The town musicians hired for the occasion seemed to be in tireless fettle. The event served to reassure everyone that all was well and that no clash of wills could ever have occurred.

Most attending Virginia ladies found that Lady Dunmore, even after having birthed seven children, was still a charming, attractive, and genial woman; a few of them remarked in private that she deserved a "better circumstance," that is, a worthier, more admirable, and certainly a less boorish husband. They reserved judgment on the royal couple's three older sons (the youngest had been left behind in England) and three daughters, who also were present at the festivities; they seemed well-behaved but a tat condescending, especially Lord Fincastle, who was attending the College. "As full of himself as his father," whispered many.

Beneath the gaiety, gossip and music, however, ran an undercurrent of concern and regret — regret that such an occasion might never be experienced again, and concern about the Governor's intentions. The concern was more often discreetly expressed by men in the piazza than in the crowded chamber, away from all the inquisitive ears there.

Near the statue of Botetourt, two gentlemen, one young and one old, discussed the Governor and his actions. "He claims that the Pennsylvania government is lax in protecting the western settlers from the Indians," observed the younger gentleman in reply to the other's indiscreet and somewhat ribald remark about the Governor, "and that the settlers there would likely prefer to be governed by Virginia. He commissioned a chap by the name of John Connolly to act as governor there."

"Prefer to be governed by Virginia?" scoffed the older. "Say, rather, by Lord Dunmore! And how long would that happy union last, once they got to know His Excellency's means and aims?"

"He plans, I am told, to rename Fort Pitt after himself, and will send Connolly to occupy it."

"The hubris of him! What has he in mind? A war between our two colonies? What blindness! What temerity! His Majesty won't stand for it, not for a moment! He'll intervene, and then perhaps we'll be blessed with a wiser governor and more just laws!"

The first gentleman demurred a reply to this latest aspersion, and instead effortlessly redirected the conversation. "I have heard that a Shawnee chief by the name of Cornstalk intends to wipe out our settlements along the Ohio, and perhaps carry a war into western Virginia, as well. The Governor could only do his duty and call for the militia in answer."

"Perhaps he must, sir! But, wouldn't that fit nicely into the Crown's designs, to keep us penned east of the mountains?" said the older gentleman with bitterness. "I know it would please His Excellency no end! Going to war with the Shawnees and Ottawas up there would distract our attention from his designs here, and cast him unfairly in the role of savior and hero! Then his *earlish* prerogative would allow him the pick of patented lands that others have already paid for! Royal robbery, I say! We know what he's up to!"

Again, the first gentleman ignored the calumny. He accounted for it by supposing that his companion owned patented land west of the transmontane, which he could now not even lawfully visit, let alone exploit. He delicately raised the topic of a possible rebellion against Crown authority. "I am told that he opines that any rebels would be pinched betwixt loyal subjects and indifferent ones, not only here, but throughout the colonies. I am afraid he may be correct in that assessment. One may observe no unanimity in dissent in the colonies."

"Did he now?" The other gentleman looked quizzically into his companion's face. "Zounds! You are a mine of information, sir!" He paused to take a generous sip from the stoneware mug he held. "Speaking of western settlers, what of our own? No new counties may be created by the Assembly without Crown approval, and no approved county could be represented in the Assembly! More robbery!"

The other gentleman ventured ruefully, "Why, they would be *virtually* represented in your Assembly, just as nine-tenths of the populace of Britain are represented in Parliament."

"Bosh! What *Assembly*?" dismissed the second gentleman with a wild gesture to the House chamber with his mug, whose contents flew out and splashed to the ground. "They are intent on committing *liberticide!*"

It was the first time the other gentleman had heard the term, though he needed no definition of it. He knew that his companion was emboldened in his incautious remarks by the potent rum punch being served this evening. Drunk for a penny, nearly under the table for tuppence! But angry, as well; perhaps rightfully so, he reflected. Still, one thing he had learned during his years as a diplomatic attaché, was that diligent sobriety in many upright men was an iron door whose key was often simply a few judicious bumpers of excellent wine. Skillfully, liberally, and patiently applied, spirits could nearly always open that door to bare the soul and most secret thoughts of the most guarded courtier, confidant, or envoy.

With a smile he gently removed the mug from the gentleman's hand and placed it on a corner of the pedestal. Like most of the other drinking vessels being employed at the ball this evening, the mug sported a cameo silhouette of John Wilkes on one side, and "No. '45" on the other. He supposed that the presence of these mugs was a subtle act of defiance by the burgesses, but one apparently lost on the Governor. His companion did not seem to notice the courtesy. "Who, sir, is committing liberticide?"

"All the men upholding Crown authority!" The gentleman again studied his companion more closely with squinted eyes, and inquired, "Who *are* you, sir? I don't recollect your name or viz."

The handsome, equally well-attired gentleman smiled and replied, "Roger Tallmadge...of Boston. I am touring Virginia in search of a purchase, perhaps a tired plantation I might revive."

"Well, you'd better hurry, sir, before our Governor beats you to it!"

Tallmadge nodded to his companion. "I should agree with you about that, I am told, as well." He smiled again and asked, "And you, sir? With whom have I the pleasure of speaking?"

"Reece Vishonn, sir!" boasted the gentleman. "I am master of Enderly plantation in Queen Anne County!" Vishonn put a friendly hand on Tallmadge's shoulder. "If you plan to pass through my parts, please accept my hospitality! I must warn you, though, there is no property there for sale!"

"Thank you, sir. If I happen in that direction, I will surely pay a call." The captain was tempted to ask his companion if he knew Hugh Kenrick, but decided against the query.

Much of his "hearsay" was communicated to him by Lord Dunmore over supper at the Palace the previous evening. He had been personally invited by the Governor to the ball tonight. He had accepted, half hoping that Hugh might be in attendance. But, his friend was not here.

And, he had accepted because his estimation of Lord Dunmore's character and governing policy was growing more and more negative. The man seemed prone to churlish vindictiveness. He was certain that to have refused the invitation would have sent the Governor into high dudgeon. He concluded that the man's character was so overbearing and sensitive to abrasion that, had he declined the invitation and incurred the man's animosity, it was likely that the Governor would have broadcast his identity as a serving officer in the Crown, and his mission, as well.

After a few more minutes of conversation with the planter, whom he left leaning against a column in a besotted but pensive mood, Tallmadge returned to the ballroom and took his leave of the Governor and his lady, thanking them for the invitation and informing His Excellency that he would depart Williamsburg early in the morning. The couple wished him Godspeed and a fruitful journey.

When he returned to Maupin's tavern later that evening, he found affixed to the door of that establishment a freshly printed broadside entitled "An Association, signed by 89 members of the Late House of Burgesses," bearing today's date. He gently removed the broadside from the door, folded it, and put it inside his frock coat. Inside, after a brief exchange of pleasantries with the proprietor, he ascended the stairs to the room he shared with Lieutenant Manners. Here he reopened the broadside and read it with some amusement but little offense, and searched through the numerous, densely packed rows of names printed at the end of the statement. He did not see Hugh Kenrick's.

He thought its absence very curious.

"How was the ball, sir?" asked the junior officer, who sat in his nightshirt at a small desk in the corner, reading a military manual by candlelight, Clarke's 1767 translation of Roman general Flavius Vegetius Renatua's treatise, *De Re Militari*. Tallmadge had read that, and many French army manuals, plus Frederick the Great's own military treatise years ago, and insisted that his aide read them on the mission for "diversion" and "edification."

"Instructive, Mr. Manners," answered Tallmadge. "Very instructive. If His Excellency has his way, this colony may well need to adopt 'Land of the Leal' as its particular anthem."

"Bloody, greedy Scots!" muttered the lieutenant.

Tallmadge mildly rebuked his aide. "Be kind, Mr. Manners. They are half the backbone of the empire, in commerce and in troops."

Captain Tallmadge and his aide rode out of Williamsburg the next morning, the rising sun on their backs, and reached the Hove Stream bridge outside of Caxton by mid-day. The captain asked a passing farmer on his way to Williamsburg with a wagon of produce for directions to Meum Hall. Soon, in the distance, over a rise on Freehold Road that paralleled the stream, they could see the undulating red pennant and furled topgallant sails of the masts of a merchantman at rest, and, beyond them, a broad gray-blue streak of the York River.

*   *   *

Jack Frake sat in his library, estimating on paper the number of tobacco seedlings that were now being transferred from the seedbeds to the fields by the tenants. He glanced up now and then to watch them at the task through his window. The rye and barley sown last winter were coming up, and the corn and oats had already been planted. Together with an uncertain political situation — all of Caxton knew that the Governor had dissolved the Assembly two days ago — it was becoming more difficult to plan the proportions of his crops now, because of the uncertainty of their markets and transportation.

There was a knock on his door, and Ruth Dakin, a house servant and wife of Henry Dakin, the cooper, opened it and stood at the threshold. She exclaimed excitedly, "Master Frake! Look who's come home!" She stood aside to reveal the figure of John Proudlocks, who wore a broad grin.

Jack dropped his pencil and rose instantly to go to his friend and former tenant. He took the man's hand in both of his and shook it vigorously. "Welcome back, John!" he laughed.

Proudlocks also laughed. "It's good to be back, sir!"

"*Sir*??" queried Jack with astonishment.

Proudlocks shook his head. "I have learned to avoid unintended assonances, Jack."

Jack waved his friend to a chair in front of his desk. "How was the crossing?"

"Uneventful," Proudlocks said, coming in. "Six weeks before a good set of winds. Mr. Geary called them soldiers' winds. He will come up shortly with your mail."

Jack said to Ruth Dakin, "Ruth, some port, please."

The servant nodded and left the room to fetch the refreshments.

When he was settled in his own chair behind the desk, he studied Proudlocks, who was garbed in a fine frock coat and other gentleman's wear. Proudlocks removed his tricorn and put it on Jack's desk. His hair had been barbered, and was tied in back with a brown ribbon.

Jack noted a great difference in his friend, one that not even their frequent letters between Caxton and London over the last three years could have prepared him for. He saw a broader wisdom, a vaster knowledge, and, somehow, a completion in the man whom he thought had been complete when he saw him board the *Sparrowhawk* to begin his voyage to England to study law.

Proudlocks braved the scrutiny with an amused smile. "I have not changed, Jack."

"No, you haven't," answered Jack. "Did you come here directly from the waterfront?"

"No. I stopped at Sachem Hall first, to look at the place." Proudlocks paused. "I have not yet reconciled myself to the fact that the place is mine. I left so soon after Mr. Reisdale's passing."

"Mr. Corsin has kept it going properly," said Jack. Enolls Corsin was the business agent and steward of the late Thomas Reisdale's plantation. "I helped him dispose of some of your crops, and Mr. Dakin and Mr. Topham repaired some of the outbuildings." He grinned. "You know, your staff has taken to referring to you as 'Prodigal Proudlocks.'"

"Yes. You mentioned that in one of your letters. I *have* been the absentee owner, haven't I?" remarked Proudlocks with a chuckle. "Where is Etáin?"

"At Mr. Kenrick's, talking music with Reverdy. She'll be delighted to have you back. You must stay for supper."

"I will, thank you." Proudlocks added, "I brought her a bundle of sheet music."

"She will thank you for it." Jack sat back in his chair. "Well, was it worth the time?"

"Yes, it was well worth the time."

Ruth Dakin returned with a tray holding two mugs and two bottles of port. She served the men, then left the room.

After a sip of his port, Proudlocks said, "I shall miss London. I almost felt as though I belonged there. There is so much to see and do there. It is a stimulating city. I must accustom myself again to Caxton's more leisurely ways."

"I once thought that about London," Jack mused. "I saw it just the one time, with Redmagne."

"Hugh's parents send you their regards, and hope you will write them even though I am no longer there." Proudlocks paused. "I shall miss them, as well. They are fine people."

Jack nodded agreement. "I will write them."

They did not need to discuss politics. Among his other and numerous observations about Britain, Proudlocks had written Jack that there existed a certain fickleness both in the law he studied at Gray's Inn — Garnet Kenrick had been instrumental in having Proudlocks admitted for study there — and in the populace itself. "The laws for liberty here are happenstance and circumstantial in nature," he had written once. "We cannot depend on them to guarantee our own liberty, nor on any justice to argue for us. Those few who do argue for us, such as Lord Camden, are checkmated on a chess board of kings and bishops and little men." Now he said, with a special, sad smile, mixed with some wonderment, "Jack, all the while I was there, after I had grown accustomed to the place, I was daily struck by how right you have been all these years, from three thousand miles away."

Jack nodded in acknowledgement of the compliment. "About the likelihood of war?"

"About that, and about the reasons." Proudlocks paused. "About the differences between their people and ours." He frowned. "About the necessity for independence."

Jack sipped his port. "While you were away," he said with a sad smile of his own, "more men have caught up with me in that respect — to put it in Etáin's words." For a moment, he seemed to ponder the thought, then to reach a decision. Abruptly, he put down his mug and picked up a candleholder as he rose. "Come with me, John. I must show you something."

He led Proudlocks to the cellar of the great house. With the candle he lit a lantern that hung from a hook on the wall inside the cellar door, and left the candleholder on the dirt floor. With the lantern he threaded through stalls of plantation supplies and household necessities. There was a crude plank door with an iron lock at the end of one row of stalls that indicated a chamber that had been extended beyond the cellar. With a key he took from his pocket, Jack opened the door. The chamber was small and cool; it had brick walls, a brick floor, and a low plastered ceiling. Several crude square boxes sat stacked on the floor on one side. On another, a sail-cloth tarpaulin covered some long objects.

Jack motioned Proudlocks closer to the boxes and held the lantern next to one of them.

Proudlocks stooped to read the lettering on a side of the box: "Barret's Volley." He turned his head and squinted a query.

"Musket balls," said Jack. "Poured and fashioned from Mr. Barret's seized type by Mr. Crompton in his brick kiln." Aymer Crompton was Mor-land's brickmaster. Jack stood up and nodded to the other boxes. "More musket balls, and powder, courtesy of Mr. Ramshaw on one of his Barbados trips." He turned and gestured with the lantern at the tarpaulin across the chamber. "Open it, John," he said.

Proudlocks, hunched over beneath the low ceiling, moved to the tarpaulin and jerked it away. He saw long boxes that could only contain mus-kets, and a swivel gun and all the accessories for firing it — a box of ord-nance to load into it, a rammer, linstock, sponger, wadding, and a water bucket. Proudlocks put a hand on the brass length of the swivel gun and glanced at Jack.

"From the *Sparrowhawk*," Jack said. "Before he retired, Mr. Ramshaw retired that, as well."

Proudlocks also noted a long-gun and its stanchion. It was an over-size musket that could fire the same size ball as the swivel gun, and had twice the range of a firelock. "Where did you find this?" he asked with amaze-ment, running a hand along the monster barrel.

"Mr. Ramshaw bought it in Jamaica from a planter there."

Proudlocks replaced the tarpaulin and faced his friend. He gestured to the chamber. "You have not told anyone about this?"

Jack shook his head. "Only Etáin, and certain of my staff who helped me stock this room. Everyone else believes I have constructed an ice cellar."

"You did not mention this armory in your letters."

"That is because I have heard that the Crown is reading correspon-dence to and from the colonies. Mr. Ramshaw warned me of that outrage, as well."

"And Mr. Kenrick — does he know?"

"No."

"May I ask why not?"

"He has not quite caught up with me." Jack nodded to the contents of the chamber. "This is for those who have."

"He is your friend, as well. And mine."

Jack briefly closed his eyes. "That is another matter." After a moment, he added, "I will tell him about this when I think it is proper. Forgive me for asking you to keep this a secret from him."

Proudlocks nodded once. "It is not necessary for me to forgive you, Jack." He did not pursue the subject. He moved over to the box labeled "Barret's Volley." He smiled. "He would have approved of this use of his type." After a pause, he looked mischievous and added, "You have ensured that he and the *Courier* will have the last word, if I may fashion a pun."

"That is my literal intent, John," answered Jack with a faint smile. "No pun intended." After a moment, he said, "Well, enough of this. You've seen it. Let's go back to my study and you can tell me more of your London adventures. Etáin should return shortly."

\*   \*   \*

Although Meum Hall had been described to him by his friend in letters over the years, and he had seen many larger plantations on his journey from South Carolina, Roger Tallmadge was still impressed by the size of the place, and by its oddly utilitarian beauty. He and Lieutenant Manners stopped for a moment at the end of the estate near the Hove Stream before proceeding through the fields to the great house they saw in the distance. He grinned with some pride and remarked to his aide, "My brother-in-law's property. We shall stay here a few days, before continuing, Mr. Manners."

After a moment, Manners asked, "Do you think we would be welcome, sir?"

Tallmadge frowned. "Why should we not be?"

The lieutenant shrugged. "Well, considering our purpose in these parts, and considering what you said about him, his being a patriot and all, and the trouble he has caused in the past...." Manners left the rest unsaid.

"Fear not, Mr. Manners," said Tallmadge. "He is a friend as well as a relative. We have discussed politics often in our letters, and it has not come between us."

The lieutenant cocked his head in dubious concession. "On paper, perhaps not, sir."

Tallmadge shook his head. "Perish your thoughts, Mr. Manners. Let us move on."

They followed a path through the fields that paralleled a line of brick supports and lengths of thick bamboo, which some of the plantation's tenants, black and white, were assembling. Tallmadge recalled Hugh's description of the conduit he had designed. As they neared the great house of Meum Hall, he observed a woman driving off in a riding chair, and another woman waving goodbye to her from the top step of the porch. This woman's head turned in the direction of the visitors and she stared at them inquisitively. She waited for them to come closer.

Roger Tallmadge recognized Reverdy Kenrick, *née* Brune, whom he had not seen since the end of the late war, over ten years ago.

# Chapter 4: The Schism

"They say that Lady Dunmore influenced the Privy Council," said Reverdy, "on which she has a brother-in-law, to have her husband appointed to the governorship of Virginia, simply because the New York governorship did not pay as much as the Virginia, and had far fewer privileges."

Roger Tallmadge nodded in agreement. "I have heard that Virginia governors are the best paid of all the governors here."

He sat with her and Lieutenant Manners in the breakfast room, which overlooked the lawn and the York River. A tea service and a plate of biscuits sat on the table between them. Hugh Kenrick was in Caxton on business, at the waterfront and in search of some tools for the tenants. Reverdy had received Tallmadge warmly, once he had identified himself, and assured Roger that her husband would be ecstatic when he returned and saw his old friend.

Hugh had traveled to England four years ago to attend the marriage of his sister Alice to the captain. Reverdy had remained behind, weakened by a miscarriage. Roger reminisced with her for a while about their years in Danvers, but out of courtesy to Manners, who knew nothing of those years, changed the subject to contemporary affairs, at the moment the muted tension he had observed between the Governor and his wife, which he had already discussed with his aide.

"Yes, that is true," Reverdy answered. "And, Lord Dunmore need not share his salary with an absentee governor, and he has another steady income from fees and parts of prizes from the Navy's seizure of contraband, as well." Reverdy paused and grinned. "I'll wager that his lordship was furious with his wife when his new instructions reached him in New York! Doubtless he knew who was responsible for them! I have heard that besides indulging in every imaginable bachelor's vice and indiscretion, Lord Dunmore had the same designs on land up there as he has exhibited here. Apparently, it has taken the couple three years to mend their relations, once he was convinced that Virginia was not so bad an appointment, after all, and once she was persuaded that he had found his mark and would become a *steady* husband." She sighed. "I can't speak of the Governor this way with Hugh, Roger. He so despises his lordship that he says the man has forfeited even the honor of caricature."

Tallmadge was tempted to agree with that estimate, but kept the thought to himself. "Brothers-in-law and conniving wives!" he exclaimed instead. "They are the bane of a nation when they have influence! Roman history is strewn with their depredations and follies!"

"*And* our own, as well!" Reverdy reminded her guest. "Do not forget the bitter rivalry between Lord Chatham and the late Mr. Grenville."

"Of course, not," Roger replied. "One can only imagine the course of our recent history if they had agreed on something, and shared only half the kind of affection that Hugh and I do." He paused to sip some tea from his cup. "Perhaps the colonies and Parliament would not be near fisticuffs, and the mutual bitterness that exists now between them would never have had cause to arise."

Reverdy smiled at him, then furled her brow. "And, you say *you* had supper with the Governor? Why were *you* so privileged?" she asked, shaking her head. She had been so delighted to see her childhood friend again that until now she had forgotten to inquire into the reason for his presence in Virginia.

Roger Tallmadge sighed, and, glancing once at the silent Lieutenant Manners, put down his teacup. "Reverdy, please accept my apology, but that is something I must first relate to Hugh in especial confidence."

Reverdy looked thoughtful. "You are still in the army, and a captain, no less. But, Hugh said that you had been on several diplomatic posts." She paused, then her face brightened. "Are you a secret emissary of His Majesty?" she speculated half seriously. "A spy, perhaps?"

Roger simply grinned at her, his expression communicating nothing. It was an art he had learned in the courts of Denmark, Prussia and France.

"You are not in uniform, and that tells half the story," teased his hostess.

"It is not from shame that we are not. Mr. Manners's and my uniforms are in our baggage, milady," replied Roger. He paused and shook his head. "Perhaps we are simply two gentlemen at leisure, and have no reason to don them. For the moment, I ask that you accept that explanation of our presence. I can say no more."

Reverdy nodded in concession. "For the nonce. But it was your fault for boasting of your supper at the Palace. How could I not wonder why you were so favored by a man who is notoriously difficult to see, even by his cronies and his Council?"

Tallmadge smiled in defeat. "I am not known for spontaneous indiscretions of the moment, but that was one of them." He said, "It was a magnificent ball, Reverdy. I was disappointed not to see you and Hugh there."

"I had wanted to attend, but Hugh would not think of it," Reverdy sighed.

Tallmadge sensed that something more serious than regret moved his relative to reply so plaintively. He chuckled. "Hugh can be cruel in his principles. I saw him in Williamsburg two days ago, marching with his fellow burgesses to a tavern after Lord Dunmore dissolved the Assembly."

"Why did you not greet him?"

Tallmadge shook his head. "He seemed too happily immersed in the business of the moment, which was cocking a snook at His Excellency with the rest of his fellows."

"Yes, he would be immersed." Reverdy abruptly changed the subject. "Have you written Alice?"

"Every other day, almost. I hope to write to her again while I am here."

"How does she fare in your mysterious absence?"

"Well enough. She will stay with her parents until my return. Then we shall find our own accommodations." Tallmadge did not want to discuss a subject that was painful to him. Ideally, he would rather have been reassigned as an artillery instructor at Woolwich, so he could be with her. "I hope to find a bundle of her letters to me waiting in Annapolis. And I must remember to ask her to write me at General Gage's headquarters." This time he changed the subject. "Who was the lady I saw leaving just as we arrived?"

"Etáin Frake, Mr. Frake's wife. She is a musician. We visit each other frequently for practice. I can sing, you know, and she has taught me to play the pianoforte, at least better than I ever learned to at home. Hugh bought me one, in France. I have my own music room upstairs. I must show it to you."

"Yes, Hugh wrote me all about that. I should like to hear you sing and play."

Reverdy grinned. "Then, perhaps Etáin and I can arrange a special concert for you and Mr. Manners."

They chatted about other things, mostly the storm five falls ago that had caused extensive damage in Queen Anne and neighboring counties, with torrential rains that leveled crops and winds that blew down houses and drove four merchantmen aground on the York. "They were the two most frightening days of my life," said Reverdy. "I was certain that the winds alone would smash this house, as they did half the tenants' dwellings. We lost several windows on this side of the house from branches that must have blown clear across the river from Gloucester! Hugh's water tower was knocked atilt and was so battered that he had to replace it. He was not able to salvage most of the crops that year. All the planters here suffered losses. Mr. Otway's plantation further up the river, as large as Meum Hall, but which is on lower ground, was flooded. The invading waters were so violent that they brought down half his great house and carried away most of the outbuildings. He abandoned the entire place. He salvaged what he could from the ruins and moved his family to Richmond town to begin anew."

"There are no storms like that in England," remarked Tallmadge. "When Lieutenant Manners and I passed through Surrey on the James, people told us about a spring freshet two years ago that roared down that river and wiped out several homes and took many lives."

Reverdy clasped her hands together. "But, enough of the weather! Such a prosaic subject!" She turned to the lieutenant. "Mr. Manners, you have been treated to a portion of our lives and have exhibited a commendable patience, but I am afraid we have neglected you. Tell me something of yourself."

The junior officer blushed and fidgeted in his chair. "What do you wish to know, milady?"

Some minutes later the breakfast door opened and Hugh Kenrick came in. "Roger!" he exclaimed, rushing to meet his friend. The two men met in the middle of the room, shaking hands and slapping each other's shoulders.

"What are you doing here?" exclaimed Hugh, standing back to spread his hands in happy, helpless wonder.

\*   \*   \*

"I am here at the behest of the secretary-at-war, Lord Barrington," answered Roger, who had managed to defer an answer in the midst of welcoming also Elyot Geary, captain of the *Sparrowhawk*, who had followed Hugh into the breakfast room, having accompanied him from the waterfront, and during the subsequent introductions and pleasantries.

Roger and Hugh sat in the study with glasses of Madeira. "I am, essentially, spying on the colonies, to apprise their ability to wage war — against the Crown. Lieutenant Manners and I have since January wound our way up from Savannah. Perhaps by August, we shall reach Boston and report to General Gage." The captain looked contrite, adding, "I apologize for not having warned you of my presence in the colonies. The Earl of Rochford and Lord Barrington impressed upon me the necessity for secrecy. Not even Alice or her parents know the true reason I am here. They believe I am escorting a Crown survey party in search of timber for the navy."

"I see," answered Hugh. He frowned. "How could you accept such an assignment?"

Roger shrugged. "Serving officers must accept their orders and perform their duty." He paused. "Naturally, I am not happy with the assignment. But, it gives me a chance to see this part of the world, which I otherwise would not have had the means to visit." After another pause, he added, "I wished to see *your* country." He reached into his coat and pulled out an oversize sheet of paper. It was the Association broadside. "I saw you in Williamsburg the other day, trooping with the burgesses to that tavern. Later the next day, after I had left the Capitol ball, I found this fixed to the hostelry door. I had expected to see your name here, and was oddly disappointed that I did not." He held up the broadside for Hugh to read.

"And you would have seen it," Hugh exclaimed with disgust, "had I not believed it already there! You see, I debated the points contained in that document, won some arguments and lost others, and volunteered to help prepare several drafts of it for Mr. Randolph and his committee, correcting the grammar and pointing, and when it was ready for Association signatures, I naturally believed I had already signed it!" He laughed and shook his head in self-mockery. "What a trick of the mind! I was exhausted that day, but determined to spend not another night in Williamsburg, and did not wait for copies to be printed and distributed." He smiled at his friend. "Well, it is done. May I see it?"

"Or, not done," remarked the captain, amused. Roger handed him the broadside over the desk. "I am obliged to take it with me, Hugh, and include it with my report. I have collected a number of such broadsides, from Georgia and the Carolinas, every one of them certain to displease General Gage."

Hugh read it, shaking his head, but commented, "Doubtless from the press of Mrs. Rind, of the other *Gazette*. We had voted her late husband's paper the official purveyor of Assembly news the very day the Governor dissolved us." He handed it back over the desk to his friend. "By all means,

Roger, give it to General Gage, and let him dare be displeased with the mettle of true Englishmen! Although, he has probably already been sent a copy by certain loyal members of the House as evidence of sedition."

Roger carefully refolded the sheet and returned it inside his coat. "I can guarantee that he will read it, and that he will be displeased."

"So be it." Hugh paused. "Are you still sitting for Bromhead?"

"Yes, of course. I must own that I am feeling some guilt about that, since I am not there to represent the place. With good fortune, I will return to London in time for the next session." Roger looked thoughtful for a moment, then said, "You know, Hugh, some years ago, when we were hunting game on the heath, you said to me that you looked forward to the empire that Mr. Pitt had in mind then, an empire stretching from Margate to the Mississippi. You don't seem to believe in that now."

"I remember that day, Roger," said Hugh. "It was an empire of reason I spoke of then, not of slavery. And, I still believe in it." He paused to sip his Madeira. "Until now, Roger, our political wisdom has been drawn from England. But, the time has come for the colonies here to impart some harsh wisdom to England."

Roger grimaced. "The Crown may harshly dispute you on that point." He leaned forward to say, "Hugh, I must own that although wisdom is wanting in London, the wisdom you and other pamphlet writers have to impart is *not* wanted." He sat back in the chair. "The men who would be receptive to your wisdom are not in office, nor are they likely to be appointed to it." He smiled sadly, and nodded up to the framed crayon portrait of the late member for Swansditch on the wall, next to the group figures of the Society of the Pippin he had last seen in Danvers many years ago. "There was our mutual friend Mr. Jones, of course, but you know what happened to him." After a pause, he added, "I am convinced that your uncle was somehow responsible for his murder."

"I have never been able to persuade myself otherwise," said Hugh. "He is a distant, incurable canker." Garnet Kenrick had written to him over the years since Dogmael Jones's murder that his brother, Basil Kenrick, Earl of Danvers, had become ambitious enough to even deign to speak frequently in Lords in support of all the legislation that now oppressed the colonies. His bloc of votes in the Commons had grown since repeal of the Stamp Act and adoption of the Declaratory Act in 1766. The Earl, Garnet Kenrick reported, had become much more active in politics, and had even been briefly appointed to the Board of Trade and Privy Council in the confused transition from the Grafton to the North ministry. Basil Kenrick had not been invited to the wedding of his niece Alice to Roger. Garnet Kenrick communicated rarely with his brother, and did not even know how the Earl viewed his nephew's marriage to Reverdy Brune.

Roger ventured, "I think I wrote you about all the officers who voted against these Parliamentary actions, and who were punished, as a result, with dismissal from their regiments or appointments or with removal from their seats in the Commons. Many have resigned their commissions, or have threatened to resign them, at the prospect of warring against their countrymen here."

Hugh cocked his head in acknowledgement of the fact. "Yes, you did write me about that. One can only hope that they are the ablest officers."

"Not necessarily all. I showed some of the pamphlets you sent me to other officers, who were either outraged by them or too witless to comment. If there is a conflict, and they are sent here, they would perform their duties with ardor and at times with imagination, according to their lights."

Hugh frowned. "Would you, Roger? Would you resign, rather than war against your countrymen?"

"I cannot yet say, Hugh. I, too, believe in the empire. Like you, I have not given up on the idea. The question of whether the colonies are right to flout the law is one that confounds my sensibilities. I agree with you that a permanent union of the colonies here is neither practical, nor even imaginable, considering the contentions and rivalries I have observed on my travels here. They remind me of all the odd alliances in Parliament that are precipitated by a crisis in England, but which fly apart again when the crisis is past." Tallmadge paused. "It is a question I cannot entertain an answer to, not until I have returned to England. It might be that I *would* resign, and take up your offer to join your father's bank in London."

"You flatter me by remembering it, as well. Gads, it seems like ages ago!" Hugh said. "Then, before you leave, I shall write a letter of recommendation for you to give to my father."

Roger nodded. "Thank you."

Hugh sat twirling his top on the green baize blotter of his desk, weighing the wisdom of introducing Roger to Jack Frake and Etáin. He was unsure of the reception Roger would receive. He decided to postpone a decision, and said, "Well, are you too tired for a tour of the plantation, Roger? Lieutenant Manners is invited, as well, if you aren't. But, it can wait until tomorrow."

"I am not too tired, thank you. Your company has refreshed me. All these years, I have tried to imagine what Meum Hall looked like, and here I am! We came through the fields from the stream that borders your south pasturage." Roger beamed. "Reverdy is looking well. We were having a glorious chat before *you* interrupted!" he added in mock accusation.

Hugh smiled dolefully. He announced with reluctance, "Reverdy will soon sail for England, Roger. She has not seen it or her parents for nigh on ten years. Her family are near frantic to see her again. You know that she was too ill to accompany me to your wedding, and on my brief visit to the Continent." He sighed. "The troubles here have made her homesick." He added woodenly, "And, she…disapproves of my actions."

"It saddens me to hear it, Hugh," Roger replied after a stunned moment. The character of some of Reverdy's comments now made sense to him. After a pause, he remarked, "I am surprised by this. She gave me to believe that she shared your views on Lord Dunmore."

"She is critical of the man, not of his office." Hugh shook his head. "Well, we have agreed that perhaps some time away from here, and away from the strife that is sure to continue, may allow her to more calmly reflect on the matters at hand."

Something in Hugh's manner and words told Roger that the subject was not to be pursued. "Well, *elder brother*," he said cheerily after he had emptied his glass of Madeira and put it down on a stand, "show me your realm!"

*     *     *

The next morning, under an overcast sky that promised rain, Hugh made his excuses, left Reverdy to entertain his guests, and rode to Morland Hall. Jack Frake, he learned there from Etáin, had gone to Yorktown on plantation business, and would not return until the next day. He saw Etáin in her own music room, where she was working on a harp transcription of William Boyce's first symphony. As Ruth Dakin served them tea at a corner table, Etáin said, "I do not ever expect to play it through to the end. It is much too long. But, there are certain passages in the opus that beg for performance."

"I should like to hear it some time," said Hugh. "The last I was in London, I heard the entire symphony played in the opera house."

"And, you shall hear it, once I've finished the task," Etáin assured him, as Ruth Dakin left the room. Then Etáin remembered something. "Oh! Mr. Proudlocks is back from London! He arrived yesterday, on the *Sparrowhawk*."

"Oh," Hugh said with interest. "Captain Geary did not tell me. Where is he now?"

Etáin laughed. "Why, at Sachem Hall, of course! While he was away, Mr. Reisdale's brothers filed some papers with the Louisa County court about two years ago concerning Mr. Reisdale's property in the Piedmont. They seek his written assurance that they have rightful title to it. Mr. Proudlocks will not contest their claim. He says that Sachem Hall was enough of a bequest." Etáin looked reflective. "Mr. Reisdale's brothers did not bother to come here to inquire, so I do not think they knew Mr. Proudlocks is an Indian. If they knew, I believe they would take a suit to the General Court."

"This is true," said Hugh. "The law is quite explicit on that matter." He smiled. "I must ask him about his sojourn in London, the next I see him."

Etáin sensed that, although Hugh and Proudlocks were close friends, at the moment seeing their mutual friend was the furthest thing in her guest's mind. "And, to what do I owe this visit?"

Hugh put down his teacup. "I know that you would answer for your husband, and so, in his absence, I must pose the question to you, instead. An answer is quite imperative."

"What question?"

"My old friend, Roger Tallmadge, is staying with us for a few days, before continuing his travels."

Etáin smiled, delighted. "You have told us much about him. We would be happy to meet him."

"He is a captain in the army, Etáin. He is accompanied by an aide, Lieutenant William Manners."

Etáin waited for her guest to continue.

Hugh said, "He has been in the colonies since January, gathering information on colonial military prowess and strength. By summer's end, he will report to General Gage in Boston, and send his conclusions to London, as well. His mission is... secret. He has seen the Governor."

Etáin put down her teacup. "And, what is your question, Hugh?"

"Whether you and Jack would be willing to meet him." Hugh paused. "He is a dear friend, and I should like you both to meet him as such, but the reason for his presence here — and both his presence and his purpose were a surprise to me — requires that you know his circumstances. I would not want to introduce him under false pretences."

"I see." Etáin sat for a moment, thinking. Then she said, "As much as I would like to meet your friend, Hugh, I don't think Jack would share my curiosity. We would all find ourselves in an awkward circumstance, even your friend." She added, after a moment. "I am sorry, but given the greater circumstance, his company would not be welcome. I am certain Jack would agree with me."

"I concur." Hugh hastened to add, "Of course, there is nothing for me to forgive in the smaller circumstance, and so I ask that you not beg pardon for the special refusal, if one could call it that."

Etáin smiled at him. "One could call it honesty."

"Yes. One could call it that."

Etáin reached over and refilled Hugh's teacup. "Does Reverdy still plan to leave for England? She did not mention it yesterday, when I visited her."

"Yes," sighed Hugh. "Perhaps even on the *Sparrowhawk*, when Captain Geary comes back down the river from West Point." He sipped the tea that his hostess had just poured. "She will take Dilch with her. She and Reverdy have become fast friends, as you know. Reverdy gave her a book of poetry by that black prodigy from Boston, Phillis Wheatley." Dilch, who once worked in the plantation fields, had become his wife's maidservant. The mistress of Meum Hall had years ago, as a corrective to her boredom, taken it upon herself to enlighten the reticent former slave. Dilch, in gratitude, subsequently became Reverdy's devoted companion.

For a moment, Hugh seemed lost in thought. Then he remembered Etáin, put down his teacup, smiled and rose. "Well, I thank you for your honesty, Etáin. I must return to my guests. Please give my regards to Jack, when he returns. You needn't show me out."

# Chapter 5: The Interlopers

It did not rain. Later that day, Hugh rode into Caxton with Roger Tallmadge and Lieutenant Manners. After they had stabled their mounts at Safford's King's Arms, Hugh led his companions on a leisurely tour of the town. He nodded in greeting to townsmen who knew him, including Reece Vishonn, who rode by on horseback. The master of Enderly touched his hat in recognition of Hugh, but seemed to frown in confused, doubting recollection of one of the gentlemen with him.

"I don't know if I should be your guide on this tour, Roger," said Hugh as they strolled down one of the "sidewalks" that was a gift of his to the town. "You may conclude that Caxton would be a peerless venue for a camp of occupation."

Roger glanced at his friend, unsure of the humor of the remark. But, he reciprocated with, "Hardly, Hugh. I have studied my maps. Not even Yorktown would suit that purpose. In a circumstance of *force majeure*, the army and navy would need to act in complement to each other. So, a camp would be established closer to that sea you folks call Chesapeake Bay, say, in the easternmost part of Hampton. There the army could procure supplies from Crown warehouses, and from the navy itself. Vessels could more readily transport troops to places where they were needed. And, the navy could more easily impose authority over the waterways and towns along them. It's quite a perfect place to headquarters such a presence. It is no accident of design that the navy and Customs make it a permanent rendezvous. Who controls the Roads, controls all, from Norfolk to Baltimore town."

Lieutenant Manners, who walked behind them, opined, "Besides, sir, how could His Majesty's army be one of 'occupation' in his own country? It is a very strange perspective you voice."

Hugh turned to the officer as he continued on. He said with icy cordiality, "It has been another country for some time, Lieutenant. It is my hope that it can be reunited with the Crown under more felicitous terms."

"Of course, sir," replied the officer, startled. He did not venture again to contradict or correct his host.

Hugh asked Roger, "You have exchanged more words with him than I have, or would ever want to, Roger, and so you must have a better understanding of his character. Do you think the Governor would abdicate his appointment, as Governor Hutchinson has in Massachusetts?"

Tallmadge smiled. There was another instance of his friend's troubling sentiments, his employment of the term *abdicate*, as though Thomas Hutchinson had been a king. "No," he answered, "I do not think he would *resign*. He is quite determined to stay on here. He has bought property all about this region, I understand, and sees many other advantages of a personal nature, though he would pursue them in the name of the Crown. He is a man inclined to govern, whatever the cost. And if he cannot govern, I am afraid he could be very...vindictive."

"I am willing to credit you the assessment."

"Thank you. And, you forget that Mr. Hutchinson was a scholar, and an historian, and not of a combative nature, except in chambers, and then only as a fumbling sneaksby. His Excellency Lord Dunmore, however, is of more imperial mettle. I can promise you that if there is trouble here the likes of which occurred in Boston, he will be very blunt, poetically and literally, in his response."

"I've no doubt of that," replied Hugh.

Roger asked, "When will I meet this famous friend of yours, Hugh? Mr. Frake? You've written to me so much about him for so long. Is he still a 'Son of Liberty'?"

Hugh nodded. "As am I," he replied. "I queried his wife on the matter, Roger, and was obliged to tell her why you are here. I am afraid a meeting will not be possible."

Roger guessed the reason, and did not pursue the subject. They had walked the length of Caxton, and now stood on the rise on Queen Anne Street that marked the bluff overlooking the riverfront. "Does this county boast a committee of correspondence?" asked the officer. "Many of the counties Mr. Manners and I have passed through seem to be ruled by them."

"Not yet," Hugh sighed. "Caxton is predominantly loyal, as is most of the county." He shook his head. "However, I am sure that the Governor's dissolution of the Assembly will spur the creation of one in Williamsburg. He has left the colony without a government, and something must replace the one he dissolved."

"That's as may be," Roger said. "However, I am obliged to note in my final report the excesses of these committees complained of by many a subject. They smack of mob rule. Many chaps have been ruined because they did not sign this or that petition, and had their goods or houses burned, or themselves subjected to physical abuse." On a more apologetic note, he added, "If I am to submit a report that reflects the temper of the situation here, I cannot but include those episodes."

Hugh shrugged. "It would be your duty, Roger. Caxton and Queen Anne here have fortunately been spared that unseemly behavior. I do not believe in bullying a man into agreement with a cause, however worthy it may be."

"Given the sentiments I read in the Association broadside, I am surprised that you are still serving tea."

Hugh was startled by the observation, and recalled also Etáin serving him the beverage earlier in the day. "What chests of it we have will be the last we will enjoy, unless we can lay hands on some Dutch tea."

Standing also on the bluff, across Queen Anne Street from them, near the edge of Sheriff Cabal Tippet's backyard, was Reverend Albert Acland, pastor of Stepney Parish Church. The minister glanced now and then at the trio. He did not attempt to greet Hugh and his companions. Hugh had no interest in introducing the minister, and did not wonder much about the man's presence. He ignored the man, as he had for years. The man had grown more rancid over time; he had heard that his sermons had become more and more indictments of anyone who defied Crown authority, equating that defiance with defiance of God and the church.

Hugh grimaced in distaste at the recollection, and pointed out the warehouses, billets and offices below them, and the piers of the principal plantations up and down the river. In time, they noticed a frigate-sized vessel coming up the York. "I don't recognize that one," remarked Hugh.

"I can make out her name," said Roger. "It's the *Fowey*."

"I wonder where it's headed. Probably for West Point to rummage some home or warehouse for contraband."

"Twenty guns, and I see marines on deck," commented Lieutenant Manners.

Roger said, "Speaking of rummaging, Hugh, I encountered one of your fellow planters at the ball, the gentleman we saw earlier. The master of a place called Enderly. He was bitter in his cups, but lucid enough to echo your own sentiments, after a fashion. His comments on the Governor were refreshingly indecorous."

"Ah. Mr. Vishonn. Well, he is bitter. The progress of the empire has disappointed him, and nearly ruined him. Some time ago the Customs caught him transporting lumber and iron bar from his mine in the Piedmont to Philadelphia, in his own vessel, without having declared it for tax, and misrepresenting the amounts on the cocket, and consequently fined him severely."

They watched the *Fowey* glide past the riverfront up the York, and when the warship was at a distance, saw crewmen begin to climb the shrouds. "I do believe they are about to take in sail," remarked Roger. "The captain means to stop somewhere up there."

"It is beginning to heave to larboard," said Hugh, watching the warship angle towards the riverfront. "I wonder...." Then he turned to his friend. "Roger, we must go. I am certain this means no good. We must return to Meum Hall."

"Of course." Roger and the lieutenant watched their host walk quickly back up Queen Anne Street, heading back to the stables. The two officers followed.

Reverend Acland watched them go, and cackled. He watched the *Fowey* as it slowed, and as crewmen began to prepare a galley boat to lower on its larboard side.

*    *    *

Reverdy, in her upstairs music room, did not observe the *Fowey* as it glided past the pier of Meum Hall. She was engrossed in a copy of *Gentleman's Magazine*, which she could not give her full attention. The pressing question of whether or not to begin preparing for a journey to England distracted her thoughts. Dilch happened to pass the window in the course of tidying up the room for the private performance that her mistress planned to give her master's guests. She stopped in amazement, because she had never seen a warship come this far up the York River. "Milady," she said, more confused than alarmed, "a ship with many guns has just gone up the river."

Reverdy rose and joined her maidservant at the window. The warship was now drifting in the vicinity of the pier of Morland Hall. She saw a galley boat being lowered down one of its sides, and men on the deck waiting to descend the rope ladder to board it once it was in the water. A number of the men wore red coats. An anchor was being lowered from the bow, and crewmen in the shrouds were adjusting the sails to counteract the prevailing winds. "Dilch, ask Bilico to prepare the riding chair." Bilico was a stable-hand.

"Is it trouble, milady?"

"It may be, Dilch. Hurry."

Dilch swept from the room.

\*     \*     \*

At Morland Hall, Etáin had interrupted her task of transcribing Haydn's "Serenade" to go to the kitchen and instruct Mary Beck what to prepare for supper, when Henry Dakin, the cooper, and Mouse, his young black assistant, came rushing in. "Mrs. Frake! There's a navy ship just dropped anchor off of Mr. Frake's pier!" exclaimed Dakin. "They've lowered a boat and marines are climbing into it!"

Etáin rushed outside from the kitchen and around the corner. Over the trees that lined the riverfront lawn she saw the tops of the ship's masts. Dakin, Mouse, and the kitchen staff had followed her out. She turned to face them. "Henry! Go and warn everyone! Tell them to come to the house! Mouse! Take a horse and ride to Yorktown and tell Mr. Frake! He's at the Swan Inn there! Go!"

Mouse bobbed his head once. "Yes, ma'am!" The boy bolted away for the stables.

Henry Dakin's eyes were wide with worry. "Mrs. Frake, do you think they know about the new cellar?" He had helped his employer dig, insulate, and stock the secret arms cache.

"I don't know, Mr. Dakin. Please hurry! The more people who stand in their way, the less likely they will want to make trouble."

"Yes, ma'am!" The cooper nodded once and rushed away on his mission.

Etáin calmly instructed Mary Beck and her servants to continue preparing tonight's supper, then walked briskly to the small house near the front lawn that was the home of Obedience Robbins, the business agent, and William Hurry, the overlooker and steward. The two men were sitting at a table in the common room, smoking their pipes. She saw that she was interrupting a card game. She said, "We are about to be called on by some marines, sirs, and probably by Customsmen. A navy ship has stopped at our pier."

After a moment, Robbins asked, "The cellar?"

"I don't know, Mr. Robbins."

The two men glanced at each other, then slapped down their cards and rose to retrieve their muskets. "Well, Mrs. Frake," said Hurry over his shoulder as he left the room, "the least we can do for uninvited guests is to give them a warmish welcome!"

"If you have a spare musket, I'll take one, as well, gentlemen."

Hurry stopped at the door and glanced at his colleague. He said, "All that's spare is a fowling piece, Mrs. Frake, and all it's ever brought down are foxes, squirrels, and pilfering hawks."

Etáin shook her head once. "Then it may need to notch a Customsman or two."

*     *     *

Hugh led the way past Meum Hall when he saw that the *Fowey* had not stopped at his pier. Roger Tallmadge and Lieutenant Manners followed him to the trail that connected Meum Hall with Morland Hall. A rider approached them along it, and Hugh recognized Mouse, who was riding saddleless. They paused long enough for Mouse to exclaim, "Mista' Kenrick, there's soldiers come to Mista' Jack's place! I'm goin' to Yorktown to fetch him now!" and then dug his heels into the horse's flanks and was off again before Hugh could acknowledge the message.

"How long a ride is it to Yorktown?" Tallmadge asked as they moved on.

"About an hour, if his mare doesn't fail at the pace he's got her going."

When they emerged from the cluster of trees that bordered the trail, they saw a dangerous tableau at the great house. Etáin Frake stood on the porch together with the business agent and steward, all of them armed. At the bottom of the steps stood a group of men and seven red-coated marines, six of them standing at attention with muskets at the shoulder, awaiting orders.

Hugh concluded that they must have just arrived, having come up the rolling road from Jack Frake's pier. The man who seemed to be in charge of two other regularly dressed men and of the marines stood at the bottom of the porch steps, apparently about to state his business. Then they all heard the approach of the newcomers, and all eyes turned to Hugh and his party.

Hugh rode past the marines up to the man in charge, a tall, stocky man with black hair and thick black eyebrows over black marble eyes. Hugh nodded to Etáin, who nodded silently in reply.

"Who are you, sir, and what is your business here?" asked Hugh, looking down on the man.

"I am Jared Hunt, inspector of the Customs, sir. I was about to ask the lady of the house for her name. I am here on official business."

"Which is...?"

"Which is none of your concern, sir."

"But, it is, sir. If you enter this house, or attempt to search it or otherwise trespass on any portion of this property, I shall be obliged to stop you."

The inspector scrutinized the intruder. "Are you the owner, sir?"

"No."

"If you are not the owner, then I strongly advise you to desist in your verbal protest of my duties, before you are tempted to interfere with them, and thus oblige me to arrest you for a criminal action."

Hugh shook his head. "I strongly advise that you, sir, desist in your criminal action, before you violate the constitution." He paused. "Or perhaps you would rather become the subject of protracted deliberations on that subject? I should warn you that the courts in these parts are very friendly to that constitution, and in them your name will be often taken in vain."

Hunt frowned. This stranger would not be bluffed or intimidated. He glanced at his two colleagues from the Customs office in Hampton, then said, as officiously as he could, "We have received information that this place contains contraband. Our source is unimpeachable. I might add that my duties, sanctioned or not by you, would not come under the consideration of any local court, or even the General Court, but under the authority of the Admiralty." He reached into his coat, pulled out a folded sheet of paper, and waved it in the air. "I have here a writ of assistance, signed by the commander of His Majesty's naval forces here, as he is authorized to do in his capacity as a member of the Admiralty."

Hugh shrugged. "Another violator of the constitution."

Hunt smirked. "So you say, sir." He returned the document to his coat, and nodded to the lieutenant and his marines.

The lieutenant of marines ordered his men to advance their arms. The six redcoats smartly brought their firelocks from their shoulders and held them level in both hands at the ready, pointed in the direction of the intervening horsemen.

"There, sir, are the upholders of the constitution! Dispute my authority with them, if you dare!"

A new voice spoke, condescending, condemnatory, and commanding. "You are a scamp, a rogue, and a coward, sir."

Hunt scowled and turned to look up at the gentleman who spoke. He scoffed once, and asked, "Are *you* the owner, sir?"

"No. I am Captain Roger Tallmadge, Grenadier Guards, on Crown business of my own here…"

Lieutenant Manners, looking worried, leaned forward. "Sir, do you think it's wise — "

Tallmadge waved a hand without glancing at his aide, who stopped speaking. "Mr. Hunt, my friend here is quite within his rights to be outraged by your proposed action, and if he sees fit to interfere with it, I shall lend him my avid assistance."

"If you interfere with *my* Crown business, sir, I am authorized to instruct the lieutenant to reply in kind, and if you survive, you will be cashiered from your precious Guards!"

Roger grinned carelessly at Hunt. "That, sir, will be a matter between my superiors and me, and you are surely not one of my superiors."

Hugh said, "Well, Mr. Hunt, if there is to be a civil war, then let it begin here. I can assure you, however, that you will not live long enough to witness the outcome of this skirmish, or of the larger conflagration it is sure to precipitate." He smiled wickedly. "History will judge you according to Mr. Tallmadge's description of your character. I am willing to accept responsibility for such a cataclysm. Are you?" Then he calmly reached down, undid the hasp that secured his sword to its sheath, and drew out the weapon. He rested the blade on his shoulder and waited.

Roger Tallmadge emulated him, and drew his own sword. He exchanged a brief smile with his friend, with whom he had never had a chance to share such an adventure.

They heard the rustle of movement behind them. Both men turned and saw a gathering of Morland Hall tenants, black and white, nearly fifteen of them, ranged in a semicircle that encompassed the tableau. Some carried muskets, which they had "advanced" in the same manner as the marines. Others brandished pitchforks and hoes. Roger glanced at Hugh again; he was more startled by the demonstration than was his friend. Neither of them noticed Lieutenant Manners, who studied the tenants disapprovingly.

Hunt was stunned. He was sweating now, and stood fingering the hilt of his undrawn sword. His two colleagues stood watching their feet shuffling in the dirt. He had observed, at first with unconcern, the collection of men who looked like tenants and slaves of the plantation here. They carried mostly farming tools and implements, but a few sported muskets.

Whether or not these weapons were charged to fire, he could not tell. But his party was clearly outnumbered, and these tenants and slaves looked determined to support the two gentlemen on horseback. He swallowed once in the knowledge that to continue to press his duty now would be a folly he did not want to answer for; indeed, one he might not survive.

To further complicate the situation, a woman, obviously a lady, had appeared on a riding chair and sat in its seat on the fringes of the tenants, watching with obvious horror.

He heard sounds on the porch of the great house. He turned and saw that two more men had gathered on it behind the finely dressed woman with red hair, presumably the mistress of the house, whom he had not even had the chance to address. They carried pistols at the ready, and those pistols were cocked.

Hunt had not counted on such resistance. The letter he had received about a possible cache of arms hidden in this house did not hint at the resolute defiance he might encounter, although he had thought it prudent to request the assistance of the marines from the naval commander. Even if the lieutenant could fire a volley, he and his men could be overwhelmed in the midst of reloading. The situation had become dangerous and humiliating. It was time to concede defeat. The Customs inspector turned back to the strangers. "Who *are* you, sir?" he asked with impatience.

"Hugh Kenrick, master of Meum Hall," said Hugh, pointing vaguely in the direction of the plantation with his sword, "and burgess for this county."

In spite of his angry red pallor, the Customs inspector seemed to smile, and his black eyes become animate with some secret knowledge. The two intruders studied him with curiosity, for they could not account for his change in demeanor. He derived a small satisfaction from that.

Hunt abruptly turned to the marine lieutenant. "Shoulder your men's arms, lieutenant, and prepare to march them back to the boat! We are done here!"

The lieutenant, a young man whose eyes were wide with fright, immediately complied with the request and gave his orders. A barely suppressed collective sigh of relief blew from the squad of redcoats. When his men's weapons were shouldered, the lieutenant looked to Mr. Hunt for further instruction.

"March them out, thank you, lieutenant. We will follow."

The lieutenant left-faced his men, strode to the head of them, and quick-marched them away. The tenants parted to let them pass. Hunt's two colleagues followed without their own superior's leave.

Hunt waved a stern finger at the two horsemen. "Do not doubt me, sirs! I will write the authorities about this incident, make no mistake about that! There will be consequences!" Without waiting for a reply, he turned on his heel and followed his party.

Hugh and Roger reined their mounts around and followed the Customs inspector a short distance. It was only then that Hugh noticed his wife in the riding chair, and the mask of bitterness in her expression.

She looked away from him, turned the chair around, and rode away back to Meum Hall.

# Chapter 6: The Antagonists

Hugh wanted to follow her, but resisted the impulse. He knew what she was thinking. He also knew it was necessary to punctuate the episode with an assurance that the Customsmen would not return. Instead, he rode with Tallmadge in the wake of the marines and Customsmen down the rolling road to the pier and the waiting galley boat tied to it. Lieutenant Manners trailed behind out of curiosity. There they stopped to watch the party board the boat. A pair of *Fowey* crewmen rowed them back across the water to the warship.

Hugh glanced behind him. Some of the tenants had followed them down the road. Others were gathered on the lawn over the bluff. He saw Etáin, Robbins and Hurry among them. He sheathed his sword, dismounted, and led his horse to the foot of the pier, where he leaned back on a post. Tallmadge grinned, and did the same, leaning on the opposite post.

Everyone waited until the *Fowey*'s anchors had been hoisted and its sails reset to catch a westerly breeze in mid-river.

"Well, elder brother," asked Tallmadge, "what now?"

Hugh shrugged. "We wait until Mr. Hunt has truly departed."

"What do you think he expected to find?"

"I don't know, Roger."

"If he was able to search for contraband, and found it, how could he have taken it away?"

"By seizing Jack's draft horses and a wagon to cart it to the pier, and using some of his axes and other tools to do it. These men are brazenly proprietary in their use of other men's property."

They all watched the warship's bow slowly turn in the current, and the intruder begin its return trip back down the York.

Hugh sighed. "Well, I must return to Meum Hall, and see what troubles my wife." He grinned almost apologetically to Roger and moved toward his mount. He saw the Morland Hall tenants and bowed his head. "Thank you, sirs."

Then he saw Etáin, Robbins and Hurry coming down the rolling road. Etáin also thanked the tenants, and turned to Hugh. "Mr. Kenrick, I am grateful for your gesture. Jack will be pleased to hear about this." She turned to Roger Tallmadge, who stood behind Hugh. "Mr. Tallmadge, you introduced yourself. I am Mrs. Jack Frake. You must know that I had asked Hugh not to bring you to Morland. But I believe now that I must revoke that request, and apologize for the inhospitality. You are welcome at Morland Hall. My husband would be interested in meeting you."

Tallmadge was startled by this frank statement, even though he had been told of the refusal. But he doffed his hat and nodded. "Thank you, madam." He glanced inquiringly at Hugh.

Hugh said, "Forgive me, Roger, but I did think it necessary to inform Mrs. Frake that you were a serving officer in the army, and of your purpose here."

Tallmadge looked bewildered, but amused. "Of course."

Without further word, Hugh took his leave, mounted his horse, and cantered back up the rolling road.

Both Tallmadge and Etáin guessed the reason for their friend's concern, but did not speak of it.

*       *       *

Jared Hunt stood on the deck, his sight fixed on the tableau of figures at the pier, and waited for the crew to hoist up the galley boat. The marines and other Customsmen had scattered on the deck to loiter and speculate until the *Fowey* got under way again. He congratulated himself for not having let his temper get the best of him, and temper he had. Patience was a virtue he had learned to acquire, exercise and appreciate during his years at Windridge Court, London, and in Danvers, Dorset. He knew he had made a wise decision. There would be another time, perhaps a better time, to impose his authority. He had been warned, by both his colleagues, and by the informing letters, that there might be an altercation, and that he might of necessity be the cause of it. But the scale of the opposition here surprised him and his colleagues from the Hampton Customs office.

His colleagues, of course, now wondered what they should do. He told them he would merely report what had happened. It would not have mattered if he had been accompanied by a regiment of marines; he would have retired from the situation. He was not going to be responsible for a "Boston massacre" here. No such disaster would ever be put on his head.

He owed his present position to his father's influence with members of the American Board of Customs Commissioners in London, and had been appointed Customs Inspector Extraordinary. The position and commission came with special discretionary powers, and allowed him to pursue matters of his own judgment and choosing. He had learned, upon his arrival here months ago, that the regular Customsmen did not wish to deal with Jack Frake or any known "Son of Liberty" anywhere in the region. In the past, he had accompanied them when they ventured out to search the properties of suspected contraband traders. These expeditions were rare, for it seemed that as the Crown became more omnipotent, the less it could exact obedience and revenue from the colonials. The Customsmen, he knew, feared for their health; often for their lives. Consequently, they were very selective in the properties they chose to raid, deciding to visit only those traders and inhabitants known to be neutral or passive insofar as Crown authority was concerned.

So-called Committees of Safety were also multiplying in many counties and exercising an exasperating authority not even enjoyed by local sheriffs or courts in more civil, abiding times. It seemed that no matter what discreet precautions were taken by the Customsmen here before carrying out a search, no matter how stealthy their preparations, armed parties would anticipate their arrival and appear to challenge or harass them. No shots had been fired yet by either side, although some incautious and headstrong officers had been seized and tarred and feathered by these renegades, or beaten to within a breath of their lives, or otherwise humiliated or threatened with ominous reprisals. Some had even been coerced into signing promises to resign their commissions or posts under the threat of having their houses pulled down and their surviving property seized by the vandals to pay other Crown taxes and imposts.

Reports of such unfortunate incidents came from many of the port towns up and down all the rivers of the Roads. He had journeyed *incognito* to some of these places to evaluate their reputation for violence or their potential for trouble. He had gotten to know the country and its inhabitants, and had grown to dislike them. Everything was too raw here; he had yet to encounter a colonial who was not crude, or peevish, or insolent. Oh, how he ached for the abundant and sophisticated fleshpots of London, whose cosmopolitan ambience catered to every whim and pleasure!

But, thought Hunt — and he had thought it many times, and even wrote his father and his patron on the Customs Board about it — the contentious situation in the colonies, and in Virginia especially, could lead to only one end, as the clamor of authority opposed the hue and cry of resistance. They clashed repeatedly and would reach a deafening, ineluctable crescendo: war. He could almost smell it in the air.

He had believed it after having spent only a few weeks here. He believed it still. He smiled now, because others were certain of it, as well. Such as Hugh Kenrick. And probably Jack Frake. His informants had suggested that the master of Morland Hall was assembling a private armory of illegal weapons and ordnance. That was what he had wanted to find and confiscate, and to arrest that planter.

He knew about Jack Frake, and had known about him for years, and of his friendship with Hugh Kenrick. His father had in his possession political pamphlets the two men had written years ago, and also had collected information about them from a variety of sources, including from members of the Commons and Lords. His father had marked the pair for misery and was determined to extinguish their influence and existence in the realm of things that mattered.

Of course, he would not commit the action himself. He was averse to violence and other disagreeable matters. He remembered standing frozen in debilitating horror as he watched the murder of Dogmael Jones years ago, and being physically ill for some time after the event. But, he had proven quite adept at arranging such things to the satisfaction of all interested parties.

His own allegiance to the Crown was unshakable, founded largely on the promises of his father, the Earl of Danvers, of his own house in London, of a knighthood, of a lucrative sinecure, and perhaps even a seat in the Commons — all that if he could arrange the unfortunate demise of Hugh Kenrick, his father's nephew and his own cousin, in such a way that would bring shameful pain to the young man's father and his family, yet not cast any suspicion of culpability on the Earl. Until now, Hugh Kenrick had been a mere abstraction, a face in a family portrait. He had postponed seeking out this young man until he had accustomed himself to his new circumstances, and saw what was possible and what was not.

He had taken quick stock of the brash young Kenrick — whom he did not at first recognize — during that brief confrontation. He had been subjected to a taste of his character, and could now plan how to fulfill his father's wishes. It would not be easy, and it would take time. He knew that he had time.

War would not happen for a while.

As the *Fowey* gathered way down the river past Caxton, he speculated how much damage could be done to the town by the ship's guns. He thought: They wouldn't even need to aim.

*     *     *

Reverend Acland observed with surprise the party that had debouched from the *Fowey* returning to it so soon. He could see the Morland pier upriver, and noted that no objects had been deposited on it to be loaded into the galley boat and then taken to the warship. That was very curious, as well. He could see only the outermost part of the pier, and Morland's small flatboat and ketch moored on the other side of it, and the riverbank not at all.

As the warship coasted back down river, the minister paced back and forth on the bluff, deep in speculation. He wondered if the precipitate departure of Hugh Kenrick and his friends from the bluff had something to do with this development. He was certain that Jack Frake had been secreting something illegal. He had observed, from his home near Stepney Parish Church, strange nocturnal comings and goings over the last few months.

He had heard that the master of Morland had dug an ice cellar, a very strange project to have undertaken so close to spring, when there would be no ice to bring down from the Piedmont. Reece Vishonn of Enderly, he knew, stocked his ice cellar with ice in January, when the frozen stuff was transportable, and often available and plentiful in the brooks and streams that bordered his plantation. The minister hoped that he had not made a fool of himself and erred in his judgment. After all, he had signed the letter with an ebulliently sanctimonious relish.

The minister learned later, by means of jubilant gossip overheard in some of the shops he patronized, that the Customsmen had been foiled in their mission to rummage the great house of Morland by none other than Hugh Kenrick, his friends, and the tenants themselves.

In his private moments, the minister queried God about why He had chosen to place him in such iniquitous company. Then, by the logic of his beliefs, he answered the query himself, knowing that he was here to do His and the Crown's bidding. He took satisfaction in knowing that he was a tool of divine and imperial intervention, but managed to persuade himself that this personal felicity was of the virtuously disinterested kind. "My malice is pure and heaven inspired," he often thought to himself, "and it will be sated according to His merciful justice."

\*      \*      \*

Edgar Cullis, also a burgess for Queen Anne County, sat in his father's library at Cullis Hall, which neighbored Enderly, reading back issues of the two *Virginia Gazettes*, desiring to catch up with news from abroad and from the northern colonies, unaware that His Majesty's servants had attempted to heed his written advice to raid Morland Hall for what he suspected were contraband arms. He, too, had heard about the new ice cellar at Morland Hall, and had paid some of his father's servants to spy on the goings-on there. They had reported that at night, small fishing vessels and other river craft had called on the Morland pier to unload longish crates, kegs and other suspicious-looking cargo, and that they had been met by Mr. Frake and some of his tenants, who carted the goods to the great house.

Edgar Cullis had not spoken of any of this to his father, who was inclined to sympathize with Hugh Kenrick and other recalcitrants in the House. But the law was the law, he thought, and until an arguably oppressive law was repealed, or amended to correct its severity, flouting it deserved a commensurate penalty. Neglecting to enforce it could only lead to anarchy, mob rule, and destruction. Jack Frake, for as long as Cullis had known him, had been a leading flouter of the law. And now he was a ringleader in a concerted movement to defy the Crown. It was time he was reined in and taught the value of obedience. With his incarceration and punishment, the "patriot" movement in Queen Anne County would collapse, and the county would not suffer the reprisals that were certain to be visited on other lawless counties and towns, once the Crown decided to restore order in its dominions.

Edgar Cullis, attorney, loyal citizen of Virginia and steadfast subject of the Crown, believed in moderation in all things.

\*      \*      \*

"I see you hurtling toward some needless tragedy, Hugh," she said, not looking at him, but at the *Fowey* as it passed slowly downriver, "and I don't want to be here to witness it."

"Hurtling?" he answered. "Yes, I concede that I am hurtling towards something. To a needless tragedy? No. Rather, towards necessary action."

When he returned to Meum Hall, after a search in the great house, he found Reverdy standing alone near the edge of the riverfront lawn. He knew how disturbed she was; she was absently worrying the riding chair whip she still held in both hands, having left the conveyance at the stable. And all he had said to her, as he came to stand by her, was "Reverdy." And she had answered.

"It is your friendship with Roger," she continued in answer to an unasked question, "and how you greeted each other yesterday, that led me to think that perhaps I was wrong to want to leave. You, and he, and his being in the army, and why he is here — they all led me to think that perhaps I was mistaken, that perhaps some meeting of the ways was possible." She added with some bitterness, "But then I saw the both of you just now at Morland, with all those weapons at the ready, and I realized that I was deluding myself."

Hugh shook his head. "What you were afraid would happen, did not. If that incident were emulated all over, on larger scales, throughout the colonies, then what you are afraid of, will not — cannot happen. The Crown's determination must be doubly matched by our own, and then there will be no tragedies."

"By your *own* determination," said Reverdy in the manner of a mild accusation. "And I am certain that some day, some time, in such a circumstance as you describe, someone will be angry enough to fire his musket, a friend or an adversary, and you will be there, and that will be the end...."

"Or perhaps the beginning...." remarked Hugh wistfully.

"Must you turn round everything I say?"

"You know that is my style. It has usually amused you." Hugh allowed himself a smile. "Perhaps the present unpleasantness can be turned round, as well." He paused. "I wish you to stay to see that, my dear...to help me accomplish it."

"You will not accomplish it, Hugh. You will only bring...retribution, and grief, to us, to everyone we know, and ruin to everything we hold dear."

Hugh reached over and took one of her hands. "I may well not accomplish it, if you...are not here. That would be my grief."

"You will not accomplish it, whether or not I am here."

"Such prophetic gloom," he sighed, "and such an intimate reproach."

Reverdy winced, as though hurt. "It is not a reproach, Hugh! It is...*caring*!"

Hugh took Reverdy by the shoulders and held her. "My dear, you applauded me in the past, when I composed and signed petitions against the Crown, and when I spoke in the House against the Crown, and advocated boycotts of the Crown's merchants, and assailed the Crown in seditious pamphlets. You have even regaled visitors with the story of how I led the obstruction of the stamps at Caxton pier years ago. What is the difference between all that, and now? How can you care the less?"

Reverdy shook her head. "I care the *more*, Hugh. And, if one is so certain of the fate of a particular thing, is it so wrong to express a natural prophetic gloom?"

Hugh let her go. "No, perhaps not, my dear. But, for my part, such certainty is the better part of resolution. I have been gloomy over events for many years, but I have always managed to turn the gloom into glory. You know that."

Reverdy bowed her head in defeat. "So many words to compose an epitaph! My fear is that you will oblige me to order a stonemason to carve them into a tombstone — yours!"

Hugh frowned, and replied, partly in defiance, partly in anger with her bitterness, "Or, in an epigraph, etched in gold letters on the finest mahogany, to affix above my study door, at Meum Hall!"

Reverdy glanced up at him, hurt in her eyes, and tears. Then she fell against him, resting her head on his chest, her sight locked on the menacing *Fowey* growing smaller on the river. "The simple explanation, Hugh, is that...I am a coward!"

Hugh's arms encircled her, and he crushed her to him. He buried his face in her hair, and whispered into her ear, "What courage it took to confess *that!*" After a moment, he held her away from him, but grasped her shoulders. "Reverdy, you shall go to England. To rest from me, from the circumstances here, to recover the balance of your spirit. And then you shall return here to me, to Meum Hall, your true home, renewed and reinvigorated from the perspective of distance, and encouraged to stand with me again."

Reverdy sobbed once, and embraced him with passionate gratitude.

Hugh held her close, thinking suddenly of the time he was last in London, and was wandering through Vauxhall Gardens when he chanced upon a concert. He remembered standing in a crowd, listening to an opera singer in a box above them, performing with an orchestra behind her Scarlatti's "Christmas Cantata." Reverdy had sung it for him years ago, and shamelessly told him afterwards that the cantata more suited him than its original subject. He remembered being enthralled by the singer's performance, but thinking also that Reverdy sang it so much more convincingly than that opera singer. He remembered how hearing the cantata then struck him with a wrenching homesickness.

That was the Reverdy he wanted back. He was certain that some time in England would cause her to rediscover him and become equally anxious to return.

# Chapter 7: The Guests

"Thank you for your gallantry, sir," said Jack Frake, "and for your honesty."

When he had ridden back to Meum Hall with Lieutenant Manners, he had found Hugh and Reverdy returning to the great house from the riverfront lawn. He had conveyed to them an invitation from Etáin to supper at Morland that evening.

At the supper table now, Roger Tallmadge nodded in silent acknowledgement. He had just finished explaining his presence in the colonies to his host.

Jack Frake had returned with Mouse early in the evening, before supper and the expected guests, and was immediately besieged in the front yard by Etáin and others with the story of the confrontation with the Customsmen. As he absorbed the details of the incident, the anger in his eyes abated as his sweaty mount regained its wind from the hard ride from Yorktown.

Now he looked bemused. "Which leaves me to wonder, Mr. Tallmadge: Why did you draw your sword against that man? Your loyalties seem to be divided."

Roger smiled and glanced once at Hugh down the table. "Not at all, Mr. Frake. In all the years that Hugh and I have been friends, I had never had the opportunity to join him in a caper, not until today." He paused, then added, "There was that, together with a dislike of the man we faced."

"Had you never before witnessed Customsmen at their calling?"

"No. I confess I have not. Not even in England."

"A press gang?"

"Once. At Great Yarmouth. A brutal and ignominious affair."

"Why do you think those men appeared here, and not at some other plantation near Caxton?"

Roger shrugged. "Presumably they received information that you ought to be searched. For what, I can only imagine. Perhaps it was for a cache of French muskets and powder, or a chest or two of Dutch tea. Or bolts of Italian cambric."

Jack Frake smiled. "Would you have objected to my possessing any of those commodities? Illegally, of course."

"Personally, no. When I have attended the Commons, without exception I have voted with the free-traders in the House, scarce as they are, and against every act that now burdens these colonies." Tallmadge smiled in modesty. "I owe that record to the persuasiveness of Hugh here, and to that of the late Sir Dogmael Jones. And, to that of Hugh's father."

"Yes," remarked Jack. "Hugh has boasted of your record in the Commons. Well, sir, perhaps, when you have completed your mission here, you will return to London and vote in that manner again."

Tallmadge could not decide if his host's words were friendly or hostile. He knew that his host was making an exception for Hugh's sake, not for his own, by allowing him to sup at his table. He replied, "That is my earnest hope, Mr. Frake. Why, upon my return, I may even resign my commission, and seek employment with Hugh's father's bank." Tallmadge paused. "Or, I may apply for a posting as a consular military attaché on the Continent. It's plum duty, and I could take my wife Alice with me. Her father would gladly supplement my half-pay to ensure a comfortable residence. And I'm certain that promotion to major would come with it, for the examiners of my past postings have given me exemplary marks in the diplomatic." But the gaiety of his words seemed to shatter on the rocky reticence of his host's expression.

After a long moment, during which he seemed to be making a decision, Jack Frake said, with some genuine humor, "I earnestly hope that you succeed in one of those ambitions, Mr. Tallmadge. It may save me the trouble of facing you with a drawn sword, as well, in the event that war comes."

Tallmadge answered with reciprocating humor, "In that event, sir, I shall endeavor to remain beyond its point."

Lieutenant Manners spoke up, and remarked leisurely. "Begging your pardon, sir, but it is not likely that *war* will come. That is too grandiose and undeserving a name for it, it seems to me. When mobs cause chaos and jeopardize lives and property in London, as they often do, His Majesty simply approves a request from the authorities to employ troops to restore order. That is not *war*. Wars occur between nations, and none of the colonies is a *nation*. They are all dominions, as much as any English county, and if their inhabitants misbehave themselves, deserve the same modest civil corrective."

The table became silent. Tallmadge's face flushed red with anger and embarrassment. Hugh stared with disbelief at the junior officer. Jack Frake eyed the lieutenant with steely contempt. Etáin glanced with sudden worry at her husband, knowing that he was within a breath of demanding that the officer leave. Reverdy stared into the remains of her supper on the plate in front of her, bracing for an explosion she was sure to come. Even the waiting servants, Ruth Dakin and Israel Beck, stood blinking in shock.

Tallmadge removed his napkin and dropped it on the table beside his plate. Without rising or looking at his subordinate, he said, "Mr. Manners, you will please apologize to Mr. Frake for those unsolicited and unkind remarks."

Lieutenant Manners looked stunned. He gulped once, and asked, with diminished audacity, "Do you wish me to withdraw my remarks, sir?"

Tallmadge turned to face the officer, and replied with an ice that matched his expression, "Or yourself from the company, sir, if you cannot oblige him or me."

The junior officer glanced around the table and saw no defenders. He gulped again, uncontrollably, when his eyes met those of Jack Frake's; the hard gray eyes of that man caused him to imagine that a pair of musket barrels was aimed at him. Unlike his superior, Manners had never experienced combat; he had the wild idea that his present paralysis was what he would feel facing an enemy's fire the first time. He had chanced an opinion, but lost the bluff. He seemed to collapse into himself. With a quick, furtive nod to Jack Frake, and with a reddened face, he stammered, "I withdraw my remarks, sir." He did not look up for the rest of the occasion. It was the first time Captain Tallmadge had ever upbraided him for his behavior, at least in front of others.

"Thank you, Mr. Manners," said Tallmadge. He glanced down the table to Jack Frake. The host nodded briefly once in acceptance. Tallmadge smiled tentatively, then said, in an effort to change the subject and relieve the tension, "Where is this Mr. Proudlocks Hugh has written me so much about? I know that he was in London, reading law, and that he has returned."

Etáin asked, "You did not meet him when he stayed with Hugh's parents?"

"No," Tallmadge replied. "Only once, and briefly, on the fly, at Hugh's parents' home in Chelsea. But, I was shuttling between London and the Continent on various diplomatic postings, and on my way to another then. Alice has written me that he is quite the gentleman and scholar."

The conversation continued on that and other subjects for the rest of

the evening. It was cordial but muted talk, dampened by Lieutenant Manners's remarks. When Hugh, Reverdy and the officers prepared to depart
for Meum Hall, it was with a curious relief felt by all. Hugh did, however,
extend to Jack and Etáin an invitation to supper at Meum Hall on June 1
in order to observe the day of "fasting and prayer" voted by the House of
Burgesses.

"We shall commiserate with the Bostonians in our own fashion," said
Hugh, "with bountiful fare and good cheer." They stood on the porch of the
great house. Lieutenant Manners had gone to the stable to fetch his and
Tallmadge's mounts, while the captain sat waiting in the riding chair with
Reverdy. Etáin stood by the conveyance, chatting with them. "And Etáin
and Reverdy will perform for us, as well."

Jack replied, "Of course. As long as Mr. Tallmadge's companion opens
his mouth solely to fill it with your fare." He paused. "You don't know how
close I came to chucking him out the door."

"I've a very good idea, Jack. But, trust Roger to instruct him in some
rules of civility."

Jack Frake studied his friend for a moment, then said, "Your friend is
a man of honor."

"Yes, he is. It is my hope that you both may become better acquainted,
in less circumspect times."

Jack nodded. After another moment, he remarked, "When they've
gone, I have something to show you."

"What?"

"That will become evident, when you see it."

*      *      *

That evening, in the room they shared at Meum Hall, Roger Tallmadge told
his subordinate, "For the balance of our journey, Mr. Manners, until we
arrive in Boston, you will please stay your tongue in all matters political,
when we are in company."

"Yes, sir," replied the lieutenant, who sat at a side table with an open
book. "But, must the Crown remain silent when its character is
besmirched?"

Tallmadge's face became taut with amazement. "Mr. Manners, *you* are
not the Crown. It rests on the wisdom of His Majesty and his counselors to
decide if it is in conflict with the colonies or at war with another nation,

and to prescribe, as you put it, the proper corrective."

"Yes, sir." Manners mechanically turned over a few leaves of Flavius Vegetius Renatua's treatise, *De Re Militari*, without seeing a single word, then resolutely closed it shut and said, "Forgive me the insolence, sir, but you must think me less than diligent if, when I witness your actions at Morland Hall today, and hear the sentiments expressed by you this evening, I am not led to suspect that, as Mr. Frake himself put it, your loyalties are divided."

Tallmadge frowned, and said with sharpness, "If they are, Mr. Manners, that is between me, my conscience, and the Crown. I will not answer your or anyone else's speculation on the matter. The subject is closed to discussion."

"Yes, sir." The lieutenant turned in his chair and opened the book again.

*　　*　　*

In another part of the great house, Reverdy asked, "When do you think Mr. Geary will return to Caxton?" She stood at the bedroom window, contemplating some lights that shown faintly across the York. She was still shaken by the near-disaster at Morland Hall.

"In a few days. He has cargo to lade at West Point, and then some lumber and oats here."

"So...I must begin preparing for the journey. Dilch will help me pack."

"Yes, of course." Hugh stood studying her figure at the window for a moment. "Well, I am to the study, to draft some letters you may take with you to post. Will you go to London first, or to Danvers?"

"I think I shall see my parents first, in Danvers, then journey up to London to stay a while with Alex's parents. Or with James and his wife. They have a fine house on Berkeley Square." Alex McDougal was her late husband, who had died years ago during a foiled robbery. James Brune was her brother, a merchant and trader with the McDougal commercial interests.

"You would surely be welcome in Chelsea," suggested Hugh. His parents lived at Cricklegate, a spacious house in Chelsea, just west of London on the Thames.

"I know," answered Reverdy. "I will call on your parents...once I have regained some peace."

Hugh smiled tentatively. "It's very odd that you will be seeing the McDougals. I have never met Alex's parents."

A moment passed before Reverdy answered, "You were never meant to, Hugh." It almost sounded like a reproach.

Hugh sighed. "Yes. Of course not." He paused. "Well, I will be downstairs for a while." Then he turned and left the room.

*     *     *

John Proudlocks called on Meum Hall the next day and offered his apology for not having visited Hugh and Reverdy sooner after his return from England. "I am a man of property now, and, as Jack has told me many times in the past, property is a demanding mistress."

"Well worth the attention, I trust, with commensurate rewards," Reverdy teased him.

Proudlocks was stunned by this risqué reply. He laughed once, "What an unladylike sentiment!"

"That is what happens when a lady is permitted to peruse gentlemen's literature, as I do. There would be more and better ladies and mistresses, if our sex could widen its reading. And, I might add, more *contented* husbands." Reverdy grinned at the helpless look on her guest's face. She laughed. "Well, you will need to neglect your own mistress for a while, Mr. Proudlocks, and join us today on a picnic on the front lawn, and tell us all about her and London."

Proudlocks stayed for the rest of the afternoon, and made better acquaintance with Roger Tallmadge. Tallmadge asked about Alice, whom he had not seen in over a year. Proudlocks assured him that she was in perfect health and in good spirits. It was a perfectly balmy day for the picnic. The house servants set up a table on the lawn near the bluff overlooking the river. Hugh, Reverdy, Tallmadge, and Proudlocks chatted happily over a meal of sweetmeats, tea and wine. Lieutenant Manners, not trusting himself again in the company of his superior's friends, was granted leave by Tallmadge to ride into Caxton to find amusement there. The conversation ranged from the possibility of a drought to the rising prices in the shops in Caxton and Williamsburg as a result of the stricter enforcement of taxes and regulations by the navy and the Customsmen.

The conversation eventually turned to speculation on the identity of "Junius," author of a series of letters published in the *Public Advertiser* in

London between 1769 and 1772 that criticized the Grafton ministry. The letters not only scandalized the Duke of Grafton, but St. James's Palace, as well.

Hugh said, "I am only now finding the time to read the newspapers that Captain Ramshaw was kind enough to send to me. Well, the letters do not so much argue against corruption and the mendacity of Grafton, as attack him with invective and insinuation. Hardly a practical means of bringing men to justice. His letters are too coy to my taste."

Roger added, "He has also attacked Viscount Barrington."

"And the whole of the king's party, and His Majesty, as well," added Proudlocks.

"It is a wonder to me that the ministry never moved against the *Advertiser*," said Hugh.

Roger shook his head. "No wonder at all, Hugh. Lessons have been learned from the Wilkes imbroglio. Now that the Commons' debates can be reported, ministers and members are chary of bringing charges against publishers and printers. I believe a new era of accountability has dawned in England. Who knows where it will lead?"

Hugh shrugged. "For the moment, in more immediate ministerial doings, to more covinous stealth," he remarked. "Who do you think it was?" he asked.

Roger shook his head. "I could not speculate with any certainty. Your father believes it was Sir Philip Francis, in the War Office. Others think Lord Shelburne." The captain looked ironic. "If I had spent more time in the Commons, instead of traipsing about the Continent, I might have had a better candidate to suggest, such as a discontented Whig surgeon in the army!" he added with a laugh.

"Yes," replied Hugh with amusement. "My father wrote me about that. He also noted that wagers were made on Junius's identity." Then he sighed. "Well, the public reporting of the Commons business, and the plummeting of actions against printers — they are both posthumous victories of Mr. Jones."

The conversation turned to the James Somerset case at the King's Bench of two summers ago. "Ah, yes! There's another cause he would have taken up with consummate alacrity!" exclaimed Hugh.

Proudlocks had followed the case while he was in London, taking a special interest in it and other cases of slaves attempting to gain their freedom in the courts. "I was present at the King's Bench in Westminster

Hall when Lord Mansfield read the final decision on Mr. Somerset," he said. "After consulting his many other deliberations on the subject, I concluded that he is a timid, cautious man. And, the decision has been misinterpreted by slaves and freedman alike." Proudlocks sipped his wine. "Mr. Somerset's case was championed by Mr. Granville Sharp and a brace of sergeants who matched his ardor on the issue. Mr. Sharp in particular has represented many blacks in Britain. He has also turned his attention to abolishing press gangs, another form of slavery. I have met him. He has even endorsed the American cause."

"Lord Mansfield is no friend of liberty," Hugh remarked. "I don't wonder that he wished to tread softly on the matter of a man's liberty. He belittled colonial authority and recommended passage of most of the Acts passed by Parliament after the late war with the French. But, how was he misinterpreted?"

"Everyone believed the freeing of Somerset a universal emancipation of slaves in Britain. That was not Lord Mansfield's intention. He simply discharged Mr. Somerset in a ruling that he hoped avoided precedent. But, it is seen as one, nonetheless. I have heard that he strenuously objected to the misreading of his finding. However, most freedmen, slaves, and abolitionists continue to remark that Mr. Somerset's situation was similar in many respects to that of any slave who ran away, was recaptured, and who subsequently sued for his freedom."

"What were Mansfield's reservations?"

"He was cognizant of the consequences of a universal emancipation, in Britain, at least. He dwelt on the enormous loss of property by slaveholders there, especially in the port towns, and imagined large bands of ex-slaves roaming the Isles to enslave whites or steal their employment." Proudlocks laughed. "It was a most amusing predicament that Lord Mansfield found himself in. He could not deny the logic and justice of Mr. Somerset's cause, and could not but concur with it, however, under protest!"

Tallmadge chuckled. "Well, it seems that Lord Mansfield played the quack physician by prescribing a vial of mercury to cure the patient of an insufferable complaint. But, he accomplished the patient's demise, instead, quite to the surprise of both parties!"

Hugh raised his wine glass in a mock toast. "Here's to Lord Mansfield, then, and to all such quackery!"

The company laughed and joined him in the toast.

Proudlocks said, "Of course, the greatest advocates of the re-enslavement of runaway blacks were the West Indian planters. The Attorney-General and Solicitor-General sided with them, accepting their petitions to oppose emancipation and abolition." Proudlocks looked thoughtful. "Your friend, Glorious Swain, lived in a legal purgatory not dissimilar to that of most blacks in Britain today, imprisoned between Chief Justice Holt's ruling in 1706 that once a black set foot in England, he could claim his freedom, and the Attorney-General's contention, which conformed with the common legal opinion that this was not true, that neither a black's baptism as a Christian nor the lapse or extinction of feudal villeinage in Britain nullified his status as a slave."

"Glorious was born in London, as well, on London Bridge," Hugh mused. He looked pensive for a moment, then turned to Roger. "Well, a portion of His Majesty's personal budget relies on the slave trade, and what justice or Parliament would ever dare deny him it?" He paused again, and asked Tallmadge. "When you supped with the Governor, Roger, did the subject of slavery arise in your conversation? His Excellency also derives a fractional share in that trade."

Roger shook his head. "No. Not once."

"Another reason I dislike that man is that a year or so ago he is alleged to have remarked that all the runaways here and throughout the colonies could be encouraged by the Crown to exact their 'revenge' on their former masters and anyone else who opposed the Crown's conquest of the colonies."

Proudlocks said, "He could not encourage them except by promising them their liberty."

"Precisely," Hugh answered. "What another pair of shoes that would be! A tyrant proclaiming liberty!"

"The liberty to serve the Crown," agreed Proudlocks, "and little else."

"Why, Hugh!" exclaimed Reverdy, "There's an idea for a dark comedy you could compose!"

Hugh smiled wanly. "No, my dear. I have advanced beyond satire. But, perhaps you shall see its like in London."

Reverdy, usually sensitive to the nuances of her husband's moods, was in too gay a spirit today to note the muted bitterness in his reply. She glanced away from him and espied a figure coming from the great house. "Oh! Here comes Mr. Spears, looking very urgent!" she said. The valet and major domo of Meum Hall approached the group and stopped before Hugh. "Sir, a courier from Williamsburg has just called and left this for you." He handed his employer a sealed sheaf of papers.

"Thank you, Spears," replied Hugh, taking it. Spears bowed once and returned to the house.

Hugh broke the seal and opened the papers. After a moment, he said, "It is a dispatch from our committee of correspondence, calling for a convention on August, first, to discuss another association for the nonimportation and non-exportation of goods vis-à-vis Britain, and our joining with other colonies in that project. This, on the advice of other colonies' committees. 'Things seem to be hurrying to an alarming crisis,' it reads. That is an understatement." He smiled. "And, here is a note from Mr. Jefferson, appending a copy of the broadside I neglected to sign, and chiding me on that account." He handed the papers over the table to Proudlocks. "Mr. Randolph and the committee are also requesting that we former burgesses 'collect the sense of our respective counties.' By that, I suppose they mean resolutions. The citizens of Williamsburg have already sanctioned a convention and nonimportation measures."

"Mr. Cullis will not help you compose resolutions," Reverdy warned. "And I doubt that Reverend Acland will lend you his church for a meeting of the freeholders to agree on any, either."

Proudlocks nodded. "I agree with you, milady," he said. "Mr. Cullis is a tepid patriot."

"This is true," Hugh sighed. "Still, I will call on him to discuss the matter. And, the freeholders can always be called together in one of the taverns."

Later that afternoon, Hugh rode alone to Cullis Hall on the other side of Caxton to advise Edgar Cullis of the convention news, only to learn from the burgess's mother, Hetty, that her husband Ralph and her son had departed the day before for the Piedmont on a wolf and deer hunting outing. She did not expect them back for another two or three weeks. "They had planned to leave after the General Assembly had adjourned," she said, "but were able to go sooner than they had planned."

This had happened often before, when Hugh needed to confer with his fellow burgess on pressing House business. He thought it too convenient, this time, but did not express his suspicion to the woman that Cullis wanted to distance himself from what he regarded as treasonous actions of the House. Cullis had been the sole burgess to argue and vote against the day of fasting and prayer, which was tomorrow. He thanked Mrs. Cullis for the information and reclaimed his mount from the stable hand.

His next stop on the way back to Caxton was Enderly, where he found

Reece Vishonn riding through one of his vast fields, supervising some of his tenants and slaves in moving young tobacco plants from their seed beds to hundreds of hills.

Vishonn was not so much startled by news of the call for a convention, as disturbed by it. "And Mr. Cullis is away," he said. "Well, that puts you, as our remaining burgess, in an awkward patch, does it not? Speaking as a justice in our own court, I would question the legality of calling a meeting of the freeholders, with only one of you present. Should they vote on a resolution to approve the convention and that other business, Mr. Cullis would surely sue you or the county for having acted without his consultation. Besides, neither of you is truly a burgess, now that the Assembly has been dissolved. Neither you nor Mr. Cullis would have the authority to call a meeting, or to take any political action at all, not until you were reelected after His Excellency had signed a writ for new elections."

Hugh grimaced. "That, apparently, is the Governor's intention."

"*What* is his intention?" asked Vishonn with a curiosity that sounded offended.

"To cast us all beyond the pale of legal action. To put us outside the law." He was silent for a while. "Well, I must agree with you about the dubious legality of calling a meeting. But, I had not expected Mr. Cullis to bolt so soon after the alarm. If we are to flout the Crown, we must have some semblance of unanimity."

Vishonn shook his head. "I am afraid unanimity will not be found in Queen Anne, my friend."

Hugh imagined that he heard a note of relief in Vishonn's words. He thanked the planter for his time and rode back across Caxton to Morland Hall, where he spoke with Jack Frake. "He's right," said Jack. "Half the planters and freeholders here would not agree to a general meeting without you *and* Mr. Cullis calling for it."

Hugh stood in Jack's study. He smacked his open palm with a fist. "What a shame! And ours was the county that foiled the stamp men, yet it cannot bring itself to defy a greater beast!"

Jack nodded in agreement. "Mr. Vishonn is right about no quorum of the citizenry being possible here, Hugh, even though he is wrong to be happy about it. The day is coming soon when the Governor will dissolve the House permanently, and then we must form our own lawful assembly, without the Crown's leave." He watched his friend pace back and forth before his study windows.

Beyond, at the far end of his fields, his tenants were busy planting the last tobacco seedlings from the beds, on both sides of the irrigation trench he had dug years ago. "We could at least call a meeting of the Sons of Liberty, Hugh, to advise them of the news. They represent about one quarter of the freeholders in the county. Not that any resolutions we might pass would be countenanced by Mr. Randolph and his committee."

"Nor recognized by him as being in anywise legal. He was, after all, once the Attorney-General." Hugh stood before Jack's desk for a moment, looking thoughtful. Then he picked up his hat and snapped it on. "Well, Beecroft and I can pen some notices, at least, for the Sons, and post them on the courthouse door and at taverns. To meet at Safford's place. What day would you recommend?"

# Chapter 8: The Observance

"Fasting, humiliation, and prayer? Three guarantors of weakness and submission!" exclaimed Jack Frake at the supper table at Meum Hall the following evening. "I have never understood how those expressions of virtue could ever be regarded as sources of strength and resolve in the face of tyranny."

"Hear, hear!" echoed Hugh Kenrick. "And let their companion, *moderation*, also be stricken from the catalogue of virtues — except in science!"

Proudlocks proclaimed, "The Crown's tyrannical policy shall wreck itself on the Godwin Sands of folly and war, and the disparate principles of England's constitution, like ruptured bulkheads, shall fill up with water and drowning men!"

"Hear, hear!" replied Jack Frake quietly with a smile at his oldest friend.

"What a sad sentiment to wish on your countrymen," Reverdy remarked in mild reproach.

Jack Frake leaned forward and said, "We do not wish it upon them, Reverdy. It is what must happen, in time."

"And happen here first," added Hugh. "And, if our countrymen are fortunate, *there*."

The supper table of Meum Hall, cleared now of the finished main courses, was resplendent with some of the finest Delft and creamware table furniture and cutlery in the county, resting on a shimmering, oblong plane of thick, French-made linen. Candelabra, silver candlesticks, and wall sconces lit up the table, the room, and the company. In the precise middle of the table reigned the silver epergne that Hugh had used years before to explain and praise the British Empire. Its many-layered dishes were piled with sweetmeats, biscuits and fruit. Dessert consisted of slices of pineapple, peach and pear in a cream sauce and brandy-flavored wine cake. The wine itself was the best Bordeaux from Hugh's cellar.

Captain Roger Tallmadge and Lieutenant William Manners sat together at the table. Around them sat the other guests: Rupert Beecroft and William Settle, of Meum Hall, and Obedience Robbins and William Hurry, of Morland Hall. Tallmadge said nothing in reply to the exclamations of Jack Frake, his friend Hugh, and John Proudlocks. He said very little at all; he merely smiled, and observed, and was happy that he knew such men. He would like to have seconded his hostess's remark, but thought it wiser to keep his own counsel. Lieutenant Manners merely ate and appeared indifferent to the talk.

While the rest of Queen Anne County — indeed, while much of Virginia, at the behest of parish ministers and returning burgesses — observed the day with fasting, humiliation, and prayer in protest of the closing of the port of Boston, Hugh had decided to protest in his own manner, by celebrating the prosperity that was to be denied Boston.

Most of Williamsburg's citizens had turned out to hear Speaker Peyton Randolph deliver a noontime address from the steps of the courthouse on Market Square. Then they followed him and his colleagues to Bruton Parish Church to hear a sermon delivered by the House chaplain, the Reverend Thomas Price. This person replaced Reverend Thomas Gwatkin, the principal of the grammar school at the College of William and Mary, who had declined the invitation by the House to endorse the protest with his own sermon. He was later to become Lady Dunmore's personal chaplain, and ultimately leave with her in a pique of self-exile for England.

In the warm confines of Stepney Parish Church in Caxton, Reverend Albert Acland stood at his pulpit and delivered his prayers and sermon. He was pleased that so many of his flock had decided to attend this special service, even though he had opposed the idea. But Moses Corbin, mayor of Caxton, had appeared at his doorstep early yesterday morning and requested in a curiously insistent manner that he accede to the wishes of many in the county.

The minister today decided to be cautious but outspoken, and delivered a sermon that was not overtly hostile or critical of the day of fasting, prayer and humiliation. So many in his congregation agreed with the purpose of the observance. Also, he knew that many here today had heard of the confrontation between Etáin Frake and the Customsmen at Morland Hall two days before; word of the incident had spread throughout the town and outlying plantations and farms.

Today, instead of donning his vestments of office, he wore a plain cassock, to seem to personally reflect the spirit of the occasion. He read from two "thanksgivings" from the prayer book.

"Let us beseech our Savior to grant us peace and deliverance from our enemies, and to help us restore public peace at home. O Almighty God, who art a strong tower of defence unto thy servants against the face of their enemies! We acknowledge it thy goodness that we were not delivered over as a prey unto them. O Eternal God, who alone makes men to be of one mind in a house, and stillest the outrage of a violent and unruly people, we bless thy holy Name, that it hath pleased thee to appease the seditious tumults which have been lately raised up amongst us...."

Moses Corbin and his wife Jewel were not the only couple that exchanged discreet whispers that their pastor had mixed his texts from the prayer book. And many other parishioners seemed to frown in suspicion of whom he referred to as their enemies and unruly people.

Acland then turned to his sermon, and in it dwelt on the necessity of all present to accept a Lenten mode of sackcloth and ashes. He dared to equivocate between the Bostonians doing repentance for their "sins" and his parishioners doing penance for them.

"It is first noted in Genesis, chapter thirty-seven," he said, "the willingness of men to grieve in that abrasive attire. Can we, many millennia removed from those times, do no less for our intransigent brethren to the north? For in praying, fasting and gratefully conceding our smallness and the vanity and meagerness of our hubris in the face of God's will, we shall redeem our souls as well as theirs. Our prodigal brethren to the north, prompted by the designs of scepsical scoundrels, it seems will be reduced to sackcloth and ashes and beggary as the justice of a *greater power*. So, my friends, let us pray and fast today so that they may be welcomed again into His benevolent and forgiving embrace.... "

In the course of his delivery, Acland noticed a face in the congregation he had never seen before. It was probably a traveler who had decided to attend the service. He thought, however, that the stranger looked incurious, and not particularly pious.

That person, sitting in a pew in the rear of the church, was Jared Hunt, who had journeyed on horseback up from Hampton to spy on the parties who had informed him of the necessity of searching Morland Hall. Acland was one of those informants. Hunt, listening to the pastor drone on, was satisfied that Acland was a "true patriot," and could be used somehow in the future.

When the service was over, he was the first out the door. He did not wish to meet the minister, not now. He rode next to Cullis Hall. Here he introduced himself as a citizen of Williamsburg and an acquaintance of her son whom he had met during the late session of the General Assembly, and said that he had spoken with that esteemed person about some legal matter.

He was informed by the mistress of that plantation that her husband and son were away. The woman offered him some tea, but he wisely declined and bid her good day.

When he rode back into Caxton and searched for a place in which to have a drink and a meal before he journeyed to Williamsburg to seek an audience with Governor Dunmore, he saw that all the taverns and inns were shut but one, the Gramatan Inn. Over a bottle of port there, he asked the young wench who served him why this establishment was open, and none of the others.

"It's this day of starvin' and mumblin'," the woman said. "Mr. Gramatan said he'd have no part in it, it was treasonous and such, and wait 'til His Majesty hears of it, they'll all get what for. His very words, but don't say I said it."

"What do *you* think of it?" asked Hunt.

The woman shrugged. "Makes me no never mind, sir," she said. "I got five years left in my 'denture, and I don't plan to starve or mumble much of that time. It's none of my business, all this hootin' and shoutin' they do around here about rights and liberty! Well, I ain't got either, and I ain't goin' to risk havin' years added to my 'denture, you can wager on that!"

"Are you a felon, or a redemptioner? What's your name?"

"I ain't no convict! It's Mary Griffin," the woman retorted with flashing eyes, "and I bought me passage, if you please! From an agent in Cheapside, right there by the Guildhall, a fella who signed a whole bunch of us up for passage!"

He thought so. Her accent was too pronounced. Probably a true Cockney, if there was any truth in her protest, born and raised within earshot of the bells of St. Mary le Bow. There was no one else in the place except the barman, who was dozing for lack of custom. He asked her a few discreet questions about Jack Frake and Hugh Kenrick, and was rewarded with some derisive commentary on those gentlemen. Satisfied that those men enjoyed some disrepute in these parts, he ceased his queries, for he had pledged to draw the least amount of attention to himself on this expedition. He apologized unnecessarily for the presumption of her felonious status, and Mary Griffin left him to tend to his guinea hen roasting on a spit in the fireplace.

When he had finished his meal, he lingered for a while over another bottle of port and read some newspapers he took from the rack — Maryland and Virginia *Gazettes*, and even some old London papers — then left to reclaim his mount from the Inn stable hand, who had fed and watered the animal. He estimated that he should reach Williamsburg by dusk and be able to find a room there for the night.

*   *   *

The concert that evening at Meum Hall was an oddly subdued, almost dispirited affair. Etáin played her harp as beautifully as always, and Reverdy sang some arias from operas, among them Scarlatti's "Pastoral on the Nativity" and Bononcini's "The Glory of Loving You," favorites of Hugh. Etáin ended the evening with Haydn's "Serenade," "Brian Boru's March," and "Hugh O'Donnell" — the latter for the host and hostess, who were soon to part for a long period of time. She was pleased to see them holding hands as they sat listening to her play that number. But, while all the performances were acknowledged with the appropriate applause, something was missing from the usual enthusiasm. Etáin thought that it was because everyone knew that this would perhaps be the last time they would sing and play together.

"That was a melancholy time," remarked Jack Frake to Etáin as they rode back in a riding chair to Morland Hall after saying their goodnights late in the evening. Etáin's harp was strapped to the back of the conveyance. Robbins and Hurry rode behind them. "The company was nearly funereal."

"Mr. Tallmadge is departing with his friend tomorrow, and Reverdy perhaps in a week, when Mr. Geary returns from West Point. That must explain their own melancholy. But, ours?"

Jack Frake shook his head. "There will be no more concerts for a long while."

"No," sighed Etáin, "I suppose not." After a moment, she said, "Mr. Proudlocks was in fine form tonight. I could see that Lieutenant Manners was biting his tongue."

"Yes, John was in his best form." Jack glanced at her once. "And you were in fine form yesterday. Would you have shot that Customsman if he had tried to force his way into our home?"

"Yes, of course." After a moment, Etáin added, "I was afraid, Jack."

"Of course, you were. So were Mr. Robbins and Mr. Hurry, and all our tenants, as well." He reached over with one arm and held her shoulder. "You might have started the war ahead of time."

Etáin grinned. "Yes. I might have, at that." Then she frowned. "There will be a war, won't there?"

"Yes. There will be a war."

"Ahead of time? Is there a proper time to begin a war?"

Jack nodded once. "From what my friends up north have written, I'm not the only one who has collected a personal armory in expectation of one, and General Gage is on the alert to find those other collections and to rob us of the means of fighting a war." He paused. "Somewhere, somehow, it will begin when the army moves to seize those means, and is opposed by another."

"An army of men who have caught up with you, Jack."

His hand had not left Etáin's shoulder. He smiled and squeezed it once in silent confirmation. Her hand reached over and rested on top of the hand in his lap that held the reins.

*   *   *

"Well, *elder* brother, we bid *adieu* again," said Captain Roger Tallmadge to Hugh.

"*Adieu*, not farewell," answered the latter. "Remember that, *younger* brother."

"Well, brother-in-law, we may meet again soon, and in London!" laughed Reverdy.

The officer stood with Lieutenant Manners in the front of the porch steps of the great house of Meum Hall. Their two mounts and the pack-horse that carried their bags were held by a stable hand at a distance.

It was early morning and dew still glistened on the leaves of trees and on blades of grass. The four had just finished breakfast. The last hour had been filled with the minutiæ of preparing for the officers' departure. The last minute instructions about the best routes to take northward — "Ride to the Pamunkey River, take a ferry across it to West Point, then another ferry across the Mattaponi," Hugh had told him over breakfast, "or perhaps the simplest way, straight up the road to Richmond town from Williamsburg" — the filling of the officers' canteens with water and the assembling of a basket of biscuits and dried fruit for them to take with them, the shoeing of one of the horses whose shoes had come loose, and silence-filling small talk, all disguised the dampening regret Hugh, Reverdy and Roger felt that they must part.

The breakfast had ended on a highlight, however, with an exchange of gifts. At the table, Roger presented Hugh with an inscribed copy of a book he had translated during his years at the Woolwich academy, Guillaume Le Blond's "Treatise on Artillery" from his larger work, *Elements of War*, published in 1747. "You are not the only one to pen words," he said to Hugh. "Please accept this, without it being an overture to the difficulties here." He laughed. "Consider it a gift from Lieutenant Manners, as well. It is one less book for him to read during our journey!"

Hugh took the book and read the inscription inside: "For a friend who knows how to range his targets so as not to strike his friends. Capt. Roger Tallmadge, a friend forever." It was followed by the day's date.

"Thank you, Roger," Hugh said. He handed the manual to Reverdy, then reached inside his coat and took out an object. "I have something for you, as well, sir. Your promotion." He handed it over the table to his friend. "Our late mutual friend, Dogmael Jones, once held this rank."

Roger took it with a slight gasp of surprise. It was a tin replica of an officer's gorget, with a hemp cord to affix from around the neck. A crude inscription read: "A Paladin for Liberty." Beneath it was a rough silhouette of a seated Britannia. Roger glanced up at Hugh with a pleased smile.

Hugh said, "I asked Bristol, one of my tenants, to fashion that the night of the incident at Morland Hall."

Roger acknowledged the gift by immediately fitting the gorget over his head and around his neck.

Now, in the yard, he said to Reverdy, with a wan smile, "Perhaps we will meet in London." He reached out and traded embraces and busses with her, then turned and firmly shook Hugh's hand. "Let us not write a bad play scene here, my friends. We will be on our way." He put on his hat. "Mr. Manners, are you ready?"

"Yes, sir," answered the lieutenant.

Hugh said to the junior officer, "Mr. Manners, look after Captain Tallmadge here, and do not let anything untoward happen to him."

The lieutenant grinned. "That has been one of my constant tasks throughout this journey, Mr. Kenrick. Yes, I will look after him." He nodded once each to his host and hostess, then turned and strode to his mount.

As Roger was about to turn and follow, Hugh said, "Roger."

The captain stopped. "Yes, Hugh?"

"Make certain that when you have reported to General Gage and finished with your business, you find yourself passage home."

Tallmadge saw the seriousness in Hugh's eyes, and knew what he meant. He nodded again. "Without a doubt, that is what I shall certainly see to. Goodbye."

Tallmadge lifted himself onto his mount, and bid Lieutenant Manners to lead the way out. He turned once in the saddle and fingered the gorget. "I shall sport this for the remainder of our journey. If anyone questions me about it," he said with a grin, "I shall ask him to peer closer and see that it is self-evident." Then he reined his mount around and followed Lieutenant Manners out of the yard.

Hugh and Reverdy exchanged lingering waves with their friend until they could no longer see him in the foliage that bordered Meum Hall. Hugh put an arm around Reverdy's waist, and they leaned slightly against each other. "Over the hills, and far away, he goes," said Hugh wistfully.

Reverdy thought, but did not say, "I shall soon follow, my love." She was remembering the day, so many years ago at the Parade Grounds near Whitehall in London, when Hugh had pointed to his forehead: *A mind can accrue honor, too, and carry its own colors*, he said then. *I am an ensign in our country's most important standing army — for how secure can a country be without its thinkers?*

And you wear a gorget of intellect and integrity, she thought. But a war of thinkers was so very different from the one that is looming now over our lives, so very and so safely apart from everything else. And your words have helped to bring about what I witnessed at Morland Hall. Your words have wrought something I haven't the courage to face. Forgive me, but I haven't Etáin's mettle.

*  *  *

Two days later the *Sparrowhawk* came down the York River and tied up at the Caxton pier. Captain Elyot Geary planned to depart again in another day once he had loaded waiting cargoes of lumber and oats into the vessel's hold.

By then, everything that Reverdy had planned to take with her to England had been packed into trunks and even into a few cases marked "Brune-Kenrick, Danvers, Dorset." It was all carted down to the pier to be loaded and put into the hold with other baggage.

The next morning, after some tearful goodbyes and best wishes between Reverdy and the staff of Meum Hall, Hugh drove her and Dilch in a carriage to Morland, where Reverdy exchanged farewells with Jack Frake and Etáin. When they passed Meum Hall again on their way to the pier, Reverdy watched the great house with some sorrow in her expression as they passed by.

Dilch carried two canvas bags stuffed with her clothes, a few books, and other necessities.

At the pier, Hugh accompanied them aboard the vessel, and was amused to see that Captain Geary had assigned her the same tiny cabin that he had occupied when he first came to the colonies on the *Sparrowhawk* with Captain Ramshaw years ago. He could not help but remark on the irony of it to Reverdy. "What a fickle vessel she is."

"No," Reverdy answered. "It's the same one I occupied when I came here with James. He had to settle for a hammock the whole voyage."

"I didn't know."

Reverdy sat in the cabin's only chair, while Hugh leaned against the tiny table, and they chatted for a while. Dilch sat on a trunk, listened, and did not interfere. At one point, Hugh turned to her. "Miss Dilch, you will take care to see that your mistress comes to no harm, and that you come to no harm yourself."

"Yes, Mr. Kenrick," said the woman. Hugh knew that she felt free to travel to England. Her mother had died years ago, and she had no other relatives here to concern herself about.

He rose, smiled, and bowed before her. "You are a princess, madam." Then he took one of her hands and kissed it.

Dilch smiled in return. "And you are a prince, sir. But, mind you not to behave like Hamlet to milady here," she added, nodding to Reverdy, "or I'll give you a piece of *my* mind! She is no Ophelia!"

Hugh knew that she had read the play. "Hamlet? No," he replied, laughing. "I shall endeavor to emulate Prince Hal!"

The bursar appeared then and informed them that Captain Geary and the pilot were ready to push off. Dilch rose and left the cabin for the deck above, knowing that the couple wanted a last moment alone together.

Hugh crushed Reverdy to him and kissed her long and passionately. For a moment, they were lost to time. Then the sounds of hurried footsteps above them reminded them of where they were. They let each other go, and left the cabin to ascend to the desk. At a place near the shrouds, Hugh passed a lingering palm over Reverdy's face, then turned and spoke with

Captain Geary for a moment. The captain assured him that he would take every care to ensure Reverdy's comfort. Hugh said, "Well, we'll see each other again, perhaps in the fall. You're welcome to stay with me, of course. And please see if you can scare up another chair for milady's cabin."

Hugh shook hands with the captain, and with a last glance at Reverdy, forced himself to walk down the gangboard to the pier. He remained in the middle of the pier to watch the gangboard taken up by the landsmen and the hawsers cast off by the dockhands.

The *Sparrowhawk* drifted out on the current, then slowly turned and picked up speed as one by one its sails were dropped to catch the wind. Reverdy stood at the shrouds with Dilch, waving occasionally to Hugh. She blew him a number of kisses. He could not see her expression. Soon her face was just a plain white oval beneath a broad brimmed hat with red ribbons that streamed in the air. Then, he could not even distinguish that.

Hugh stood motionless with his hat in an outstretched arm until the *Sparrowhawk* reached a bend far down river. A passing dockhand caused him to remember to drop his arm. He turned and walked back down the pier to his carriage, forgetting that he still clutched his hat in that hand.

# Chapter 9: The Decision

Alull in politics, at least in Queen Anne County, was accompanied by a colony-wide drought that lasted from late spring through midsummer. "We are abused by nature, as well as by the Crown," remarked Hugh in answer to a complaint about the weather during a meeting of the Sons of Liberty, to which all other interested parties had been invited some days after June 1st.

It was a sparsely attended meeting, for many planters and farmers chose instead to tend to their crops in a desperate attempt to salvage what they could of them. Hugh advised the company of the Association's call for a convention in Williamsburg on the first of August.

"Its purpose is two-fold, gentlemen: to sanction another round of non-importation resolutions, and to agree to select delegates to a congress of the colonies in the fall." He grimaced. "I am told that many Virginia counties are drafting resolutions and instructions commensurate with the spirit of boycott. Unfortunately, we have not a quorum of freeholders here to discuss what resolutions we might add to those of other counties. Nor is Mr. Cullis here to discuss this business. Nor may we discuss instructions to delegates to this convention, those delegates being Mr. Cullis and me. Until we are reelected by the Governor's writ, he or I may attend this convention *ex officio*, but without knowing the true sentiment of the county."

The meeting was held in the Olympus Room of Steven Safford's tavern. Those who came noted that his signboard over the entrance had been altered. Blotted out with black paint was "King's"; printed neatly in yellow over the paint was "Safford's."

The tavern owner, after the meeting, remarked to Hugh and Jack as he put two complimentary glasses of ale in front of them at a table, "It seems that the Loyalists in these parts, *in absentia*, have voted down any further action by the county. And the others are dispirited and resigned to hardship."

"Mr. Cullis's hand may be detected in that vote, even as far away as the Piedmont, where he pursues deer and wolves," said Hugh with irony.

Safford nodded. "I hear that he rode about the county after he returned from Williamsburg, talking to the freeholders here about the Governor's dissolution."

"Doubtless to instill in them a fear of His Excellency, or of God and the courts if they defy him."

Jack turned to John Proudlocks and said, "Well, John, it seems that you've studied law, only to return to a lawless country."

"For the nonce," Proudlocks replied with a smile.

Reverend Acland, in his sermon one Sunday during that dry spell, cited the surprising snow in early May, which was followed by a frost that damaged most rye and oats crops, and killed countless tobacco seedlings that their planters had not been careful or quick enough to bed in straw. It was all, according to the pastor, the work of God. "The extended denial of rain is His third and most distressing message to us this sorrow-filled season. We have caused Him to frown on our actions. Only obedience to Him and His temporal representative will mollify our Savior, and then we shall again merit His benevolent countenance, and prosper in our humble lives."

Several men in the congregation abruptly rose from their pews and walked out of the church with their wives and children. Stunned, Acland and the rest of the congregation watched them leave. One of the men paused at the door to turn and shake a finger at Acland, who stood frozen in his high pulpit. "Whose 'benevolent countenance' will we merit, Reverend? God's, or the king's? I don't know about God's intentions, but it seems the only thing that'll make His Majesty happy is if we all obeyed him into our own starvation!" Then he spun on his heel and followed his family out the door.

The pastor merely blinked in speechlessness, and after a moment, glanced down with a pained expression at his flock. He was visibly annoyed and offended by the demonstration, and stammered throughout the rest of his sermon.

Two weeks after Reverdy's departure, Hugh remembered, almost without cause, something that Jack Frake had said to him on the evening of the celebration. He rode to Morland Hall and asked him what it was that he wanted to show him.

When his friend opened the ice cellar door and led him inside with a lantern, Hugh gasped in immediate recognition. He did not need to guess the contents of the powder kegs and what lay beneath the long shapes of the tarpaulins. "Oh, Jack! This is…dangerous."

"This is what those Customsmen must have been after," said Jack.

"Yes. Of course. I am surprised that they have not returned." He faced his friend. "How long have you been collecting this armory?"

"For the last three years." Jack walked over to the crate that was marked "Barret's Volley." He nodded to it. "Actually, I began collecting all this when I bought Mr. Barret's seized type."

Hugh lifted the tarpaulin that covered the long-gun. "Where did you get this?"

"Ramshaw found it in Jamaica. It's old, but in very good condition. I took it apart and cleaned it inside and out. And the swivel gun is from the *Sparrowhawk*." He raised another length of canvas.

Hugh grinned, stood over to it and ran a hand over the brass length of the swivel gun that rested next to the long-gun. "Not the same one you used to blow off that pirate's head?"

Jack Frake nodded. "The very same. It seems I've not yet finished with it."

Hugh replaced the long-gun's tarpaulin. "Jack, why did you not tell me about this sooner?"

Jack dropped the canvas atop the swivel gun. "Would you have approved?"

"No."

Jack Frake leaned against one of the walls of the cellar and folded his arms. "Are you saying that it is permissible for the Crown to assemble troops and weapons in Boston to better enslave us, but that we may not reciprocate in kind?"

"Three years ago, Jack, there was a chance to mend our differences. There is still a chance."

"There was never a chance, Hugh. I knew that some ten years ago, after we received word of the Proclamation that locked us east of the mountains and turned the continent into a Bridewell Prison."

"That is an unfortunate description of our predicament."

"*Your* very words, Hugh, when you argued with Mr. Henry for the Resolves in the House, nearly ten years ago."

Hugh stood in amazed recollection. "So they were." After a moment, he gestured to the room at large. "Jack, it may well be that Mr. Hunt will return, determined not to be foiled. I recommend moving this armory to a more secure place. Perhaps to the Otway place, to one of the out-buildings that had not been ruined by the river."

"I've thought of that," said Jack. "Will you help me in that task, when I'm ready?"

"Of course. Send word to me, and I shall be there."

*   *   *

When he returned to Meum Hall, Hugh reviewed Mr. Beecroft's account ledgers, then turned to whittle down the stack of correspondence that had accumulated over the past weeks. Mixed in with the correspondence were a dozen political pamphlets by tractarians both for and against Crown actions and policies, and a half dozen of both *Virginia Gazettes* that contained perorations in a similar vein, some on the mark, others hysterical, but all angry. Noteworthy among the latter was a series the letters in the Rind *Gazette* from a "British American," thought by some to be Thomson Mason, recently elected burgess for Loudoun County.

On top of the pile was a letter from his father, dated early May, which he had only glanced at earlier, and saw that was another confession of failure in politics:

"My dear Hugh: I have learned in the most humbling manner imaginable that the Commons is not my best venue. I am more comfortable discussing rabbit warrens with our wardens in Danvers than I am addressing the mass of members here. I dither and stammer when I rise to speak, often resorting to making disconnected points I had earlier labored to thread together and practiced on your patient mother and your sister Alice. On more than one occasion I have provoked mocking members to remind me to address my words to the Chair. My remissness in this regard has given some cruel members leave to make sport of my lapses in House protocol. I confess that I am not only ineffectual in the House, but very likely an embarrassment and impediment to our cause.

"Oh, how I long for Sir Dogmael's confident eloquence, whose thoughts and sentiments were *en rapport* with his oration! What ease of expression, embedded in so ordered a mind! We so miss his pleasantly innervating company! I sometimes wish it were possible for him to speak through me from his final reward, that I could be his Delphic oracle. Even though his skill often proved a liability, I am certain that in these critical times it would now make a difference. He was a knight, a paladin, and I have been but his fumbling squire in this art...."

He finished the letter, which contained news of more dangerous mischief by Parliament, some family news, a brief report on his uncle the Earl's activities, and worried comments on the state of trade between England and the colonies. Hugh sighed in sympathy with his father. What a burden he had taken upon himself, he thought. And a futile one, as well! He glanced at the pamphlets and *Gazettes* that awaited him. He sighed again, this time tiredly. His sight rested on the pile of tracts and pamphlets he himself had written against all the legislation that was now old news.

He reread another *Gazette* that carried the announcement from Governor Dunmore who, having issued a writ for new elections for a General Assembly to be convened in mid-August, after the convention, now prorogued it until early November. A letter from Colonel Munford explained that it was part punishment for calling the convention, even though only the Assembly could vote money for the militia that the Governor intended to call up for his planned campaign against the Indians on the western frontier. "It matters little to him that we cannot renew the law that pays our sheriffs and coroners and other officers," wrote Munford, "and that most of our courts as a consequence are effectively closed. We cannot fathom how he will meet the militia's expenses, although we are certain he will not volunteer them from his own purse."

He tossed the *Gazette* aside and reached for the next letter that sat next atop the pile.

He frowned when he recognized the handwriting on the sealed paper: It was Reverdy's.

Very gently, he broke the seal and opened the page. The letter read:

"My beloved Hugh: It takes what seems forever to find the words for this letter, and I think parts of me die when I find them and put them down on this paper. I must first thank you for being so understanding of my predicament, and allowing me to journey home to better ponder our situation without the distraction of crisis. It is no thoughtless thing I do here, leaving this missive among the papers you are sure to peruse after I have gone. It is the pensive coward in me, for I could not command the courage to tell you what I write here. And because I have not the strength to prolong the pain of writing these words, I shall be mercifully brief for both our sakes.

"I cannot return to you and Meum Hall until reconciliation has been reached between our England and the colonies. I cannot contemplate returning to our normal bliss, not until bliss has been restored in the damnable politics that lately has occupied so much of your energy and concern. All I see ahead are ruination, and misery, and the demise of so many people and things close to us. You seem to be made for that kind of existence, and have been since the idyll of our childhoods. I confess I am not so made. I have never told you, but I have had nightmares of visitations of hell on Meum Hall, and on Jack and Etáin, and everyone we hold dear, the flames of perdition rising to consume everything, followed by the sound of endless dirges of death assaulting my ear, the same nightmare, over and over...."

He slapped the letter down as he shot from his chair, exclaiming, "*No!*" — to her sense of foreboding, to her willingness to surrender their happiness together, to Jack's certainty of war, to Reece Vishonn's resignation to war or submission to Crown authority, to the deadening sense of futility that smothered so much ambition. "No!" he thought, it shall not be! None of it shall come to pass!

At that moment, he decided. He rushed from his study and the great house and found Beecroft in his office in the senior staff's quarters. "Mr. Beecroft, what England-bound ships are at the riverfront here?"

The astonished Beecroft blinked once, and replied, "The *Osprey*, sir. And the *Anacreon*. They're loading what they can. I believe they both plan to leave directly for England in a few days. The *Osprey* took on what the *Busy* could not. It had ample space in the hold." The steward paused. "Sir, I've spoken with their captains and masters. They don't think they'll be back this way for a while, not until the troubles are settled."

"Of course not. Well, be kind enough to go down and enquire of them if they have room for a passenger."

After a moment, Beecroft, again astonished, answered, "Yes, sir. Is it you?"

"I must return to England for a while, to right some wrongs."

*   *   *

"Why?" asked Etáin

Hugh shrugged. "For many reasons," he said. He rode to Morland Hall later that afternoon to break the news. Beecroft had managed to reserve a place for him on the *Anacreon*, which was to set sail for England in two days. Hugh had given him and Spears instructions on what to pack for the voyage, and they were now busying themselves in that task. Hugh stood with his friends in the supper room.

"First, I will not be able to attend the convention in Williamsburg in two weeks, except, perhaps, to audit it. But, I would be out of sorts, since the county has no resolutions to present to the Association and no delegates to instruct on the matters to be voted on. In any event, no instructions. I would be a mere spectator. After my career in the House, that role would be intolerable, nearly an offence. I have been spoilt by the privilege of speaking my mind to my peers."

Jack Frake smiled. "That's no reason for going to England."

Hugh grinned in concession. "As you know, the Governor has already prorogued the General Assembly. He is likely to do it again. The House may not sit again until spring of next year. I cannot brook artificial idleness, especially one enforced by that scion of the Stuarts."

"Still not a good enough reason," said Jack, amused.

"I wish to see if I can help my father in the Commons. He writes that Parliament will sit again in late November. Perhaps I can speak in his place." Hugh paused, and added with less confidence, "And, there is Reverdy. She…left me a note saying that she cannot return here until there is a reconciliation. It may be possible that I can have a hand in effecting one."

To this, Jack and Etáin had no immediate reply. They were not certain which reconciliation their friend meant, but they doubted the likelihood of either of them if they were mutually dependent. After a moment, Jack remarked, "Hugh, if you speak in the Commons, you will not be addressing your *peers*."

Hugh nodded once. "I will accept that as an unfortunate compliment."

"It was a compliment. What is unfortunate is that you think it necessary to address them at all."

"I will not argue that point with you, Jack. I must try."

"Still trying to salvage the epergne of empire?"

Hugh shut his eyes for a moment at the slight. Then he realized it was not a slight. He replied, "If as notable and esteemed a gentleman as Benjamin Franklin believes in it, I can only second him."

Jack shook his head. "It's not like you to defer to authority, Hugh, not even to one as esteemed as Mr. Franklin's."

"I do not defer to his authority. I have been here longer than he to witness the events of the last fifteen years, and my appraisal is based on my own authority."

Jack said nothing more.

After a moment, Etáin said, "We shall miss you, Hugh."

"And I shall miss both of you. I should return by early spring." He smiled and picked up his hat. "Well, I will visit Mr. Proudlocks now. My plan is certain to displease him, as well," he added lightly. "Is there anything you want from London?"

Jack said, "Their recognition of our independence."

"We are not displeased with you or your purpose, Hugh," Etáin said. "We are saddened that you should choose to leave at such a time." When she saw the controlled hurt in her friend's expression, she rushed to add, touching his arm, "We shall see you off at the pier, of course."

"Thank you." Hugh turned and left the room.

*   *   *

Two days later, he boarded the *Anacreon*, and stood at the shrouds, waving at the crowd of friends on the pier as the merchantman gained the river current. Jack and Etáin, John Proudlocks, Beecroft and Spears, William Settle — who had already proven his ability to look after Meum Hall during his past absences — even his housekeeper and many of his tenants, were there to bid him farewell.

Other planters were there, too: among them Reece Vishonn, and Jock Fraser, whom he had encountered in Safford's Arms the day before, when he went there to ask for any last mail that might have been left. Jock Fraser had treated him to a pint of ale, and boisterously sung him a song that underscored his best wishes for a good voyage and safe return, "Will Ye No' Come Back Again." When Hugh, laughing, asked him what he meant, Fraser slapped him on the shoulder. "It's a Scots marchin' song, laddie! I will tell you that I'd like to hoot it to that devil in the Palace when he leaves for the frontier. I'd mean something else by it, though," he had added with a wink.

The last words Hugh heard, before the growing distance between the *Anacreon* and the pier reduced the farewells and Godspeeds to mere sounds, were Jack's, who waved his hat up at him, shouting, "Come back to Hyperborea!"

Hugh waved his hat in answer, and shouted, "Hyperborea forever!"

A while later, as the vessel rounded a bend in the York, he watched Caxton vanish and blend into the summer haze.

# Chapter 10: The Interview

Jared Hunt, in the meantime, came away from his interview with Governor Dunmore less satisfied than he might have been, but content with the results nonetheless. Upon his arrival in Williamsburg, he had been made to wait for it for two consecutive days in the grand foyer of the Palace. His Excellency, explained the officious Captain Foy, the Governor's secretary, was busy with the onerous gubernatorial business of the colony, and in addition was making preparations to march to the frontier to put down an Indian uprising.

Contrary to his expectations, the documents he had brought with him did not expedite an audience with the Governor. He was not sure if they served him well or ill. These were his letter of introduction, signed by the Earl of Danvers, and his extraordinary commission, signed by the Earl of Rochford, Secretary of State for the Southern Department, and the Earl of Dartmouth, Secretary of State for the Colonies, under the signature of the president of the American Board of Customs Commissioners. This second document gave him discretionary authority over any and all Customs officers in the colonies.

Hunt speculated that the Governor was overwhelmed by all the power represented in the signatures, and postponed a meeting with the bearer of those instruments in a peevish demonstration of his own importance.

When at last Hunt was escorted to the Governor's office, His Excellency remarked, "What a broadside of recommendations, sir! You must be a man of *particular* talents." He handed the papers back over his desk to his visitor.

Hunt smiled, rose from his chair, took the papers and put them back inside his coat, then reseated himself. He was sensitive to the sneer beneath the compliment and its insinuation that his talents, while practical, worthy of emulation and perhaps even to be envied for, were hardly laudable in the normal sense. But he was not offended. His talents were his career. He replied with brazen lightness, "I am fortunate that my modest abilities are recognized and commended to broader service, your lordship. I have been in the personal service of his lordship the Earl of Danvers for many years now."

"Danvers? Don't know him," remarked the Governor with perfunctory haste, shaking his head.

"Of Dorset, your lordship," said Hunt, certain that His Excellency had lied. "The Earl has been a champion of the policy of exacting deference from the colonies for as long as I have known him. And he was one of those in Lords who some years ago campaigned to have Mr. Pitt elevated to reduce his obstructing influence in the Commons. The consequences of that elevation are known to all but Lord Chatham himself, whose influence in Lords is predictably negligible, even when he manages to attend."

"Yes, *Lord* Chatham," said Dunmore, groaning with stressed boredom. He had indeed made the acquaintance of the Earl of Danvers, but did not wish to concede his visitor's obvious familiarity with political machinations, of which that specific one he himself had full knowledge. "Yes. Fie on the foolish man. Now, what is your purpose here, Mr. Hunt?" He leaned back in his chair, as though prepared to listen to his visitor's plea and to weigh whether or not it was worth considering.

Hunt paused to cross his legs and to choose his words carefully. "I am here on a special mission, your lordship, to foil the designs of some gentlemen to deny His Majesty and Parliament rightful sovereignty over these colonies, and over Virginia, especially. You have noted that my Customs commission grants me latitude in that purpose. These gentlemen have been conspiring to stir up disaffection with the Crown."

Dunmore scoffed. "I daresay half the burgesses here are guilty of stirring up disaffection! Even some of my Councilmen, not one of whom, by the bye, moved himself to castigate the villains behind that offensive day of fasting and prayer. But, pray, *which* gentlemen?"

"My profuse apologies, your lordship, but I am not at liberty to divulge their identities. My instructions in that respect are strict. Were I to be asked that question by His Majesty, I could not make an exception even for him. However, I can safely tell you that they are Virginians — no more are they Englishmen! — and that when I have foiled them, you shall know it."

Hunt had no instructions of the kind. He had taken stock of His Excellency and suspected that if the Governor knew the name of Hugh Kenrick, he might be tempted to act himself, and have the man either hanged, jailed or otherwise ruined, just to exercise his power. The Earl, Hunt knew too well, might be half pleased with such an episode, but at the same time feel cheated. His employer was obsessed with personally and directly punishing his nephew Hugh Kenrick and thereby hurting his own brother, the Baron of Danvers, for offenses that he, Jared Hunt, did not permit himself to think merited such vindicatory purposes. Hunt knew that his future security rested on catering to that obsession. It was none of his business what the Earl did to assuage his injuries.

He noted without surprise that His Excellency did not like his delicately put answer. The man's face, rigid in resentment, grew a shade red in anger.

But Dunmore decided that tact was the better part of discretion. He sniffed in feigned indifference to the answer, and asked, somewhat imperiously, "Well, sir, what is it you want from me?"

"Nothing, your lordship. It is a courtesy call I make, merely to inform you that Virginia is on the Crown's mind, and that it is taking appropriate action to retain this His Majesty's most prosperous dominion."

The Governor hummed in tired approval of the Crown's concern. "Yes. Well, all sorts of strangers are calling on me these days. Not two weeks ago an army officer on his own secret mission called on me to ask for militia figures."

Hunt frowned. Army officers were less numerous in this colony than Customs officials. He could not recall encountering a single one since his arrival in Virginia, except at Morland Hall that shameful day. He asked, "Your lordship, was it a captain in gentleman's garb?"

"Yes, sir. It was."

"Was it Captain Roger Tallmadge, perhaps, of the Grenadier Guards?"

Dunmore looked interested now, and sat forward. "Why, yes, I believe that was his name. I don't recollect his regiment, but his papers were in order. Had him to supper, and invited him to my ladyship's ball at the Capitol. An amiable chap, but too stealthy to my tastes."

Hunt smiled. Here was an opportunity to wreak his own vengeance. He braced himself and related to the Governor the incident at Morland Hall.

When he was finished, Dunmore was livid. "Well, that is a chargeable offense!" he bellowed. "Interfering with Crown officers in the performance of their duty! And siding with a rebel! What disgraceful behavior!" The Governor paused. "Now that I think of it, it might explain some of his comments to me in this very office, which at the time I placed no importance on. Something must be done about him. What was it you were searching for, sir?"

"Arms, your lordship. The office in Hampton had received information that some suspicious activities were to be observed at that plantation."

"Did you return to it?"

"No, your lordship. Doubtless the contraband, if it exists, would have been moved soon after my visit and secreted elsewhere. And one of the gentlemen it is my task to compromise and bring to justice was involved in that treasonous behavior, as well. Apparently, he is a friend of Captain Tallmadge's. He is very much esteemed in that county, and to move against him now would be tantamount to inviting open rebellion by many of its inhabitants. I would not act so recklessly, and would rather wait until conditions are in my own favor."

The Governor hummed in thought. "Which vessel brought you and the marines up?"

"The *Fowey*, your lordship, captained by Mr. Montague."

"I see." Dunmore pounded a fist once on some paperwork in front of him. "Well, Mr. Hunt, I shall write General Gage in Boston about this incident so that he may prepare a surprise for Captain Tallmadge! A court martial and a hanging will end that chap's duplicity!"

"Thank you, your lordship. I have also written General Gage about the affair."

After some further chitchat about the weather, the charms of Williamsburg, and how His Excellency planned to deal with Cornstalk, the Shawnee chief behind the frontier uprising, Jared Hunt left the Governor's office in a good mood. The next day he rode out on a journey to Richmond, and from there to Petersburg, to note the condition and temper of the people in those towns, and returned to Williamsburg nearly two weeks later. After another night there, he ventured back to Caxton before beginning the ride back to Hampton.

Cautiously he reconnoitered Meum Hall, which he had seen only once from the *Fowey* the day of the incident at Morland. He did not want to encounter any of the parties who had participated in that affair. Following the directions of a passing Indian curiously attired in colonial dress and who rode a horse on a fine saddle, he drew up his mount at Hove Stream, where some slaves were busy pouring buckets of water from the stream into some contraption that seemed linked to a length of bamboo. The gray-green arm of bamboo stretched into a vast field of tobacco and corn, until it disappeared halfway through them, its most visible end pointing to a cluster of houses the size of pebbles in the distance.

The slaves paused to study him. He asked them if the large house was

Meum Hall.

"Yassuh," replied the slave who held a rag flag on a stick. "That's Mista Kenrick's place."

"Is he about? I'm an old friend, and may pay him a visit."

"He gone sometime, Mista, on a boat. For England. Won't be back 'til spring."

Hunt managed to repress his disappointment. "Well, I'll call on him then." But anger and curiosity got the best of him. "*Why* did he go to England?" he abruptly demanded, as though his prey had no justifiable right to move beyond his power.

The slave with the flag shrugged. "Don't know, Mista. Not our business. Heard he might talk in the big burgess house there, and he went after Missus Reverdy, too, to bring her back. That's what we hear."

Hunt nodded thanks, reined his mount around, and began the ride back to Williamsburg. Damn! he thought. The whelp has sailed for England! That meant either pursuing him in another vessel, or writing the Earl a letter that contained the unpleasant news. Now he would need to amend his own plans and postpone a triumphant return to London. Either alternative would upset the Earl, for Hunt knew that his employer and patron wished Hugh Kenrick to meet his end or his disgrace beyond the help of his caring and anxious father.

Hunt resigned himself to writing a report to the Earl. And what would he do with himself until Hugh Kenrick returned, other than accompany Customsmen on their raids? It had become so dull an occupation! How could he justify his time to his patron, and explain his inactivity? Something tickled his memory, and he recalled the oddly attired Indian who had given him directions to Meum Hall. That was it! He could claim that His Excellency, Governor Dunmore, had pressed him into service on the frontier campaign! How could he refuse such a request? The Governor planned to end the uprising by the end of December. That ought to kill so much time! And then spring would be upon him in no time! Hunt even convinced himself that it might even be an interesting adventure!

Jared Hunt felt much less angry, now that he had hit upon a plan. He would again seek an interview with the Governor to volunteer his services on that campaign, in whatever capacity His Excellency wished to accept them.

The extraordinarily commissioned Customsman urged his mount into a trot on the road back to Williamsburg.

John Proudlocks, watching from the woods that bordered the road, wondered when and where he had seen the stranger before, and what possible business he could have at Meum Hall.

# Chapter 11: The Chamade

On July 8, two days before he departed on a tour of some of the Piedmont counties, and before he left again in September to campaign against the Indians, Governor Dunmore prorogued the General Assembly until November. His action was part punishment of the burgesses for scheduling the August convention; and part convenience to the Governor, for once the convention was concluded, the burgesses would have no reason to assemble again in Williamsburg during the months he expected to be absent. He would not need to worry about further rebellious mischief they might concoct behind his back. The Governor liked to keep a close ear to the political keyhole and a hand firmly on the latch of assembly.

Of course, he believed that everyone understood that he would brave the rigors and dangers of a campaign as his duty to protect the westernmost reaches of His Majesty's dominion of Virginia. He did not entertain the possibility that perhaps many Virginians suspected that the Cornstalk uprising was precipitated by his seizure earlier in the year of western Pennsylvania. The Shawnee chief Cornstalk, Pontiac's successor, knew that the British army was forbidden to protect settlers who ventured west of the mountains. What else could he do, but take steps by calling out the militia — not the army — to protect those settlers and to restore order?

Dunmore appointed a Crown crony, John Connolly, a physician of dubious talent, in Pittsburg to govern the newly acquired land. He even proposed to rename Fort Pitt after himself. But Connolly barely had enough time to set up shop at Fort Pitt when he was arrested by Pennsylvania authorities. In the meantime, war had broken out between the settlers and the Indians in the Ohio territory.

And, the Governor may or may not have had at the time of his departure for the west a copy of the Quebec Act, passed in Parliament on June 22, which made Canadian all land west of the Ohio River and on the east bank of the Mississippi clear to the Gulf of Mexico, and Roman Catholicism that province's official religion. The Act sanctioned the arbitrary annexation of land claimed by Virginia and other colonies but put in abeyance by the Proclamation of 1763.

Dunmore had personal plans for the Virginia lands. If he had knowledge of the Act, it did not seem to trouble him. After all, he was the Crown, His Majesty's viceroy, and the Crown could redraw boundaries at will and at the king's pleasure. And he must have noted with worried envy that the Crown was already granting enormous parcels of land to favored, well-connected British and colonial speculators. Only the year before the Board of Trade had bestowed upon the Grand Ohio Company 20 million acres in exchange for some £10,000, the region to become another proprietary colony with the curious name of Vandalia.

"Dunmore's War" — a generous designation for a campaign that saw but one battle, a near disaster at which the Governor was not even present, but for which he was responsible — was a microcosm of the French and Indian War in terms of Crown motives and ends. This time the colonials, especially the Virginians, while grateful for their Governor's concern, were more perceptive and alert to those motives and ends. As in the past war, the campaign's ostensible purpose was to remove or at least neutralize a mortal threat to better ensure British sovereignty. But because of the political turmoil of the past ten years, the colonials did not automatically assume that the war was waged and won for the sake of their security and for British liberty.

Tactless, bellicose, and crudely sly, almost from the beginning of his tenure Dunmore seemed to them a caricature of the Crown's true motives. He was insensitive to that insinuative mockery; he did not care a fig for what his subjects thought of him. He was a Stuart, and he would govern. Most Virginians had heard that the Governor had advocated, in a letter to Lord Dartmouth, Secretary of State for the Colonies, the employment of not only slaves, but Indians, as well, to terrify recalcitrant colonials into deference and obedience, should matters get out of hand. A few of them privately entertained the idea that the Governor's "war" had a dual purpose: to cause a crisis requiring Crown intervention to resolve the dispute between Virginia and Pennsylvania over western Pennsylvania, to better to enforce the Proclamation of 1763, and to resolve it in the land-hungry Governor's favor; and to test the mettle of the Virginia militia, and to divert it from any possible action against himself.

John Murray, Earl of Dunmore, was not a model of benevolent despotism. In the course of his campaign, he prorogued the General Assembly three times, the last time to early February next year.

Jared Hunt approved of these actions. He did not regret his offer to accompany the Governor on the campaign, even though he was again obliged to wait two days before being granted an interview. His Excellency had accepted the offer with alacrity, but advised the extraordinary Customsman that he must bring his own weapon and that he would march and camp "at his own or the Customs' expense."

When the Governor pressed him for an explanation of his eagerness, to the neglect of his other Crown duties, Hunt had replied that, while he was investigating other venues of smuggling and impropriety, he returned to Williamsburg only to learn that his quarry had sailed for England, removing himself from the likelihood of making that journey in shackles to face trial in London for treason. "He is expected to return in the spring, your lordship," he had told the Governor. "I will snare him then. As for my other duties, my commission does not oblige me to apply myself in that regard." The Governor sympathized with such dedication. He advised his visitor to rejoin him in Williamsburg in late August or early September, when he planned to leave for the west.

Jared Hunt then returned to Hampton, and scoured that port's shops for extra clothing, a musket, and other campaign necessities. He later returned to Williamsburg to join the Governor's retinue. He did not mind following in the Governor's footsteps on the arduous march west. The Governor spoke with him as his father, the Earl of Dunmore, did not. They were men of like mind, disposed to like action. He enjoyed lavish meals at the Governor's field table, plentiful drink from the Governor's private stock, and ribald conversation with the Governor and his staff about the fickle colonials.

For an aristocrat, thought Hunt, Dunmore was not such a bad fellow.

\*   \*   \*

Nor was John Randolph, brother of Peyton and the king's Attorney-General for Virginia, such a bad fellow. A graduate of London's Middle Temple, he was clerk of the House of Burgesses when Patrick Henry introduced his Stamp Act Resolves in 1765. Originally elected burgess for Lunenburg County in 1769, he was later returned, through Governor Dunmore's intercession, as burgess for the College of William and Mary, a much more convenient and preferable constituency. The College, like abandoned Jamestown with its single burgess, was the Virginian counterpart of a Parliamentary rotten borough. It was virtually a lifetime sinecure for whoever held it. Also, it kept him close to his brother, burgess for Williamsburg and

Speaker of the House.

The Governor was pleased to assist John Randolph in changing his constituency because the Attorney-General was the epitome of moderation and a champion of Crown authority. Randolph abhorred the course his brother and the rest of the House were following. He was an apologist for the status quo. "We ought to declare, in the most public manner, that the act of the Bostonians in destroying the property of the East India Company, was illegal, and ought not to be countenanced." The investment of British troops in Boston, he asserted in a tract written in July and published in the Purdie and Dixon *Virginia Gazette* while the convention was sitting, was but "a check to that growing disorder which appeared to be licentiousness instead of freedom, and which must endanger the peace of the British Empire in America, unless it was smothered in its infancy."

He argued that the reparations expected by Parliament for the destroyed tea were only a matter of justice and civil government. Reconciliation between the mother country and her colonies was possible and a mutually profitable and amicable readjustment of their relationship could be arrived at "without noise" by rebellious rabble. The political mechanism of the Empire could be infinitely cobbled and caulked to the satisfaction of all parties. But, he warned, "Let us make every effort, exert every nerve, in order to terminate a dispute which is big with the fate of both of us," before it was too late.

After all, he reasoned, if Great Britain and her colonies separated, the mother country would "fall into ruin; and America, that once hopeful and promising soil," would "become subject to the will of some despotic prince, and be of less importance than it was whilst in the hands of the savages." Moderation and accommodation were John Randolph's watchwords. He believed that the status quo could be amended indefinitely to sustain everlasting imperial harmony.

A despotic prince, however, with the connivance of Parliament, was already attempting to subject the colonies to his will. Randolph, though, was unable to conceive of a greater vista of the crisis. He refused to ascribe to the Crown a shred of fault, culpability or villainous intent, and would concede only a tiny measure of thoughtless foolhardiness in some of its legislation. His disenchantment with the march of events was experienced by numerous other colonial gentlemen, whose world of genteel class distinctions, prestige, and Crown-blessed security came to an abrupt and embittering end. John Randolph eventually abandoned Virginia and his family and exiled himself to England, as did other "Tories."

The convention in Williamsburg, held in the Capitol instead of the Raleigh Tavern to seat over one hundred elected and reelected burgesses and delegates, began on August 1 and adjourned on August 6. Several rounds of voting chose the delegates who would travel to Philadelphia to attend a general congress unanimously endorsed by the convention: Peyton Randolph, Richard Henry Lee, Patrick Henry, George Washington, Benjamin Harrison, Richard Bland, and Edmund Pendleton. It was an unlikely but working union of men who in the past were hostile political antagonists.

Of the seven, Henry was the keystone. He had been the most consistent in his political convictions over the years; the others had been exemplars of caution and "moderation."

The convention sired a new Association whose twelve resolutions reflected as near a declaration of independence as Virginians would then allow themselves: No purchases of British imports after November 1; no slave purchases after that date; no imports of British tea, nor any consumption of it, even in one's own home; no tobacco or other colonial exports to Britain after August 10 of the following year; a more vigorous husbanding of sheep to fashion clothing, and a reduction in sheep slaughtering, to eliminate dependency on British-made apparel and textiles; no "price gouging" by traders and merchants for goods made scarce by the boycott; the social and commercial ostracizing of merchants and traders who refused to sign the Association after November 1; the publication of the names of any person who violated the Association's resolves; an appeal for donations and contributions to relieve the distress of the citizens of Boston; and the naming of Robert Carter Nicholas, Treasurer and burgess for James City County, to replace Peyton Randolph as head of the ad hoc convention, in the event the latter died.

The instructions given to the delegates to the general congress underscored the Association's resolutions. Aside from naming the delegates, they reiterated most the injustices committed by Parliament, with the king's approval, since the Proclamation of 1763, and expressed a hope that the king's ministers would see reason. They also expressed regret for resorting to a boycott of British commerce. Further, they caustically criticized General Thomas Gage, the new governor of Massachusetts, and warned that if he attempted to enforce his edict — which he was empowered to issue under the coercive Massachusetts Governing Act — deeming it a treasonable offense to assemble to form associations or to express or discuss American grievances, such a "proclamation will justify resistance and reprisal."

What was intended to be a prologue to the publication of the convention's resolutions, was instead printed by the Rind *Virginia Gazette* as a separate epilogue, Jefferson's anonymously penned "A Summary View of the Rights of British America." Jefferson, who had planned to present it to the convention for consideration, fell ill on his way back to Williamsburg, and forwarded it to Peyton Randolph, who in turn "tabled" it for anyone's perusal. Most delegates found it too severe in its accusations and language, and nothing in it was adopted. Jefferson's "Summary" expanded on the Crown's offenses and the colonists' grievances, traced the origins of liberty and the proper relationship between king and subject to pre-Norman Conquest times, and ended by appealing to His Majesty to check Parliament's powers and revoke all its oppressive legislation, as most colonial charters required and expected him to do. "Let not the name of George the Third be a blot in the page of history," wrote the thirty-one-year-old Virginian.

After tactfully blaming George the Third's counselors for all the troublesome legislation, and not His Majesty himself, Jefferson appealed, "This, sire, is the advice of your great American council, on the observance of which may perhaps depend your felicity and future fame, and the preservation of that harmony which alone can continue both to Great Britain and America the reciprocal advantages of their connection. It is neither our wish, nor our interest, to separate from her. We are willing, on our part, to sacrifice every thing which reason can ask to the restoration of that tranquility for which all must wish."

The "Summary" was the precursor of a monumental document its author was to compose two years later. Before the end of 1774, it was reprinted in Philadelphia and London.

The seven deputies, instructions in hand, returned home to their counties to prepare for the journey to Philadelphia, where the first Continental Congress was scheduled to convene on September 5. Georgia was the only colony that did not send delegates, and New York delegates attended *ex officio*. Henry traveled with Pendleton and Washington to Philadelphia, where they joined Peyton Randolph, Benjamin Harrison and Richard Bland. From a tavern they walked together to Carpenter's Hall, the site of the congress. Richard Henry Lee arrived the next day.

In one of history's ironies, Peyton Randolph, the man who had been willing to pay five hundred guineas for a single vote to defeat Henry's fifth Crown-defying Stamp Act resolve nine years before, was subsequently chosen to be president of the first Continental Congress. Over time, the virtue of "moderation" had become to him less and less a practical answer to Crown encroachments.

And it was Henry who made real for the other delegates and for the rest of the colonies the enormity of their peril and the unique position in which they found themselves. On the first day, after all the delegates had presented their instructions, he spoke to a hushed congress:

"I go upon the supposition that government is at an end. All distinctions are thrown down. All America is thrown into one mass....The distinctions between Virginians, Pennsylvanians, New Yorkers, and New Englanders, are no more. I am not a Virginian, but an American!"

This was an expression of what many Crown ministers had known for a long time, and hoped in vain that no one in North America would ever grasp. It was an identification of the fact that America was indeed another kingdom, another country, and that its inhabitants were no longer Britons.

Few of the men who opposed Crown policies and impositions could imagine, let alone welcome, a complete political break with Britain. Many who could imagine it viewed the prospect with horror. John Randolph was one of these, asserting that the animosity engendered by dubious Parliamentary legislation did not justify violence, separation or independence. The preservation of the Empire was of paramount importance. Independence would lead, if not to military strife with the mother country, then to anarchy within each former colony or strife between some or all of them, if they were not first conquered by France or Spain.

Still others devoted their imagination to a closer, more intimate political union of the colonies and Britain, as did delegate Joseph Galloway of Pennsylvania, speaker of its legislature. At the Philadelphia congress he proposed that a central, elective colonial legislature could work with Parliament, headed by a president-general appointed by the king.

The "grand council" of legislators would be "inferior" to Parliament but exercise veto power over Parliamentary acts and even originate legislation for Crown approval. It would embody a mandated share of genuine power with Parliament and act under a special colonial constitution that complemented the British constitution. If the colonies could not be literally or even virtually represented in Parliament — he certainly agreed with many "intemperate" radicals on those points — Galloway's answer was simple: Create a truly representative government that was nearly Parliament's equal in legislative authority.

The idea of governing the colonies in such a fashion was questioned by many delegates, most notably by Patrick Henry, who, having observed corruption of his own General Assembly, argued that while such a "grand council" would insulate the colonies from direct Parliamentary influence, such an association would surely infect it as well and create new opportunities for oppressive skullduggery of a greater magnitude. Bribery and subornation of the grand council by Parliament and the king's ministers were guaranteed by the connection. A royally appointed president-general who served at the king's pleasure — and served the king's purposes — was by itself a malodorous aspect of the scheme. Where would his allegiance sit: With St. James's Palace, or with the colonies?

But, without even admitting that likelihood, many at the congress dismissed such a scheme as mere "virtual" independence, as contemptibly specious a notion as "virtual" representation in Parliament. Others saw in Galloway's plan of union salvation of themselves and of the Empire.

Galloway's plan was narrowly rejected as untenable. Instead, the congress adopted the Suffolk Resolves, brought hastily to Philadelphia by courier Paul Revere from Massachusetts. These were more in the spirit of Henry's position. They declared the Coercive Acts unconstitutional, called for the citizens of Massachusetts to form their own government, advised all the colonies to form and arm their militias, and endorsed stringent trade sanctions against Britain. On October 14 the congress issued its own Declaration and set of resolves. These ten resolves condemned the Coercive Acts as well as the Quebec Act, all the legislation passed by Parliament since 1763, asserted the right to life, liberty and property, and the right to self-government without Crown interference.

On October 18 the congress created a continental association, modeled on the Virginia Association. When it adjourned on October 22, the congress resolved to meet again in May of 1775 if by that time the Crown had not acted to address American grievances. The Declaration and resolves were sent to London. The delegates packed their bags and journeyed home to await a reply.

Galloway rode back to his farm in Pennsylvania to pout. Later, he volunteered to assist General Howe in governing Philadelphia when that general occupied the city. In 1778 he joined the growing number of American loyalists in England, and became their spokesman. He nurtured a special animus for Samuel Adams, the intransigent radical of Boston, whom he blamed, in an unintended compliment, for the defeat of his plan of union by intriguing with factions at the congress. "He eats little, drinks little, sleeps little, thinks much, and is most decisive and indefatigable in the pursuit of his objects."

The Declaration and resolves of the First Continental Congress were to be the last major appeal to reason that Americans would make.

*    *    *

In the meantime, Governor Dunmore completed a successful campaign to pacify the Indians. He saw no action himself. That was seen by General Andrew Lewis, of Botetourt County and a veteran of the French and Indian War, whose column of Virginia militia, over 1,000 strong, was supposed to have rendezvoused on September 30 with the Governor and his column of equal strength at Point Pleasant in the Ohio territory, at the juncture of the Ohio and Kanawha rivers. Lewis arrived there on schedule, after a grueling march through unmapped wilderness, and encamped to await Dunmore, who took the wagon roads cleared by Braddock nearly two decades before to Fort Pitt. There Dunmore met with some apprehensive Delawares and concluded a minor treaty with them. Impressed with his own obvious gift for peace-making, he decided to march further west to an Indian town called Chillicothe to parley with its natives. He sent orders to Lewis a hundred miles down river to join him there.

While Lewis's militia was preparing to obey, it was attacked on October 10 by Cornstalk and an army, "five acres" shoulder to shoulder of them, of Shawnees, Mingos, Iowas, Delawares, Wyandots, and Cayugas. After a fierce all-day battle, Lewis sent Cornstalk fleeing across the Ohio River with what was left of his warriors. The Virginians lost 75 men in the battle, including Lewis's brother, Colonel Charles Lewis.

The general then marched with part of his force to join Dunmore at Chillicothe, only to receive word from Dunmore to return to Point Pleasant and await orders. He marched on, however, with the bitter certainty that had His Excellency kept to the original plan, their combined armies could have dealt Cornstalk and his allies an even greater blow. When he faced the Governor, he tactfully proposed that this could still be done. Dunmore instead ordered him and his militia back home and his troops mustered out. Lewis contained his anger and obeyed. Dunmore remained near Chillicothe on the Scioto River for two more months, concocting treaties, he thought, with as much skill as any Indian commissioner, moved by expectations of lavish Crown gratitude in the form of exclusive land patents and other royal rewards.

But when he returned to Williamsburg in early December, he encountered a number of surprises. His wife, Charlotte, after whom he had named his camp at Chillicothe, had given birth to their ninth child, a daughter, christened at his insistence Virginia in a transparent ploy to win public affection. Also, a special quorum of the House and Council voted him mere thanks for his conduct in the west, instead of showering him with praises of heroism. He must have realized then that it had been a mistake to send General Lewis home so soon, for that veteran had forwarded to Williamsburg a truer account of the campaign than the Governor would have liked.

Finally, a letter from Lord Dartmouth had arrived in his absence expressing the king's extreme displeasure with the campaign. The Secretary explained that his action was not only a violation of past treaties and of His Majesty's good word, but an intrusion into Canadian territory where the Governor had no authority, as well. Stung by this unexpected chastisement, the Governor wrote letters to Dartmouth and the king detailing his accomplishments in the west and expressing surprise that the Crown would frown not only upon actions he had taken to protect and benefit this most important of His Majesty's dominions, but his initiative to resolve the matter of western Pennsylvania, one that had been festering ever since the late war.

With his wisdom questioned and his political influence in jeopardy, the Governor's mind was in too fey a state to be bothered by a report from a Council member that, as a consequence of the August convention, new companies of militia were being raised throughout the colony, and by the news that Virginians had held their own "tea party" in Yorktown, having on November 2 boarded the recently arrived merchantman *Virginia* and tossed from it two half-chests of tea, purchased by a Williamsburg merchant, into the York River.

Jared Hunt returned with the Governor, as well, spent another night in Williamsburg before continuing on to Hampton, and was oblivious to his host's new crises. The extraordinary Customsman had thoroughly enjoyed the diversion, and during his martial sojourn had even discussed with the Governor various means of enforcing Crown authority. He could hardly wait to return to Hampton to compose a letter to the Earl in which he would describe these ideas and his time with his lordship.

In the event that matters could not be settled peacefully, he proposed to the Governor that men loyal to the Crown — who were numerous — be recruited to form a squadron of cavalry that could strike anywhere on short notice. Throughout his travels, he had observed the fine quality of Virginian horse stock, which could be drafted or bought for that purpose. He also informed the Governor that the Hampton Customs office was expecting to receive soon a sloop, the *Basilisk*, that had been seized in Maryland in an Admiralty tax judgment, and since converted into an eight-gun sloop-of-war. It could patrol the rivers around Chesapeake Bay more easily than the navy's larger warships.

The Governor had thought these excellent ideas, and promised to allow Hunt some role in their implementation, if the need arose.

*     *     *

The *Anacreon*, after an uneventful voyage, reached Falmouth in Cornwall in mid-September, at about the time Lord Dunmore was halfway along his march to Fort Pitt, Cornstalk was assembling his five acres of warriors, and the first Continental Congress was debating the Suffolk Resolves. From there Hugh Kenrick took a series of coastal packets to Poole and Danvers in Dorset. He did not venture to his family's home at Danvers — too likely his uncle the Earl was in residence before he left for London and Parliament, which was scheduled to sit again in late November — but called on the Brunes. Robert Brune, Reverdy's father, said his daughter had spent a while with him and her mother, but many weeks ago had gone up to London to stay with her brother and his wife.

After a day's rest with his parents-in-law, Hugh took another coastal packet from Poole to Dover, and from there a coach to London.

It rained all the way from Dover to London. The city's normal, irregular canopy of smoke had merged with one of rain clouds. The city was darker, as a consequence, but somehow cleaner, the rain washing the soot and grime from the air directly into the ground. During the coach ride, he wondered if the drought in Virginia had finally given way to rain. Then it struck him somehow that it was incongruous to think of London and Virginia in the same thought.

And he wondered what the convention in Williamsburg had accomplished. What was likely done and said there, he thought, as the coach neared Charing Cross and Westminster, would clash violently with what he knew was done and said in the Parliamentary buildings on the Thames.

That, too, was an incongruity. In the city he knew so intimately, he felt like a stranger visiting it for the first time.

From the coach inn he took a hackney to Chelsea. At last he reached Cricklegate, his parents' home up river on the Thames. After another joyful reunion with his surprised parents and sister Alice, he later stated the purpose of his visit to his father in the latter's study. "I am here to salvage my country's honor, and to reclaim my wife."

Garnet Kenrick smiled sadly. "I wish you well with Reverdy, Hugh," he said. "Your mother and I both wish we could help you in that regard." He did not elaborate. Reverdy had always mystified him and Effney Kenrick; they could not penetrate her attraction to a man they both suspected she should be repelled by. Then he frowned. "Your country's honor? Which country, Hugh? This one? God knows, its honor lately has been begging for salvation."

"America, father. I can't decide if its honor needs salvaging or recognition. Or if I am truly an American." Hugh stood at the study window and gazed out at the Thames that was barely visible through an ashen fog. After a moment he turned to ask, "Would it be possible for me to speak in the Commons in your stead? Could that be arranged?" New elections for the Commons were to be held for a new Parliament, as required by the Septennial Act. His father could merely reelect himself. The nature of the borough permitted him to do that.

The Baron nodded, intrigued by the proposal. "Of course. I shall merely retire and elect you the new member for Swansditch, that is all." He paused to sip his coffee. "But, what would you say there, Hugh, other than what I have struggled to say there?"

Hugh shrugged. "*Laissez-faire*, father. Leave us alone."

# Chapter 12: The Patriots

About the time Hugh Kenrick arrived at Cricklegate, Samuel Johnson was hurrying back to London from a tour of Wales with his companions, Henry Thrale, a noted brewer, and his wife Hester, on word of the dissolution of Parliament. Thrale, member for Southwark, wished to be reelected. On his behalf — or perhaps at the behest of the ministry — Johnson went to work on a pamphlet addressed to British electors, "The Patriot," which discoursed on the nature of true and fraudulent patriotism, the mendacity of Americans, the Middlesex elections, and the disgraceful conduct of the Commons over John Wilkes, whom in any event he thought ought to be thoroughly and repeatedly dunked.

"It is the quality of Patriotism to be jealous and watchful, to observe all secret machinations, and to see public dangers at a distance. The true Lover of his country is ready to communicate his fears and to sound the alarm, whenever he perceives the approach of mischief."

That the Americans were, by those criteria, true patriots, was not conceded by him. His remedy for the American troubles was to require of them unconditional submission to Crown authority, in payment of a debt of gratitude.

One afternoon, during a stroll with his father through Westminster Hall, Hugh Kenrick purchased a copy of the pamphlet at a bookseller's stall there. They made their way to nearby Purgatory Tavern, to mark Hugh's election with a dinner in honor of Dogmael Jones. He perused the pamphlet while they waited for their meal. He threw the pamphlet down on the table. "Contemptible blather," he remarked. "I am surprised that Lord North has not contrived to find him a seat in Parliament."

Garnet Kenrick picked it up and glanced through it. "Very likely he was approached on the matter. But I hear that Dr. Johnson is too irascible to sit in the Commons. As irascible as Mr. Wilkes."

"Mr. Wilkes is irascible in action, but Dr. Johnson is ignorant of his own venality. Mr. Jones was a *true patriot*." Father and son toasted the memory of the late member for Swansditch. After dinner, they hired a hackney to take them to Blackfriars Bridge, where the Baron pointed out some of the block stones from the family quarry at Portland that had gone into construction of the bridge.

John Wilkes, while serving his 22-month sentence in King's Bench prison for publishing the *North Briton No. 45* and his obscene parody, *Essay on Women*, conducted an election campaign from his cell, and in 1770 was not only elected an alderman of London, but in 1771 sheriff of London and Middlesex, and in 1774 Lord Mayor of the metropolis. In 1774 he finally became member for Middlesex in the Commons, after that body voted him expelled three times, in spite of his overwhelming victories at the polls.

On the fourth ballot, the Commons arbitrarily declared his opponent, Colonel Henry Lawes Luttrell, the victor, the former member of Bossiney having received about one-third of Wilkes's votes. Luttrell had been bribed to run for the seat against Wilkes by the Duke of Grafton, with His Majesty's blessing. The Commons, weary of opposing Wilkes and the enmity of his numerous supporters, did not contest the former convict's fifth election. His companion member for Middlesex was John Glynn, a lawyer and a "radical" spokesman for the Bill of Rights Society and also an advocate of the colonial cause.

Wilkes's motion in February 1775 to have the resolution of 1768 declaring him unfit to attend the Commons and expelled from it expunged from the House journals was defeated by a large majority, much to the pleasure of Lord North and His Majesty.

The colonists esteemed Wilkes as a hero and a true patriot, a man who had defied the Crown and won after a seemingly endless struggle against the formidable hydra of corruption, preferment, and the king's will. In England and in the colonies, drinking mugs and punch bowls bore his likeness or "No. 45," boys were given his name, and a town was named after him. His victory proved that it was not fruitless to oppose the Crown and helped to encourage the colonials in their own resistance. It also proved the depth of corruption and arrogance of Parliament. After a decade-long contest, it begrudged a single man a single seat in the Commons; would it deign to begrudge the colonies their rights? A growing number of men in the colonies did not think it would.

Henry Luttrell returned to representing Bossiney, becoming a staunch supporter of Lord North.

"The die is now cast," wrote George the Third to North in early September about North's Coercive Acts. "The colonies must either submit or triumph. I do not wish to come to severer measures, but we must not retreat. By coolness and unremitted pursuit of the measures that have been adopted, I trust they will come to submit....I am clear there must always be one tax to keep up the right, and as such I approve of the tea duty."

The political establishment in London during the summer and early fall of 1774 was as oblivious to the gravity of the colonial situation as it was to it in the summer and fall of 1765. The first hint of trouble was a report in October from the ambassador to The Hague that a consignment of cannon and powder had been loaded onto a Rhode Island merchantman in Amsterdam. But the vessel was intercepted and the episode dismissed as a bothersome anomaly.

Otherwise, Lord North and the king devoted their time and energies to forming a reliable "king's party" in the Commons, now that a new Parliament was to be summoned for November, the general election scheduled for the second week of that month. The announcement took by surprise many of those who held seats and offices, and also those who wished to hold seats and offices, precipitating an undignified scramble from holidays and diversions to formulate alliances and plans.

Fletcher Norton, the Speaker of the Commons, had to be cajoled to stand again and continue in that role. Influential peers, such as the Duke of Athol and the Earl of Morton, had inconveniently died, as well as the bishops of Bangor and Worcester, and the candidates and members in their trains had to be persuaded to remain in the court party. Preferments and places had to be shuffled amongst, withdrawn from, or awarded to court party men. The office of Cofferer to the king was an especially difficult one to fill, its former occupant having decided to enter the polls for a seat in the Commons. Candidates had to be solicited, vetted, and bribed to stand for seats, necessitating the cooperation, arm-twisting, or bribery of sponsoring peers. Vacancies occasioned by death, resignations and refusals had to be filled.

It was very exhausting and frustrating work. But, in the end, Lord North and His Majesty triumphed — except in Middlesex, which John Wilkes at last captured — and ensconced in the Commons a bloc that would obstruct any move to placate the colonies or any motion for a substantive conciliation with them.

Also in February, the king wrote Lord North that he was pleased with the proposed Commons address to His Majesty that the colonies were in a state of rebellion. "I should imagine that after the very flagrant outrage committed by the province of New Hampshire (the capture of Fort Constitution earlier that year by "rebels" and the sending of its ordnance to Cambridge), some notice ought to be taken of it, for whatever difference prudence may devise between the New England governments and those of the rest of North America, this cannot extend to New Hampshire."

Hugh Kenrick and his father observed the business from a distance. Hugh wrote a letter to the *London Evening Observer*, in which he railed against "decayed peers and superannuated peerages, and a conniving throne." On November 11 Hugh was "elected" by his father as the new member for Swansditch. He presented his credentials to a House committee, and took the loyalty oath. The oath did not matter to him.

In the meantime, news continued to assault Parliament and St. James's Palace. General Gage had the temerity to make some recommendations to the policymakers. His Majesty wrote Lord North in mid-November, after the new Parliament was in session, "I return the private letters received from Lieutenant General Gage. His idea of suspending the acts appears to me the most absurd that can be suggested. The people are ripe for mischief upon which the Mother Country adopts suspending the measures she has thought necessary. This must suggest to the colonies a fear that alone prompts them to their present violence. We must either master them or totally leave them to themselves, and treat them as aliens. I do not by this mean to insinuate that I am for advice for new measures; but I am for supporting those already undertaken."

In another note to Lord North, George remarked, "The line of conduct seems now chalked out; the New England governments are in a state of rebellion. Blows must decide whether they are to be subject to this country or independent."

A month later he wrote his first minister, replying to a suggestion that the government suspend regulations for the colonies, and send commissioners there to "examine the disputes," that he frowned on the notion, saying that such actions could be interpreted by the colonials as signs of self-doubt and weakness. "I cannot think it likely to make them reasonable. I do not want to drive them to despair but to submission, which nothing but the inconvenience of their situation can bring their pride to submit to."

Already, in December and January, George was reviewing proposed lists of army regiments to distribute between Britain, Ireland, and Boston, and exchanging notes with North and Viscount Barrington, the Secretary-at-War, on which generals to send to North America. The king had already approved of a speech to be delivered in Lords by Mansfield that detailed a plan for conducting a war in America.

\*   \*   \*

Throughout it all, Hugh Kenrick moved like a man in a dream. He had written Reverdy at her brother's place on Berkeley Square, advising her of his presence and his wish to see her. James Brune replied, expressing delight that his brother-in-law was in London, and saying that he had forwarded his letter to his sister, who had gone down to Bath for a month or so. Hugh had supper with James Brune, and they traded memories of happier times. He treated his sister Alice to a production of Handel's *Alcina* at the Opera House, and helped her grasp the meaning of some passages from Goethe's *The Sorrows of Young Werther*, a novel which she was struggling to read in German. Alone, he attended plays at Covent Garden and Drury Lane. His father was an acquaintance of a member of the Royal Academy, and together they attended lectures there by Joshua Reynolds and other speakers.

At Lion Key in the Pool of London, he and his father discussed with Benjamin Worley the dismal future of colonial trade. Garnet Kenrick outlined a plan to increase Worley's European trade to compensate for the expected loss of colonial custom. "My son and I do not expect the Americans to relinquish their liberties in exchange for a mess of British pottage," he warned the agent. "So, we must look elsewhere to keep up our fortunes."

Hugh added, "If the government does not alter its policies, Mr. Worley, you should expect it will think to prohibit any measure of trade with any portion of North America, excepting Canada. For all practical purposes, a state of war already exists between the countries."

He accompanied his mother and sister on shopping tours in London. In one emporium, they admired an exhibition of Josiah Wedgwood's lines of terra cotta and his first examples of jasperware. The clerk who showed them the meticulously crafted blue and white vases and tableware excitedly described the Herculean effort that Wedgwood's factory in Etruria was making to fill an order by Empress Catherine of Russia for over 960 pieces. "They say that Mr. Wedgwood's product has become the reigning *ton* in France, as well," said the clerk, "and threatens to replace Sèvres porcelain there in the best houses, much to the consternation of King Louis!"

One evening, over a banquet, the Duke of Richmond said to his guests, among them Garnet Kenrick and Hugh: "You will have observed that, in recent governments, all the ministers imbued with some measure of audacity have been cursed with short longevity in the career of first minister. I include that invidious rascal, the late Mr. Grenville, and that stalwart but cloudy advocate, Chatham *née* Pitt." He leaned forward to whisper, "I will even include milord Rockingham in that unfortunate company." Then he sat up again, and continued. " But Lord North, I am afraid, will be with us for some duration, because he is not audacious, but rather a meek, fawning puppet of a malign consension." He paused, then said with finality, "As for his policies vis-à-vis the colonies, they are a hotch potch of opaque, careless futility. There will be a war."

"And not just with Massachusetts, your grace," remarked Hugh.

The Duke smiled and nodded agreement. "No, sir. Not just with Massachusetts. With your Virginia, as well. Perhaps a more formidable foe than may be Massachusetts. But, please, do not convey that sentiment to the gentlemen of Boston. I would not wish to provoke them to pen pamphlets about *me*. Far be it from me to claim they steal the thunder first heard clapped in your own capital so many years ago." He signed tiredly. "Well, all I can assure you, sirs, is that in Lords I shall oppose every coercive measure that comes up from the Commons, and every one birthed in my own House. Such measures will be numerous."

William Pitt, Earl of Chatham, proposed in Lords an address to the king to remove British troops from Boston. His proposal was defeated. He then moved that the Continental Congress be recognized as legitimate, as well as many of its grievances. That proposal was rejected, as well. General opinion in the Commons, in Lords, in the press, and among the electorate was correct in the assessment that Chatham's influence in Parliament was not merely negligible; it was practically nil.

Instead, Parliament declared Massachusetts in a state of rebellion, and a few days later passed the New England Restraining Act, which forbade New England, and later colonies south of it, from trading with any nation other than Britain. Parliament was in no mood to compromise.

*       *       *

It was inevitable that Hugh would encounter Sir Henoch Pannell and Crispin Hillier on the first day of the new Parliament on November 29. He did not seek them out, but was espied by them in the Palace Yard in a light fog among the throngs of members who milled about before leaving in groups to take their seats in the House. He stood with his father apart from most of the groups, Garnet Kenrick pointing out to his son some of the members he knew or was acquainted with.

"We meet again, sir, in the same circumstances, it seems."

Hugh and his father turned to note Sir Henoch Pannell, member for Canovan. A mixture of genuine surprise and smug congeniality stretched the wide face. Behind his large figure stood the diminutive, somber Crispin Hillier, member for Onyxcombe. Both men were in the Earl of Danvers's bloc in the Commons, a bloc that allied itself frequently with the court and North's parties. Pannell smiled with pointed gregariousness. "I believe our exchange then concerned our Britannic flora, which has turned somewhat thorny of late." Pannell nodded in greeting to the Baron.

"Very much so, Sir Henoch," answered Hugh with cold reserve. "I recall our encounter then."

"I have mellowed somewhat since then, sir. And you?"

"I have grown sharper thorns."

After he, too, nodded to the Baron, Crispin Hillier spoke. "We did not know you were in town, milord Hugh," he said, his words seeming to include a third party who was not present and which rendered Henoch Pannell's presence coincidental. "Have you paid your respects to your uncle?"

"I have no respects to pay him, Mr. Hillier," replied Hugh.

"I am sorry to hear it," remarked Hillier.

"Perhaps as sorry as may be my brother," said Garnet Kenrick, "when he learns that my son is in town to attend the Commons."

"I wouldn't know, milord," replied Hillier. "I do not presume to audit his lordship's moods."

Feeling left out, Pannell jumped back into the conversation. "Well, milord," he said to Hugh, "I am afraid you will be tempted to nap in the gallery today. Nothing shattering will be said or done in today's sitting. All droll procedures and calendar business." He grinned. "I do not expect to speak today, so there won't be much for you to take me to task for, as you did last time. No botanical matters to prune at all. I will be spared a prickling by your thorns."

"I don't expect to speak either, Sir Henoch," answered Hugh.

Abruptly, Pannell frowned in confusion. "Oh...?" Hillier took a step closer, his own expression wrinkled with knowledge of an answer he was reluctant to believe.

"My son is the new member for Swansditch, Sir Henoch, Mr. Hillier," the Baron said. "I have conceded that Hugh's oratory is more biting than my own. He shall speak for me, when the time comes, and I shall hear him from the gallery."

Pannell blinked once, then recovered quickly from his shock. He mused with a sigh, "Well, more injurious eloquence by way of Swansditch? I thought that had passed away with Sir Dogmael, rest his soul."

Hillier's brow furled. "Milord, are you not a burgess in your Virginia assembly? I believe there may be some legal conflict here, in your possibly representing two different governments."

Hugh smiled wickedly. "There may be a conflict, Mr. Hillier, if you truly own that my government is of another nation, and not a handmaiden of the Crown. However, the General Assembly was dissolved, and its members will not be burgesses again until it meets again. Governor Dunmore will not likely call it back until the spring. In any event, I am not there to be reelected, if he chances to call it sooner." He paused. "Besides, am I not a citizen of the Empire?"

This was too much for the member for Onyxcombe to answer in so short a time. He answered, rhetorically and without conviction, "That remains to be seen, milord."

"Well, if you do speak, milord," said Pannell, "mind what you say. Our oratory may now be reported in the newspapers through this Hansard creature. I voted against that scuttling of our privilege, you know. Its only consequence is to open our private thoughts to endless ridicule and contempt."

"I am not surprised that you opposed it," answered Hugh. "As for the ridicule and contempt, too often they are deserved."

Garnet Kenrick smiled. "It is only a matter of justice, Sir Henoch. No longer must the electorate rely solely on caricatures to gauge the character and ends of the elected."

Again, Henoch Pannell's eyes widened in surprise. The Baron's remark called to him the unwelcome memory of the two caricatures that ridiculed him and the Grenville government during the Stamp Act debates a decade ago. The memory silenced him, even though he wished to reply. He had always been certain that the Baron and Sir Dogmael Jones were responsible for the caricatures.

Hugh Kenrick, after a brief study of Pannell's expression, turned to his father. "Sir, you underestimate your skills. Shall we go in?"

The father and son nodded in parting to the members for Canovan and Onyxcombe, then turned and crossed the Yard in the direction of St. Stephen's Chapel.

"Well, Mr. Hillier," sighed Pannell as they watched them go, "what do you make of that?"

"His lordship will be *very* displeased," commented Hillier ominously.

"Doubtless. But what mischief do you think they are up to?"

"Windmills, Sir Henoch," Hillier said. "Windmills. I believe the younger Quixote has agreed to tilt at us for the older. But the younger wields a much more effective lance."

Henoch Pannell's brow furled at the allusion. He had never read *Don Quixote de la Mancha*, but did not want to confess it.

*       *       *

That evening, Crispin Hillier called at Windridge Court and asked to see the Earl of Danvers. Basil Kenrick received the attorney in his study, where he was making notes for the opening of Lords. Hillier bowed once to the Earl, then said, "I have some upsetting news, your lordship."

"What news, Mr. Hillier?"

"Your nephew is in London."

Basil Kenrick smiled. "Yes, I know."

"How, your lordship?"

"I received a report from Mr. Hunt two days ago."

"I see," replied Hillier. "Then he could not tell you that your nephew is now the member for Swansditch. Your brother elected him. Sir Henoch and I saw them at the Commons this morning. Your nephew took a seat next to Colonel Barré." Hillier paused and chuckled. "Swansditch and Calne. An unlikely pairing, but they will agree!"

"Excuse me, Mr. Hillier?"

"Calne, your lordship. It is Colonel Barré's new seat. It is a market town in Wiltshire, on the Marden River." Hillier paused. "Colonel Barré is expected to speak against the government's colonial policy with his usual frightening mode."

"I see. My nephew will speak against it, it is to be expected. Perhaps I shall attend the Commons when he is there. I have not seen him in years."

Crispin Hillier did not wish to dwell on why the Earl had wished him to arrange for his son's appointment to the Customs service and be sent to

Virginia, just as he had never dwelt, all these eight years, on the Earl's or
Mr. Hunt's role in the death of Sir Dogmael Jones after the Stamp Act had
been repealed. Nor did he dwell on the matter of why the Earl sustained
such a hatred for his nephew, for the incidents that had caused the hatred
were forgotten by everyone long ago. Instead, he asked, "How is Mr.
Hunt?"

The Earl considered the question impertinent, but answered it anyway.
"He has been drafted by Governor Dunmore there to participate in an
Indian campaign. Perhaps he will acquire some martial sense from the
experience. It may come in handy when we find it necessary to reconquer
the colonies."

Hillier cleared his throat. "Can we be so certain of *war*, your lordship?"

"Of course," dismissed the Earl. "Look at my nephew. He, like his
fellow traitors over there, has not nurtured a proper sense of his duty. He
needs be taught it with compulsion. Or perish." He grinned, and added, in
the manner of boasting, "Just as Sir Dogmael perished."

Crispin Hillier winced at the reference. Even though he and the Earl
had never, all this time, discussed the late barrister's murder, he wished his
lordship had not said that. It gave him a feeling of complicity.

# Chapter 13: The Arrangements

Except for infrequent home leaves, he had been in North America for over ten years, and was at the peak of his military career. As a captain, he had been with the Duke of Cumberland at Culloden in 1746; as a major, he served as an aide to George Keppel in Flanders at Maastricht at the end of the War of the Austrian Succession; he was a colonel under General Braddock and survived that officer's disastrous defeat on the Monongahela in 1755. He had commanded light infantry at Ticonderoga, and took part in the taking of Quebec under Wolfe. In 1760, Major General Jeffery Amherst, after securing Canada for the Empire, appointed him governor of Montreal.

He had married a colonial woman, Margaret Kemble, daughter of the president of the Council of New Jersey. In 1761 he was promoted major general, and two years later succeeded Amherst in New York as commander-in-chief of all British forces in North America, which included over fifty garrisons from Newfoundland to the Caribbean.

When he returned from leave in England on the *Lively* in April 1774, he carried with him his appointment as governor of Massachusetts Bay and a copy of a draft of the Massachusetts Government Act, both documents giving him absolute power over that colony. Accompanying these was a letter from Lord Dartmouth, instructing him in the scope and importance of his new duties, the most important of which was securing the absolute and unconditional submission of Massachusetts to the Crown.

He was a tall, thin man, with a longish, angular face that was a mask of frigid patience wedded to an unimaginative and unmovable resolve to obey his instructions to the letter. He was a capable administrator, and while not sympathetic to the unrest in his appointive realm, was not entirely blind to the dire political and military situation that grew worse by the week. The few discreet recommendations he made to his superiors in London to perhaps lessen the harshness of the recent Acts, so as to alleviate a crisis he did not think could be resolved militarily, were consistently and curtly dismissed. The fault was his, for his worried, accurate and detailed reports on the colonial crisis merely served to stiffen the resolve of his superiors to exact total due deference from the colonists.

His name was Lieutenant General Thomas Gage, and he was now fifty-three years old.

It was late September. Before him at his desk in Salem, to which most of Massachusetts's government had been removed as part of the punitive closing of the port of Boston, sat a much younger officer, Captain Roger Tallmadge, who had arrived in Boston four days ago only to be directed to the smaller port town north of the chastened city. The general had been advised months ago of the mission and imminent arrival of the captain and his aide, Lieutenant William Manners, by Lord Barrington.

The captain and Manners, riding into Salem, had immediately found a room, changed into their uniforms after a hearty meal in the tavern below, then reported to Gage's headquarters to deliver the report on colonial military estimates. They were told by a staff aide to amuse themselves until the Governor had time to read and evaluate the report, and then they would be sent for.

Traveling together for months had not made the pair fast friends, and they were only too glad to part for a while from each other's company and find separate diversions. They were warned not to journey alone into Boston, especially not in uniform, except in the company of at least a platoon of soldiers. Manners was absent for long periods of time; Tallmadge did not enquire about the lieutenant's diversions. Then, three days into their wait, the lieutenant vanished.

Late in the afternoon of the next day, Gage sent for Tallmadge and complimented him on the thoroughness of the report. He smiled and patted the top of a bound sheaf of papers. "An invaluable assessment of the circumstances here, Captain. Your observations concur with my own. I shall certainly commend its value to Lord Barrington."

"Thank you, sir."

"Your report is in two different hands, sir. I presume they are your own and Lieutenant Manners's."

"Yes, sir. That portion of it in Lieutenant Manners's hand was dictated by me."

"Of course." After a pause, Gage cleared his throat and with almost tired reluctance brought up another matter. He reached for another short pile of papers and placed them in front of him. "Captain Tallmadge, I have here before me letters from Governor Dunmore and from a Mr. Jared Hunt of the Customs in Virginia, in addition to letters from a Reverend Acland, pastor of a church in Queen Anne County, Virginia, and a Mr. Edgar Cullis, an attorney and burgess for that county in the assembly down there. They all report an action you took during your brief stay in those parts. The action you are accused of by them is, unfortunately, a court martial offense — you were an officer in the field at the time, not acting in any private capacity — and I am certain some attorney for the Customs could concoct an argument for a civil offense, as well."

The general paused. "In addition to these letters, I have before me the sworn testimony of Lieutenant William Manners, your companion and aide the last several months, citing the same offense, and who further asserts, in addition to detailing your action, that you harbor a secret sympathy with the rebelliousness here. His testimony substantiates these other accusations."

"What action, sir?" asked Roger hoarsely, knowing immediately what it was. Now he could account for the lieutenant's absence and disappearance.

"Obstructing a Crown official in the commission of his duties. Obstructing Mr. Hunt, to be precise." Gage paused to turn a page of the sheaf and perused the next. "At a plantation known as Morland Hall, where Mr. Hunt suspected he would find a cache of arms and powder collected by a Mr. Jack Frake, to be likely used against His Majesty's forces. You committed this action in the company of a Mr. Hugh Kenrick, another planter there, whom Mr. Hunt also suspects of numerous offenses against the Crown. You drew your sword, together with this other gentleman, against Mr. Hunt. An *unwise* gesture, sir." He let the page drop and sat back. "Do you deny or confess your action, sir?"

"I admit the action, sir," Roger answered.

Gage nodded. "Why did you so act?"

Roger cast about in his mind for an explanation that would make sense. "I decided to aid the friend of a friend, sir," he replied. "I have no fondness for Customsmen. You perhaps know, sir, that when Customsmen rummage a vessel or private abode, they cause much damage for which they are no longer accountable and for which there is no compensation to the searched party, whether or not contraband is found. Mr. Hunt, as I recollect, was obnoxious and blustery. He threatened and insulted me.

"As for his lordship Governor Dunmore, I reported to him out of courtesy in Williamsburg, before the incident at Morland Hall, and even supped at his quarters. I disliked him on sight, and he, me. He is an ambitious man and I believe he will cause the Crown more regret than I think it would wish to tolerate. Amongst his mischief, he is alienating the affections of the inhabitants of Virginia, and is planning to campaign against the Shawnees in the proscribed territories, perhaps in opposition to Crown policy, and certainly without the concordance of the General Assembly, which he dissolved out of spite."

Roger paused. "I do not know either Reverend Acland or Mr. Cullis, sir. And, Mr. Kenrick is also a burgess in the General Assembly." He paused again, weighing whether or not to mention his friend's status. "He is the nephew of the Earl of Danvers. We grew up together in Danvers, Dorset. We are brothers-in-law."

Then he thought of something that he believed would lessen the seriousness of the charge, something that Hugh had said to Mr. Hunt that day, and something which he thought the general would appreciate. "I am certain that the stand Mr. Kenrick and I took prevented the occurrence of a violent incident, sir, one that could have had unfortunate consequences throughout the colonies. The inhabitants of the plantation were armed, as well. They vastly outnumbered Mr. Hunt's party, which included a squad of marines, and would have traded blows with them, with tragic and ominous results."

Gage frowned. "Governor Dunmore mentioned the marines, but Mr. Hunt did not. Curious omission." He paused. "A friend of a friend, you say? I see," mused Gage. After he again cleared his throat, he continued. "I would dismiss Mr. Hunt's and Governor Dunmore's intelligence as shallow nastiness. I myself have never met a Customsman I liked. And I have no feeling for Governor Dunmore, except some grave reservations for his mode of governance. In some quarters he is regarded as a grasping ogre, and the stories I collected while I was in New York tend to confirm that estimation. I *am* aware of his schemes in the west and have written Lord Dartmouth about them. Perhaps the Crown will call him to account for *his* actions."

The general seemed to realize that he was musing out loud and that he had said more than he had intended to a subordinate. He sighed, and continued. "However, I cannot ignore Lieutenant Manners's testimony concerning your actions at this plantation. Consequently, I must grant all the intelligence before me here some credence. What have you to say to it, sir?"

Roger closed his eyes for a brief moment. "Only that I admit the action, sir, and do not regret having taken it."

Gage hummed and scrutinized his subordinate for a moment. Roger could not penetrate the opaque expression. Then the general reached into a desk drawer and took out an object, which he placed on top of the damning letters. "Lieutenant Manners asserts that your friend gave you *this.*"

Roger gasped. It was the tin gorget that Hugh Kenrick had given him as a parting gift. He remembered removing it when he and Manners had changed into their uniforms in the tavern room, and then forgetting it. The beast! thought Roger. The two-faced, thieving, tattling coward!

Gage hummed again. "'A Paladin for Liberty.' A quaintly dangerous sentiment. A present from your friend, Mr. Kenrick? Lieutenant Manners asserts in his affidavit that you wore this throughout the rest of your journey. Do you deny it?"

"No, sir," answered Roger. He added, "I judged it a prudent ruse to stave off over-curiosity about Mr. Manners and myself. Indeed, it saved us a number of scrapes, sir, as we passed through several counties under the government of committees. Intrusive and somewhat belligerent colonials took it for the accoutrement of a colonial officer. When asked, I claimed that we were in the militia of South Carolina and were on a mission to see some rebels in Boston. That seemed to allay their hostility."

"I see." Gage dropped the gorget and reached for a carafe and a glass to pour himself some wine. Silently he gestured to the carafe to Roger, who shook his head. After he took a sip, the general said, "Tell me a little about yourself, sir."

With some shyness, Roger recited details of his life. He concluded, "In my father's last letter to me, which I collected in New York, he assured me that he would arrange for my reelection as the member for Bromhead."

"Minden? Artillery? Politics?" Gage had studied the young man while the latter spoke. He sighed, then said, "Now, I know that you are eager to return home, to your wife, to the comforts of England, and to your seat in the Commons. God knows, you have roughed it for the last six months and are deserving of some relief. But you are in a bad patch in this affair. Governor Dunmore and Mr. Hunt, you see, had the foresight to send copies of these letters to the War Office, to Lord North, and to Lord Barrington, as well. Reverend Acland noted that he sent a copy of his letter to me to the Bishop of London." The general shrugged in unsmiling amusement. "So, if you returned to England now, a court martial would await you there, or at least a demand for your resignation, which would amount to dismissal from the service and a disgrace. Very likely you would need to surrender your seat in the Commons, as well, or even be expelled from that body. If you were asked to resign, I would not recommend that you demand a court martial to exonerate yourself. It would not go well for you.

"As for me, I would be expected to take some action. If I did not, I would never hear the end of it." Gage looked stern and strangely compassionate. "I propose that you remain here on my staff for another year, until next October, as an aide or in some other useful capacity. You were an instructor at Woolwich, you say, and so you must have some pedagogical talent. I have among the ranks here some stragglers and regimental orphans who should be trained properly in discipline and fighting. You could perhaps assume command of them. I will write London about this...punishment."

Gage noted the crestfallen expression on the officer's face. "Come next October, you will be free to return to England, carrying a letter from me exonerating you of the charge of sedition and whatever other charges could be laid on you. I have that discretion." Gage raised his eyebrows. "However, if that is not to your liking and you do not agree to this proposal, I will have no other choice but to call for a court martial. You are an able officer, and that would be unfortunate. It would be a shame to lose you." The general sat back and waited for the captain to reply.

After a long moment, Roger forced himself to say, "I accept your proposal, sir."

"Good," replied Gage with some relief. "A *wise* decision." He picked up the gorget, studied it once more, then held it out to the captain. "You may have this, but do not wear it in public. It was a gift, and is irrelevant to the matter at hand." He attempted some levity. "Perhaps when you return to London and take your seat, you could wear it to the debates in the Commons, to better flaunt your...sympathies."

Roger rose, took the gorget, and dropped it into one of his tunic pockets. Gage folded his hands over the letters. "That is all, Captain Tallmadge. I will not respond to Governor Dunmore's and Mr. Hunt's letters, nor will I communicate this matter to any of the other officers here. You should acquaint yourself with them, in the meantime, to better assess the troops and the situation here. I will send for you when I have made some arrangements. Good day to you, sir."

Roger stood up. "Yes, sir. Thank you." He hesitated for a moment. "Sir, Mr. Manners left my company a day ago, and did not say where he was going. He left not so much as a note. His effects are gone from our room. He was still under my orders. Have you any knowledge of his...whereabouts?"

A slight smile broke the ice of Gage's temperate expression. "At his request, I have reassigned him, and sent him to Montreal to report to the officer in charge of the garrison there. He left yesterday aboard a mail packet bound for Quebec Province." The general chuckled. "After so much time in the tropics, I thought a good dose of a Canadian winter would do the puppy some good."

Roger screwed up his face in disbelief. "Did he request that particular assignment, sir?"

Gage's smile broadened. "No, Captain. The order came as a surprise to him. I expect he was wanting to be sent to Barbados, or to some other salubrious clime."

Roger was secretly pleased that the general had not liked Manners, either. It was just as well that the lieutenant was out of his own reach now. "Yes, sir," Roger said. "I shall await your orders, sir." He saluted, turned smartly, and left the general's office.

When he returned to the tavern, he took out pen, ink and paper and began to compose urgent letters to his wife, Alice, to his father, and to Hugh Kenrick. Days later, after he had introduced himself to other army officers in Salem, he had practically memorized his response to the rumor, apparently begun by Lieutenant Manners and propagated by members of the general staff who arranged Gage's interviews and screened correspondence to the general, that he was a traitor and sympathizer with the rebels: "Stuff and nonsense, sir. You will note who was ordered to Canada, and who remains here."

He sentenced the tin gorget, wrapped in a length of torn hose, to the bottom of his baggage.

*     *     *

A chill, late October gust swept off the York River and caused them to lean closer to each other. Jack Frake and Etáin were taking what they knew would be one of their last evening strolls this season on the grounds atop the bluff of Morland Hall. In the gathering twilight, faint, shimmering yellow lights were beginning to appear on the opposite bank in Gloucester.

As they moved along the path that paralleled the edge of the bluff, Jack turned to gaze at the lights in the great house. It was too dark for his wife to see the frown in his expression. He said, without warning or preamble: "I do not want you here when it begins. For my own peace of mind, I must know that you are in the safest place possible."

"Where?" Etáin did not need to ask what he was talking about. His study desk was strewn with Williamsburg *Gazettes* and newspapers from other colonies, and correspondence from other chapters of the Sons of Liberty. This afternoon, John Proudlocks, Jock Fraser, and other men had come to meet her husband in the study, where they discussed the resolutions of the August convention in Williamsburg, and news of the debates in the congress in Philadelphia that was beginning to filter south.

She did not intrude on the meeting, but quietly served the visitors ale and cider and left the room. She had stayed long enough to hear her husband say, "Some counties are not even waiting for a second congress. They have passed resolutions to recruit militia companies and to stock up on powder and ball. We have ample stores of those, but have no effective militia. Mr. Vishonn is the colonel of this county's militia, but he will not commit himself to calling it up. He is holding out for reconciliation, or a civil answer to the congress's petition. So, we are on our own, and must make our own arrangements."

She left the room then, knowing that the news was dire and that Jack would tell her it. Her husband, John Proudlocks, William Settle, and many of the tenants had helped move the powder, ball, and arms from Morland's ice cellar to the cellar of the abandoned Otway place shortly after the raid by the Customsmen.

"In the enemy's camp," Jack said without emphasis.

Etáin furled her brow in confusion.

He looked down on her face. He could not see it well in the hastening dark, but he could sense the question in it. "With your parents, in Edinburgh. For the duration." After a few years in Glasgow, her father's firm, Sutherland and Bain, had reassigned him to Edinburgh to oversee the North Sea and Baltic trade.

Etáin shook her head. "I wish to be here, with you, when it begins, and for the duration."

Jack said, with finality, "No." He paused. "You are one of the things I shall be fighting for. You, and Morland, and liberty. Morland may perish in the fight. We may even be conquered, and liberty vanquished, for a while. I may need to go into hiding, or I may become a prisoner. But you will remain sacrosanct. I wish to carry with me at least the knowledge that you are apart from it all...from all the bloodshed, and destruction, and cruelty that are sure to come." He paused. "With you safe from harm, my mind will be clear and my hand free to act."

Etáin stopped and said with sudden anger, "Or, you may die somehow, in the fighting, or be hanged or shot, as a prisoner! You are asking me to possibly never see you again, to be apart from you, and to imagine you, beyond my reach, beyond my help, amongst all that bloodshed, destruction and cruelty! Imagination can be worse than the reality, Jack!" She was angry with him, the first time ever, and did not feel the tears in her eyes.

Jack turned to face her and smiled for the first time this evening. "True. Imagination can be worse. And, yes, I might even die." He raised a hand to touch her face, and felt the tears, then held her by the shoulders, his expression turning grim with determination. "Or you, if you remained here. You see, if anything happened to you, I am not sure I would want to go on fighting...or living. If Morland were destroyed, it could be rebuilt." He gripped her shoulders more tightly. "*You* cannot be replaced."

"Nor *you*, Jack," whispered Etáin. She moved closer to him and rested her forehead on his chest. She was remembering her governess, Millicent Morley. It was said that she flung herself off the cliff into the sea at Tragedy Point at Falmouth, after Redmagne was hanged and gibbeted. All this time, she was never sure why her governess believed she could not live without Redmagne. For her, it was a subject of occasional and brief wonder, for Jack had always been here, in the great house, or in the fields, or in Williamsburg. The question had seemed superfluous, because he was always somewhere close.

She trembled now, because she no longer wondered why Millicent Morley had flung herself into the sea.

He drew her close to him and said into her hair, "I want you here with me, always, Etáin," said Jack. "And you *will* be with me, always, when I am alone, doing what must be done...in the coming years." He paused. "Just as Skelly and Redmagne have always been with me, all these years." He chuckled softly. "You reminded me of that yourself, Etáin, some years ago, when you thought then there would be war, and I told you I wished they could be here."

She nodded in recollection. "And you will be with me, whatever the distance between us," she said. She realized only after she said it, that she had surrendered to his wish, and would go to Edinburgh.

"It will be for years, Etáin," he warned her. "Many years."

She did not look up at him. "I will write my parents. When shall I leave?"

"Early spring," said Jack.

# Chapter 14: The Annulment

One evening in December, about a week after the new Parliament had opened, Hugh took Reverdy to Covent Garden to see a restaging of George Colman's comedy, *The Jealous Wife*, a loose adaptation of Henry Fielding's *Tom Jones*. He did not care for Fielding's novel, but had selected the play from a number of productions as the most promising. He had heard that Colman's plays were well done. It was their fourth meeting since Reverdy's return from Bath. She seemed happy to see him again, but there was an oddly bleak manner in her delight that he could not yet fathom.

To his surprise, Reverdy eagerly approved of the choice. "They say that Mr. Colman is beginning to eclipse Mr. Garrick in the theater," she said to him the afternoon he proposed the outing, "and that he is raising the theater to the stature it once enjoyed." She chuckled in amusement. "Mr. Garrick, it seems, is too busy *acting* as a messenger between Lord North and that protégé of Lord Rockingham's, Mr. Edmund Burke. Mr. Burke and Mr. Garrick are members of Dr. Johnson's club, which is very odd, for I have heard that Dr. Johnson cannot abide Mr. Burke's politics."

"Perhaps not," Hugh demurred with an invisible shrug. He did not care to discuss Dr. Johnson at the moment. Nor Edmund Burke, the new member for Bristol whom he thought likely to become Lord Chatham's heir in oratory in the Commons. He had met him briefly in the coffee room of the House the second or third day after the new Parliament opened, and was impressed by his apparent advocacy of the colonial cause. "The theater will revive entirely, once the office of Lord Chamberlain is abolished, and when the theater licensing act is repealed."

"Must you always color a subject with politics?"

"Yes, when the subject has been the object of politics, as the theater has been. You know that politics is not incidental to my interests. And, there is no Lord Chamberlain in America."

She was tempted to reply that there was little produced in America that a Lord Chamberlain could censor or approve. Instead, she remarked, "It is unfortunate that Mr. Garrick has not been knighted. Perhaps someday notable artists will receive proper recognition for their contributions to the nation."

Hugh said, "He has done well enough without being bestowed the king's pleasure."

A cold drizzle was falling when they emerged from the theater. They waited with others beneath the theater porch for a hackney to take them back to her brother's house on Berkeley Square, and stood apart from the hubbub and jostling of the crowd. Hugh did not vie with the other theatergoers for a vehicle. He did not seem to be in a hurry.

Reverdy pulled up the hood of her cape and sighed, "Well, that was a suitable play for us to see."

"Why so?"

"*I* am a jealous wife."

"I did not intend any personal allusions in my choice of this play," answered Hugh. "I chose it on Mr. Colman's reputation." He paused. "*Our* marriage cannot be described as a farce, as this play can be."

"No, it cannot," agreed Reverdy. "Perhaps, then…as a sentimental novel?"

"No. Our…union has been too fierce for mere sentiment." He looked at her face, which was in partial shadow from the light of a nearby lamppost. "What are you jealous of, Reverdy?"

She answered almost immediately, "Your other wife, Hugh. Politics."

"Do not ask me to choose between you," he replied. After a moment, he added, "You are an element of a trinity of principal concerns in my world. Politics, or the liberty that may be had from it, is another."

"What is the third element?" asked Reverdy.

"My life," Hugh answered with a solemnity his wife had not heard in him in a long time. Nor in anyone since her return. The solemnity made her uncomfortable. She resented it. And with a bitterness she could not disguise, she answered, "Yes. Of course, there is always *that*."

The slight did not escape Hugh's notice. He said nothing for a long moment. Then, at his gesture, a free hackney approached them and stopped. He helped Reverdy into the vehicle, gave the driver the address, and boarded after his wife to take the seat opposite her.

A while after the hackney jerked forward, Reverdy asked, "Do you not think Mr. Colman stages a worthy play?"

Hugh shrugged. "The play is worthless, but it was well staged. And, many worthy plays are sadly ill-staged."

Reverdy sighed in defeat. "Well, perhaps next week we can come again here, Hugh. The newspaper noted that Mr. Colman is staging *The Clandes-*

*tine Marriage,* which I believe he wrote with Mr. Garrick. Perhaps it will be a more appropriate one for us to attend." When Hugh did not respond to this remark — she sensed that he refused to — Reverdy said, to fill the awkward silence, "Alice must be distraught that Roger has not returned, and afraid that he might be caught up in the troubles in Boston."

Alice Tallmadge was inconsolable for several days after receiving Roger's first letter in mid-November. She had since received a series of letters from her husband, expressing his hope to be able to see her again the next fall. "She is both. Well, at least he was not court-martialed."

"It was foolish of him that day, siding with you against that Customsman! He should have known it would be reported!"

Hugh shrugged. "Perhaps he did know. But it was important to him to take that action. A right thing for him to do." He smiled, for the first time this evening. "How is Miss Dilch?" he asked.

"She is fine. After reading about that Wheatley woman's visit here, she has written a pound of poetry. One verse was even published in the *Evening Standard,* two months ago. James may try to find a publisher for her work." After another long silence, Reverdy asked, "Have you seen your uncle?"

"No."

After a moment, Reverdy braved, "I have, Hugh."

Hugh turned in surprise to face her. "Why? Did he send for you?"

"No. I called on him, at Windridge Court, some weeks ago, shortly after I returned from Bath, after I got your letter there. I called on him when I knew he was not entertaining others."

"But, *why?*"

"To see if some reconciliation between you and him was possible."

Hugh shook his head. "It is not possible."

"He agreed," sighed Reverdy. "I abandoned that purpose early on. But our conversation was otherwise cordial. He asked many questions about you, and us, and Virginia."

"My uncle's curiosity has been proven many times a lair for the unsuspecting, Reverdy. Beware of his hospitality." Hugh paused. "You should not have volunteered any intelligence about us or Virginia. Under the present circumstances, he is an enemy — ours, and the colonies'."

"You are being unfair to him, I think," ventured Reverdy in protest. "I could see plainly that he was miserable. He has not seen his brother your father and his family in years. He has communicated by messenger only with your father for so long. For company, he is surrounded by fearful servants and conniving politicians and peers. His very words to me."

Hugh scoffed in dismissal. "His *preferred* company for as long as I have known him."

Reverdy ventured, "I think that if you made a gesture of conciliation to him, sunlight and peace would enter into all our lives, and all would be well...and we could be happy again."

"Reverdy!" exclaimed Hugh with angry sharpness. "That is a contemptible idea!"

Reverdy seemed to cower in fear away from him to the corner of the compartment. It was the first time he had ever spoken to her in that manner. She was shocked.

Hugh continued. "Have you forgotten all the misery he has caused me, and caused the family? Have you forgotten that he was probably responsible for Sir Dogmael's murder? Have you forgotten that he would prefer me to be a toady, instead of the man you love? Or *dead*?"

Reverdy could not reply to this scolding outburst. She sat stunned. Inside her fur muffler, her hands clenched each other anxiously. She was afraid.

Hugh said, "You should not be taken in by his misery. There are two kinds of that condition, Reverdy: The one caused by injustice and endured by innocents, and the other is the natural companion of an evil person. Of course, my uncle is miserable! He is plagued by his own malignancy!"

Reverdy said nothing, but looked out the glass into the passing darkness. It seemed safer to watch nothing than the severe reproach on her husband's face, which made her feel like a criminal.

They did not speak again until the hackney arrived at the steps of James Brune's residence on Berkeley Square. Hugh handed her out of the vehicle, told the driver to wait, and walked his wife to the door.

On the steps, Reverdy asked suddenly, "Are you still determined to speak in the Commons?"

"Yes." They had discussed the subject during their last meeting. She did not approve of the idea. She thought he would merely make more enemies.

"When will you return...to Virginia?"

"In early spring. Perhaps sooner, if circumstances permit."

"What circumstances, Hugh?" asked Reverdy.

"Whether or not you wish to return with me. And whether or not I see anything to be gained by staying here to audit Parliament."

Reverdy braved a bold look into his face. "You would not stay here for me?"

Hugh shook his head. "If there is nothing to be gained by it, no."

"Not even for the...politics?"

"If I conclude that Parliament is deaf to reason, no."

Reverdy turned to face the ornate door, reached up, and yanked the bell-pull. She said, not turning to face him, "It seems that you are married more to 'Lady Liberty' than to me, Hugh."

"You must own that she has been more a mistress to me than you have been of late, my dear."

She was surprised, not by his words, but by the tenderness and regret in them. Any other man, she knew, would have uttered them with a growling, cutting bitterness meant to hurt. She resented his not having said it that way, for it left her no excuse to reply in kind. She fought the knowledge, and replied, "You asked me not to demand that you choose between us. I won't. *You* have made that choice, Hugh. I cannot tolerate this rivalry. I have tried to, all these years...you know that...but never could."

They heard a bolt being moved then, and the door opened. A servant greeted her. Without looking back at Hugh, Reverdy hurried in. The servant, who knew him, raised his brow in silent question, waiting for Hugh. Hugh shook his head once. The servant nodded in answer, and closed the door. Hugh heard the bolt slide home.

Upon hearing that sound, he thought: *That is the end of it.*

Since seeing her again after she returned from Bath, he had observed, at first with alarm, then with an imposed dispassion, a kind of mathematics at work in their relationship. Numbers represented facts, and all those facts represented an unalterable sum. That sum was reached tonight. She had been seduced by the city, by all it had to offer. All the things that concerned her, from its politics to its society, the city's countless, incidental distractions, were facts that now outweighed any value she might have seen in him. In consuming them, they had consumed her soul. She saw the unalterable in him, and did not want it.

It was she who had made a choice, he thought. She was not what he had always thought she was, or could be. The thing that he saw in her, he asked himself: Could he blame his imagination? Or a desperation to see it? Perhaps both. Perhaps once it had lived, but it had since died. For the first time since he had known her, he acknowledged a chasm that could never be bridged. He knew that he must accept that fact, as well, in time.

Hugh heard someone inquire, "Sir?" He turned to look up, and saw the hackney driver scowling down at him from his perch. Hugh nodded once to the man, strode back down the steps into the drizzle to the vehicle, and said, "To Chelsea."

During the ride back up the Thames, he sat watching the darkness pass by through the glass, feeling desolate, filled by an emptiness that was at the same time a great weight of grief.

*    *    *

It was late when he arrived at Cricklegate. Everyone had retired: his parents, Alice, and even the servants. He let himself in with his own key. When he reached his room, he found a letter sitting in a salver on his desk. It was from John Proudlocks, written in late October. He lit a lamp, opened the letter, and read it.

Proudlocks dwelt on news of their friends and of the troubles in Virginia and in the colonies, and then brought up another subject. "His name is Jared Hunt. I saw him near Caxton, on the road to Williamsburg. He was leaving the vicinity of Meum Hall, after having enquired about your whereabouts of some of your laborers. He is the same man that your father says is your uncle's secretary. We saw him twice in the Turk's Head tavern there in London. He is the man who attempted to rummage Mr. Frake's house. Mr. Frake and I are curious about his presence here. We are certain that he is here at the behest of your uncle, Lord Danvers. To what purpose, we can only guess."

Hugh put the letter aside. He would ask his father about it tomorrow. He could not now devote any time or energy to wondering about his uncle's machinations or this Mr. Hunt.

# Chapter 15: The Epiphany

Rupert Beecroft, the business agent at Meum Hall, forwarded Roger Tallmadge's letter to Hugh, penned in Boston. It reached London in late November.

After describing his circumstances and Lieutenant Manners's betrayal, the captain wrote, "Boston is a pretty town, but now it bristles with hostility instead of bustling with commerce, and looks emaciated for the closing of the port. I interviewed with General or Governor Gage in Salem, but shortly thereafter he moved the government back to Boston, as well as his headquarters, for the smaller town proved untenable. Only the most essential elements of his government had been moved there by the time Lieutenant Manners and I were directed to it, so the General's affairs were not much affected by the move back. Salem was also taken over by a provincial 'congress,' instigated by Mr. Samuel Adams, and a leading merchant here, Mr. John Hancock, and a Dr. Joseph Warren, all of them very fiery fellows among a host of them, and very much the objects of General Gage's attention. This new 'congress' asserts that it, and not General Gage's, is the true government.

"I am assigned a billet in Boston, in the house of a Mrs. Brophy, a sea captain's widow, with two other officers, both senior to me, much against the will and means of the lady, for the new act gives her no choice in the matter. She receives pittance in compensation, if any at all, from the army and the other officers. I have tried to help her out with whatever coin I can spare. I believe she is appreciative of the gesture, and I would do more, but a gesture is all my purse can afford as penance for the imposition.

"The army here is quite useless and impotent, unable to move at will without risking a violent encounter with the rebels, which the General wishes to avert. However, he has ordered discreet forays into the surrounding countryside and hamlets to seize or destroy arms and powder cached there. But these expeditions seem futile, for your friends the rebels seem to have an infinite supply of these provisions. There have been no clashes yet between them and our troops, but backs are up on both sides and tempers grow short, and I fear that some violence is inevitable.

"I have been put in charge of training some regulars from broken regi-

ments and companies reduced by sickness and desertion, and have persuaded the General to pay them from his own budget. They are a good company, although the worst recruits in it are the American loyalists, whose
ardor to smote the rebels greatly surpasses their capacity for discipline, and
they give me the most trouble.

"I do hope that nothing happens while I am here. I am of two minds in
my predicament: I would hesitate to fire on the people here, for their grievances are in the main legitimate. But I am also reluctant to tolerate abuse
by them of my fellow Britons who wear the King's scarlet, for our rank and
file are mostly ignorant of the causes of the troubles. Even many of the officers, who boast some education, are confounded by the heat of defiance
exhibited by their cousinal countrymen, but like me, determined to do their
duty. Other officers are contemptuous of the rebel militia companies here,
and are spoiling for a fight, hoping for a chance to bloody a few heads. Most
of my fellow officers have no field experience to credit them, and I have
cautioned them on the horrors of war, and also that if we come to blows
with the inhabitants, very likely the Americans will not oblige us with a
purely European mode of fighting it, as I noted in my report to Lord Barrington.

"I am fortunate that General Gage attaches much importance to my
report, and to my career, as well, so that I am not sitting in arrest awaiting
the judgment of a court martial. One of his staff suggested to me, in an ine-
briate and indiscreet moment in a tavern, that Manners was despatched to
Montreal to avoid the chance of a duel between he and me. There was not
much chance for that, for dueling seems to me a vain and wasteful way to
recoup one's honor. In any encounter with him, I would have merely
shown my back and opened a window to express my contempt...."

The morning after his last evening with Reverdy, before joining his
family downstairs in the breakfast room, Hugh reread Roger's letter and
others from Jack Frake and John Proudlocks, to divert his mind from the
loss of Reverdy. He took the time to draft replies to all of them.

Over breakfast, he did not discuss her, but showed his parents Proudlocks's letter. Garnet Kenrick's face grew red in anger. "He has sent this
man to harm you!" exclaimed the Baron. "And found him a place in the
Customs in your parts to disguise his purpose! I shall speak to the Earl
about it — after I have made some inquiries."

"Do you wish me to accompany you, sir?" asked Hugh. "I should like
to see his face when he learns that he has been found out."

"No. I do not wish him to set eyes on *you* ever again."

Effney Kenrick studied her son over the breakfast table. "How is Reverdy, Hugh?" she asked with guarded gentleness.

Hugh replied with some uncharacteristic woodenness, "It is finished, madam. We were married in Virginia, and if there is a court open there when I return, I shall seek an annulment."

"I'm sorry, Hugh. For the both of you."

Hugh merely nodded in acknowledgement, then abruptly changed the subject. "I bought Lord Chesterfield's *Letters to His Son* on Duck Lane yesterday. Quite an interesting self-portrait of the man. It is unfortunate that he died last year. He could have perhaps seconded Lords Chatham and Richmond in Lords on the American business. I believe Mr. Jones consulted him on some matters years ago. Much of his advice to his son, however, is arguably vacuous or too precious for words. Still, I hope to finish the book during the cessation of hostilities at Westminster." He would be idle until Parliament met again after the Christmas recess.

From that moment on, Hugh sought neither advice nor consolation from his parents about Reverdy, and his parents thought it wiser not to offer any.

On the morning before Christmas, while snow fell, Garnet Kenrick journeyed alone by hackney to Windridge Court, his first visit there in years. Alden Curle answered the door, and for a moment was too astounded to do anything but gape stupidly at the Baron.

"I am here to see the Earl," said the Baron sternly.

Curle stammered, "He...he is...indisposed at the moment, milord."

"I saw him just now in his bedroom window, Mr. Curle. If you do not admit me, I shall admit myself."

Still stunned by the visitor's presence, Curle merely blinked and remained immobile. The Baron sighed impatiently and brushed past the *major domo*.

He climbed the wide stairs and strode directly down the passageway to his brother's room, unbuttoning his great coat as he went. He opened the door to the chamber without knocking.

His brother was still in his nightgown and nightcap, standing by the fireplace, a cup and saucer in his hands. Claybourne, his valet, was laying out the Earl's garments on the spacious bed. Both men looked up in shock at the intruder. The Baron noted that his brother had not aged gracefully. He thought it could be said that his brother had decayed. There was a noticeable curve in his back, and a pronounced stoop to his shoulders that had not been there the last time the Baron had seen him. His long, fox-like face had, it seemed, grown narrower and paler, the eyes recessed behind a confused map of lines and creases.

"Brother!" exclaimed Basil Kenrick with disbelief. "What...?"

"I will be brief, Basil," said Garnet Kenrick without preamble. "Your secretary, Mr. Jared Hunt, is in Virginia. Is this not true?"

"I...what are you talking about?"

"What is his purpose there?"

"How...?....I don't know what you are..."

Garnet Kenrick spoke before his brother could complete his protest. "I enquired at the offices of the Commissioner of the Revenue and Customs Board, Basil, and learned that you secured Mr. Hunt a place in Virginia, one giving him some special authority there. I am certain that such an appointment came at a price. I learned further that Sir Henoch Pannell interceded on your behalf in those offices to secure the appointment. To what purpose, Basil?"

Basil Kenrick stood still, and said nothing. His eyes narrowed in petulant defiance.

Garnet Kenrick, taking a step forward, raised a hand and emphasized his words with a stabbing finger. "Hear me well, Basil: Should anything happen to my son that reveals your hand, either here or in Virginia, I shall hold you responsible, and call you out to pistols, swords or bare knuckles. It will not matter to me, which. And when I have finished with you, I shall seek out Mr. Hunt, wherever he may be found, to the same end. Am I clear?"

The Earl glowered at his brother. He remembered the cup and saucer in his hands, then flung them aside at the fireplace, where they crashed into the firedog with a tinkle of shattered porcelain. The flames and the hot iron fizzled angrily from the spilt tea. Claybourne, witnessing this confrontation, cringed and took a step backward.

The Earl's hands opened and closed in trembling fists. He, too, took a step closer, his head lowered as though he meant to pounce. He demanded in a taunting growl, "Are you *threatening* me, Garnet?"

Garnet Kenrick shook his head once. "No, I am warning you. It is my son you threaten. Good day." He squared his shoulders, spun around, and walked out.

\*    \*    \*

The Christmas holiday season in the Kenrick residence was subdued, almost dour. In the midst of her preparations for it, Effney Kenrick toyed with the idea of inviting James Brune, his wife, and Reverdy to Cricklegate for at least one day to share roast goose and plum pudding. She asked Hugh what he thought of the idea.

Her son had merely shrugged with indifference. "If you wish their company, I will not mind. James can be trusted to be entertaining on such occasions."

Effney abandoned the idea that very instant. She knew that she could not invite the Brunes without inviting Reverdy. She was about to turn and leave Hugh's study, when Hugh asked, "Mother, you have not seen her, or tried to patch things up between us in any way, have you?"

"No, Hugh. I have not seen her in months, nor written her. Nor has your father."

"Thank you."

Alice Tallmadge had composed a melody to go with the words of a doggerel, "Out of the Tavern." On Twelfth Night, after supper, she entertained her family and neighbors with a performance of it on a pianoforte in the sitting room. Taking sips between stanzas from a glass of rum punch, she sang, in a pleasant, contralto voice:

*Out of the tavern I've just stepped tonight.*
*Street! You are caught in a very bad light!*
*Right hand and left hand are both out of place!*
*Street! You are drunk, 'tis a very clear case!*

*Moon! 'tis a very queer figure you cut;*
*One eye is staring, while the other is shut!*
*Tipsy, I see, and you are greatly to blame.*
*Old as you are, 'tis a horrible shame!*

*Then the street lamps, what a scandalous sight!*
*None of them soberly standing upright.*
*Rocking and staggering! Why, upon my word!*
*Each of the lamps is as drunk as a lord!*

*All is confusion! Now isn't it odd,*
*That I am the only thing sober abroad?*
*Sure it is rash with this crew to remain!*
*Better go into the tavern again!*

Alice earned a round of laughter and applause from the company. While she bowed in acknowledgement, Hugh remarked to his father, who sat beside him, "What an appropriate Parliamentary psalm that would make! Amending the title, of course, to 'Out of the Commons'! Shall I propose it to the House chaplain? I can see it now, he intoning those words for all those pious, bowed heads before they proceeded to their rancorous business!"

Garnet Kenrick smiled without humor at the jest. He had never known his son to be so bitter. He wished it were in his power to make things right for him. He wondered what Hugh would say in Parliament, when it reconvened after the holidays.

# Chapter 16: The Riddle

The holiday cheer that animated men since Christmas was spent in members of Parliament by the time they reassembled in Westminster in mid-January 1775. The seasonal good will they might have bestowed upon their friends, families, neighbors, servants and tenants dissolved in a wink on the question of what to do about the rebellious North American colonies, a friendly sprite that vanished in the glum presence of niggling obstinacy and offended parochialism.

Hugh Kenrick was disconcerted by the abrupt transition from the constant benevolence of his family to the passive belligerence of the men he encountered again in the Commons. He sought to acquaint himself with those who were in the least sympathetic with the colonial cause. He found them, but soon realized that most of them were men of disparate parts; no glue held them together as a bloc, and no consistency could be found in their positions.

He vented his exasperation on his father one afternoon while they supped together in the Purgatory Tavern after leaving the Commons. "I do not understand how these people can proclaim the liberties of the colonies, but in the next breath demand that the Crown assert its authority over them at the price of suspending those liberties."

"Have patience with them, Hugh," cautioned his father. "They haven't your advantage."

Hugh scoffed. "What advantage have *I*?"

"You have lived a…freer life than most of your colleagues in the House. In Virginia." Garnet Kenrick paused. "And a more valorous one, in the cause of liberty."

Hugh smiled and nodded in acknowledgement of the compliment. "That may be said of Mr. Jones, as well."

"Of course," agreed his father. "Every year, I have remarked it to your mother, on the anniversary of his murder."

"I am beginning to appreciate the contempt he held for the House." Then he shook his head. "It is as though they had ridden on pentagonal wheels all their lives, father, and could not conceive of round ones! Or, having conceived of them, are opposed to them! They are comfortable with the vexations of *conditional* liberty, with the fetters and shackles of pro-scription and regulation, and nurture an envious resentment of anyone who does not wish to be similarly hobbled."

"It is an appropriate riddle you posit, Hugh," sighed the Baron, "but I fear I have no answer to it." Garnet Kenrick's expression brightened then. He paused to lean back in his chair and study his son with new interest, as though a mystery of his own had just been solved. "The answer to it rests in you, son. I believe it has lain there, undiscovered, all these years…from the very first," he mused, as he remembered his six-year-old son fighting John Hamlyn to reclaim his brass top from the thief in Green Park, where the city had thronged one evening to celebrate another peace, in another age, it seemed. He paused again, and leaned closer over the table and added softly, in a confidential near-whisper, "Surely you know that a riddle is composed by its creator for an answer he already knows." He smiled and reached over to pat his son's shoulder. "You have the answer to that riddle, and to your others, as well. Some day, you'll find the words. And then you may tell *me*."

And Hugh was thrust back in memory to the day in Glorious Swain's garret, after the Pippins had been arrested, tried, and sentenced to the pil-lory and penal servitude for a crime they did not commit. He remembered Swain, the gentle but menacing sage, telling him: "*You do not know what you are. The name for you has not yet been devised. The answer lies in you, and only you can put it into the right words. Someday, you will….*"

Hugh blinked in wonder at the memory, and then in astonishment for how much two men who had never met had in common. He raised his glass of ale, and in the first warm gesture he had made in weeks, said, "A toast to you, father, and to the five hundred of you who do not sit in the Com-mons."

This time it was his father who stared back in astonishment, and blushed in acknowledgement of the compliment.

*    *    *

From that day on, Hugh had the sense that he was waiting for something to dawn on him, and that the answer depended on his diligent presence in the Commons. He did not think of it in those terms; it was a vague premo-nition he was unable to articulate. He sensed that when it happened, it would be momentous. He did, however, note a growing distance between himself and the men and events in the Commons, a distance measured by impatience and indifference, coupled with a reluctance to let them color his judgment of the Commons and the men who sat in it. He wondered if it was connected somehow with his estrangement from Reverdy. He initially thought the notion absurd.

He experienced that conflict when he spoke with the most promising advocate of the colonial cause in the Commons, Lord Rockingham's man, Edmund Burke, with whom Hugh initiated a tentative and guarded acquaintance. Burke found time in his busy schedule to reciprocate the interest, chiefly because the new member for Swansditch had also represented his Virginia county in the General Assembly. In the Commons lobby Burke introduced him to Henry Cruger, a merchant and his fellow member for Bristol, the second largest commercial port in the nation. "Born in New York," remarked Burke, "and an alumnus of King's College there."

Cruger, a large, garrulous man, shook Hugh's hand. "Sir, have no fear! Mr. Burke and I shall endeavor to persuade the House to follow reason," he said with a laugh, "he eloquently, and I plainly, in what he has called a rhetorical flanking movement, to catch the mob unawares here on both sides!"

*   *   *

On January 20, Hugh stood near the bar in Lords and heard Chatham introduce a motion to withdraw troops from Boston, and his speech urging reconciliation with the colonies. When Pitt touched on Boston and the coercive measurements taken against Massachusetts for the opposition there to Crown authority, he said, "The indiscriminate hand of vengeance has lumped together innocent and guilty, with all the formalities of hostility has blocked up the town, and reduced to beggary and famine thirty thousand inhabitants....But His Majesty is advised that the union in America cannot last. Ministers have more eyes than I, and should have more ears; but with all the information I have been able to procure, I can pronounce it a union, solid, permanent, and effectual...." He discussed the futility of what amounted to martial law in Massachusetts. "...Proceed not to such coercion, such prescriptions; cease your indiscriminate inflictions; amerce not thirty thousand; oppress not three millions, for the fault of forty or fifty individuals. Such severity of injustice must forever render incurable the wounds you have already given your colonies; you irritate them to unappeasable rancor. What though you march from town to town, and from province to province; though you should be able to secure the obedience of the country you leave behind you in your progress, to grasp the dominion of eighteen hundred miles of continent, populous in numbers possessing valor, liberty and resistance?"

Hugh's hopes rose when he heard Chatham proclaim: "The spirit which now resists your taxation in America is the same which formerly opposed loans, benevolences, and ship-money in England…and by the Bill of Rights vindicated the English Constitution; the same spirit which established the great fundamental, essential maxim of your liberties — that no subject of England shall be taxed but by his own consent."

And Chatham caused Hugh to remember the speech that Isaac Barré made in the Commons years ago in debate over the Stamp Act, a transcript of which speech Dogmael Jones had sent him. But he remembered it with regret. Chatham said, "Let this distinction remain forever ascertained: taxation is theirs, commercial regulation is ours….I recognize to the Americans their supreme unalienable right to their property, a right which they are justified in the defence of to the last extremity….When your lordships look at the papers transmitted us from America, you cannot but respect their cause, and wish to make it your own….I have read Thucydides, and have studied and admired the master-states of the world — that for solidity of reasoning, force of sagacity, and wisdom of conclusion, under such a complication of difficult circumstances, no nation or body of men can stand in preference to the General Congress at Philadelphia. I trust it is obvious to your lordships, that all attempts to impose servitude upon such men, to establish despotism over such a mighty continental nation, must be vain, must be fatal."

Chatham prudently blamed the king's ministers for the present crisis, not the king himself. After all these years, even after the Wilkes affair, the king still could do no wrong, though some men in and out of Parliament said in private that he could and had done wrong, since he had signed all the measures that were responsible for the crisis. He warned that the bad counsel he was receiving would lead to disaster. "I will not say that the King is betrayed, but I will pronounce that the kingdom is undone."

When Chatham resumed his seat, the chamber was quiet. Hugh glanced around the place — he saw his uncle, the Earl of Danvers, seated in a line of berobed figures, all of them still as death — and thought that it was a silence of petulance, not of persuasion or speechlessness.

The motion to require General Gage to withdraw his troops from

Boston was defeated in that chamber by a humiliating and telling majority.

On February 9, the Commons approved an address to the king advising him that "a state of war" existed between the mother country and the colonies. Hugh was one of a tiny minority in the House who voted against it. He accosted Edmund Burke hurrying from the House to rendezvous in Lords with his patron, Lord Rockingham. "You know, sir, that the address just endorsed by our House is an implicit recognition of American independence."

Startled, the member for Bristol glanced at Hugh, and peered at him for a long moment through the diminished light of a cloudy day. He removed his spectacles and chewed thoughtfully on the end of one ear-catch. At length, he queried, "How so, sir?"

"America is another country, another kingdom. A nation may declare war on another nation, not on its own kith and kin," Hugh answered. "May I ask how you voted?"

"Why, against it, of course."

"As did I, sir. But, we erred in that action. It occurred to me just a moment ago that we ought to have voted for it."

"Why?"

"To agree with the majority that America is another nation."

"What novel reasoning," mused Burke. Then he smiled grimly, and gestured with his spectacles as he replied, "Well, I shall endeavor at some future point to dissuade the majority of that notion. I am laboring on some corrective measures to introduce as resolutions. I hope you will vote for them. You could not err in endorsing *them*. They are the only salvation I can conceive." He nodded once, then turned and hurried off to his appointment, leaving Hugh with the sudden certainty that the member for Bristol disapproved of that notion.

On February 22 Hugh took pleasure in voting for John Wilkes's resolution to expunge from the House record of the last Parliament the resolution that he was incapable of sitting in the Commons. The House defeated the motion, but that event did not rob Hugh of the satisfaction. It was what Dogmael Jones would have done.

On the evening of March 22, Edmund Burke rose to speak for over three hours on why Lord North's colonial policies were foolhardy, how those policies violated the Constitution, and how the "spirit of American liberty," even though it might be admitted that it was at variance with the English spirit, could be accommodated with conciliation and concession.

Hugh sat listening with special attention, and midway through Burke's oratory, glanced up at the gallery to his father, and shook his head once.

In the lobby of the House, Hugh was oblivious to the jostling of him by members rushing out at the late hour for home, supper, and drink. His thoughts were abruptly broken by a jovial greeting. "Well, milord," proclaimed a boisterous voice, "I had expected you to second Mr. Burke with a speech at least half as long as his! I must say I am very disappointed that you did not. I took particular pains to remain awake throughout his elevated oratory, tempted though I was to emulate so many of my colleagues, and stretch out over some empty seats to nap! Did you not notice that as the hours went by, Mr. Burke's audience diminished by half?"

Hugh stopped to look at the speaker. He was so deep in his own thoughts that it took a moment for the face and name of the member for Canovan to register. With Sir Henoch Pannell stood Crispin Hillier, his uncle's man for Onyxcombe. Hugh blinked once, then said to Pannell, "If you were indeed awake during his oration, sir, you will recall that Mr. Burke noted that 'A great empire and little minds go ill together.' You, sir, are another little mind, and with your fellows, you have doomed the empire. Good evening." He brushed past Pannell and went outside to wait for his father outside the lobby.

Pannell sniffed once at the slight. "Well, what do you think of that?" he asked of his companion. "What airs! It is no wonder to me that his lordship does not like him!"

Hillier cocked his head with a wan smile. "You must own, sir, that you have the enervating habit of intruding on others' cogitations. I myself have complained of it often enough."

Pitt, Burke, Wilkes, and all the others who professed affection for the colonies and championed their cause, Hugh realized now, had futilely committed their allegiances between Britain and America. He could not see any of them grasping that futility. He could no longer endure witnessing that division, for it could have only one end. Because they could not reconcile the elements of that division, and because they wished to retain Crown authority over America, the logic of the events must end in a choice of force.

He recalled Burke's assertion, early in his speech, that the colonists were not only "devoted to liberty, but to liberty according to English ideas and on English principles." He did not think that was entirely true. There was a difference between the English and American ideas of liberty. He thought that the answer to the impossibility of reconciliation — indeed, the root cause of the conflict — lay in that difference. What was it?

It was futile to imagine reconciliation, he thought, because there were two radically different and clashing notions of liberty: the notion of it handed down and preserved, in some respects, in the Constitution, common law, and tradition; and that notion of it proclaimed by the colonies.

He was done here. He had nothing to say here. All these men would be deaf to his logic for liberty, as he had witnessed Burke and Chatham struggle to convey. The speeches of the colonies' advocates were inexorably bound in the logic of force. He was still deep in these thoughts when his father tapped him on the shoulder outside the lobby door to let him know that he had joined him.

They walked slowly from the Commons, through Westminster Hall, to the Palace Yard to find a hackney to take them back to Chelsea. Hugh felt a dull sadness, one rooted in a profound indifference, wishing he could care, but knowing that he could not. By the time they reached the Yard, Hugh said, "I am going home, father," he announced, "on the next available vessel."

His father said, "But, son, you have not spoken in the Commons, as you wished to."

Hugh could only reply, "No longer. There is nothing to say. Nothing I could say would make a difference. Even if I possessed the skill of Cicero, it would be useless there. They want to hold the colonies within the empire, but it cannot be done. And Mr. Burke noted himself that even should the Crown conquer America, what it would possess at the end would not be what it had fought for. It would be a ruined land — depreciated, sunk, wasted, and consumed in the contest." He paused. "His very words. You heard him. And, even with that wisdom, the House voted against his conciliation resolutions, overwhelmingly." He shrugged. "But, because the Crown will not be able to conquer America, that is more likely a description of this country, after the contest."

"Yes. That is all true," remarked Garnet Kenrick. He sighed and added with irony, "Well, I suppose you must resign the seat, and I must reelect myself to it."

This remark caused Hugh to remember Wilkes's diatribe against the corruption that had denied him his seat in the House, and Sir Henoch's smug boast at Windridge Court that he could reelect himself to his own, and Jones's disdain for the House, and his own father's sentiments. And he remembered something else his father had said, years ago: "It is a corrupt system, our Parliament, but we shall attempt to either overcome the corruption, or make it work for us...for liberty." He knew now that neither was possible. After listening to the debates these past months, and observing how insipid was the opposition, he concluded that he had nothing to say here, because whatever he could say, would have no effect. Corruption worked only for the corrupted; corruption could not sire its antipode, virtuous liberty.

He wished to return home now, where he would find it.

\*    \*    \*

Benjamin Worley at Lion Key secured passage for Hugh on the *Regulas*, a merchantman that would call on Norfolk, Virginia, before continuing on to Savannah and the West Indies with cargo. The vessel was expected to leave the Pool of London in two weeks, and its captain was confident it would reach Virginia in early May.

During his preparations for the voyage, Hugh limited his communication with Reverdy to a short letter advising her that he would seek an annulment of their marriage in a Virginia court. Effney Kenrick gently queried him, "You will not see her again, Hugh?"

"No."

She did not pursue the subject. In the midst of packing his trunk with books, prints, clothing and other items he had bought in London, it did not occur to Hugh that he had received no reply to his note. It did occur to his parents, and they asked him about it. He shrugged. "I love Britannia, but I am leaving her, as well." He would say no more about Reverdy. His parents did not raise the subject again.

The morning arrived when his family accompanied Hugh to the Pool of London and Lion Key to bid him farewell. They all silently cursed a thick, dirty fog that enveloped the Keys, thick enough that they could not see halfway across the Thames. Alice Tallmadge gave him a letter to send to her husband Roger in Boston, and Garnet Kenrick gave him a letter to deliver to John Proudlocks in Caxton, and also a bundle of invoice letters to various merchants in Virginia and Maryland to forward. "I don't expect these to be paid," said the Baron. "They are just a formality. Perhaps they will see to them after things have been settled, if they are able to."

The farewells were anxious and melancholy, for they were all certain of war, and did not know when they would unite again. "It may be years, Hugh," said the Baron.

"It may be years," Hugh agreed. Then he embraced his mother, bussed his sister Alice, and shook hands with his father and Benjamin Worley, who had accompanied them on the wharf. A crewman from the *Regulas* came then and requested Hugh to follow him. Hugh tipped his hat once again, then turned and went up the gangboard.

He stood at the shrouds, out of the crew's way, waving his hat in answer to the waves of his family on the wharf. As the *Regulas* gained the middle of the Thames, the figures on the wharf and their surroundings became blurs in the fog, and then indistinguishable from it, until all he could see was a darker band of gray beneath a lighter one.

\* \* \*

He could not know it, and would learn of it long after the event, but the day after Hugh listened to Edmund Burke plead with the Commons to see sense and adopt a policy of conciliation with the colonies, another orator, speaking to a much smaller assembly in a plain wooden church atop a hill in Richmond, Virginia, had touched on matters he had wrestled with these last several months.

"It is natural to man to indulge in the illusions of hope....Is this the part of wise men, engaged in a great and arduous struggle for liberty?....For my part, whatever anguish of spirit it may cost, I am willing to know the whole truth, to know the worst and to provide for it....

"It is in vain, sir, to extenuate the matter. Gentlemen may cry peace, peace — but there is no peace! The war is actually begun! The next gale that sweeps from the north will bring to our ears the clash of resounding arms! Our brethren are already in the field! Why stand we here idle? What is it that gentlemen wish? What would they have? Is life so dear, or peace so sweet, as to be purchased at the price of chains and slavery? Forbid it, Almighty God! I know not what course others may take; but as for me, give me liberty, or give me death!"

The speaker glanced around the crowded assembly of men, fellow burgesses all, and in a silence broken only by the patter of rain on the roof above and the rush of it outside the windows, noted the looks of transported speechlessness in the faces. Then he became aware of a murmur of men gathered outside in the rain, a murmur mixed with excitement, anger and exaltation.

Patrick Henry shut his eyes briefly and sighed with the knowledge that his work was done, and that his call to arms would be heeded. He nodded once to the assembly, and took his seat again.

# PART II

# Chapter 1: The Farewells

No one in Britain would learn of Henry's speech, a call for the formation of a militia and for taking a "posture of defense" against the Crown, for at least a generation. Hugh Kenrick would hear snatches of it almost immediately when he returned to Caxton, that Henry raised a hand holding an imaginary dagger, and at the end of his last sentence, plunged it into his heart. He would hear many things about the second Virginia Convention and the resolutions Henry introduced in it, all seconded by Richard Henry Lee. He would learn that the one hundred and twenty men who attended the seven-day convention went as elected delegates, not as burgesses, and that Queen Anne County earned the shameful distinction of not having been represented at it.

During the voyage, when it was not raining, Hugh would often pace the deck deep in thought in the stiff, bracing spring winds. The captain and crew of the *Regulas* began to refer to him as "the worrier." They knew that he was a man of importance, a Virginia bashaw, a former member of Parliament, and a man not to be toyed with or mocked to his face. They sensed that he was unhappy, perhaps even angry, and that he was not receptive to idle chatter. But Hugh was simply pondering his past and his future — his marriage, his conduct, Meum Hall, Virginia, his life. At times he wondered why no one engaged him in conversation, except, tentatively, the captain of the *Regulas*. He was not aware of the frown that seemed to be etched on his face.

He could not know that the second Massachusetts provincial congress in Cambridge, dominated by John Hancock and Joseph Warren, had in early February called for the formation of militia. Nor could he know that Lord North's conciliatory plan, endorsed by the Commons on the same day a bill was introduced for the New England Restraining Act, was ultimately adopted and sent to committee for emendation, but that the Restraining Act passed on the very day he set sail for Virginia. Two weeks later the Act's provisions, which forbade New England from trading with any nation but Britain and its colonies in the British West Indies, were broadened to include Virginia, Pennsylvania, Maryland, New Jersey, and South Carolina.

He knew only vaguely, through letters his sister Alice had read to him, that his friend Roger Tallmadge was chafing in Boston, commanding a company of soldiers and hoping that his superior, General Gage, would keep his word and allow him to return home in October. But he and Roger were both ignorant of the secret letter sent to Gage in January by Lord Dartmouth, Secretary of State for the Colonies, in which the minister chided the general for asking for 20,000 men to "conquer" Massachusetts, Connecticut, and Rhode Island, and claimed that the general's 4,000 troops were certainly equal to that task. Dartmouth opined that even should the "rude rabble" of troublemakers form the semblance of a disciplined army, a "single action" between them and His Majesty's forces ought to be a sobering experience for the "rabble," they having exhausted their resources and resolve in such an encounter.

Dartmouth stressed, however, that His Majesty agreed with his ministers that the first important act to reestablish Crown authority in New England was to arrest and imprison the "actors and abettors" of the provincial congress for treason and rebellion. The Secretary of State, like so many in the ministry, was oblivious to both the seriousness of American unrest and the scale of intercolonial organization created by those "actors and abettors," and wrote to the hapless general: "I must again repeat that any efforts of the people, unprepared to encounter with a regular force, cannot be very formidable; and though such a proceeding should be, according to your own idea of it, a signal for hostilities yet...it will surely be better that a conflict should be brought on, upon such ground, than in a riper state of rebellion."

He did not know that the rebellion had already reached that state of ripeness. "Absentee hubris!" muttered the general, who did know it.

The *Regulas* was nearly halfway across the Atlantic when Hugh Kenrick read Edmund Burke's revised *A Vindication of Natural Society*, one of the books he bought in London after his first brief meeting with the author in the Commons, but had not found time to read until now. At the end of the tract he encountered a line he thought best applied to his troubling conflicts over the last few months:

"We first throw away the tales along with the rattles of our nurses; those of the priest keep their hold a little longer; those of our governors the longest of all."

It was true, he thought: As I have grown wiser, I have disowned the rattles, the priests, the governors, and all their tales.

On the other hand, Hugh recollected, Burke's wisdom did not extend to all subjects. The member for Bristol had remarked to him over supper at Waghorn's Tavern in Westminster, in response to a dismissive comment of Hugh's that an atheist was likely more moral than any Christian sitting in the House, "Atheism must be removed root and branch. But, I am otherwise broadly tolerant."

Hugh, in turn, had replied that such tolerance was generous in the least, given that his supper companion defended an intolerant state church. For his part, he expressed an indifference to God; and more, a moral and scientific objection to the notion of an all-knowing, all-powerful deity. "It is a belief that when He completed His creation, He retired from active interference in it. That is as absurdly pointless an enterprise as my having worked to restore my plantation, then retiring in hopes it will not ever fall back into ruin."

Burke had no reply to that, except to say that he found the analogy odious and repellent to all his "articles of decency and good sense. We are not imbued with a power beyond mere reason, as He is. Further, while He is privileged to measure us, we are neither privileged nor able to measure Him."

And Hugh remembered Burke's fellow member for Bristol, Henry Cruger, saying, "Our constituency is the second largest port in this country. It is an interesting town. Perhaps your father's firm could send us some of his custom. We send serge to the colonies, and fustian, and tobacco pipes, and numerous other manufactures. Cargoes of Negroes are regularly bartered for cargoes of sugar."

No more, thought Hugh then. Even then, in the emptied chamber of the Commons, in the grand space of Westminster Hall in the evenings, in the hushed silence of the metropolis's theaters, in the quiet privacy of his room at Cricklegate, he knew that the empire was dissolved, at an end. He did not know it then, and could not know it now, but he often reiterated in his mind now what he had remarked to his father only a month ago, Lord Dartmouth's advice to General Gage in that secret letter, that force "should be repelled by force." There was no longer any question in his mind about whose sword had first been unsheathed and raised, and what was the proper response to that action. Reason was powerless against men whose actions were moved by maleficent ends.

And on April 19, neither Hugh, the captain, the crew and passengers of that vessel, a little more than halfway across the Atlantic, would hear the "shot heard 'round the world" on the Lexington Green in Massachusetts.

A week later, on another sunny day, during one of Hugh's turns on deck, the watch in the crow's nest alerted the crew to a vessel passing in the opposite direction not a mile away. The captain came up from his cabin and used his spyglass to observe the ship. Hugh happened to be standing beside him. "It's the *Friendly*, out of Liverpool," remarked the captain, handing the glass to Hugh, with whom he had a courteous relationship and whom he had had to supper on numerous occasions. "I know the master, Brian Kelly. She's heavy in the water, though. Wonder if she was able to unship her cargo."

"Where does she usually call?" asked Hugh, using the glass to study the indistinct figures moving on the other vessel's deck, some of which seemed to be women. He could not see the faces that peered back at the *Regulas*. The sun flashed on glass. He guessed the *Regulas* was being observed, as well.

"Hampton, Norfolk, and thereabouts," the captain answered. "Usually imports a hotchpotch of goods, and manages to trade them for profitable bulk for the Indies or home. Bloody nonimportation business! It's the bane of everyone's trade! Hope things have calmed down, and Mr. Kelly's carrying back lumber and lead to Liverpool. Well, I've no worry. All I need to unship in Norfolk are you passengers."

Hugh doubted that the *Friendly* was carrying exported cargo. The Continental Congress had adopted nonimportation measures effective last December, and all exports to Britain, Ireland and the West Indies were to cease in September. He thought that perhaps Mr. Kelly had been able to negotiate a barter of goods with the Scottish merchants in Norfolk. But he did not say so to the captain. Instead, he replied casually, "Oh, yes. I have noted her mentioned in our *Gazette*. She trades mostly on the James River, if I am not mistaken." He and the captain tacitly avoided discussing politics. Benjamin Worley had judiciously warned him that the man was a staunch patriot, and likewise warned the captain that his special passenger was a "patriot in the colonial sense."

One of the specks on the deck of the *Friendly* was Etáin Frake. And in Hugh's baggage in the hold was sheet music he had found in London for her, including some dances and *divertimenti* by Wolfgang Mozart, arias by the new court composer to Emperor Joseph the Second in Vienna, Italian Antonio Salieri, and some cello concerti by Luigi Boccherini that Hugh was confident Etáin could adapt for her harp.

*    *    *

In March, the *Friendly,* after making surreptitious arrangements with merchants in Norfolk for disposal of her cargo of miscellanies, sailed up the York to Yorktown, West Point, and finally Caxton, in a furtive quest to unload the balance of it in trade for anything to take back to England. The captain and master of the vessel were not successful; the county committees on the upper James River and on the York were diligent and threatened to seize the cargo for auction if any attempts were made to unship it.

The captain and master decided to take passengers back to England, for ready money only. They received more applications for berths than they had room to accommodate. Many Virginians were electing to go into self-exile, the captain and master observed. They agreed that it was not likely the *Friendly* would plough these waters again for a long time. One of the first applicants for a berth was a planter in Caxton, Jack Frake, who was sending his wife to Scotland.

Jack Frake had been adamant in his decision to send his wife away. After their initial discussion in October, Etáin ventured the proposal that she go to Philadelphia instead, or New York, or up-country to Richmond or one of the western counties. But Jack insisted that the safest place for her was with her parents in Edinburgh.

"Every one of those towns is likely to be occupied by British troops," he had countered. "Perhaps even laid waste and their inhabitants left to fend for themselves as beggars. You've read the accounts in the *Gazette*s of how much the people are suffering in Boston. Every port town between New Hampshire and Georgia could be seized by the British, and made to endure the same punishment. As for sending you up-country, the counties there would be at the mercy of Loyalist marauders and Indians. No one knows if Dunmore's peace will hold when war is declared, and there will certainly be no peace with the Loyalists." He shook his head. "No, the safest place for you is behind enemy lines."

"And what is the safest place for *you,* Jack?" she asked, the anger and concern coloring her question with uncharacteristic harshness.

Jack had merely smiled the disarming smile of certitude and finality that had always ended their infrequent arguments, and replied, "There is no safe place for me, while tyrants roam our countryside."

"No tyrants roam our countryside," Etáin protested.

"They've always roamed it, Etáin. I said as much during the late war, at Mr. Vishonn's place, when Hugh arrived here."

"At Enderly." After a long moment, she sighed. "So you did. It was how you two met."

"Where you posed your riddle to us."

That was in the fall. The winter had passed, and early spring arrived. Jack kept a close watch on the ship arrivals and departures posted in the two *Gazettes*. He remembered when entire pages of the *Gazette* and the *Courier* were filled with notices of vessels' arrivals and summaries of the goods they brought, and of their impending departures, accompanied by solicitations for passengers and cargo to take to England. These notices had dwindled to less than a column.

Then in March the *Friendly* braved a stop at Caxton. Obedience Robbins, who was in town on business, chanced to have dinner with the master, Brian Kelly, in Safford's Arms Tavern. Robbins subsequently informed Jack of Kelly's and the captain's intentions. Jack, who a week before had observed from the riverfront lawn of the great house the vessel making its way up to West Point, immediately rode into town to accost Kelly and arrange for Etáin's billet. Kelly said he would raise anchor in two days, once he had victualed his stores for the journey back to England. He would make no more stops before exiting the Capes, except to be inspected for contraband at the mouth of the York by one of His Majesty's ships.

Susannah Giddens, the housekeeper at Morland Hall, helped Etáin pack her trunks. A farewell dinner was hastily arranged for the day before her departure, and invitations sent out to John Proudlocks, Jock Fraser, and other friends in Caxton. At one point during her preparations for the journey, she called Jack into her music room. "I must leave my instruments and music behind. There is not enough time to properly fix them for the voyage."

"I knew that." Jack shook his head. "No. You are leaving them to remind me of you."

Etáin nodded. "Yes." She paused. "Be sure Mrs. Giddens dusts the room once a week. And please loosen the strings on the harp, after I've left. It may be…years before I touch them again."

After the dinner, in her music room, Etáin gave one last concert on her harp. "You all look as though you were wearing mourning blacks, but I will perform no sad songs," she said to her audience, which included all the Morland Hall house staff. "Just the songs that have brought us together, and will always bring us together."

And that afternoon she played, among other melodies, "Brian Boru's March," the tune she had dedicated to the town's defiance of the stamps nine years ago, and which she had dubbed "A Meeting at Caxton Pier." She played another melody, one she had performed at the victory celebration at Enderly the year Hugh Kenrick arrived in Caxton. She saw the questioning frowns on her listeners' faces. "It is called 'Hearts of Oak,' but now someone has called it 'The Liberty Song.' I am sorry, but while I have heard there are new words to it, I do not know them."

"We'll find them," said Jack.

Jock Fraser then asked her to play "Will Ye No' Come Back Again," the song he had bellowed out to Hugh Kenrick in Safford's Arms the day he left for England, and insisted on accompanying her. Everyone laughed but applauded his performance, for he could not sing well. John Proudlocks remarked, "If it were not for the modulating influence of the rum punch, we would have thought you were practicing a speech!"

"A speech of mine you have not yet heard, laddie!" laughed Fraser. "When you do, you'll note the difference, and beg my pardon!" And the company laughed with him.

Etáin smiled at Fraser. "I will come back, Jock, when you, and my Jack, and John there, have won us our own country." She glanced down at her gloved hands, and the strings she knew so well. Then she looked up and said, "I shall play my last number now, as a farewell to my husband."

Jack Frake frowned in wonder about what she meant.

Etáin played her transcription of "See, the conquering hero comes."

When she was finished, the room was quiet for a while. Then Jack rose, came to her, and kissed her forehead in thanks. It was only then that she let the tears that had begun to blur her vision as she played roll down her cheeks. She reached up for his neck and brought his lips down to her own. Then she whispered into his ear, "My north."

*     *     *

It was the same company that saw Etáin off on the *Friendly* the next afternoon. Her baggage had already been taken down that morning by Obedience Robbins and Mouse, the apprentice cooper and stowed, and her tiny cabin — for which Jack Frake had paid Brian Kelly extra to ensure her privacy and solitude — outfitted with the things she would need during the voyage. On the pier, she said her farewells to the Morland staff that had come down, and bussed John Proudlocks. "Take care of Jack, look after him, won't you?"

"Like a brother," Proudlocks replied. "I will write you about his doings, if he won't."

"Thank you."

"Give Hugh my regards and my regrets, when he returns," she said to Jack.

"Of course," said Jack. "When he returns, he will be surprised and disappointed that you are not here."

"I know. And you will look after him."

Jack Frake grinned. "Like a brother." Then he turned to Proudlocks. "John, I'm going aboard with her to see that her cabin is suitable. Wait for me, will you?"

Proudlocks nodded once, then reached out and took one of Etáin's hands. "*Adieu*, milady. We will work as fast as possible to see you back in your own country."

Etáin solemnly inclined her head. Then Proudlocks turned and strode back down the pier. Jack took her arm and led her up the gangboard.

Inside the cabin, he looked around and nodded approval of her billet, then took Etáin in his arms and kissed her passionately. They stood together for a long moment, clutched in each other's embraces, until the captain's steward appeared and informed them that the vessel was about to leave.

On the pier, Jack Frake watched the *Friendly* sidle out into the river. Etáin waved to him from the deck. Jack removed his hat and held it at his side. He stood like a statue and watched the vessel until it rounded a bend and was gone.

# Chapter 2: The Gunpowder

Just before dawn on April 21, Jack Frake picked up a lamp, left his library, and crossed the breezeway to Etáin's music room. He sat in her chair at the desk where she worked on her transcriptions. By sitting there, he imagined that he could hear her practicing her music. The house had been silent for nearly a month. Hearing her practice, he realized now, had been as much a part of his daily routine as paying his employees or sketching out on paper for William Hurry, his overlooker and steward, the next season's plantings in the fields beyond. She was a presence, her music a fixture. Both were gone now, and the house seemed so much emptier. He felt the quietude of loneliness.

He was anxious about how she was faring on the voyage to England. Once the *Friendly* stopped at Liverpool, she would need to find passage up the Irish Sea to Glasgow, and then take a coach across Scotland to Edinburgh on the North Sea. The captain had assured him that he would arrange the swiftest journey possible for her to Glasgow on one of the coastal vessels or packets. Months ago Etáin had written her parents about her impending arrival, asking her father, Ian McRae, to arrange with a brother-in-law and merchant partner in Glasgow to fix her transportation from the River Clyde to Edinburgh.

In turn, Etáin was aware of his anxiety. She herself was not outwardly concerned, though the voyage itself would be fraught with risks and dangers. A sudden storm on the Atlantic could swamp the *Friendly*, or even sink it, or a fog could cause it to ram a sandbar, rocks or another vessel off the coast of England. She had tried to relieve his worry by saying that she missed her parents, and was happy that she would see them again after so many years. She knew, as well as he, that it was an irrelevant assurance, but it was all she could offer him.

It struck him now that he had crossed the ocean only once in his lifetime, when Captain Ramshaw brought him here as an indentured felon on the *Sparrowhawk*. Since then he had traveled much of the seaboard, from New York to Wilmington. But he had never been tempted to recross the ocean. He had no parents to miss, and no reason to return to England. No, he thought, he might still have a parent, his mother, Huldah, who might still be alive. He remembered the last time he saw her, when he stood at the door of the cottage in Cornwall, waiting for some sign that she had not betrayed him to kidnappers who were subsequently murdered by his assumed father, Isham Leith. He remembered her and that man with indifference, as though they were strangers. It was so long ago, in another age.

His glance happened to fall on Etáin's bookshelf and the three spines of the *Encyclopædia Britannica* that her father had sent them some years ago, it having been published in Edinburgh and her father having been one of its original subscribers. The set had been intended for his library, but he had no room for the volumes. He had often come to her room to peruse it. Well, he assured himself, if that could make it safely across the ocean, Etáin could be in no danger. He smiled at his self-deception; that assurance was irrelevant, as well. He knew he would stop worrying about Etáin when he received letters from her from Liverpool, Glasgow, and Edinburgh.

He became aware of the rhythmic thumping of hooves on the ground outside, then through Etáin's window he saw a bobbing flambeau and an indistinct figure approach the porch. He rose with the lamp and strode back down the breezeway to the front door, and opened it just as John Proudlocks was dismounting. His friend came up the steps. "Jack," said the Indian, "there's been an incident in Williamsburg! Last night! Or early this morning! The Governor has stolen the colony's powder from the Powder Horn!"

The "Powder Horn" was the local nickname for the public Magazine. "Stolen it?"

"By some marines from one of the warships. At least, they were redcoats."

"But wasn't the Magazine being guarded by the Williamsburg volunteers?"

"It was, until early this morning. The whole town's riled up."

"Did you just ride from Williamsburg?"

"No. My cooper went to town yesterday to have a wagon wheel repaired, and stayed overnight at a tavern and planned to come back later today. He heard a commotion, and then someone beating a drum alert. He woke up, went out, and learned as much as I've told you. He hitched up the wagon and returned just fifteen minutes ago." Proudlocks paused. "He heard talk of storming the Palace and arresting the Governor!"

Jack stood for a moment, thinking. Rumors had reached Caxton that the Governor was plotting to seize the arms and gunpowder in the Magazine in Williamsburg to forestall any militia action against him. The contents of the Magazine were the colony's, not the Crown's or the Governor's, paid for by internal taxes. The Governor had no authority to touch them. And, Dunmore had prorogued the General Assembly several times since Hugh Kenrick had left for England, the last time as punishment for the Richmond convention, at which Patrick Henry had called for Virginians to take a posture of defense against the Crown.

The convention had subsequently adopted a number of measures, among them plans to manufacture gunpowder and establish foundries to fashion parts for muskets and other firearms. Jack Frake twisted his mouth in faint disgust. Henry's resolution, expressed in a stirring speech — ending with, "I know not what course others may take, but as for me, give me liberty, or give me death!" — had, like his Stamp Act Resolves nine years before, been coolly received by many of the delegates, and passed by a single vote.

Jack Frake presumed that Dunmore acted on instructions from London. He had received reports from his correspondents from other chapters of the Sons of Liberty that General Gage in Boston was making a concerted effort to seize and destroy colonial stores of arms and powder in Massachusetts.

He had always been certain of an inevitable clash with the Governor. He and many other Virginians had felt more amused than insulted when Dunmore announced with condescending gusto at a Capitol ball in January that his new daughter, born shortly before he returned from his campaign in the west, would be christened "Virginia," as though that gesture could somehow ameliorate the growing tension between Virginians and their royal governor and his tyrannical ambitions.

He said to Proudlocks, "I want to see how serious this is. Will you ride with me to Williamsburg?"

"Of course. I can saddle you up while you get ready and let your staff know where you're off to."

Half an hour later they were cantering over the Hove Stream Bridge to the road that led to Williamsburg.

When they arrived in mid-morning, they found the town almost as bustling as when the General Assembly and General Court were in session. On the Palace Green milled scores of people, while the town volunteer company and a militia company from James City County were drawn up on opposite sides of the Green. They rode towards the Palace gate, and saw that marine sentries had been posted and the two otherwise symbolic and decorative 6-pounder guns taken inside to the courtyard, one of them aimed at the gate, with boxes of powder and ball at the ready on either side of the wheels. They saw a few of Dunmore's fifty-seven slaves brandishing muskets, pistols and swords, weapons likely taken down from the armament that decorated the walls of the Palace foyer.

Jack Frake asked Captain Innes of the town's company of volunteers about the red-coated marines. The man answered, "They're probably from the *Fowey*, sir. She's anchored just off Porto Bello and the Governor's place there. It may be the whole company or just half of it. Their pieces are primed, for sure, and those fellows look like they're primed for a fight, too." The captain laughed. "Well, if that's how they feel, we'll give 'em one!"

Neither Governor Dunmore, nor the General Assembly, nor anyone in Virginia realized it, but by ordering the marines to expropriate the Magazine powder, the Governor had effectively abdicated his office and given Virginians the right to depose him or to petition London to have him recalled. Some now argued that, because of the nature of the Governor's action and the presence of armed militia on the Palace Green, he was all but deposed. The last time the colonials had raised their voices and weapons against their royal governor was during Nathaniel Bacon's rebellion nearly a hundred years before.

Later in the morning, Peyton Randolph, Speaker of the House, together with Robert Carter Nicholas, the Treasurer, and the mayor, John Dixon, rode in the Speaker's landau to the Palace and were admitted by the guards past the ornate gate. At noontime they reemerged and rode to the courthouse on the market square, the mayor first urging the crowd and militia to follow them to hear an announcement.

On the steps of the courthouse Randolph conveyed the Governor's explanation for the gunpowder seizure: His Excellency had heard that a slave revolt was imminent in Surry County across the James River, and naturally and dutifully had taken the precaution of removing the powder to prevent its illegal seizure. Randolph also cautioned the audience that any violent action against the Governor or the Palace would doubtless precipitate anarchy and invite certain retaliation by the Crown.

Jack Frake and John Proudlocks stood in the crowd. A man close to Jack Frake remarked, "Cow pasties! I'm from Surry, and there ain't enough slaves there to make trouble if they'd a mind to!"

Another man answered, "But there've been rumors of trouble in Surry for weeks, sir."

"Yeah?" answered the man from Surry. "And I heard tell for years angels can dance on pins, but I ain't seen that yet, neither! I'm sayin' there ain't nothing to it, and the Governor's a liar!"

"I must agree with this gentleman," said another man, a member of the town volunteers. "I believe the Governor is playing hot cockles with Mr. Randolph and all of us."

Although the crowd and militia were skeptical of the official explanation, they dispersed on Randolph's continued urging.

Jack Frake and Proudlocks decided to return to Caxton. "Nothing else will happen here, unless the Governor commits another blunder," said Jack.

Proudlocks studied the crowd and armed men drifting away from the courthouse. "Things are a musket shot shy of war," he observed. He chuckled. "I am confident that the Governor will think of another blunder to commit."

"He has a talent for it," remarked Jack. "We must see Mr. Vishonn and persuade him to call out the county militia."

"He has turned Tory," Proudlocks said. "He is afraid of his little man." As they rode past the College of William and Mary for the road back to Caxton, he asked, "What will you do if Mr. Vishonn refuses?"

Jack Frake shrugged. "Form an independent company and be at the ready."

"That may well reduce the county militia by half its numbers. Many of the men are Sons of Liberty."

"So be it."

Reece Vishonn, master of Enderly, was colonel of the Queen Anne militia, which in the past had been mustered and drilled on a bare, unused portion of Enderly about twice a year since the French and Indian War. Since last June, Vishonn had steadfastly refused to muster the militia, claiming that it would offend the Governor and even the General Assembly.

He still maintained this position. "I won't, Mr. Frake," said the planter in his library when Jack and Proudlocks called and were admitted. "And if I did, it would be to protect this county from the kind of rioters you described that laid siege to the Governor in Williamsburg."

"There was no rioting," Jack Frake corrected. "The Palace was not threatened."

"It may as well have been," sniffed Vishonn. "Dozens of armed men appear outside the Palace gates and His Excellency isn't supposed to arm his staff and borrow a few marines? What foolishness that would have been if he hadn't!" The planter looked petulant. "He has a family to protect, and his office to uphold. And I will not have this county accused of fostering the kind of hellish mischief they take for granted up north!"

Jack Frake sipped some of the cider his host had provided. "Do you remember John Connolly?"

"Vaguely," answered Vishonn. "He was some quack who was supposed to have claimed Fort Pitt and thereabouts for Virginia, but he was arrested by the government up there. I think the Governor sent him — for entirely legitimate reasons. You can't fault him for trying to resolve the Ohio Valley question."

Jack Frake nodded. "Yesterday I received information from my correspondents in Pennsylvania that Mr. Connolly is free again and will negotiate the final terms of the treaty the Governor arranged with the Shawnees last winter. The suspicion is that by those terms he is to enlist the Shawnees and other tribes on the Crown's side to invade Virginia if there is war. Now, if there is any truth to that, and any about a slave rebellion in the works, Virginia would go up in flames, from the Tidewater to the mountains." He paused. "You may not want to frighten the Governor, sir, but he would not scruple to frighten you and all Virginians into submission." He added, as the planter stared at him furiously, "I cannot imagine any act of betrayal that the Governor would hesitate to take if it would keep him in office and Virginia isolated from her sister colonies."

A measureless moment passed, and then the older man's face reddened in anger. At first his callers could not determine if it was because he was offended by the implication that he could be frightened, or was alarmed by the information. He rose abruptly and pointed to his library door. "Damn your correspondents and your suspicions and your Sons of Liberty! I know what you're conspiring, Mr. Frake! You have spent your welcome here, sir! I will not tolerate my character or the Governor's being so brazenly...slandered! Good day to you!"

Jack Frake put down his glass of cider, nodded to Proudlocks, and together they turned and left the room. As they rode out of the courtyard, Proudlocks shook his head. "He was offended by your suggestion that he would submit to fear."

"I expected he would be, but it had to be said," Jack Frake replied. "Well, we must have a meeting of the Sons of Liberty." They rode to Safford's Arms Tavern, and spoke with the proprietor.

*　　*　　*

That night, again under cover of darkness, Governor Dunmore sent his wife and seven children to the *Fowey,* ostensibly for their protection, but actually because he did not know what to expect next. He himself returned to the Palace.

Over the course of a week, word had spread of the incident at the Magazine, north, south, and west. In Fredericksburg, some six hundred volunteer militiamen assembled for a proposed march on the Capitol, and its captain sent a messenger to Williamsburg to obtain a first-hand account of the affair. In Hanover County, Patrick Henry was elected colonel of another force, which began to march immediately for the purpose of meeting or preventing an invasion. Henry and his men had by this time learned of the fights at Lexington and Concord, and to their minds, the war had begun. He and his volunteers stopped at an ordinary not half a day's march from the Capitol.

Henry did not yet know it, but Dunmore had since informed the mayor of Williamsburg that if harm came to him, his family, or any British officer, he would free the colony's slaves and let them destroy the town. He also informed Thomas Nelson, member of the Governor's Council, that Yorktown would be bombarded by the naval vessels on the York if the Palace or his person were attacked.

During the march from Hanover, the lawyer in Henry caught up with the colonel in him, and stayed the patriot's hand. Henry sent a courier to the Governor at the Palace with a receipt for payment for the stolen gunpowder. The Governor signed it in exchange for a warrant for £330, countersigned by the Treasurer, Robert Carter Nicholas. Henry, who had postponed his journey to Philadelphia to attend the second Continental Congress, scheduled to convene in early May, pledged to give the warrant to his delegation for presentation to the Congress or to the next Virginia convention. He led his force back to Hanover, and he returned home to prepare for the journey to Philadelphia.

The gunpowder remained on the warship *Magdalen* at Burwell's Landing on the James River.

Lord Dunmore subsequently decreed that, henceforth, no one in Virginia was to aid or ally himself with Patrick Henry. This action was another blunder, for the decree simply publicized Dunmore's animus for a man most Virginians revered. His Council, reduced by death and desertion from twelve to seven, also condemned Henry, expressing its "detestation and abhorrence for that licentious and ungovernable spirit that has gone forth and misled that once happy people of this country." The statement only earned the public's contempt for the Council. On May 12, the Governor sent for Lady Charlotte and his family to return to the Palace.

In the meantime, Jack Frake had met with the Sons of Liberty at Safford's Arms, and was the next day unanimously elected captain of a new independent company, and Jock Fraser his first lieutenant. Reece Vishonn, colonel of the county militia, saw his command reduced to a platoon. Most of the men in the new company took with them the arms, powder, ball, knives, bayonets, and other military accoutrements allotted to them by the county. On paper, Vishonn was colonel of a militia of one hundred men. Only a handful chose to remain loyal to the colonel.

And one day, in mid-May, Jack Frake read in a *Virginia Gazette* the details of the battles of Lexington and Concord. At the end of one account of the actions, the editor commented, "The sword is now drawn, and God knows when it will be sheathed."

His staff observed him pacing on the porch of the great house, his hands clasped behind his back, clutching the *Gazette*. He was pondering whether to ask his men to march to Massachusetts to join in the fighting that was sure to occur there, or to stay here, where fighting was certain to happen, as well. He had converted an unused portion of his fields into a mustering camp for the volunteers.

That very afternoon, Hugh Kenrick arrived in Caxton on a merchant sloop from Norfolk. While he waited for his baggage to be unloaded at the pier, he paid an idle boy to go to Meum Hall and tell someone there to send down a cart down for his things. Then he walked up to Safford's Arms for a lunch.

When he entered, he found the place dense with smoke and packed with citizens and armed men. It was the busiest and noisiest he had ever seen the place. He was instantly recognized and greeted by cheers and the news that he had been reelected burgess for the county, together with Edgar Cullis. The Governor the day before had issued a call for a General Assembly to meet in Williamsburg on the first of June to consider the terms of conciliation sent to the colonies by Lord North.

Hugh could hardly keep up with the news everyone seemed to be shouting at him. Steven Safford pressed a *Gazette* in his hands and pointed to the accounts of Lexington and Concord, and also to letters in the newspaper about the Magazine incident. "The Governor no longer governs," said the proprietor. "He will make war on us."

Hugh sat down at a table and read the accounts and the letters, forgetting a tankard of ale and the plate of coldcuts the man had put at his elbow.

No one in Virginia would know it for weeks, but the war had begun auspiciously that very day, with the bloodless capture of British Fort Ticonderoga on Lake Champlain by Ethan Allen, Benedict Arnold, and a small force of eighty-three men, netting the revolutionary forces artillery and great quantities of military stores. And in Philadelphia, the second Continental Congress had convened.

# Chapter 3: The Warnings

"There is no occasion for jubilation."

This warning was the opening of Hugh Kenrick's remarks to a meeting of the Sons of Liberty a few days later in the Olympus Room of Safford's Tavern. The Sons' membership included most of the rank and file of the Queen Anne County Volunteer Company, a militia that numbered about fifty men.

Hugh stood at the round table where in the past so many meetings had been convened, in between Jack Frake and Jock Fraser. Propped up on a staff in a corner behind them was the multi-striped banner altered East India Company Jack that once served as a tablecloth for the Sons, and which was carried to the Caxton pier years ago when the town foiled an attempt to smuggle stamps into the colony. Furled around its staff, it was now the Company's ensign, to be carried into action as a rallying point, as the position of the commanding officer, and as an expression of pride and identity. Sewn in black on one white stripe beneath the cobalt canton by Lydia Heathcoate, the town seamstress, were the words, *Queen Anne Independent Company, Virginia*. On another white stripe were the words, *Sons of Liberty*. And in the canton were the words, *Live Free, or Die*.

"No, sirs, there is no cause for celebration, now that the first salvos have been exchanged between troops and colonists. Difficult, spirit-wrenching times lay ahead of us. Parliament is determined to retain the colonies, by force if necessary, abetted by our alleged protector, the king. General Gage's ten regiments in Boston will be joined, possibly by summer's end, by many more. A great fleet has been assembled in Boston Harbor, and many more warships lurk off American shores, aside from the usual ones that filch our pockets and purses by means of the codified laws of tyranny. What the Crown intends for Massachusetts, it must intend for all the colonies. It is only a matter of time before armies and fleets intrude on Virginia with the same purpose: our subjugation.

"While in London, I came by information that His Majesty devoted some considerable time to the lists of regiments that may be sent here or kept in Ireland, if needed, as well as a list of generals who might be ordered to direct a campaign here. And when I last sat in the Commons, that body had approved an address to the king that the colonies were in a 'state of rebellion.' Doubtless, by now it and the king have agreed that a state of *war* now exists between us and Britain."

He paused to study the attentive faces crowded into the Olympus Room. "I must stress that we are not the rebels in this circumstance, but rather Parliament, the king, and the whole apparatus of the empire. They rebel against everything Britain once boasted of: her host of liberties, her Constitution, her reputation as the refuge for exiles from tyranny. On reflection, one could argue that it has fallen to us to resolve many of the issues of the Civil War of the last century. We are able to resolve them, for we have an advantage over the liberty-minded men of that distant age. We have the wisdom of Mr. John Locke and of his many thoughtful successors in that realm of inquiry." He paused again. "So, when perhaps you are called a 'rebel,' pray, do not accept that appellation. Regard it as an insult. You are each of you a revolutionary, unlike any in the past."

After a long silence, during which the audience absorbed the gravity of Hugh's words, one man asked, "Is there any hope of reconciliation, Mr. Kenrick?"

Hugh shook his head. "Scant hope, sir. Allow me to illustrate my pessimism. While I was in London, Lord Mansfield of the King's Bench last December found a governor-general of Bengal, Mr. Harry Verelst, guilty of gross abuses against a group of Armenian merchants who traded with the East India Company, under whose auspices he governed. It was charged that he imprisoned them for half a year in Bengal, took their property, and subsequently denied them the liberty to trade in those parts. These merchants sued him in a British court. Lord Mansfield found him guilty of 'oppression, false imprisonment, and singular depredations' and Mr. Verelst was ordered to pay the Armenians some £9,000 in damages, in addition to the costs borne by the Armenians to lodge the suit."

"That was a just finding," said John Proudlocks.

Hugh chuckled. "It was, sir. But, would that Lord Mansfield had been so fair ten years ago, when he was asked by Mr. Grenville about the justice of a stamp tax on Americans. Would that he had been so fair to us when he found in Mr. Somerset's favor fewer years ago." He shrugged. "We, of course, cannot sue the Company for gross abuses of our liberty by way of its tea. Nor can we confidently sue for our liberty, as Mr. Somerset did, by merely setting foot on English soil. Nor can we sue the Crown for the greater false imprisonment it intends for us — indeed, has imposed on us for nigh a generation — for taking our property, and for the many singular depredations that are sure to come."

One man asked, "Is it true that the Governor wanted the Shawnees to defeat General Lewis and the militia at Point Pleasant and his men last fall? Some here are saying the Governor wanted to make sure no one could fight him if he gave Virginians cause to. General Lewis and his men were the ones to do it, if it came to that."

"I have heard that rumor. If such connivance of the Governor's is true, it damns him."

"He is damned even if it is not true," said Jack Frake.

"He is behaving like the Emperor Nero," said Proudlocks.

Jock Fraser said, "We'll know for sure when that Connolly fellow sends the treaty down to the General Assembly."

"Beware of skullduggery," said Hugh. "It is alive in the Palace. Even in the House."

Nearly everyone in the room understood who was the object of Hugh's last remark: Edgar Cullis, whose treachery had nearly scuttled passage of the Stamp Act Resolves in the House ten years ago, and who was suspected of having informed Lieutenant-Governor Fauquier of Wendel Barret's role in broadcasting the Resolves to the other colonies. Fauquier closed the Caxton *Courier* and suspended Barret's printing license. The editor and printer shortly thereafter died of a stroke.

"We've a drummer and a fifer for the company now," said Jock Fraser. "Do you remember Travis Barret?"

"Mr. Barret's apprentice printer," said Hugh with a smile, knowing what prompted Fraser to raise the subject.

"He ran away from his aunt's family to join our company," said Fraser, "and brought his black friend Cletus with him. Mr. Jude Kenny there taught him the fife, and Will Kenny over there taught Cletus the drum," he added, pointing to the brothers in the room. "They're staying at my place. I've put them to work, since I need a few extra hands in the fields and the cooperage."

"Can they bear arms?"

"Of course," laughed Fraser. "When they aren't tootin' and tappin', they'll be shootin'!"

The men all laughed.

Another man said, "We've been debating whether or not we should march north to Massachusetts to help lay siege to Boston, Mr. Kenrick. But

Mr. Frake here — I mean, *Captain* Frake — says he expects there'll be enough business here to keep us busy, the Governor is sure to get himself evicted from Williamsburg, the way he keeps combing the cat the wrong way. What do you think, sir?"

"I agree with Mr. Frake. It is only a matter of time before volleys are invited here, as well. There will be another convention held here in Virginia, and I am sure that by that time, it will become our *de facto* government. So many other colonies have already established civil authorities apart from the legislatures. These new authorities have jurisdiction over armed forces, as well as civil law. I expect that the convention will conclude that Virginia must have her own army, and not merely a militia."

                              *       *       *

He had been given a warm welcome home by his staff at Meum Hall, and by Jack Frake, John Proudlocks, Jock Fraser and others who knew him well. At Morland, Jack Frake had arranged for a special supper to mark Hugh's return. Proudlocks was the first guest to arrive. He asked, "Did you speak in Parliament? You wrote us that your father had chosen you to replace him."

"No, I did not speak. I realized that there was nothing to say to that body." He grinned in self-effacement at Jack. "Of course, *you* knew that already."

Jack merely answered with a grin of his own, then said, "You might have plenty to say to the House when it sits in June. Half the membership hails from the Piedmont and outlying counties now. The Tidewater is in the minority for the first time, if the election returns in the *Gazette* are to be credited." Then he asked, "Did you see Reverdy?"

"Yes," answered Hugh. "Often. However, she will not be returning." He spoke frankly and without hesitation, with no sign of emotion, as though he were commenting on the weather. Jack Frake sensed that this was not a subject to be pursued. But he and John Proudlocks especially had noted a new element in the mien of their friend, one that had colored his words and actions since his return: a somber, fastidious melancholy. Proudlocks was puzzled by it, but Jack Frake thought he knew its cause.

He and Proudlocks discreetly observed this dour youth who had somehow, in the time between Reverdy's departure and his own return, lost his youth. They both sensed that Hugh Kenrick had for the last half-year endured a crisis of soul, of mind. They had concluded, by their own inferences, that he planned to divorce his wife. But only Jack Frake was certain that Hugh was also divorcing his country: Britain. He could not help but recall Hugh's exuberant assertions of years ago, when the master of Meum Hall had happily and confidently proclaimed an empire of reason, a Pax Britannica stretching from Margate to the Mississippi and beyond. That empire was now unraveling and flying apart. He wondered how a man could carry the burden of such an error without it draining him of the wish to live.

And Jack Frake also wondered if he himself was a reproach to his friend, for he had always been certain of the empire's inevitable and violent demise, and had said so to Hugh many times over the years. At times, he caught Hugh staring at him with a curious look of reluctant envy, curious because it seemed to be an unconscious envy.

When the remaining guests arrived, the talk centered on political and local matters.

Hugh asked, "What is Reverend Acland up to? And Mr. Cullis?"

"Mr. Acland has gone quite mad," said Jock Fraser. "To hear him preach, the world is coming to an end, and the York will turn into a river of flame and our fields will be watered by brimstone."

"Mr. Cullis is keeping his own counsel. He hasn't said much about anything all the while."

"I must call on him before the General Assembly," said Hugh, "to see what he has to say."

While at Morland, Hugh gave Jack all the sheet music he had bought in London for Etáin. "I think you were wise to send her away," he said to Jack Frake. "However, I shall miss her and her music."

Jack Frake smiled and took the leather portfolio of sheet music. "If we are fortunate, we shall both miss her for only a short while. She will play for us again…when this is over."

"I must write her a letter, charging her with causing us both misery," said Hugh in affectionate jest.

Proudlocks had written Hugh when he was in London about the mysterious "Mr. Hunt." Hugh asked about him now. "Have you seen him since then?"

"No," answered Proudlocks. "But I did inform Mr. Hurry and Mr. Beecroft to be alert to such a man loitering around Meum Hall. He has not been seen in these parts since then."

                              *     *     *

At that moment in Hampton, Jared Turley, known to his Customs colleagues in Hampton as Jared Hunt, paced up and down the deck of the sloop-of-war *Basilisk*, proud as a captain. Formerly a privately owned merchant vessel that ran contraband, and named the *Nassau*, it had been converted into a warship by shipbuilders at Annapolis contracted by the Customs Service. It had been seized by the navy, and its owner, a notorious smuggler with "patriotic" sympathies, was charged with gross violations of the Navigation and other Acts by the Admiralty Court.

Hunt had chosen the new name for the vessel, a mythological serpent that could kill with its breath and glance. Hunt took the liberty of writing Governor Dunmore about the quality of the acquisition, boasting that it could probably better police the rivers of the Roads than any naval vessels or Customs cutters currently on duty in the Bay. "She is as slick as a trout in the water, sir, and I believe she has a glorious career ahead of her in service to the Crown. She will be managed by a loyal captain from the Eastern Shore, and he has assembled for the *Basilisk* an eager and hearty crew. He has also employed a Negro pilot who claims to know every rock, eddy, and sandbar in the Bay and in the rivers. She sports eight guns deck-side, in addition to a swivel. She is not impressive to look at when seen alongside a man-of-war, but she could level Norfolk or any town in this region just as thoroughly as one of His Majesty's best ships."

                              *     *     *

The next morning Hugh rode to Cullis Hall to see Edgar Cullis. Hetty Cullis, Edgar's mother, answered his knock. He half expected her to inform him that her son and her husband Ralph had left for the Piedmont on a hunting trip. It had happened so often in the past. And he was almost surprised when the woman invited him in and showed him to her husband's library. "Mr. Cullis, my husband, is in Norfolk on business," she said. "Edgar is preparing himself for the next Assembly. May I serve you something?"

"No, thank you, Mrs. Cullis. My stay will be brief."

"I understand that you have just returned from England, Mr. Kenrick," said the woman. "You must tell me something of your stay there! How is Mrs. Kenrick?"

Hugh chatted with the woman for a few moments without revealing anything personal or important. He thought that his icy cordiality moved Mrs. Cullis to relent and lead him to the back of the great house.

Edgar Cullis rose from his father's desk when his mother showed Hugh in. Mrs. Cullis turned and left the room. "I saw you coming up the coach path," said the other burgess. "Have you come to berate me again? And, by the way, welcome home."

Hugh removed his hat. "Thank you. No, I have not come to berate you. I am here simply to tell you what I plan to do in the Assembly, and perhaps what I will say about Lord North's 'Olive Branch' proposals. I hope you will reciprocate."

Cullis nodded and waved Hugh to a chair in front of the desk. Out of courtesy, Hugh obliged. Cullis remained standing. "Have you seen this?" He took a sheet of paper from a pile of documents and handed it over to Hugh. "Mr. Corbin was kind enough to send me a copy."

Hugh read it. It was the Governor's Council statement condemning Patrick Henry's actions over the gunpowder incident. Hugh made a scoffing sound. "It is the Governor's actions that are detestable, abhorrent, and licentious," commented Hugh, "moved by an ungovernable spirit of tyranny." He handed the sheet back over the desk.

Cullis cocked his head. "I had expected to hear such a sentiment from you."

Hugh shrugged. "The Council has rendered itself redundant, and it little matters what it has to say about anything." Then he frowned. "Why are *you* so privileged as to be sent a transcript from the Council's journal?"

Cullis grinned. "Because there are vacancies on the Council now...and my name has been mentioned to fill one of them."

Hugh screwed up his face in amazement. "The Board of Trade and Privy Council must approve of such an appointment, and then secure His Majesty's signature. Have you any influence or friends in London?"

It was Cullis's turn to shrug. "Enough there, and enough here, sir. Mr. Corbin, Reverend Camm, and Mr. Wormley have all promised to write letters of recommendation, should my name be settled on." The three men were on the Council.

Hugh laughed. "Mr. Cullis, you may as well hope for a cardinal's hat! In a year's time, perhaps less, when those bodies bother to consider your candidacy, and whether or not they endorse it, I venture to say there will be no royal government here, no Governor's Council, and no Governor!"

"Then I shall be found on the side that will fight to reestablish those authorities!" replied Cullis with defiance.

"And I shall be found on the side that will aim to tether those authorities, or to abolish them if they will not submit to a harness." Hugh paused. "Mr. Cullis, have you no notion of the gravity of events? My God, the war has already begun! Some eighty soldiers died on the retreat to Boston last month, and nearly a hundred Massachusetts men! Both sides have drawn blood from each other, and there will be no reconciliation or thought of peace. That is but the beginning. Do you seriously think the ministry in London is going to devote any time to considering names for appointments to a colonial council, when its aim is to abolish all the charters here?" He paused again. "And here is what I will say in the House about Lord North's proposals: that they are a subterfuge worthy of Jonathan Wild!"

Cullis bridled at this outburst. His whole body stiffened, and he looked over Hugh's head to reply, "And I shall argue that Lord North's proposals comprise a hand extended in friendship and charity. I shall argue that their rejection would amount to criminal ingratitude."

Hugh rose. "You may argue that, sir," he said as he put on his hat, "but you will persuade only fools and dishonest men."

After a sharp glance at his visitor, Cullis turned his head away to stare out a window. "You may leave now, Mr. Kenrick. And I would thank you not to call on this house again."

"You may rely on me to honor that request. Good day to you."

Hugh Kenrick rode back to Meum Hall.

*     *     *

Two days later, on Sunday, at Stepney Parish Church, Reverend Albert Acland read from Samuel in the Old Testament. "...And the Philistines had captured the Ark of God, they brought it from Ebenezer to Ashdod, and there they carried it into the temple of Dagon and set it beside Dagon himself. When the people of Ashdod rose next morning, there was Dagon fallen face downwards before the Ark of the Lord; so they took him and put him back in his place. Next morning when they rose, Dagon had fallen again face downwards before the Ark of the Lord, with his head and his two hands lying broken off beside his platform....Then the Lord laid a heavy hand upon the people of Ashdod; he threw them into distress and plagued them with tumors, and their territory swarmed with rats....There was death and destruction all through the city...."

He snapped the Bible shut and glared at his congregation. "Need I elaborate on the parallels in our own Ashdod, my good people? We will not be spared the Lord's heavy hand! We are already plagued with the tumors of dissension and flagrant disobedience and the pestilence of lawlessness, and our once happy land now swarms with rats — who are called *patriots*! And the time is not far off when we also shall see tears, and hear the wailing and weeping and gnashing of teeth, which now distract the mothers and daughters in Massachusetts in lament for the husbands and brothers who dared visit violence on His Majesty's servants, and met death themselves! And that will be the Lord's justice and retribution, as well, and this punishment shall be passed on from generation to generation...!"

\*     \*     \*

In Mecklenburg, North Carolina, the provincial congress on May 31 adopted resolves that suspended the power of all royal authority in North Carolina, and sent them to its delegates at the Continental Congress in Philadelphia. The colony thus earned the distinction of being the first to declare its independence from Britain, more than a year before the United Colonies — or, as Patrick Henry preferred to refer to them, "The United States" — declared their independence.

Early in the morning of June 1, there disappeared from in front of Sheriff Cabal Tippet's house on the bluff overlooking Caxton's riverfront, the old cannon from two wars ago. Sheriff Tippet that day made some formal inquiries about the theft, but did not investigate the matter with much energy. He suspected who was responsible. He secretly approved of the theft, and wondered why it had not occurred sooner.

# Chapter 4: The Soldiers

Two evenings later, Jack Frake rode to Meum Hall. He found Hugh sitting on the south porch with a tankard of cider, looking out over his fields. Another chair stood on the other side of a small table, which held a pitcher and some books. Hugh waved a welcome to him.

Jack Frake nodded, dismounted, tied his mount to a hitching post, and joined his friend, taking the vacant chair. Hugh offered him a draught from the tankard. Jack Frake shook his head once, then rose and paced once before saying, "We are going to Boston."

Hugh could not hide the surprise in his question. "When?"

"Tomorrow morning."

"How?"

Jack Frake smiled. "On the *Sparrowhawk*. At first light."

"She's here?"

"At Yorktown." Jack Frake paused. "She sailed from Plymouth before news of any of the recent troubles reached England. She has some cargo not covered by the non-importation resolutions. We'll march down before dawn, board her, and stow ourselves below decks out of sight." He paused to take out a seegar and light it with a match. "Geary's already been cleared by the Customs cutters and the navy, chiefly because he also carried military stores from Plymouth to Hampton, so it's doubtful he will be stopped again. He'll take her straight up the Bay to Baltimore. There we'll disembark and march north. Jock Fraser has the route all mapped out. We will provision ourselves as we go along. We should reach the town by the middle of June."

Hugh studied his friend for a moment. "I thought you were opposed to going to Boston."

Jack Frake drew on his seegar. "I still am. But the men want to pitch in, and voted on it yesterday. They've made some good arguments. If the army up there can be holed up in Boston or defeated there, there's a good chance that the British will give up the effort after one encounter, after their noses have been bloodied, whether or not they have reinforcements. The more men and guns they see opposing them in the field, perhaps the less likely they will seek a military resolution, and resume their cajoling and procrastinating. I can't disagree with that reasoning. But I'm not entirely convinced by it, either."

"Nor am I," Hugh said. "Britain has had her nose bloodied in battle more than once, but has always recouped her losses and ultimately won. You know that better than I. You were with Braddock twenty years ago."

"Yes. But another thing that must occur to them is that, this time, many of the Americans they will be facing are veterans of the last war, as officers and in the ranks. It is not a mob of Londoners they'll be riding down over cobblestone streets with drawn swords, but men who can give as good as they get. That was proven at Lexington and Concord." Jack Frake sighed, and added doubtfully, "All that may give them pause for thought."

Hugh nodded in doubt, as well. "How were you able to arrange transport on the *Sparrowhawk*? She was due to arrive this month, I know, but is Captain Geary behind this?"

"Ramshaw arranged it. He wrote me some months ago. He saw which way Parliament was going, and made a gift of powder through his connections in Norfolk, England. Geary is sympathetic. His only son was pressed into the navy there some years ago, and died at sea. He's also been arbitrarily fined by the Revenue for various niggling infractions. Geary was planning to settle in Boston to begin his own trade in a few years." Jack Frake grinned tentatively. "There's even half a chance he'll offer the *Sparrowhawk* to the Congress as the foundation of a navy, or apply for a letter of marque to sail as a privateer to raid British shipping. We've discussed it. He has Ramshaw's blessing. Ramshaw still owns a quarter interest in the *Sparrowhawk*. But Geary hasn't decided yet on either course."

After a moment, Hugh said, "I almost envy you, Jack. I am feeling neglected."

"Don't envy me. You will be here at the General Assembly, opposing the Governor."

"Don't envy me *that*," said Hugh with a short laugh. "It may be that he is a more formidable foe than General Gage." He paused. "May I accompany you to Yorktown to see you and the men off?"

"Of course."

"Have you enough munitions?"

Jack Frake nodded. "We are taking paper for cartridges, and mouldings to fashion ball. We will add to our pouches some of His Majesty's powder, as well, courtesy of Geary and Ramshaw. Geary showed the Customsmen and the navy altered cockets. Ramshaw taught him all his old smuggling tricks. So, we'll be busy making munitions as we sail up the Bay." After another moment, he added, "Every man in the company has been given a few balls from Barret's Volley."

Hugh understood. The "Volley" was a mound of musket balls cast from Wendel Barret's *Courier* printing type, which was seized by Lieutenant-Governor Fauquier as punishment for having broadcast the Stamp Act Resolves. Jack Frake secretly purchased the type after the Lieutenant-Governor returned it after Barret's death years ago. "Are you taking Mr. Tippet's cannon, or the swivel?"

"No. They would only slow us down. I am supposing that if the Massachusetts men are besieging Boston, there will be guns enough."

They sat for a moment in silence. Then Hugh asked, "What will happen to Morland...if anything happens to you, Jack? I mean, if there is more fighting up north?"

Jack Frake shrugged his shoulders once. "Etáin will inherit it. I've discussed it with Mr. Proudlocks. He'll see to it."

"Is he going with you?"

"Yes. He commands a platoon. Nominally, he is a sergeant."

"Do the men mind?"

"Not that I've noticed. Not that he's noticed. The men respect him. He can cite laws and statutes most of them have never heard of. Many of them wish to hire him as their lawyer. But, he is not certain when and if he will be able to follow in Mr. Reisdale's footsteps, and open his own practice."

Hugh chuckled. "The sergeant-at-war is a sergeant-at-law, as well. The legal profession is redeeming itself, Jack."

\*   \*   \*

In the darkness early the next morning, Hugh rode with Jack Frake and the Queen Anne Volunteer Company to Yorktown, the company marching behind with Jock Fraser in the lead. William Hurry, Jack Frake's steward and business manager now, accompanied them to return to Morland with his employer's mount.

The men of the company wore a mongrel collection of fringed hunting shirts, frock coats, leggings, and a variety of headgear ranging from tricorns to round-brims to flat brims with one side pinned to the crown with a cockade. As befitted musicians, Travis Barret and Cletus wore red coats, which someone had found for them, although the coats were too big for them. Jock Fraser was dandily dressed as though for a ball at the Capitol, and carried the ensign. All the men were armed with muskets, and hanging from them on shoulder belts were powder horns, sheathed knives, pouches with ball and extra powder, canteens, and bayonets. All wore packs, to which were strapped sleeping rolls.

Jack Frake was similarly armed and attired. But fixed to his belt also was a sword in its scabbard. It was the first time Hugh had ever seen him wear such a weapon. He said so. Jack Frake replied, "It was John Massie's. I brought it up from the cellar and spent an hour last night removing the rust from the blade and the guard." John Massie was the planter who bought Jack Frake's indenture decades ago, and was the former owner of Morland Hall.

Hugh looked grim. "Well, we should both hope that the enemy never gets near enough to you that you would need to employ it."

"My hope, as well," agreed Jack Frake.

Hugh smiled, and said, "Then you need something to complement your rank as an officer." Under the light of flambeaux at the bottom of the gangboard to the *Sparrowhawk*, and as the men of the Company filed singly from the pier up the gangboard to the vessel, he reached into his frock coat and presented Jack Frake with a steel gorget on a hemp cord. As his friend held the object and studied it with pleased astonishment — the gorget was in the standard crescent shape — Hugh added, "I had planned to give it to you some time later, when I saw the Company on parade or at drill. Mr. Zouch fashioned it from the plates and the damaged lock on a broken musket I found in one of my cellars." Zouch was Meum Hall's brickmaster.

Jack grinned when he held the gorget closer under one of the flambeaux to read the engraved inscription, which was in Latin: *Sapere aude.* "My Latin is very poor," he said.

"Have the courage to use your own reason," said Hugh. "It is the watchword of our age."

"It has always been my own," replied Jack Frake. "Thank you." He then lifted the symbol of command and fitted it around his neck. "There. Now I am a true officer."

Hugh reached over and adjusted the gorget over his friend's shirt, and needlessly pulled one of the coat lapels straight.

Jock Fraser, curious about the exchange between the men, came over and, when he saw the gorget, stopped and saluted Jack Frake. He ran a finger over the gorget, then said, "Steel? Well, if nothing else, sir, at least it might stop a ball or two."

John Proudlocks came down the gangboard and approached them. He noticed the gorget, and paused to salute his commander. "Captain Geary sends his compliments, Jack, and says he is ready to cast off. He wants to round Mobjack Bay by mid-morning."

"All right, John." Jack Frake extended his hand to Hugh.

Hugh shook it firmly, then shook hands with Jock Fraser and Proudlocks as Jack Frake spoke a last time with William Hurry. Hugh took a step back to watch them ascend the gangboard. The rest of the Company had already gone below deck. Jack Frake, Fraser and Proudlocks stood at the rail.

Hugh could not decide if they were looking at him or at Yorktown on the bluff behind him, perhaps for the last time. No, banish that somber thought! he told himself. Jock Fraser, in a final gesture of farewell, unfurled the ensign and waved it at Hugh. Hugh raised his right hand to the tip of his tricorn in a vague salute. "When you take on the Governor," shouted Fraser down to him, "be sure to leave a bit of him for us to chew on!"

As dawn began to give the shapes on the riverbank the substance of buildings, sand, and water, the *Sparrowhawk* raised anchor and drifted out from the pier. Then crewmen in the masts dropped sail and the vessel began its trip back down the York.

Hugh watched it diminish until, in the rising sun, the *Sparrowhawk* was a mere speck of white sail on a false horizon of blue-gray water. All he could hear now were waves lapping on the beach.

Then a voice queried, "Well, Mr. Kenrick, shall we return to Caxton?"

He turned to William Hurry. "Yes," he answered. "Let us depart before anyone here wonders about our presence."

As they turned to their mounts, neither of them noticed a lone rider on the bluff above them. This figure turned and galloped off in the direction of the Swan Tavern in Yorktown.

When the rider returned to his accommodation at the tavern, he quickly penned a note. "Mr. Jack Frake, master of Morland Hall, has boarded the *Sparrowhawk* with his vigilance gang for a destination one can only presume is Boston to join the rebels there. It is likely the vessel will take them up the Bay to Baltimore. I cannot imagine a more expeditious route. The captain of the *Sparrowhawk* has obviously conspired with Mr. Frake in the commission of treason, or at least of sedition, for your correspondent observed no sign of commandeering or forced possession of the vessel by Mr. Frake...."

When he was finished, he folded and sealed the letter with wax, and addressed the top fold to "Mr. Jared Hunt, of the Revenue office, in Hampton." He did not sign it, except as "A Loyal Patriot." He had brought with him on a separate mount a slave servant from his father's household staff to act as valet. He instructed this man to ride to Hampton with the note, and gave him money for expenses. "There is a crown in it for you if you deliver this by tomorrow morning," he said to the man. "Do not return here. Come to Williamsburg, to my cousin's house. I will be there preparing for the next session."

It was Edgar Cullis.

*    *    *

Hugh returned to Meum Hall to finish reading correspondence that had collected while he was in England, a chore he wanted to complete before leaving for the General Assembly in Williamsburg. More letters had arrived on the very vessel that brought him to the York River and Caxton. There were several from Roger Tallmadge in Boston, whose plight he had become familiar with while in London. The top letter seemed to be the most recent missive. He opened it. It was dated April 21.

"Dear Hugh:

"It is with some reluctance that I pen this letter, but hope it finds you in good health and imbued with some charity for the revelations I describe here. As you know, I have been detained here in Boston by General Gage for my actions at Morland Hall, and also because Governor Dunmore, Lieutenant Manners and that functionary of the Revenue all wrote unflattering reports of my conduct there and elsewhere, which the General could not but help give some credit, though he is keen enough a judge of character to suspect that personal rancor moved the authors of those reports and colored the thrust of their charges. Else why has he been lenient and allowed me to act as a detached serving officer here, instead of recommending my discharge or a court-martial? He has promised to allow me to return home in October, for he places great importance on the report I handed him upon my arrival here, and cannot think me the caitiff that my informants, in their cat's-cradle of insinuations, would have anyone believe I am.

"Still, I now imagine that the penalty could not be harsher, for I took part in the retreat from Lexington and Concord Bridge, at least in the last phase of the encounter. I had not seen such fighting in Europe, when tens of thousands were engaged in the regular style of warfare, but the fewer numbers in this instance do not render the consequences less terrible.

"I do not know precisely how it began — the stories from officers and ranks wildly contradict each other about what happened on Lexington Green. I was not present there, but either some militiamen fired first on Colonel Smith's expedition, which was enroute to destroy some martial stores, or his men fired first. I am sure your newspaper there in Virginia has reported the blaming details of the event on the Green that sparked the tragedy, perhaps fairly, perhaps not. Colonel Smith accomplished his task, but his command suffered a great penalty.

"My company was ordered to escort Earl Hugh Percy's two guns in the relief foray on the road along which the colonel's troops were retreating from Lexington. But, about seven miles from Charlestown, and seeing our grenadiers and light infantry being assaulted from both sides, I instinctively saw a means to relieve their agonizing gauntlet, and prevent a rout (which it very nearly became), at least on one side of that road, and offered to lead my company of regimental orphans, whom I had drilled mercilessly during months of idleness, in a defensive flanking of our troops, to drive the militiamen from the woods and hedgerows and fences from which they fired at Colonel Smith's men.

"I myself carried a musket, but was so distracted by the tactic that, even though it was primed, I neglected to use it. I advanced the company through fields and over the undulating terrain in good order, having the men in platoons advance several paces to fire, and each platoon then overtaken by the next, so that they fired in turns. We advanced rapidly this way in the opposite direction of the retreat on the road below, and killed or wounded numerous militiamen who would otherwise have pursued our men to inflict more casualties. Appreciating the success of this maneuver, my men were hot for it, and many of them were eager to use the bayonet on wounded militiamen brought down by our fire or from the road, but I forbade it.

"I do believe that many of our troops were spared death or injury from the action because of my company's valor, and also that of flanking parties sent by the grenadiers and regulars. When we saw the last of our troops on the road retreating, I retired the company in good, unhurried order as well, retracing our steps, and the militiamen kept their distance for respect for our fire. Two of our company perished, and several were injured but were helped back by their fellows. This action reduced my company from thirty-one to twenty-two effectives.

"I have been commended by Lord Percy for my diligence, bravery and initiative, and he has sent his remarks up to General Gage. I am of two minds of this development, for it may mean that the General will see my true loyalties and allow me to depart for home and Alice; or he may conclude that I am too valuable an officer to let go. In any event, my company is grateful for my leadership, for they have proven their mettle when other officers disparaged their soldiering. From my own purse, I bought them all extra pints of spirits, and ordered extra rations of victuals for them from the commissary soon after we were ferried back to Boston from Charlestown.

"I come now to my main point. One incident during my company's advance will haunt me all my days, I believe, and I have not related this to anyone else but Alice, whom I wrote yesterday. When we had fired our ninth or tenth volley, the platoons advanced again about twenty paces, loading their pieces as they walked, as I had trained them in Boston. The militiamen we had last fired on had fled their cover of trees and boulders in a thin wood.

"We came upon one of their number, leaning against a tree. There was a gash in his chest, and his coat and shirt were red with blood. One arm, his left, hung inert from his shoulder, though no blood issued from the hole in his coat there. His rifle — not a musket, but one of those hated rifles — had apparently been struck by ball, as well, for the stock had been smashed and severed from the lock. You know the fearsome accuracy of these Pennsylvania rifles, and so very likely that weapon had brought down a dozen of our men on the road. I am not certain if our volley struck him in turn, or one answering from the road. He saw us advance, and I had never seen such a look of defiance in a man's face, except perhaps on your own, my friend. He sat there, still holding his useless firelock at the ready, as though he would use it.

"My sergeant cursed and raised his musket and made to run the fellow through with his bayonet. 'You devil's spawn! You cowardly villain! I'll teach you to fight proper!' he growled with a hatred I had not before heard in him. But I restrained him from this pointless action before he could take many steps. And, instead of expressing thanks, the wounded fellow shouted — and it must have cost him strength — 'You damned bloody-backs! Leave our country!'

"I confess I was startled by his words, but instead of resenting them, I felt some strange pride and respect for the fellow. I ordered my sergeant to advance the men by platoon again, then took my canteen and bent to offer this Yankee some water. But he made no answering gesture, and at that moment, even though he still stared defiantly at me, I knew he had died. With his last breath, he had fired words at us! How can one pity such a man? Pity is such a cheap, cowardly recompense for bravery!

"As I reached to close his eyes, I felt my own well up with tears. Please credit me with this. I have been in battle, as you know, and seen so many more men die horribly, even needlessly, through incompetence or cowardice, but this was the first time I could not contain my emotion. For a moment, I was oblivious to the roar of Lord Percy's guns and the musket fire between Smith's men and the militiamen. Then I rose and wiped my eyes with my sleeve, and followed my company through the woods, and caught up with them.

"The incident will haunt me, my friend, because this defiant Yankee resembled you in his features and demeanor, so much so that he could have passed for your older brother. No! Let me be frank! In that moment, I imagined I was looking at you! It cannot be said that I am a devout man, but I have prayed to Almighty God that this coincidence is not a portent! A war has begun here, one Lord North cannot forestall, he can no longer act as a broker for peace between the colonies and the mother country, but I most earnestly hope that it is not a war between us."

Hugh sighed and put the letter down on his desk. Oh, Roger, he thought: I wish I had a God to pray to for the same purpose. That is the extent of prayer I am capable of.

# Chapter 5: The House

Hugh read the rest of his friend's letter, only half focused on its contents, which were estimates of British casualties — one hundred and fifty, with seventy-three dead, and more than twenty missing or captured — and speculation on how long the British army would be arrested in Boston, not daring another attack against the Massachusetts militia until reinforcements arrived, which Roger did not expect to see until the next year.

He also confided in his letter that Lord Barrington, the Secretary-at-War, had received and read his report on colonial military strengths, and wrote him a letter of thanks and appreciation. Roger related that the Secretary was of the opinion, based on his report and other intelligence, that an army campaign would be too costly, perhaps even futile, and that the best way to subdue the colonies was with a sea war and a naval blockade of all the port towns. The Secretary also wrote that the Adjunct-General, Edward Harvey, the king's aide-de-camp, had privately dismissed the land war favored by the king and Lord North "as wild an idea as ever controverted common sense."

"My friend," continued Roger, "this is the bleakest spring I have ever known. The troops here, where before they were indifferent to their posting, are now bent on revenge for the Lexington affair. But there are only about four thousand able troops now, and the provincial congress here has approved an army of some thirteen thousand, and appointed a politician and farmer, Artemas Ward, its commander. It has sent appeals to other colonies for volunteers for this army. Our patrols have returned with news that the colonials are truly answering the appeal; bands of armed men have been seen heading from many directions for Cambridge, Ward's headquarters. Bleak also, is Lord Barrington's news that the ministry is entertaining the employment of German troops to supplement our own, and, should that expedient be barred, it is even contemplating approaching Empress Catherine of Russia for the loan of her troops....The talk among officers here is that the ministry is sending some generals to relieve or assist General Gage....Bells are to be heard ringing in the towns, and today it is not even Sunday...."

Hugh put the letter aside, then rose and left his study. Under the blue, late May sky, he took a tour on foot of the fields, where his tenants were busy with the spring plantings of corn, tobacco, and horse oats. On a few acres he was experimenting with English red wheat, to see if it would come up so early in the year, and stopped long enough to inspect the shoots that were pushing up through the soil. He paused at the special shed constructed to house the disassembled conduit, which was being repaired and readied for the summer by his tenants. As he walked, he nodded in answering greeting to the men and women in the fields, and went on, hands clasped behind his back, deep in thought.

One thought kept returning to him: Roger, you are dangerous. Or is it our circumstance that is perilous? Will I ever see you again? *Can* we ever see each other again? And he thought of Reverdy, and the gulf that separated them. Somehow, he thought, the two conflicts were connected. Their commonality eluded him.

He stopped when he tripped slightly on an object. He looked up to see that he had made a complete circuit of the fields, and was standing before the great house. His only thought now was that in two days, he would be absent from it again, attending the next session of the General Assembly.

\*     \*     \*

The General Assembly that met in Williamsburg on June 1 was a contentious, almost surly gathering of men who, in past times, placed paramount value on decorum and civility. It sat now at the beck and call of a man whom most of its members had come to despise, or at least not trust. It sat because Governor Dunmore wished it to peruse the terms of Lord North's "Olive Branch" proposals, and then approve of them in the name of loyalty, good will, and peace, so that he could send a report to General Gage, to the Board of Trade, and to the Privy Council as proof of his good governance — and also as a means to reinstate his teetering authority and prestige on more stable grounds.

The majority of burgesses, however, were in no mood to curry the Governor's favor by doing his bidding, even though, as a body, they expressed courteous concern for the safety of the Governor and his family, regretting that they had sought refuge on the *Fowey*. A few of the burgesses wore hunting shirts, and sported tomahawks tucked into their belts. The House no longer sat in awe of his rank, power, and place. It mechanically observed all the formalities and rules of the House, and did not worry whether or not the Palace or the Council would approve or veto any of its business. A handful of the burgesses were certain this was the last time this particular Governor would call for a General Assembly.

And a few were certain that this would be the last General Assembly to sit under the aegis of the Crown. Hugh Kenrick was one of those few.

Thomas Jefferson, burgess for Albemarle, preparing to journey to Philadelphia to complete Virginia's delegation at the Congress, was not. He still held out for "the blessings of liberty and prosperity and the most permanent harmony with Great Britain," despite the fact that he had been recently informed by Peyton Randolph that, as a consequence of his controversial pamphlet, *A Summary View of the Rights of British America*, he had been named in a bill of attainder passed by Parliament, together with Randolph, John Adams, Samuel Adams, and John Hancock, among others.

During a recess on the second day of the Assembly, Hugh found a few private moments with him over dinner in the Blue Bell Tavern. At one point in their conversation, Hugh remarked, "In fact, Lord Dunmore is deposed. Or, rather, he abdicated his office when he sent his family to the *Fowey* and barricaded himself in the Palace."

"You would be hard put to convince *him* of that, Mr. Kenrick. And many of our colleagues in the House labor under the delusion that His Excellency is merely misbehaving. The act of contrition present in his address to us on the first day here was meant to convey that impression. Well, my friend," sighed Jefferson, "no more concerts in the Palace! Not because I don't think His Excellency has a musical ear — I doubt he has — but because I think I would refuse the chance to play for his patronizing delectation."

Hugh smiled. "Could you stay long enough to hear them discussed in the House, would you refuse Lord North's proposals, as well?"

"I will postpone my journey to Philadelphia long enough to speak and vote on the matter," answered Jefferson. "My cousin the Speaker advises me that Mr. Nicholas and Mr. Wormley may concoct a move for approval. As I have grasped their meaning, yes, I would advocate their rejection. Yet, I still hold out hope for a mutually amicable reconciliation. Otherwise," mused the tall redhead, his expression darkening, "we are docketed for terrible times...and we are at a disadvantage in all respects."

"This is true," agreed Hugh. "But, live free, or die."

"A succinct and worthy sentiment," Jefferson said after some thought.

"Did you compose it?"

"No. It was composed by outlaws in England. It is the motto of my county's volunteer company."

"By English outlaws, you say?" Jefferson chuckled. "How appropriate! Would that it had been adopted as a standard toast, over 'Long live the king'!" He frowned sternly. "His Majesty is a traitor, a willing partner to Parliament's depredations, and not worthy of any well-wishing."

Hugh smiled again. "That is not the sentiment I read in your *Summary View*, sir. You had a more generous notion of him in it. You appealed to his reason."

Jefferson shook his head. "My premise that if His Majesty has any reason to address, it is whittled down with each passing day. I can no longer rest sole blame on his counselors and ministers."

Hugh studied the pensive, freckled face across the table from him for a moment. "Sir, I make this prediction: As Mr. Henry has been called by some the 'trumpet' of our cause, some day you shall be called its 'pen.'"

Jefferson shook his head again. "You bequeath me too much honor, sir."

"No, I do not. That abundance of honor will become evident when you accept that there can be no reconciliation. Then you will find words grander than those in your *Summary View*."

Jefferson did not contest the proposition; nor did he deny its possibility. He took a sip of his ale, then asked, "Do you remember the first time we met and talked, outside the Palace, during one of Mr. Fauquier's concerts? It seems so long ago, in another age! We have both matured, in some respects, but are still as young. I cannot account for the phenomenon, but we are imbued with some constancy. Perhaps it is an ambition to remain unaffected by men and events, to preserve the blameless youth of our souls." And they talked for a while about matters other than politics.

Peyton Randolph had recently returned from Philadelphia to serve as Speaker. He had been elected president of the Congress in Philadelphia, but resigned that position upon receiving word of the new General Assembly. John Hancock was elected to succeed him. Randolph was not present at the Congress when, on May 29, it voted to send addresses to the inhabitants of Canada, the Floridas, and the British West Indies, asking them to join in the resistance. He would probably have frowned on such an action. He had hastened back to Williamsburg to ensure that Virginia did nothing rash to incur further Crown displeasure. And, he had the contradictory task of ensuring that Virginia did nothing that would put it at odds with the Congress. At the insistence of some burgesses and Council members, he agreed to put Lord North's Olive Branch proposals on the agenda for debate at the House's leisure.

The House worked steadily on desultory matters carried over from the last session, when, in the early hours of June 5, an incident occurred that obviated for a few days concerns for mundane legislative business. Fearing that the Governor would expropriate the arms in the Magazine, as well, several young local men broke into the building, and were greeted by musket fire. The place had been booby-trapped with trip wires leading to spring-guns. Residents awakened by the noise rushed to the Magazine to find the young men injured. It was immediately assumed that the Governor was behind the scheme.

The incident commanded the attention of the House when it convened later that morning. As the members voted to create a committee to investigate the crime, townsmen raided the Magazine and made off with the remaining gunpowder and hundreds of weapons, ostensively to better arm the militia.

After acrimonious exchanges of blame between the House and Dunmore over responsibility for the booby-trap, it was determined that the marines who took the powder in April had rigged the devices. If true, no one doubted on whose order the marines had acted. But officials and the keeper of the Magazine had entered the structure before June 5, and neither encountered nor observed spring-guns. Nor did this observation exonerate the Governor from his suspected responsibility.

On the following Wednesday, after paying Peyton Randolph an evening social call, Governor Dunmore, again resorting to the cloak of darkness while the town was asleep, loaded his family onto carriages, and rode to Yorktown to move in with them aboard the *Fowey* anchored there. The burgesses did not learn of this stealthy action until well into the morning. As the House prepared to send another delegation to the Palace, a messenger appeared with a letter from the Governor advising it that he and his family had removed to the warship out of concern for "the blind and unmeasurable fury" of his subjects. If the House had any business for him, he could be found on the *Fowey*.

Hugh Kenrick merely shrugged at the news, and remarked to another burgess, "It is a singularly appropriate venue for him."

The Governor's Palace was, for all practical purposes, now abandoned.

Many of its indentured servants fled through the Palace Park in the rear to Porto Bello, Dunmore's lodge on the York. Most of his one hundred and fifty slaves vanished. Townsmen thronged to the unguarded Palace and entered it, most for the first time. They were quite astonished with how lavishly their former Governor lived, and with the enormity of his wealth. They also noted that at every door was a stand of muskets, primed and ready to fire — on them, in the event they tried to storm the place. Most of the visitors realized that these preparations were a measure of the Governor's hostile and condescending regard of them.

Hugh Kenrick joined a group of burgesses who took time out from the House to walk through the Palace. He had many fond memories of the place, and some sour, such as coming here years ago to plead with Lieutenant-Governor Fauquier for Wendel Barret's printing license.

"Look at all our taxes!" exclaimed one of the burgesses, who had never been invited to the Palace. They were standing in the foyer, looking into the generously stocked pantry. The burgess was pointing to a pile of fine tableware. "Why, that punchbowl, and that tea service there! Why, the price one could fetch for either one could probably keep me, my staff and my servants in stomach and style for a year, at least!"

Hugh smiled in agreement, then said, not managing to suppress the bitter anger in his words, "Do you not all concede that it seems pointless to wait on the Governor on a warship, sirs?" He paused to gesture at the foyer. "Is this not evidence that he has abdicated, and is no longer our Governor? A deposed one, if you will allow it? Is not empty, habitual formality governing the substance and direction of our situation? Why do we continue to pamper him by maintaining the charade?"

Some burgesses grunted noncommittal affirmation to his questions. Others glanced at him sharply with resentment, as though he had scolded them for an oversight they did not care to acknowledge. One burgess braved a petulant reply, "Because he still possesses the Seal of Virginia, sir, and that makes him governor still and it commands our respect and fealty."

Hugh turned on this man and wagged a finger at him. "That Seal is now an empty symbol, sir! And how do we know that His Excellency has not emulated James the Second, who tossed the Great Seal into the Thames upon his flight from London? How do we know that His Excellency has not tossed our Seal into the York, in a similar demonstration of spite and malice?"

The other burgess had nothing to say in reply.

Four days after Dunmore moved his office and quarters to the *Fowey*,
the House resolved itself into a Committee of the Whole and took up the
matter of Lord North's Olive Branch proposals. Edgar Cullis kept his
promise, and argued that Lord North's proposals were a gesture of friendship, affection, and charity, and that their rejection would amount to criminal ingratitude. "It is hoped," he concluded, "that this House will reciprocate him in these very sentiments in conformity to its noble purpose."

By chance, Cullis had taken a seat next to Hugh. Hugh turned to him
and remarked, "A fine speech, sir, one worthy of the ear of the Commons."

Cullis's face reddened, but he managed to reply, "I shall treat that as a
compliment, sir."

Jefferson rose to speak, and in a cool, dismissive manner said the proposals merely changed the mode of taxation and ignored the burdensome
Acts, and should not be taken seriously. And after other burgesses had
spoken for or against the proposals, Hugh rose and was warily recognized
by Peyton Randolph.

Hugh nodded his thanks to the Speaker. "In the last war," he began,
"our enemies were the French and Indians, and the lands beyond the
mountains were their itinerate domain where we ventured at our own
peril. Our claims to property there were therefore unenforceable and moot.
We have returned to that circumstance, only now our enemy is Britain, and
the lands beyond the transmontane are Catholic French and Indian again,
where we would venture at our own peril! And, to add salt to that wound
inflicted by new British acts, our claims are not only unenforceable, but
illegal, as well! Not even the most duplicitous Roman tyrant could have
authored such an insidious, malicious irony!"

Some of the older burgesses grumbled audibly in protest at this last
remark, but Hugh did not deign to acknowledge them. He continued, "This
'Olive Branch' is but a jester's scepter, all frills and bright ribbons and noisy
bells. No man worthy of the name would accept it as a gift of friendship.
Do not forget that, in olden times, the court jester alone could mock a sovereign with impunity. Are we kings who would tolerate such mockery, or
men? This proposal that we bleed ourselves at Parliament's behest mocks
our intelligence and seeks to suborn our quest for liberty! It seeks to bribe
any colony by abolishing taxes on some imported goods of the Crown's
choice into that amenable colony, in exchange for taxing itself for the
'common defense.' May I ask: Defense, against whom? And if the revenue
derived by such self-impoverishment is also intended to support each colo-

nial government, may I then ask: *Whose* government? One elected by the people, or a supine one slyly arranged to the Crown's satisfaction?"

After a pause to catch his breath, he went on. "But, there is a more wicked motive behind this 'Olive Branch,' and that is to breach the unity that now exists in all the colonies, by luring each one away in such an arrangement. This is a common practice among ministers and parties in Parliament — I witnessed it with my own eyes, when I sat briefly in the Commons — and that practice is now proposed here! In sum, Lord North's proposals are contemptible and too transparent in their design to be devious! There is nothing to debate concerning them. I will state this moment, that I will not vote for approval."

One burgess across the floor rose and asked, "When you refer to election of a government by the *people*, sir, are you proposing *democracy*? It seems that anyone half familiar with the histories of Rome and Greece would apprehend the dangers of that species of polity."

"I advocate no such thing, sir," replied Hugh, "and I thank you for not slandering my character by imputing that I do. What we should aspire to, sir, is a republic in which our liberties are untouchable by government. We shall need to be explicit in that matter, in future, so that we leave judges and politicians no room for thoughtless or insouciant interpretation. A *democracy*, you say? Sir, in a democracy, policy trumps every principle but one, every time."

"Which principle?" asked the burgess who queried Hugh.

"The public good, sir. The histories you cite prove that it is a whore that will sell itself to the greatest majority for the highest price."

The burgesses gasped in shock at the introduction of that indiscreet term. Hugh sat down. He had nothing more to say on the subject.

Later in the day, the House voted to reject the Olive Branch propositions as an intrusion on colonial financial self-governance, as a willful neglect to repeal the disputed Acts, and as a neglect to promise free trade with the world, freed from the prison of the Navigation Acts. And it was not lost on most of the burgesses, either, that while the Crown wished the colonies to provide for the "mutual defense" by self-taxation, it was assembling an armada and army to make war on those very colonies. Hugh voted for rejection, Cullis against it.

Some days later, as a sop to Governor Dunmore, the Assembly approved of a measure to pay the invoices of the Governor's war in the west last fall and winter, reasoning that his actions were nominally legitimate, because the territories and lands arbitrarily annexed to Canada were Virginia's. These bills included the pay of General Lewis's militia, some of whom were now guarding the Palace to prevent looting. It also ratified the treaty with the Indians arranged by the Governor's crony, John Connolly. To meet those obligations, the Assembly subsequently approved a measure to impose a special tax on newly imported slaves.

To Hugh, these measures confessed a reluctance to admit that Crown authority was at an end. He abstained from voting on them. He sat patiently on the bench, at times alone, as the days rolled by, and watched the tiresome and predictable charade. Often he did not hear what business was being conducted, for his sight was fixed on a point over the Speaker's chair, and he was lost in a reverie of that chamber's glorious moments, moments in which he had played a part.

One afternoon, during a brief recess, and after the legislation had been submitted to a committee to prepare for presentation to the Governor, Hugh stopped in the breezeway outside that connected the House with the General Court and Council chambers. Other members had come out to smoke and talk. Hugh looked up at the white marble statue of Baron de Botetourt that stood in the middle of the breezeway, and debated with himself whether or not to bother returning to the chamber. He remembered voting against the resolution to honor the late governor with the statue.

A voice behind him said, "Yes, the riddle is solved. It has claws and teeth."

Hugh turned to face Thomas Jefferson, and instantly recalled the exchange they had had over a year ago in this same spot. He smiled in acknowledgement. "Yes, it is a lion in ill-conceived disguise." He nodded to the statue. "Look at it, Mr. Jefferson. See the rich robes, and the regal deportment, and the benign visage. That is the stance of tyranny. It is a gorgeous, seductive conception, is it not? Little wonder that so many men become enamored of it. That is what must happen first, for tyranny to last any length of time. The tyrant must conquer their minds, but the minds must first be willing *subjects*."

Jefferson cocked his head in appreciation of the idea. "And, if they are not willing?" he asked.

"Then, if they still be men, there will be a war," answered Hugh.

"This has been proven true, has it not?" said Jefferson. After a moment, he tucked his leather portfolio beneath an arm and clasped one of Hugh's hands in both of his and shook it. "Mr. Kenrick, I must depart immediately for the Congress, and cannot dally here. Perhaps you would come to Philadelphia, and we could continue this discussion?"

Hugh said, "Perhaps I might. I have so little company left here."

Jefferson released Hugh's hand, and touched his hat. "I most earnestly hope you will. Well, goodbye, sir."

Hugh touched his hat in answer. "Godspeed, Mr. Jefferson."

Hugh turned his back on the statue of Botetourt to watch the Virginian rush through the piazza, turn a corner, and disappear. Then a clerk came out to ring a hand bell, signaling the end of the recess. Hugh turned and followed the other burgesses back inside. He was determined to see this session through to the end.

The legislation was taken by a delegation of the House to Yorktown and Governor Dunmore. The burgesses were told by his secretary, Captain Foy, who had also moved onboard the *Fowey* with his wife, not to wait; His Excellency must be given time to read the particulars and give it some thought. The chastened delegation journeyed back to Williamsburg.

Another day passed, and another messenger arrived with a note from the Governor. In the note he announced his veto of the legislation, claiming that only Parliament had the authority to create an import tax, and that the General Assembly had overreached its authority. He also withheld consent from the treaty ratification, claiming that action was an executive power, not a legislative one.

No one thought to ask whether or not His Excellency had sought the advice of his Council; for all practical purposes, the Council had been dissolved. And no one was surprised by the veto.

On June 24, Peyton Randolph ordered the clerk of the House to gavel the end of the session, and the burgesses filed out of the chamber into a hot, humid afternoon. Hugh Kenrick returned to his room at the Raleigh Tavern, and prepared to ride back to Caxton and Meum Hall.

*   *   *

On June 29, John Murray, Earl of Dunmore, royal governor presumptive of Virginia, oversaw the transfer of Lady Charlotte and their seven children, together with servants and other minor officials, from the *Fowey* to the naval schooner *Magdalen*. He was sending his family home to England. In the back of his mind was the intention to send for it again, once he had regained the Palace and the authority and power it represented. At the moment, he was not quite sure how he could accomplish that. But his family was a distraction and a burden, preventing him from thinking clearly about his next steps. So, it had to go.

Among those who climbed the gangboard of the *Magdalen* with Lady Charlotte was her new confidant and chaplain, Reverend Thomas Gwatkin, the former principal of the grammar school at the College of William and Mary. He had declined to deliver a sermon at Bruton Church in observance of the day of fasting and prayer the previous June, an event approved by the burgesses in support of the town of Boston over the port's closing, and for which the Governor had dissolved the Assembly.

When all was ready, both warships set sail and proceeded down the York River. The *Magdalen* was bound for New York, where Lady Charlotte and her company would take another vessel to England. The *Fowey* accompanied the schooner as far as the Capes, then turned its bowsprit and jibs in the direction of Norfolk, a friendlier town than was Williamsburg.

# Chapter 6: The Virginians

General Thomas Gage, Governor of Massachusetts, after the Boston Tea Party in 1773 opined in a report to George the Third that the colonists "will be lions while we are lambs, but if we take the resolute part, they will undoubtedly prove very meek." This was merely tactful assurance to his sovereign, whom he knew would not wish to hear otherwise; it was not good form to abuse the royal mind with sour news. Privately, the commander-in-chief of His Majesty's forces in North America doubted that those forces, directed by him or by any other general, could contain the Americans were they to rise up enmasse against the Crown. Gage's lukewarm resolve on that point in his official reports, however, merely encouraged the king and the ministry to chastise the colonies and bring them back into the empire's fold.

On June 12, he imposed martial law on Massachusetts, proclaimed as rebels and traitors anyone aiding Americans arming against Crown authority, and offered pardons to all who swore allegiance to the Crown, all but Samuel Adams and John Hancock, the new president of the Continental Congress.

At Bunker Hill, on June 17, 1775, Gage was to be proven right in his estimate of colonial character and the scale of colonial opposition to submitting to complete imperial domination. The British lion was to be badly mauled by the colonial panther.

The Queen Anne Volunteer Company arrived in Cambridge late afternoon on June 15, tired and ragged from its grueling two-week march up through Maryland, Pennsylvania, New York and Connecticut, but ready to fight. Captain Jack Frake sought out a commander-in-chief of the American forces they encountered. He was directed by a local militia captain to report to General Artemas Ward's headquarters, a farmhouse surrounded by the camps of Massachusetts militiamen. He marched the Company the short distance to that house, then told it to rest easy while he reported its presence and inquired about an assignment.

As Massachusetts, Connecticut and New Hampshire militiamen gathered around the Virginians in curiosity, Jack went inside the house. Here he found several "Yankee" commanding officers, including Ward, of Massachusetts and nominal commander of the gathering colonial army; Brigadier Israel Putnam of Connecticut; Colonel William Prescott of a wealthy Massachusetts merchant family; and Colonel John Stark, of New Hampshire.

Dr. Joseph Warren of the provincial congress sat in a corner, puffing on a pipe. It was he who two months before had sent Paul Revere and other riders to alert the country west of Cambridge of the British expedition to seize and destroy colonial military stores in Concord. He was awaiting appointment as major general and a command from Ward.

Jack Frake introduced himself, and the other men reciprocated.

"Any battle experience, Captain?" asked Ward, who sat at a table made of rough planks resting on wooden horses. The table was smothered with papers, two lanterns, and tankards of ale. Ward noted the faint scar to the side of the Virginian's forehead, and did not think it the result of a mishap with a plough or cooperage tool. Like Putnam and Stark, he was a veteran of the French and Indian War, and had seen that kind of healed wound before.

"I was with General Braddock at Monongahela, sir. In the thick of it. So, I believe, was General Gage. And Colonel Washington."

"Gage, too? I didn't know that," said Ward. "Well, he's been recalled, apparently. Lexington and Concord were his Monongahela. Three generals have come to replace him. They came on the *Cerberus* late last month with reinforcements. William Howe, John Burgoyne, and Henry Clinton, major generals all. Howe's in command here now. We expect that Clinton and Burgoyne will have their own commands. Then we have Admiral Graves with his warships down there, ready as vultures, with over a hundred guns. We have only six."

"We don't know for sure that Gage has been recalled," ventured Putnam. "He is still governor and he could be planning the mischief they're up to. He outranks the other three, anyway."

Ward shrugged. "What about your men?" he asked Jack Frake. "How many in your company?"

"Fifty, sir. Half of them saw action in the last war, as well."

"Good. Then they won't bolt when the British jump on them?"

"I don't think they will, sir."

"Why not, sir? It's not French or Indians they'll be asked to fire upon, but their own kith and kin. Their countrymen."

Jack Frake frowned. "They don't think they are, sir. Not any more."

Ward smiled, pleased with the answer. Then his brow furled, and he asked with undisguised suspicion, "How did you know to come up here, Captain Frake?"

"Newspaper accounts of the action on the Concord road, sir. And, some of my men and I are Sons of Liberty. We received information from correspondents. If anything precipitous was going to happen, it would happen here." He paused. "It was our Sons of Liberty who prevented the stamps from being introduced into Virginia, together with the citizens of our county."

"*Precipitous?*" scoffed Stark. "What a vocabulary! You must be book-learned!"

Prescott asked, "Have you brought your own powder and lead, Captain? We are a bit short of them. And of entrenching tools, too."

"Yes, sir. About fifty rounds per man. But we brought no tools."

Stark, glancing through a window at the new militia waiting outside the house, stared disapprovingly at the ensign that rippled in the warm wind. He narrowed his eyes, though, to read the motto in the canton, "Live Free, or Die." He pronounced the words once, then addressed the stranger. "Ghastly colors you carry, sir, but the motto is interesting. What inspired it?" Ward, Putnam, Warren all rose and went to the door, which they opened to see the newcomers themselves and the odd ensign.

"Friends of mine who died by the Crown's hand many years ago," answered Jack Frake.

"Soldiers?" asked Dr. Warren.

"Smugglers, sir. In Cornwall. They were hanged. I was transported."

"So! You're a damned criminal!" accused Stark.

"Aren't we all now, gentlemen?" replied Jack Frake, although it was not a question.

The American officers all laughed at this remark, because it was true.

Stark's compressed lips bent in a reluctant smile. "You Virginians have an answer for everything! You must be a damned lawyer!"

"No, sir. A planter. I own a thousand acres on the York River."

Stark grunted once and regarded the stranger with new interest. Then he pointed out the window to the ensign now resting over Jock Fraser's shoulder. "You added some stripes to that thing, sir. I guess they represent the colonies, but I count thirteen. Do you include Quebec?"

"No, sir. Georgia." Jack Frake added, "We know that is an East India jack. It was found in Louisbourg in a French billet, in the war before last."

He saw the puzzled looks on the officers' faces. "The tea flag, sir," he said.

"The *tea* flag?" asked Warren.

"It was East India tea that you fellows tossed into the harbor here, was it not?" asked Jack Frake.

"So it was," remarked Putnam. "Never saw the likes of your ensign in any port here. Well, it is as gaudy as the Union Jack. It might be adapted somehow. The British have their crosses, and we'll have our stripes. Then we'll know who's who when it comes to blows."

"Georgia!" scoffed Stark. "Those people down there are too slow to see the times. Must be the heat softening their noodles. They haven't sent anyone to a Congress yet. Quebec is more likely to join us. And if they don't, well...they might be persuaded to."

Ward glanced at Stark and shook his head once. Jack Frake, observing the silent communication, could only sense its significance, and remained ignorant of tentative plans to invade Canada and remove the northern threat to the colonies, should they pursue a course of independence.

Jack Frake said, "Georgia might join the Congress, in time."

Stark said with disgust, "Well, they'd better make up their damned minds!"

Ward sat down again and volunteered, "They just might, and soon. The other day I received a letter from a committee man in North Carolina, in your parts, Captain Frake. It seems that a convention in Mecklenburg there has already declared that colony's independence. How stands Virginia?"

"Governor Dunmore's likely actions will provoke the same public declaration there, as well."

"Likely actions?"

"He is a Stuart and a lord, sir, and determined to rule. We are quite tired of him, and he of us."

Ward studied Jack Frake for a moment, then asked him, "Why do you want to be *here*, Captain Frake? I'd have thought you would want to stay in Virginia to give Dunmore the same business we plan to give General Gage." He chuckled. "It isn't as though there won't be plenty of fighting to go around, once it begins here. There will be that up and down the seaboard."

Jack Frake paused before he answered. Then he smiled. "We Virginians began the business with the Stamp Act Resolves, sir. That was an enfilade of paper. It would only be justice if we contributed an enfilade of lead, as well, since the Crown's policies and intentions were proof against the paper." He smiled again. "It is a matter of finishing what we started. That is why we are here."

Stark shook his head and bellowed, "The hubris of you Virginians! You even rule the damned Congress! There's that Randolph fellow, and Henry, and Washington. And that Jefferson puppy with his scrivenings. Talkers and lawyers and scriveners! You all sound alike!"

Jack Frake was unsure of the intent of Stark's protestations. He answered lightly, "Well, Colonel Stark, if you don't take caution, the capital of these united colonies might someday be found in Williamsburg, with Mr. John Adams or Mr. Hancock as president."

Stark merely barked with incredulity while the other officers laughed.

Jack Frake added the remark, addressing the company, "Sirs, revolutions are not merely a matter of armies and muskets and flouting authority. Lasting revolutions are a matter of minds and ideas. It has always been my premise that this is the kind of revolution we have been making for ten years."

To this, neither Stark nor any of the other men had an answer. That was true, as well.

Ward said, "Well, Captain Frake, why don't you find your men somewhere to encamp and rest up? And please join me at supper tonight, and bring your second in command. We might have work for you on the peninsula overlooking Boston. You see, we plan to lay a stronger siege to it. Gage knows this, and will try to stop us. He plans to occupy Dorchester Heights that overlooks the harbor, and we hope to beat him to it, as well. Today, tomorrow, next week, we'll see. I'll show you the maps at supper." He rose and extended his hand over the table. He grinned. "Massachusetts welcomes you, Captain."

Jack Frake stepped forward and shook it. "Thank you, sir."

Prescott said, "We will be digging entrenchments and building a redoubt somewhere on the Charlestown peninsula, Captain. You and your men might find yourselves helping out with that."

"We are mostly farmers, sir, and have much experience in digging ditches, as well."

Stark chuckled. "You're the first Virginians we've seen who don't look like they're dressed for court or out to squire the ladies."

Ward added as an afterthought, "We're only militia here, Captain Frake, so there's no saluting or any of those other formalities. Not yet, not until Congress gets around to creating a true army. However, orders will be *obeyed*."

"Of course, sir." Jack Frake inclined his head to the other men, then turned and left the room, closing the door behind him.

Colonel Stark grinned for the first time, and nodded to the door. "I like that man," he said to no one in particular. "He talks back, the saucy Virginian!"

The next day members of the Queen Anne Volunteer Company familiarized themselves with their surroundings and with their comrades-in-arms to be. Jack Frake and Jock Fraser sat on the porch of Ward's headquarters and studied a map that the commander had loaned them. Then on foot, with John Proudlocks joining them, they reconnoitered the land overlooking the Charlestown peninsula.

To the east, they saw a small collection of buildings that was Charlestown on the southeast tip. From it led several dirt roads, merging less than a mile in the west into one that crossed the neck that divided the Mystic River from the Charles River, which widened at its mouth to form what looked like a small bay. Farther east, a little beyond Charlestown across a small body of water that was the outlet from the Charles River, sat Boston on its own peninsula, connected to the mainland by a narrow neck, as well. The only vessels they saw at sail in the water were British warships; the port remained closed.

On the map, they identified Breed's Hill northwest of Charlestown in the middle of the peninsula, the larger Bunker Hill to the northwest of it near the Mystic, and Moulton's Hill, also on the Mystic on the northeastern tip. In between Charlestown and the neck they noted fenced pastureland, clay pits and brick kilns, what looked like a swamp, high grass and a few trees. The entire peninsula looked deserted. Jack Frake used the spyglass that Hugh had given him years ago to survey the place, which was only half a mile at its widest. He shared the glass with Fraser and Proudlocks. The only moving things they saw were a few stray livestock, cattle and pigs, searching for forage. Satisfied that they had a grasp of the potential battlefield, the men returned to their camp.

There were a few other flags or ensigns that marked the campsites of other companies and regiments. Some were green, blue or yellow lengths of cloth hastily knocked together and fastened to pikes, and featured rattlesnakes, pine trees, and other devices. Most of the other men were garbed as the Virginians, in frock coats, waistcoats, breeches, and brimmed and fur hats, much of it homespun and not imported from Britain. A few officers wore uniforms and gorgets from the last war.

Jack Frake moved around the various encampments and acquainted himself with the northern men. Like his own from Virginia, they were a mixture of shopkeepers, farmers, tailors, mechanics, coopers, wheel-wrights, carpenters, teachers and men from many other trades. There were even some students from nearby Harvard. They carried a variety of firearms: muskets, fowling pieces, and some rifles. He noticed a few black men among the Yankees, also bearing arms. These were northern freedmen; they did not behave like servants or slaves, but mingled freely and easily with their white compatriots.

In the early evening Proudlocks returned to camp from a mysterious quest. A red sash draped from around his waist now, identifying him as a sergeant. He brought three more: one for Jude Kenny, the other platoon sergeant, one for Jock Fraser as lieutenant, and one for Jack Frake.

"Where did you find these?" asked Jack Frake, astonished as he tied one around his waist. The sashes were of finely made silk, and were regu-lation British army. Many of the northern militiamen's officers and sergeants wore them.

Proudlocks said, "Some of the Massachusetts men here fought the British along the Concord road. They took them from captured sergeants. I traded a few bullets for them."

Under a starry night, Jack Frake sat at a campfire with Fraser, Proud-locks and other men. As he listened to them talk, he felt anxious about what would happen tomorrow, and somehow vindicated. He could not help but think of Augustus Skelly and his gang facing British soldiers at the Marvel caves in Cornwall, and how he had wished he had been there to share the moment of supreme defiance. He fought the unreasonable notion that he was making up for that absence now. But the memory would not fade, nor the notion, and he smiled at their tenacity.

And then he thought of the puzzle that Skelly told him once he was destined to solve. He distinctly remembered the night that Skelly had joined him on the watch above the Marvel caves, and had replied, in answer to his assertion that living the life of an outlaw was more honorable than obeying unjust laws, *"'Honor' is such an empty notion nowadays. There is a better word for what you mean. The vilest rake in Parliament can claim honor. No, what moves us, Jack, is something more substantial....I'm sure you'll find the right word for it someday."*

Now he wondered if he would live long enough to know the answer.

At nine o'clock that night, Jack Frake received word from Brigadier

Putnam that his company was to join Colonel Prescott and march to
Bunker Hill to help fortify it. Before the Virginians could be roused from
their sleeping rolls, the order was countermanded by Prescott himself, who
rode up to their encampment. "I've spoken with General Ward, Captain.
We won't have enough tools, and not enough water in our barrels to spare.
It's going to be dirty, dusty work all night, you see. Thank you for your
offer. Your men have traveled far to be with us. Rest them, sir, so they'll be
fresh tomorrow."

"Yes, sir," answered Jack Frake.

# Chapter 7: The Hills

"Stand to arms, men."

The sound of guns at dawn had awakened the Virginians. It was distant fire, and as the men of the Company rose and prepared themselves to march, they wondered if the British had stolen up on Prescott, Putnam, and other units that had been sent to Bunker and Breed's Hills to fortify them. A Connecticut officer rode by and informed Jack Frake that the navy at first light had begun bombarding the peninsula, but that the warships could not elevate their guns high enough to cause much damage.

"Where do we march, sir?" asked Jock Fraser.

"Follow the sound of the guns, sir," said the officer with a smile, pointing in the direction of the peninsula, "and everyone else here, to Breed's Hill." He rode off to instruct other units.

The night had been hot, and the day promised to be hotter. The sky was cloudless and an intense blue. The rising sun promised to bake the heads of the armies and keep their powder dry.

Cletus stood with his drum by Jack Frake and beat the signal he had practiced so often. Travis Barret stood next to Cletus, nervously fingering his fife. Next to Jack Frake stood Fraser with the ensign. The men of the Queen Anne Volunteer Company quickly downed last gulps of coffee and pieces of bread, put out their fires, and rushed to form two lines. They stood at the ready, at attention, muskets shouldered.

Jack Frake addressed his troops. "We will march as smartly as we practiced in drill back home, men. Mind your sergeants' commands. They'll be mine. We will fight as well as any other company here." He smiled. "Let us show the others that Americans can hale from the south, too." Then he added, "And be sure to make your first shots a salute from Wendel Barret." In each of the men's pouches were two or three lead balls, fashioned from the Caxton *Courier*'s seized printing type long ago, and on which had been painted in white *WB*.

The men answered in unison, "Yes, sir!"

Jack Frake nodded to Fraser, who yelled, "In columns of twos, right face!" The Company obeyed. Then Fraser turned to Cletus and Travis

Barret. "Play the tune that Mr. Kenny taught you, sons." The young men nodded.

Jack Frake and Fraser walked to the beginning of the formation. "March!" shouted Fraser.

The Queen Anne Volunteer Company moved forward in perfect step. "Left wheel!" The Company moved from the encampment onto a path that led into the distance and past other units that were preparing to march. Cletus beat a marching cadence, and Travis Barret, at first haltingly, then with more confidence, played "Yankee Doodle."

"Cradle arms!"

The men swung their muskets around to rest the barrels in the crooks of their left arms.

Many of the northern men stopped what they were doing to watch the Virginians pass by. "What's that they're marching to?" asked a Connecticut militiaman.

"Sounds like the 'Anacreon Song,'" answered another. "I sung it often enough in my cups."

"No," said another militiaman. "Not at all. It's that new song I heard. 'Yankee Macaroni.'"

"Look at that ensign!" said the sergeant of a Massachusetts regiment. "As brazen as a Beacon Hill doxy! We ought to get us one of those, and put our name on it."

"'Live free or die,'" said his companion. "Well, they march a bit like the bloody-backs, but those Virginians are flying the right idea."

The Company followed other units to the Charlestown Neck, crossed it with them, passed Bunker Hill, and then marched down a road to Breed's Hill into a square redoubt that Prescott's men had built overnight. The eastern and western sides of the hill were steep, too steep for an assault, but the southern and northern sides were sloped and vulnerable. The redoubt's walls were constructed of earth, wicker baskets filled with dirt, and fascines. Field guns were being positioned at the redoubt's walls. Men were rushing back and forth to construct a breastwork on the northeast side of the redoubt. Dust from their efforts and from cannon balls that fell short of the redoubt was mixed with clouds of smoke from the warships drifting over the peninsula.

Five warships fired at the hill, and several gunboats or floating batteries from the Charles River, as well. It was eleven-thirty in the morning. Cannon balls from the gunboats had shrieked over the heads of Jack Frake's men on the Neck to plop harmlessly in the Mystic River. They still came, but fell far short of their target, the redoubt. Jack Frake saw the northern men working feverishly to construct the breastwork. He ordered his men to fall out, stack their arms, and pitch in to help complete it. This they did without hesitation.

Shortly after noontime, the roars of the British warships increased. Prescott urged his men to finish the breastwork. Jack Frake and Jock Fraser mounted the parapet facing Charlestown. With his spyglass Jack Frake counted nearly thirty barges being rowed in procession from Boston in the direction of Moulton's Hill. They were thick with redcoats, and the sun winked ominously on fifteen hundred upright, fixed bayonets and on the cap plates of hundreds of grenadiers.

Behind them, a voice said, "It will take them some time to set up, once they land." Jack Frake and Fraser turned to face Prescott. "In the meantime, Captain, do you see that rail fence there?"

Jack Frake turned north and nodded. A rough wooden fence spanned the pastureland from about one hundred feet north of the breastwork in the direction of the Mystic River. He saw militiamen working hurriedly to reinforce it with stones and cover it with hay. The fence, once fortified and manned, would protect the left flank of the redoubt and Bunker Hill, as well. "Yes, sir?"

"March your company out and join Captain Knowlton and his Connecticut men there. I have it from Ward that he's sending over Colonel Stark's two New Hampshire regiments. I'll put them on the fence, too." He paused. "I should warn you it's likely that's where Howe will concentrate an attack."

"How do you know it will be his attack?"

Prescott held up his own spyglass. "I saw him on one of the barges. I guess Gage liked his plan best, whatever it might be." He gestured to Moulton's Hill. Already there was a great clot of redcoats assembled by the small hill, and it grew bigger as the barges disgorged the troops.

"There's a gap between your breastwork and that fence, sir," observed Jack Frake.

"I know," answered Prescott. "Let's hope Howe's men don't get that far."

"Yes, sir." Jack Frake and Fraser jumped down from the redoubt. The Company's men collected their arms, formed up, and marched out of the redoubt and through the grass to join the Connecticut men. Jack Frake had made Samuel Knowlton's acquaintance yesterday when he toured the camps at Cambridge. Again, the Company stacked arms and pitched in to reinforce the fence.

At about one o'clock, when the task was nearly completed, Colonel Stark marched in along the fence with his regiments from Breed's Hill. He assigned companies of the New Hampshire men to positions with the Connecticut troops. With him was Colonel James Reed, who led one of the regiments. As he passed by Jack Frake, Stark tipped his hat in greeting. "Welcome to hell, Captain. Good luck."

"And you, sir," answered Jack Frake, tipping his hat in turn.

Stark marched with the remainder of his men to the Mystic River and the beach below a bluff, where they proceeded to erect a wall of stone on the beach to protect that flank.

Jack Frake turned and used his spyglass to observe the British. He saw them forming up in three long lines, grenadiers first, one behind the other, nearly a thousand feet away. Every one of the grenadiers carried a full pack on his back. In addition, troops were pulling artillery into place to support the infantry. Jock Fraser said, "Eight guns, Mr. Frake. Six-pounders, twelve-pounders, and two howitzers. They mean to smash us by bayonet or ball."

A slight breeze played lazily with the regimental colors of the British. Travis Barret glanced over at the Company's ensign, which Fraser had planted in some grass behind the Company. It undulated in the warm air, as well. "Wind's from the south, Mr. Frake," he remarked.

Jack Frake heard the fear in the young man's words. He smiled reassuringly at him. "So are we." Then he turned to Fraser. "Jock, tell the men to load their pieces."

Jock Fraser left to walk up and down the Company line to relay the order. John Proudlocks strode leisurely over to Jack Frake. He grinned and said casually, "Here we are again, Jack."

"Again, John? We've always been here, you and I." Jack Frake paused, then said gruffly. "Get back to your men. When they come at us up the hill, we'll give them a taste of their own discipline, and fire in successive platoons. Four. Tell Mr. Fraser that."

Proudlocks answered, "Yes, sir." He turned and walked away. He knew that his friend felt the same pit in his stomach as he did.

Jack Frake busied himself loading his own musket, and succeeded in stopping the shaking in his hands, so that only a few grains of powder fell from his powder horn to the ground as he filled the flash pan. He did not relish the prospect of killing any British. But they had made it necessary. He glanced at his men preparing themselves to fire, eyes fixed on the impressive lines of red below. He wondered what they thought about it.

And he thought of Etáin, safely in Edinburgh. He had not yet received a letter from her. Perhaps one was waiting for him at Morland Hall. He must make sure that he returned home to read it.

When he was finished loading his musket, he walked up and down the line, and his words were punctuated by the sound of guns firing from the warships. "Men, we opposed their Stamp Act and every other law they passed to enslave us. We would not obey those laws. The soldiers you see down there are just as much a part of those laws as the men who created the laws. They are how the king and Parliament always meant to enforce them. Those soldiers are the power behind the laws. That's what you should think as you bring them down as they advance."

"Shootin' legislation?" queried one of the men. "No trouble with that, Captain! Look at all those laws!" he exclaimed, pointing to the lines of red-coats. "Let's repeal 'em!"

Many of the men around him laughed at the remark.

"Yes," said Jack Frake. "That's the way to think of it today."

"Good point," said Proudlocks, who had studied law in London. "Wish I'd made it."

As the Company reformed into four lines behind the fence, the roar of guns from the warships abated, and they heard the beat of a score of drums and the faint shriek of many fifes. The lines of redcoats began to advance up the hill toward the rail fence.

Jack Frake conceded to himself that the sight was majestic. Even magnificent. He took the spyglass from his pack and swept it over the front rank, studying the faces. He could see that every British soldier looked stolidly ahead of him, brow and mouth grim, musket poised straight up to lean on his left shoulder. The grenadiers were tall, their bearskin caps made them appear taller, and their fixed bayonets soared almost two feet above the bearskins. They looked formidable and unbeatable. But he knew they were men, and that any one of them would die just as quickly as short men with a well-placed musket ball. Many of the grenadiers were handsome, worthy-looking men. He was sorry they would need to die.

He slid the spyglass back into his pack and observed his own men. Many of them stared with wide-eyed fixation on the advancing spectacle; it was a new phenomenon to them, the terrifying pageantry of parade ground warfare. Some were swallowing their spit, others wiping their brows of sweat that was not entirely drawn by the heat and sun.

John Proudlocks, in command of the rear fourth platoon, watched with calm, almost studious regard, as though he were listening to a lecture at the Middle Temple in London. Jock Fraser, in charge of the third, watched the advancing army with a faint, greedy smile, as though a meal were coming to him. Jude Kenny, in command of the second platoon, watched with disbelief. Travis Barret, in the second platoon, stood biting his lip; Cletus, behind him in the third, watched with the air of a prince.

Jack Frake glanced to his left and saw the Connecticut and New Hampshire men had made ready. Some were kneeling, muskets or rifles already aimed, trigger fingers curled to fire; others lay on the ground, the barrels of their weapons steadied atop a rail or stone.

As the British drums and the tramp of the grenadiers' boots came closer, Jack Frake yelled to the first platoon, "When they're fifty yards away, fire on my order. Don't waste your shots."

Cannon fire erupted from Breed's Hill, but the iron balls fell short of the first line, bounded uselessly, and disappeared in the grass. There were remnants of fences and large rocks, and when the tightly organized line of grenadiers encountered them their formation was broken up. As the grenadiers scrambled on command from their officers and sergeants to reform their lines, the northern men behind the fence opened fire. At the same time, the guns from Breed's Hill found their range and ploughed iron through the confused mass of redcoats. Muskets also fired from the redoubt, but Jack Frake did not think many could be effective from that distance.

"First platoon, fire!" shouted Jack Frake, and he brought up his musket to his shoulder and fired.

Many grenadiers died swiftly, silently, and fell like knocked over dolls. Others screamed in pain, fell, writhed on the ground, then were still. Others stumbled to their knees, dropping their muskets to clutch at their heads or limbs. The second line of grenadiers moved forward and became merged with the remnants of the first.

"Mr. Kenny, second platoon, please!" shouted Jack Frake as he reloaded. At first he thought he could not be heard over the deafening musket blasts on either side of him. But he was heard.

Jude Kenny shouted, "Fire!" The second platoon fired.

Jack Frake finished replacing his ramrod under the barrel. Redcoats were still falling. He saw a drummer boy in the rear swing wildly around as he was hit. When he fell, his drum came loose from his strap and rolled back down the hill. "Third platoon, Mr. Fraser!"

The third platoon fired.

"Mr. Proudlocks!"

The fourth platoon fired.

By now the smoke from so many muskets created a bluish-gray cloud over and in front of the rail fence. It was rising and thinning, but too slowly for any man to see through it yet.

"Hold your fire until we have targets, men!" shouted Jack Frake. He risked a glance at his men. Some were visibly shaken and had trouble filling their flash pans or fixing their ramrods into the muzzles. Some men took swigs from their canteens, others from black liquor flasks.

Jack Frake glanced to his left and right. The northern men on both sides of him were still firing into the curtain of smoke, certain of hitting a soldier. Then he heard an explosion of musketry from the direction of Mystic beach. Stark's men, he thought. Musket fire on the other side of Breed's Hill also grew in intensity. He had forgotten about the troops he had seen marching south in the direction of Charlestown. Howe must have launched an attack on the south end of Breed's Hill, as well.

The smoke cleared enough now in front of the Company that they could see that the grenadiers had gained ground after the first volley, but now were retreating back down the hill. Some cheering was heard on either side of the Queen Anne Volunteer Company.

"That's strange, Mr. Frake," said Jock Fraser. "None of their artillery fired."

Jack Frake shrugged. He was too distracted to speculate on why. "Perhaps they brought the wrong ordnance, or packed sugar instead of powder." Down the hill, the grenadiers had withdrawn completely out of range of muskets and the cannon at the redoubt. The grass on the slope below was littered with inert red figures. Even the firing at the beach had diminished to single, distinguishable musketry.

Jack Frake witnessed something he had seen at Monongahela twenty years ago. Soldiers were removing their officer's red sashes and using them as litters to carry their owners from the field. Most of the downed officers seemed to be dead; others gestured crazily in the air. One officer still gripped his sword and waved it as though still urging his troops on. Some grenadiers limped away from the field; others could be seen crawling. Officers ran onto the field to retrieve fallen colors.

"Captain Frake," said John Proudlocks. Jack Frake turned. "They must have got off some shots." He nodded to a man at the far end of the third platoon. The man lay on his stomach, his face turned in Jack Frake's direction, a look of surprise on it. He had been hit in the midst of reloading his musket; the ramrod protruded from the muzzle. Jack Frake knew the man only slightly; he had been a small farmer near Proudlocks's Sachem Hall.

"That's a shame," said Jock Fraser. "Someone close his eyes."

Jack Frake looked away, reached for his canteen, and took a long draught of water.

Some twenty minutes later, the grenadiers and supporting regular infantry had formed in lines again. The drums began beating the march, and they could hear officers and sergeants shout commands. The glittering red beast moved inexorably forward over the grass dotted with fallen grenadiers. It was advancing directly for the rail fence.

"This is hellishly easy," said Jock Fraser. There was a note of disapproval in his words. "If they came at us in columns instead of lines, we wouldn't stand a chance. Why don't they?"

Jack Frake shook his head. "Because their general believes them invincible. Take your place, Mr. Fraser. This is no time to discuss foolishness."

The cannon from the redoubt opened up again, cutting swathes through the ordered ranks of redcoats. And when the wave reached fifty yards, the men at the rail fence and breastwork delivered a thunderous volley and kept firing. Jack Frake's platoons this time were able to fire two volleys each.

Again the disposition of the enemy was obscured by a thick pall of smoke. And when it cleared, the grenadiers and regulars had retreated again, leaving more dead and wounded in the grass.

The northern men to the right continued to fire until they realized that none of their bullets were finding a target, but dropping uselessly among the dead and wounded below.

Jack Frake stepped up on one of the fence rails and looked to his right at the breastwork further down the line. It was almost parallel with the rail fence. He noted the gap between the fence and the breastwork, and remembered Prescott's hope that the British would not come that far.

Then he glanced back down at the redcoats, and wondered if they had enough resolve left to try. He took out his spyglass and surveyed the carnage. The grass was strewn with hundreds of British, this time with many regulars as well as grenadiers. Some of the shapes still moved. He saw another officer being taken from the field on his sash by a pair of drummer boys. Half of the man's right arm was gone, and he could not discern where the bloody stump ended and the torn red sleeve began. In the man's other hand were his regiment's colors on a broken pike, dragging over the grass and bodies as the drummers carried the man off. A ball from the redoubt must have severed both the arm and the pike. The officer's mouth was open, and he thought he could hear it emit a howl.

The sight appalled Jack Frake, and clashed with his hope that the British had had enough.

"Reload, men," he said as he stepped down from the fence, "and rest easy. They won't try again for a while." It was a redundant order. The men of the Company had already reloaded and were standing at ease. Jack Frake reloaded his musket and rested his back against the fence. When he was finished, he happened to glance up at the ensign fluttering idly behind their position. There were two holes in it that were not there before. Beyond the ensign, he saw Bunker Hill and men standing atop it.

Captain Knowlton came down the line, checking on the units. He stopped and asked Jack Frake, "How's your powder, Mr. Frake?"

"We've enough, and lead, too."

"Good. Lose anyone?"

"One man, during the first charge."

"We lost a couple, too. But I'm worried about the redoubt. Mr. Prescott has little powder to spare. General Ward's been very careful with the munitions."

"Where is General Ward?" asked Jack Frake.

"Probably atop Cobble Hill, watching it all." Knowlton took out a pipe and packed it with tobacco and lit it with a match as he spoke. "Colonel Stark down on the beach chopped up the Fusiliers who came at us that way. Half of them are still there, dead. They attacked in a column, all bunched together, there was no room for a line, and they died in bunches. They won't be coming that way again." Knowlton gestured with his pipe. "Well, I'd better check on the rest of the line. See you back in Cambridge, Captain. Or maybe Boston." He glanced at the Company. "You Virginians are steady."

Jack Frake nodded in acknowledgement of the compliment. "I'd like to see Boston," he answered. He tipped his hat at Knowlton as the man turned and made his way through the Company to the northern men on the right. He remembered then that he had a pipe, as well. He removed it and a pouch from his pack, filled it with tobacco, and lit it. Some of his men saw him with the pipe, and took out their own.

And someone remembered to remove the dead man's hat and place it over his closed eyes.

# Chapter 8: The Retreat

Twenty minutes passed. The sun beat down on living and dead alike. On either side of the Queen Anne Volunteer Company, men congratulated themselves and speculated about what the British would try next, if anything. But the Virginians said little. "Lots of laws repealed down there," remarked the man who thought of "Shootin' legislation." He said it sadly. No one laughed. Jack Frake looked at Travis Barret and Cletus. They smiled back at him, reassured that he seemed calm and unafraid.

"Look at Charlestown," said one of the men. "It's burning." Everyone turned to look in that direction. What buildings they could see were indeed afire. They had not had the time to notice what was happening on that side of the peninsula. They would learn later that a British warship had fired a carcass, or incendiary shell, at the village, which was defended by Americans who had been firing on the rear ranks of the marines and regulars assaulting the south side of the redoubt. There were no means and no time to fight the blaze, and the Americans were driven out.

John Proudlocks came up to Jack Frake. He, too, held a pipe. "It's the Monongahela again, Jack. Do you remember?"

Jack Frake shook his head once and jerked it back to the field behind him. "Look at that, John. I don't need to remember the Monongahela. One slaughter is enough."

After a moment, Proudlocks asked, "Thought of Etáin?"

Jack Frake merely smiled in answer.

After a moment of silence, Proudlocks seemed to reach a decision. "I've been thinking of Lydia," he said.

Jack Frake grinned in surprise. He asked, softly, so no one else could hear, "Lydia Heathcoate, our seamstress?"

Proudlocks cocked his head once in acknowledgement. "We've been keeping it quiet — " He stopped speaking and pointed past his friend's shoulder. "Look!"

Jack Frake turned. The British had formed up again, both grenadiers and regulars. As he watched, on commands he could not hear, the ranks grounded their muskets, lay them down with bayonets pointed at the rail fence and breastwork, removed their knapsacks, and lay them in the grass, one company after another. On more commands, the soldiers retrieved their weapons and rested them against their shoulders, ready to assault the hill again.

It was then that the British field guns, scattered from Moulton's Hill to the outskirts of Charlestown, and oddly silent until now, began firing. Jock Fraser yelled, "Guess they found a way to ignite sugar, Captain!" The howitzers lobbed balls inside the redoubt, while the two twelve-pounders and four of the field guns blasted away at the breastwork and redoubt.

The other two field guns were aimed at the rail fence. They fired consecutively.

The first ball raised dust on the unoccupied hillside above them. The second struck the fence with a crash somewhere on Jack Frake's left. He heard a scream and a shout and an instant later he and Proudlocks were showered with flying splinters. And blood. They dropped their pipes and made the platoons ready to receive the next charge. The drums had begun beating again. Jack Frake wiped his brow with a sleeve. He did not notice the blood and smudges of black powder on it that came off with the sweat.

Smoke from the British guns and the fires in Charlestown drifted toward the rail fence. Through it the Virginians saw the lines move forward, then, to their amazement, pivot enmasse to the right, like a pendulum, and sweep in the direction of the breastwork and redoubt. Not one officer or enlisted man looked in the direction of the rail fence; it was as though the men at the rail fence were not there to notice. The lines did not stop moving. On another command, the grenadiers and regulars shouted "Huzzah!" and swung their muskets down, bayonets at the ready. Then the drums beat a faster cadence, and the lines broke into a quick march, almost a trot, and rushed up the hill, quickly enough for the king's and regimental colors to ripple in the breeze. More British fell, but the lines kept moving.

Jack Frake espied a party of horsemen in red at the far end of the lines, out of musket range. The generals, he thought.

"They're passing us by!" shouted Fraser, outraged. As if to contradict him, a ball from one of the field guns struck the soil in front of the fence and splattered the Virginians with pebbles and dirt.

"They'll cut us off from Bunker and a way out of here if they take the breastwork!" added Jude Kenny. Even as he spoke, they watched the northern men at the breastwork fall back as the twelve-pounders and field guns found their mark and razed it in geysers of rails, hay and stones. Only a few muskets among the northern men fired back at the swiftly advancing British.

The guns at the redoubt did not answer.

"They're out of powder," said Jack Frake. He glanced around. On both sides of the Virginians, the Connecticut and New Hampshire men saw the dilemma as well as he did. Staying here meant entrapment on this corner of the peninsula, with no means of escape, and assault from the land and by the warships. Already the northern men were abandoning the rail and moving up the hill toward Bunker.

Jack Frake turned again and saw another column of redcoats, independent of the main attack, marching up the hill. As he watched, it swung out into two lines and advanced without missing a step. The British in it looked fresh, although a few had bandaged heads. He thought there might be four or five hundred of them. Reserves, thought Jack Frake. He did not recognize the uniforms. There were grenadiers, but they were not as tall as the ones from the first two charges. The regulars accompanying them did not share the same color coat facings on their uniforms. Probably the remnants of companies decimated in the first two charges, he thought. They were marching for the rail fence. He heard commands relayed down the line, and another "Huzzah!" as the muskets and bayonets came down.

"All right!" shouted Jack Frake. "We're finished here! Up the hill to Bunker, but in good order!"

The Virginians turned and began moving up the hill in platoons. Jock Fraser snatched up the ensign and ran ahead to lead the way. Jack Frake and Proudlocks trailed behind.

They had not gone many yards when Colonel Stark emerged from the smoke and confusion with a company of New Hampshire men. He came alongside Jack Frake and yelled as they moved uphill, as balls from the field guns fell around them, "Captain Frake, I want you to join some of my men to cover our fellows from the breastwork and redoubt — do you see? the lobster-backs are already there! — so they aren't chased down while they show tail! The British can't shoot well, but they're hell with the bayonet and we aren't! Keep them off our men until we're over the Neck. We've got to save this army to fight another day! Understood?"

"Yes, sir."

"If anything happens to me, you take orders from Captain Knowlton or Captain Dearborn here!"

Jack Frake glanced at the colonel's companion, and nodded.

They all looked down at the oncoming British. "Fusiliers, Captain Frake, or what's left of them! They're plenty mad after the licking we gave them at the beach! Left them in piles! Those regulars look like business, too! Don't let them get near you!" He slapped Jack Frake's shoulder. "Your face is dirty, guess you've been shooting! You Virginians aren't all pen and paper, after all! Good luck!" Without further word, Stark and Dearborn sprinted off to join other New Hampshire companies, leaving the one that accompanied them behind.

The supporting field guns stopped firing. The American tide flowed uphill, pursued by the red.

To the right of the Company, northern men were pausing in flight to pour volleys into the British as they swarmed past the breastwork. By now, many British were dashing over the abandoned breastwork and through the gap into the redoubt or over the parapet; others were in pursuit of the defenders. Jack Frake looked down the hill and saw the Fusiliers climbing over the rail fence the Company had abandoned only moments before. He ordered the Company to halt and fire in platoons, and each platoon to move up the hill once it had discharged its muskets.

His men obeyed without question. They brought down a soldier who carried the Fusiliers' regimental colors, a sergeant, an officer, and several rank and file. But the mass of red pressed forward. Half the soldiers were over the fence by now. The New Hampshire and Connecticut men to the Company's left were firing into the British farther down the rail fence, delaying the advance.

Jack Frake knew that as long as they kept the British at bay, they would be safe, but there was a risk that if he moved the Company too slowly uphill, they could be surrounded by redcoats, and that would be the end. A quick appraisal of his dilemma revealed that he was protecting the flank of the northern men retreating from the rail fence, who in turn were covering the men retreating from the breastwork and redoubt. He tried to keep pace with the retreating northern men, but it was difficult.

Just as he noticed that a redcoat had picked up the regimental colors, he saw a line of Fusiliers and regulars pause to take up firing positions. "Present firelocks!" shouted a sergeant.

"First two platoons, fire! Now!" Jack Frake yelled, even though he was in the line of fire. Proudlocks, closer to the first two platoons, relayed the command.

"Fire!" shouted a British lieutenant.

Thundering flame from the British muskets shot up at Jack Frake, and flame exploded from behind him. Something struck his steel gorget and blinded him for a second. When he recovered his sight and hearing a second later, he saw that several of the Fusiliers and regulars had fallen. Without taking his eyes off the enemy, he stumbled backwards and tripped on a body. He looked down. It was "Shootin' legislation"; a musket ball had pierced his neck and come out the other side. He turned and waved the Company further up the hill, then followed it. On his way up, he stepped over the bodies of two more of his men. He did not have time to see who they were.

Jack Frake, struggling against the smoke of the guns and muskets that stung his eyes and made him cough, happened to glance up at the Company ensign that now rippled in the wind over his men's heads. The words in the cobalt canton commanded his attention for a brief, eternal moment: *Live free, or die. Yes!* he thought. *Yes! I will! Yes, Augustus! Yes, Redmagne! I know! I know! I've known all these years, what you knew that day in Falmouth!* Then the thought was gone, the thought of a man who was certain he was near his end — a thought quick and fleetingly final and glorious in its dedication.

"Push on, men! Push on! They're on the run!"

He heard the voice, and turned to see, not five yards from him, a regular officer holding up a sword, looking back at a clot of hesitant Fusiliers and regulars, urging them to follow.

"Push on, men! We have them! For king and country, push on!"

Jack Frake stood to his full height, raised his musket, pulled back the hammer, readied his finger on the trigger, and aimed for the officer's heart.

The officer turned to look up. His face was taut with purpose. It was a handsome, boyish face, unafraid, confident, and enthused in expectation of victory. But the officer's expression turned, first to surprise when it saw the muzzle of a musket leveled at his heart, then to brave acceptance of the inevitable, and finally to astonishment when he glimpsed the face behind the hammer.

The officer's mouth opened in recognition of Jack Frake, and in the instant that he pressed the trigger, Jack Frake recognized Roger Tallmadge.

It was a mercifully clean shot. Roger Tallmadge jerked backwards, his tricorn flying off, still gripping his sword, then fell and rolled downhill to rest at the feet of some Fusiliers, leaving the sword behind in the trampled grass.

This time it was Jack Frake who stood in immobilizing astonishment, staring at the man he had just killed. He did not notice a Fusilier corporal rush at him with a lowered bayonet, yelling, "You bloody rebel!" He did not notice John Proudlocks suddenly appear and knock the corporal's weapon aside with his musket, then raise his musket and slam the butt end of it into the corporal's face. The corporal fell backwards into a pair of regulars.

Jack Frake regained full consciousness only when Proudlocks yanked him around by the arm and pulled him uphill.

"Are you all right?" asked Proudlocks as they moved.

"Yes," answered Jack Frake.

"I saw," said Proudlocks. "I know."

"What do you know?" demanded Jack Frake. "What did you see?"

"Tallmadge. Mr. Kenrick's friend."

Jack Frake instead ordered, "Get with your platoon! We'll fire on them again!"

"Yes, sir!"

*   *   *

By dusk, the guns, muskets, and drums were silent. The only sounds heard by the victors on the Charlestown peninsula now were the moans, wails, and pleadings of the wounded. When night fell, dozens of flambeaux moved about the darkened hills in search of those sounds.

Most of the Americans had fled across the Neck, some over the causeway to Cobble Hill on the mainland, and made their way back to Cambridge. It was a rout, but an orderly one. The Americans knew they had inflicted significant casualties on the British, who did not pursue them off the peninsula. Lacking specific information, they could not decide whether the British dared not or could not attempt to disperse them further beyond Bunker Hill. They were grateful that the momentum of defeat ended once the Neck was behind them. Most of the army had been saved to fight another day, as Colonel Stark had hoped it would be.

The British counted over one thousand casualties, a quarter of them dead. Over ninety officers perished. The victors, licking their wounds and beginning to comprehend the enormous cost of their success, could not quite savor it. General Henry Clinton, who had come across from Boston to join in the battle, and who had ridden up to Breed's Hill only to find officerless troops wondering what to do next, wrote that it was "a dear bought victory. Another such would have ruined us."

The Americans, after the militiamen and regiments completed their roll calls, estimated they had lost over a hundred dead, and counted nearly three hundred wounded. How many had been captured, they did not know. More than a score of the dead, men trapped inside the redoubt as the British poured in, were bayoneted by vengeful redcoats.

In one of the ironic coincidences of the battle, Major John Pitcairn, whose men had fired on the militia on Lexington Green in April, died with scores of his marines during a second assault on the south slope of Breed's Hill, while Dr. Joseph Warren, the man who had sent riders to alert the militia of the British march to Lexington and Concord, died while trying to leave Breed's Hill.

The Queen Anne Volunteer Company had survived almost intact. It marched resolutely back across the Neck, in formation, while hundreds of other Americans dashed across it under further bombardment by the floating batteries on the Charles. Colonel Stark, marching with his own men across the Neck, had observed the coolness of the Company in action, and now in retreat, and it inspired his further admiration.

But the mood inside the Company's camp at Cambridge was as somber as it was in all the units that camped again near the headquarters. Five more of its number had perished on the peninsula, mostly from musket fire from the pursuing British, including Jude Kenny. Once the fires had been lit to warm their food, hands and souls, a few of the men permitted themselves to cry in relief or in horror. Most men sat around their fires that night and traded anecdotes about close calls and lost friends, and speculated about what would happen next. And all of them regarded Jack Frake with gratitude, for his ruthless leadership during the retreat had more than once saved them from certain death or perilous capture.

*What will you do?* Jack Frake asked himself in his mind, over and over again.

"What will you do?" asked John Proudlocks, who sat next to him at one of the fires. He brought two battered pewter mugs of coffee from another platoon's campfire, and gave one to his captain.

Jack Frake took it and sipped the acrid brew first, before answering. "About what?"

"Captain Tallmadge."

"Tell him the truth," replied Jack Frake without emphasis.

"The captain was his friend."

*Will he remain mine?* thought Jack Frake. They were both thinking of Hugh Kenrick.

"Did you know it was him?" asked Proudlocks.

"Not until it was too late."

"Do you regret it?"

After a moment, Jack Frake answered, "No." *Not even if he does not remain my friend*, he thought to himself. He paused. "No more about it, John. I am tired."

"Yes, Jack." Proudlocks sipped his coffee.

"Thank you for clubbing that Fusilier," said Jack Frake. "I didn't see him coming."

"You already thanked me."

"Yes, that's right. I did. On the Neck, on our way back."

Jack Frake had already tortured himself in wondering if it had been possible — if the fraction of a second could have existed — to lower or shift his musket a fraction of an inch, and simply wound Tallmadge, perhaps in the arm, or in the leg, and stopped him from rallying his troops, but left him alive.

But he knew he was torturing himself needlessly; he knew that the fraction of a second never existed. By the time he recognized the face, the flint and the spark and the powder had already sent the ball on its journey down the barrel and out the muzzle.

But then, he thought, Tallmadge was there, serving the Crown, taking part in an effort to conquer the colonies. He was the enemy. Why was he there? Tallmadge himself had told him, over supper at Meum Hall the previous June, that he planned to sail back to England when he reached Boston, possibly to resign his commission in the army and work at Hugh's father's bank, or at least apply for an assignment, possibly as a consular military attaché on the Continent, that did not conflict with his reservations about what Parliament wished to do in the colonies. "It's plum duty, Mr. Frake," he heard the voice saying with a gaiety that tried to mask embarrassment.

But Tallmadge was there, and he had died.

No one else in the company but John Proudlocks knew the significance of the incident.

Jack Frake's gorget now had an indentation. A ball that was deflected from the steel had nearly obliterated *aude* in the inscription. Jock Fraser was the first to notice it, once they had reached their old campground. "God's oath, Mr. Frake!" he exclaimed as he examined the whorl in the gorget, "I was only jesting there in Yorktown! Thank God it wasn't tin or copper! You owe Mr. Kenrick some thanks for it!" Jack Frake smiled humorlessly in reply. *Make up your mind*, he thought to himself: *Thank God, or thank Mr. Kenrick. God, however, might be more forgiving; Mr. Kenrick may wish it had been tin or copper.*

Fraser examined it more closely. There was a patch of blood on the gorget, and then he noticed a cut beneath the stubble on his captain's chin. "Guess it flew up at you when it was hit, Captain."

"I guess it did, Jock."

Jack Frake removed it now from around his neck and examined the gorget. He handed it to Proudlocks. "What does your legal Latin tell you it says now, John?" he asked.

Proudlocks put down his coffee and held the gorget closer to the fire and read the inscription again. "'*Sapere aude*,'" he mused. Staring into the campfire, he reached back in his mind to the Latin lessons he had taken in order to understand much of the law he studied at the Middle Temple. After a moment, he answered, "The courage has been removed, leaving you your reason." He scoffed and gave the gorget back to his friend. "Well, I know *that* isn't true. If it were, we would not be sitting here tonight."

Jack Frake smiled in acknowledgement. He replaced the gorget around his neck, then put down his own mug. He reached into the pack beside him and found one of the seegars he had brought with him. He would have preferred his pipe, but he had left it at the rail fence, where it was probably ground to pieces under the boots of the attacking British.

Then he remembered that Proudlocks had dropped his there, as well, as they rushed to prepare for the third assault. He took out a second seegar, and offered it to his friend.

Proudlocks nodded in thanks and took it. He reached down into the campfire and took out a burning twig, and with it lit both seegars, Jack Frake's first, then his own.

Then they sat quietly together, alone in their separate thoughts.

Jack Frake thought of Etáin and Morland Hall, and contemplated decisions he must now make.

\*   \*   \*

"You and your men are welcome to stay, Captain Frake," said General Ward the next morning. "We will be moving soon to fortify Dorchester Heights.

We don't think General Gage has enough strength left to do that now. Then we'll have him trapped in Boston. He would need to rely on the navy for food and other supplies, for he won't be able to reach the farms south of him. We'll be in his way. We'll either starve him into submission, or force him to leave."

Jack Frake stood where he stood two mornings ago, in the headquarters, before Ward's makeshift desk. Prescott, Putnam, and Stark were there, as well.

Ward added, "Colonel Stark here has testified to the bravery and ability of your Company."

Jack Frake nodded to the colonel, then said, "When word of the battle here spreads, sir, you won't lack for men to replace us. And when word of it reaches Virginia, we will be needed there, as well. Governor Dunmore is certain to raise hell. So, we would like to return home to make certain he doesn't raise too much hell."

The other officers permitted themselves to chuckle at the humor.

Jack Frake added, "My Company did not come here under the authority of a committee or the Virginia convention, sir. We came of our own free will."

"I know," said Ward. "Well, perhaps we may take consolation in the possibility that another Virginian may be appointed commander of all our forces by the Congress. At least, that's the talk in my correspondence from Philadelphia, that he's the favorite. I have a note from Mr. John Adams that his proposal to the Congress that the army here be regarded as the official army of the colonies was accepted, and that he himself will nominate Mr. Washington to be its commander-in-chief, if no one else will."

Jack Frake replied, "Should that come about, sir, I am sure that Virginian will more than make up for the absence of my company." He grinned in recollection. "He and I made a very brief acquaintance at the Monongahela, sir. He saved the British there."

"Of course," said Ward. "Well, he pulled their chestnuts out of the fire then. We can only hope now that he will toss them back in!"

Jack Frake grinned again, then said, "Well, sir, with your leave, my company will depart. We have a long march ahead of us."

Ward rose to shake Jack Frake's hand. "Thank you, sir." Prescott, Putnam, and Stark came over to shake his hand, as well.

After Stark was finished, he scrutinized Jack Frake's gorget, and frowned when he noted the indentation. "What a marksman that lobsterback must have been!" he exclaimed. "Captain, you and your men can fight alongside me and mine any time!"

"Thank you, Colonel," answered Jack Frake. "Perhaps we will. We would be honored to." He stepped back, tipped his hat, and nodded to each of the men, then turned and left the room.

# Chapter 9: The Invitation

On July 5, the second Continental Congress adopted its own "olive branch" petition to send to London, in it professing allegiance to George the Third, hoping for reconciliation, and denying any Parliamentary authority over the colonies. George refused to receive the petition, and although the Commons did recognize it in November, it was subsequently rejected by Parliament as a foundation for reconciliation. The king had already declared the colonies in open rebellion. Congress replied to the proclamation with another expression of loyalty to him, but not to Parliament. George replied to that with a proclamation that closed the colonies to all commerce, effective March 1, 1776.

In the meantime, Washington was appointed unanimously by Congress as commander-in-chief of the army. Congress also voted $2 million in bills of credit to finance that army and naval matters. The "Twelve Confederated Colonies" subsequently rejected Lord North's "olive branch" on July 31.

The mails, always slow, became slower and unpredictable. Most colonial "post boys," once hired by royally appointed postmasters, now rode under the authority of a multitude of committees of safety up and down the seaboard, whose own couriers often carried and received mail, as well. Virtually the only item that British merchantmen could bring into the colonies now without it being subjected to taxes, embargos, or nonimportation measures, was mail. In Williamsburg, Alexander Purdie, publisher of one of the several *Virginia Gazettes* that had appeared in the region since the death of Joseph Royle, who published the government-controlled *Gazette*, was soon to be appointed postmaster by the Congress, together with Benjamin Franklin as postmaster general. What the Crown had taken away from Franklin, the Congress gave back.

At the end of the first week of July, a courier from West Point rode into Caxton and left mail at Safford's Arms Tavern. Safford saw some envelopes addressed to Hugh Kenrick, and sent a serving boy with them to Meum Hall. Word of the battle of Breed's Hill had traveled faster than the mails, however, and Safford anxiously looked for an envelope addressed to him or anyone else in Caxton from Jack Frake. But, there was nothing.

Hugh was in the fields with William Settle inspecting the reassembled conduit when Rupert Beecroft came out and informed his employer that several envelopes had arrived. He thanked the man, and turned back to instructing Settle to replace or repair some of the bamboo lengths, which age had begun to crack in many places. He, too, was waiting to hear word from Jack Frake, and also from Otis Talbot and Novus Easley in Philadelphia. He had heard about Breed's Hill, as well, and half hoped he would hear from Roger Tallmadge.

A letter from him was the first thing Hugh sought when he entered his study and looked at the envelopes. He found letters from Talbot and Easley, but he smiled when he found a letter from his friend. He breathed a sigh of relief, sat in his chair, and broke the seal on the letter. It was dated June 5.

"My dear Hugh," it began, "something is afoot here, for the Americans have the town surrounded, and General Gage wishes to remove them once and for all. That is necessary because the army here will need fresh food and supplies from the countryside. And, he wishes to demonstrate the Crown's power and determination. It is thought that the Americans plan to fortify the Charlestown peninsula, directly across from Boston here, and possibly turn one of the hills there closer to the town into a fort. From there they could bombard the town, though I do not think they would do anything that would injure a captive populace who have already suffered much from the port closing.

"Much to my surprise, a triumvirate of generals arrived with reinforcements last week on the *Cerberus* to assist General Gage. Soon after their arrival, I was instructed to have my company of orphans prepared to act as a reserve for an action most officers here can only guess at. It is rumored among the officers here that the ministry is not pleased with General Gage's performance. He may very well be replaced, which would leave me stranded here. For if he is recalled, the other generals would certainly take no cognizance of my duress or of General Gage's promise to release me from what has become an onerous duty...."

Tallmadge went on to discuss his wife Alice, from whom he had received several letters, and news she had written him about her family and London. Otis Talbot, the Kenrick family's agent in Philadelphia, wrote excitedly about the Congress, as did Novus Easley, a Quaker merchant there with whom Hugh had done business in the past. And both merchants discussed the various ways they were managing to stay solvent in spite of the nonimportation measures.

The talk in Caxton was that the British had suffered great casualties at

Breed's Hill. Roger's letter allowed Hugh a sliver of hope that his friend was not one of them. And the question returned to him, as he read Tallmadge's letter: Could he permit himself to remain a friend of Roger?

Other incidents filled the talk in Caxton's shops and taverns: the departure of Arthur Stannard, tobacco agent for the London firm of Weddle, Umphlett and Company. Stannard and his family departed on a merchantman from Hampton in early June because the agent's business had departed; the hogsheads of tobacco he usually bought and consigned to his firm in London were now going in other directions, all of them illegal by Crown law. And the planters who remained loyal to him were planting less and less tobacco and devoting more of their acreage instead to flax, hemp and various food crops.

The nonimportation measures adopted first by Virginia and other colonies and then by the Congress erased the tobacco trade and any reason for Stannard or any other British agent to remain in the colonies. Stannard wrote to his firm earlier in the year stating his intention to leave Virginia, "for the trade has more than vanished, it is denied me, and my presence is no longer justified. Indeed, my presence is fraught with indignities, for wherever I go now I am treated with a begrudgement that borders on base hostility. I feel fortunate that I have not been made the object of the tar and feather, as some of our countrymen have been in these parts. I must leave with my family before we are perhaps arrested and confined in a jail to await an unknown fate at the hands of reckless outlaws."

Stannard, now the father of two sons and a daughter, neglected to mention that his family consisted of Winifred, his wife, and the daughter and youngest son. His oldest son, Joseph, graduated from the Philadelphia Academy, had become a lawyer, and was now on the staff of Charles Thomson, secretary to the Congress. He called himself a Virginian. The embittered father disowned him, and refused to discuss him with family or friends.

Stannard had sold his house and the contents of his shop to a merchant in Fredericksburg. Lucas Rittles, the grocer and his next-door tradesman, had bought the valued pattern books that Stannard had used for so many years to sell his stock of miscellanies and domestic wares.

Hugh felt left out of everything. He could not attend the convention in Richmond on July 17, for Queen Anne County had neglected to elect delegates to it. That was the doing of Reece Vishonn, now the senior magistrate of the county court, who exerted great influence among the farmers and planters, and had discouraged such an election. Hugh could not join Jack Frake and his Company on the march to Boston, for he had only just returned from England, and Meum Hall required his attention.

The next morning, as he was reading account books over breakfast, Ann Vere, the housekeeper, informed Hugh that several gentlemen had arrived and wished to speak with him on "a matter of utmost importance." She mentioned the names of the visitors.

"Show them into the study, Mrs. Vere," he answered. "I will be there shortly."

"Shall I prepare refreshments, Mr. Kenrick?" asked Mrs. Vere.

Hugh thought about it for a moment, then shook his head. "No, Mrs. Vere. I suspect it is not a hospitable call." He was aware that the county's leading citizens had been avoiding him.

When he entered the study, he saw Reece Vishonn sitting with Edgar Cullis and Carver Gramatan. With them were Moses Corbin, the mayor of Caxton, and Cabal Tippet, sheriff of the county, both of whom continued in their offices in a political purgatory, since Crown authority had been suspended. They stood deferentially at the sides. Hugh went to his desk and sat down. He studied the men arraigned before him. He had the odd but certain sense that they were all cringing in his presence.

After an exchange of cordial greetings, Hugh said, "Come to your business, sirs."

Vishonn cleared his throat and announced, "We will not send delegates to Richmond for this third convention, Mr. Kenrick. Mr. Cullis here will certainly not attend. When Governor Dunmore reclaims the Palace and his authority, this county, at least, will be spared punishment for rash and treasonous actions, as many others will not be. We have persuaded many freeholders that it is in their best interests to remain loyal, and, to our minds, *patriotic*." He paused. "We have sent His Excellency a note asserting our sentiments and our loyalty."

Hugh frowned. He toyed idly with the brass top that was always there. "Was that to forestall an assault on Caxton by one of his warships?"

Carver Gramatan frowned and asked, "Why do you think he would wish to assault us, Mr. Kenrick?"

"Because if he does not reclaim the Palace and his authority, he will become a marauder. No better than a pirate."

Carver Gramatan merely clucked his tongue in disagreement and in distaste.

"Frankly, yes," braved Vishonn. "That was one of the purposes of our note to His Excellency. We wish to avoid tragic...confusion. In our note to him we also offered whatever assistance he may require and that is within our power to provide."

Hugh shrugged, then sighed. "Much of this is not news to me, Mr. Vishonn. And what news it is, does not startle me. You must know that. What is the purpose of this visit?"

Cullis cleared his throat and said, "We are forming our own committee of safety, sir, in order to counter that of the Virginia convention and any in the neighboring counties. Mr. Corbin and Mr. Tippet here have agreed to sit on that committee. We also thought it prudent to advise you that we have begun recruiting men for a militia to oppose the one that departed here some weeks ago, led by Mr. Frake."

Hugh let go of the top and rose from his desk to pace leisurely behind it. He asked, "Do you know the particulars of the Quebec Act, sirs?"

Vishonn glanced warily at Cullis and Gramatan, then said, "We are acquainted with them. Why do you ask?"

"That Act proclaims Parliamentary supremacy over Canada in all matters whatsoever, grants it no legislative assembly or power, denies Canadians the right of taxation and governance of their internal affairs, authorizes the trial of civil cases without juries, and confirms the Catholic Church as the 'official' religion. There is all that, in addition to the Act's annexation to Quebec of all territory west of the transmontane. Land, I needn't remind you, Mr. Vishonn, already claimed by Virginia and Virginians. Much of it claimed by you."

"What is your point, sir?"

"That the Quebec Act is very likely a model for how the Crown wishes to reorganize all the other colonies, so that they will be less troublesome and more servile. Surely, that must have occurred to you. Can you imagine Virginia subjected to the same enslaving strictures?"

"Yes, sir, I do," said Cullis. The other visitors grunted agreement. "But we would not asperse the Act with such a description as you put on it."

"I have not aspersed it, sir. I have described it. In the description lies the aspersion." Before any of his visitors could reply, Hugh asked, "How would you expect to profit from such a usurpation, gentlemen? Perhaps, Mr. Cullis, you still expect to be appointed to a Governor's Council. And you, Mr. Vishonn? Perhaps the Crown would see its way to recognizing your claims."

The planter looked at the floor. Cullis looked away. "Our loyalty would be our reward, sir," he said, "*and* it would be rewarded."

Hugh stopped pacing, and his glance fell on the caricature that his father and Dogmael Jones had placed in British newspapers years ago that satirized the Stamp Act, pinned to the wall beneath the framed collective portrait of the Society of the Pippin. Cullis had helped him distribute copies of it in Williamsburg during the Stamp Act debates. "Doubtless, a loyalty rewarded with bones, table scraps, and a pat on the head."

Cullis's face grew red and he shot up out of his chair.

Hugh shook his head in warning. "Do not challenge me to swords or pistols, sir! I did not invite you here! If anyone is offended by words spoken here, it is I! Every one of you shames the name of Virginia! You are all moved by a Brunswick stew of compromise, fear, and practicality!" Unbidden, but welcome nonetheless, a phrase from long ago flashed through Hugh's mind, a phrase employed by Patrick Henry in his speech for the Resolves and directed against those men in the House who sat in fear of the Crown. He added with derisive calmness, "I am surprised that none of you has donned the livery of menials. That would be your proper attire."

Carver Gramatan also rose. "I have had enough!" he said to Vishonn and Cullis. "I warned you it would be useless to come here!" He collected his hat and stormed out of the study.

Sheriff Tippet took a tentative step forward and gestured in supplication with a hand. "Sir, we have only come here to invite you to sit on the committee. You are respected throughout the county, and your presence on the committee would serve to, well..." Tippet stood there, at a loss for words.

Hugh grinned devilishly, and glanced at Vishonn and Cullis. "Serve as a dollop of 'moderation,' perhaps, Mr. Tippet?" He saw in Vishonn's and Cullis's expressions memory of the day, years ago, when they had called on him here to persuade him to run for burgess. "These gentlemen know too well the consequences of such an invitation. You see them all about you now. I must take some credit for them." He smiled at Sheriff Tippet. "Invite me at your own risk, sirs."

Vishonn sighed and rose to stand with Cullis. "We are done here, sirs. Thank you, Mr. Kenrick, for your time." He put on his hat and moved to the door. Cullis, Tippet, and Corbin followed. Cullis turned, however, and said, "Mr. Kenrick, you have rejected an invitation to help bring order to this county. We must now extend it to Reverend Acland."

Hugh scoffed. "My alternate offends me, as well, Mr. Cullis, but I am sure he will prove worthy and eager company."

The door closed behind the visitors. Hugh watched them through his window as they climbed onto their mounts and rode off.

*My world is unraveling,* he thought, *and that is my doing, as well.*

\*   \*   \*

Jared Hunt.

He had obtained the name by drawing into idle talk the housekeeper of Morland Hall, Susanah Giddens, when he encountered her outside Lucas Rittles's shop in Caxton. "That's what my husband Dorsey said the devil said, Mr. Cullis. He was on the porch with my mistress, Mrs. Frake, in earshot of everything that was said then. Jared Hunt, inspector of the Customs." That was in June of last year, a week after the Customsmen had been turned away from rummaging Morland Hall for contraband. Edgar Cullis had written down the name, and had since entered into a correspondence with the man.

Although it was not he who had initiated the correspondence. He had received a short letter from Jared Hunt some weeks after the incident, congratulating him on his loyalty to His Majesty, to Lord Dunmore, and to the Crown, and describing him as a man of "staunchly principled character, standing alone in the yammering company of misfits and miscreants otherwise nowadays called the House of Burgesses. You are to be pitied and applauded. Your servant and steadfast ally, Mr. Jared Hunt, Inspector Extraordinary of the Customs and Revenue, Hampton."

Cullis could neither imagine how the fellow had secured his name, nor how Hunt knew so much about his allegiances and standing in the House. He did not know that Hunt had patronized the Gramatan Inn often since last summer, and made a mercenary friend of Mary Griffin, the serving wench there, paying her genuine coin for information about the town's business. He had not met the man, but a cordial exchange of pleasantries had led to his supplying Mr. Hunt with information about the county's more rambunctious inhabitants. It was quite easy and safe, he thought; they were simply names he passed on to another name, one conveniently far away.

Two evenings after the fruitless and infuriating visit to Meum Hall to enlist Hugh Kenrick on the committee of safety, an hour or so before supper, that name called on him at home. Cullis was not sure he liked it. Mr. Hunt exuded power in his tall, stocky body, and sly ruthlessness in his black marble eyes. The contrast between his own tall, lithesome figure and Hunt's was overwhelming. His immediate impression was that Hunt could double him over with just a light punch to his stomach. The black eyes were watchful and appraising. He felt transparent and helpless in the man's presence.

But he welcomed the visitor into his office on the other side of Cullis Hall, away from his father's, and ordered a pitcher of punch from the kitchen. "To what do I owe this call, sir?" he asked when they were both settled in chairs.

"Sociability, Mr. Cullis," answered Jared Hunt. "Mere sociability. We have written each other for so long, I thought it about time we met. Also, I wish to inform you of my activities. I will not stay long."

"Your activities?"

"Yes. Not long ago I paid a call on His Excellency, Governor Dunmore, in Norfolk, where he is busy assembling a fleet of vessels to police that part of the Roads. I have obtained from him what one might call a special letter of marque to better police the York River to ensure the loyalty of its denizens, and to conduct affairs to my own, to his, and the Crown's satisfaction."

Cullis shook his head. "You are with the Customs, Mr. Hunt, not with the navy. I don't understand."

Hunt chuckled. "You are right, sir. His Excellency has no authority over my immediate employer, but I thought it best to secure his sanction, so there would be no conflict between us in the future. After all, we pursue the same end. He was amenable to my proposed arrangement, almost to a fault. A harried person he is, with a book of grievances as thick as the Bible."

A servant knocked on the office door then and came in with a tray holding glasses and a pitcher. The man poured Cullis and Hunt glasses from the pitcher, then left the room.

After they had each tasted the punch, Cullis asked, "How will you police the York, Mr. Hunt?"

"With a vessel that must be envied by His Excellency. The *Sparrowhawk.*" He paused when he saw the look of surprise on his host's face.

"You should not be so astounded, sir. Thanks to your vigilance, I had an excuse to seize it as it came down the Bay from Baltimore. I intercepted it with our own *Basilisk*. The *Sparrowhawk* now flies the Customs jack."

"The *Basilisk*?" queried Cullis. "What an evil name!" For a reason he could only vaguely grasp, he thought the name suited his visitor, as well.

"Isn't it, though? My idea! Formerly the *Nassau*, a sloop seized for irregularities in commerce, some time ago, and since converted to Crown purposes. She has not sailed these parts much, so I can appreciate your ignorance of her. Eight guns, eight swivels, and wonderfully crewed. The *Sparrowhawk*? Twenty guns, four swivels. Old and a bit creaky, but serviceable. I understand she was to be retired by her owners in one or two years, and broken up for parts. Seen her best days, she has, but I'll squeeze a few more from her." Hunt took another sip of his punch and continued. "Captain Geary and half his crew were dismissed. It is now mastered by a loyal fellow from Norfolk, Buell Tragle, whose merchant sloop was appropriated by His Excellency in exchange for a promissory note."

"On what grounds did you seize the *Sparrowhawk*, Mr. Hunt?"

Hunt shrugged. "I have sent the necessary paperwork to the Admiralty Court in Halifax, charging Captain Geary and the vessel with aiding and abetting sedition and treason against the Crown. For having transported Mr. Frake and his 'volunteers,' of course. Many thanks for the information! Hope he found the affair in Boston interesting. With luck, fatal. On the vessel I found not only illicit cargo laded in Baltimore, but a secret compartment containing all the instruments for forging and counterfeiting Crown documents. A pair of fellows in it were in the midst of manufacturing false documents to present to the navy here and to our Customsmen." He laughed once and shook his head. "Quite amazing that the business was not discovered years sooner! We found false cockets some thirty years old, and even a handbook of forged official signatures of men who must have gone to their final reward some time during the last war! All hanging offenses, you know!"

They talked more. Hunt dwelt on the adventures of Lord Dunmore. "He persuaded the captain of the *Fowey* some days ago to sail up to Porto Bello downriver from here to determine the disposition of his lodge. The servants still there fixed them a fine dinner, but towards the end of it an alarm was raised about approaching horsemen coming to arrest His Excellency. Throwing dignity to the winds, he and the good captain scurried to the longboat that put them ashore and were rowed back to the safety of the

*Fowey.* The horsemen contented themselves with the arrest of two of Captain Montague's crew who were left behind."

A servant knocked on the door and came in to announce supper. Cullis was obliged to ask Hunt if he would stay for it.

Hunt shook his head. "Thank you, sir, but it was not my intention to intrude on your repast." He leaned closer to Cullis and confided, "Besides, I know that you and your father are at odds over many important matters. My presence at your table would create an awkwardness, once he knew my business."

Cullis's curiosity got the best of him. "How would you know that, Mr. Hunt?"

Hunt cocked his head. "People talk, Mr. Cullis. Times, I think it's half my business, listening and sifting through people's twaddle! Mr. Gramatan's, for instance. I have exchanged a few missives with him, as well. And others." Hunt rose and snapped on his hat. "Well, I leave you now, sir. I was certain I would find a visit with you most edifying. I will spend the night at Mr. Gramatan's hostelry." He made to go, then stopped. "Oh, I must ask this: Did Mr. Kenrick agree to grace your committee of safety with his presence and wisdom?"

"No, sir. He did not."

"I didn't think he would make such a concession." Hunt grinned. "But, I believe the good reverend did?"

Cullis nodded. "With alacrity, sir."

"Excellent! A committee solidly patriotic, with no chance of a division lurking in its ranks! It pleases me more than you can imagine that you and the others have acted on my suggestion to form such a governing council! Well, good night to you, sir! Thank you for the punch! Please, attend to your supper. I will see myself out!"

Edgar Cullis stood at his desk and listened to Jared Hunt let himself out of the house. He did not think he liked the man. He felt foolish and superfluous. For some reason, he felt that he had just been patted on the head. "What a presumptuous, patronizing intriguer!" he thought.

And he could not think of a reason why Hunt had called on him, other than to pat him on the head. But he silently cursed, not his departed visitor, but Hugh Kenrick.

# Chapter 10: The Words

There was no question in Lord Dunmore's mind that, as in the past, his office gave him broad authority over naval vessels stationed in the Virginia waters of Chesapeake Bay. The Admiralty seemed to demur that authority, and by implication, the Crown, as well, for the Crown was not entirely pleased with the Governor's actions. Shortly after his misadventure at Porto Bello, the *Mercury*, a 20-gun frigate, arrived with orders from Admiral Graves in Boston for the infamous *Fowey* to proceed to that town. Captain George Montague of the *Fowey* must have breathed relief, for he was tiring of serving as the Governor's ferryman. So must have Captain Edward Foy, the Governor's personal secretary, who promptly resigned his post and departed with his wife on the *Fowey*, first sending to a Council member an incriminating letter in which he dwelt on his former employer's dubious character and actions.

Dunmore almost immediately made an implacable enemy of John McCartney, captain of the *Mercury*, by attempting to issue orders to him as he had to Captain Montague. The *Mercury*'s captain made it clear that he reported to Admiral Graves alone. The Governor had had to transfer his office and staff to the *Mercury*, but McCartney let it be known that it was on his sufferance that the Governor resided there. The captain's lack of deference and ostensive insubordination so infuriated Dunmore that he wrote a blistering letter of condemnation to Admiral Graves, who subsequently relieved McCartney of duty. Throughout the remainder of that summer and into the fall, Lord Dunmore made few friends and a multitude of enemies.

Many Virginians knew the story of King Midas, who turned to gold everything he touched. They began to say of Governor Dunmore that he was a demi-king; anything he touched was rendered worthless, or destroyed. "He has declared war on his own subjects, and is resolved to rule, even if it is as sovereign of a desolate and hostile land," commented a letter writer in a *Virginia Gazette*. Richard Henry Lee, a delegate for Virginia to the Continental Congress, when he read of Dunmore's depredations in Virginia, wrote a correspondent that if George the Third's ministers "had searched through the world for a person best fitted to ruin their cause, and procure union and success for these colonies, they could not have found a more complete agent than Lord Dunmore."

On July 17, the first day of the Virginia convention in Richmond, and a few days after he was visited by the county "committee of safety," Hugh Kenrick decided that he needed to devote some time to reflection in his study, to read and to think, as a respite from the more immediate demands of Meum Hall. He wished to find an answer to why so many men refused to acknowledge the tyranny that they were willing to tolerate — indeed, become partners with — why they would accept it as a normal state of affairs. He suspected that fear alone could not account for the phenomenon.

He had before him copies of Samuel Johnson's two latest political tracts, *The Patriot* and *Taxation No Tyranny*, given to him by his father when he was in England. His father had added his own disparaging remarks in them as marginalia. One concerned the matter of Johnson having been paid by the government to write the pamphlets. "It would seem that the pension that Dr. Johnson has collected for so many years must now be earned. Perhaps, instead, *repaid*? I never quite believed that his *Dictionary*, worthy enterprise that is was, alone had raised him in official esteem."

In rereading the pamphlets, Hugh marveled at what he deemed the "mental gymnastics" that Johnson performed to assert that Americans had no grounds for opposing Parliamentary sovereignty over the colonies. Or *sophistry*, he thought, recalling the day long ago when he inadvertently discovered it in a defense of reason against subterfuge. His tutor then had congratulated him on that discovery. Johnson opposed slavery; this he knew. But he could not understand how the man could not likewise oppose colonial slavery. Was the scale of its cunning yet outlandish subtlety beyond his grasp? Or did he condone it, but clothe it in the rubrical sackcloth of "due deference"?

On impulse, he penned a note to Edgar Cullis, whom he knew also owned a copy of the *Taxation* pamphlet, and quoted Johnson from it against that other Virginian's preference for tyranny.

"If you would do me the courtesy of perusing your copy of his tract, you will see that Dr. Johnson employs in it an observation by Fontenelle, that if twenty philosophers shall resolutely deny that the presence of the sun makes the day, he will not despair but whole nations may adopt the opinion. Perhaps, sir," Hugh wrote, "you and your fellows on the committee labor at the same set of oars, and move on the same premise, that many submitting to the same opinion creates an impregnable truth. I can imagine that in some faraway day, an embittered Machiavellian writer will compose a fable in which your descendents in mind may also allow themselves to be convinced that tyranny is freedom, that subjugation to a sovereign's will is the natural, preferred, and happiest condition of men, and persuaded that a trained and forcibly educated purblind rejection of the truth is a distinguishing mark of eternal wisdom and practical sagacity.

"But, be warned, sir: The reality of things will inevitably and inexorably intrude, regardless of the heat and sincerity of one's submission, and painfully lance such tumorous fantasies, leaving their expedient subscribers in a rueful state worse than that known by the truly ignorant. Tyrants, you must own, are oblivious or indifferent to the consequences of their actions; to them *force* is the universal corrective. One's submission to it can only be rewarded by them with the arrogant, audacious salve of allowing one to continue one's own life, a thing that was never theirs to grant or give, covet, own, or expend. When *those* truths are set in men's minds as indisputably eternal, then the revolution we are witnessing today will be deemed by future chroniclers as but a prelude or overture to a greater one."

A thought sped through Hugh's mind then, too swift for him to arrest and consider. For a reason he could only at first suspect, he glanced up at the collective portrait of the Pippins on the wall across from his desk, his sight resting on the figure of Glorious Swain. Then he remembered the task that wonderful man had assigned him, of knowing what he was, and finding its name.

He reread the note, signed it, and asked Rupert Beecroft to copy it to the letter book, then have a servant take the note to Cullis Hall.

He thought there was a clue to Johnson's rejection of the truth of the crisis to be found in other of the man's works. Hugh took down his copy of Johnson's *Shakespeare*, and reread the Preface to it.

"In the writings of other poets, a character is too often an individual; in those of Shakespeare it is commonly a species....The theater, when it is under any other direction, is peopled by such characters as were never seen, conversing in a language which was never heard, upon topics which will never arise in the commerce of mankind...." Shakespeare, wrote Johnson, created characters recognizable by the people, "with so much ease and simplicity, that it seems scarcely to claim the merit of fiction, but to have been gleaned by diligent selection out of common conversation and common occurrences....Shakespeare has no heroes; his scenes are occupied only by men, who act and speak as the reader thinks that he should himself have spoken or acted on the same occasion; even where the agency is supernatural, the dialogue is level with life. Other writers disguise the most natural passions and most frequent of incidents so that he who contemplates them in the book will not know them in the world...."

What a dreary perspective on men and the world! thought Hugh. It allowed no place for moral ambition, neither in life, nor in art, only a humble, itinerate acceptance of things and men as they are! What tragic nonsense! What cowardice! What a litany of accommodation! He thought of *Hyperborea*. I have always known the characters in that novel, and in the world! They converse in a language I have always heard, on topics more familiar to me than food, and are moved by passions to create occurrences that ought to be the common level of life! They are a measure of what one should have spoken or done on so many occasions, and *have been* spoken, and *have been* done! They are in the world, speaking and acting today!

And Hugh Kenrick suddenly realized that he was one of them. He sat in quiet astonishment at the fact, and knew that he was closer to fulfilling Glorious Swain's task.

He thought next of Edgar Cullis, who was once a friend. And of Reverdy, who was once his wife. While his mind lingered briefly on Reverdy, he put her and Cullis out of his mind, because there were Dogmael Jones and Jack Frake. And John Proudlocks. And so many men now, men he did not know, but whose words he had read; and those he did know, such as Patrick Henry, men who were rising up to claim their original rights, to overturn or reject a corrupt political system guilty of an enormous abuse!

Hugh laughed to himself for the first time in weeks. He remembered those words well, spoken by Dr. Johnson himself, when he and Dogmael Jones overheard them in a London tavern. What ironic justice! he thought. What gross contradictions in the man's art and politics! He almost felt a compulsion to write the man a letter and point them out to him.

Yes, thought Hugh. There was much to object to in Johnson's Preface, and in much of his writing, as well. He disagreed with the critic's appraisal of Shakespeare, but conceded his observation that Shakespeare had dispensed with the three unities of drama before they had even been invented.

It was as he tossed aside Johnson's pamphlets that he gasped. The thought shot home in his consciousness and seemed to lighten his very existence, causing him to rise suddenly from the chair as he made the sound. Of course! he thought. The great arguments for liberty, for life, for freedom, rested on one great necessary truth: that one must source oneself, for everything else to have any meaning! God had nothing to do with it. The Corpus Mysticum of royal sovereignty had nothing to do with it. Nor Parliament. Nor even the Congress in Philadelphia. That was the truth which the Congress must recognize when it someday convenes to establish a just and lasting polity, as surely it will convene.

Hugh stood still and retraced the trail in his mind that had led him to the revelation. Why, he had nearly said it himself in his note to Edgar Cullis! "...*One's own life, a thing that was never theirs to grant or give, covet, own, or expend....*"

After a moment, he realized that he was standing, and that he held his hands out, balled into fists, as though he were holding the idea in them, so that it would never escape him again. He glanced again up at the image of Glorious Swain. *You knew then the form of the question, but not of its answer, nor did I,* he addressed the memory. *I wish you were alive to hear the answer!* Hugh smiled in salute to the man and the memory.

There was a letter from his sister Alice, and one from his mother. The letters must have arrived shortly before he returned to Caxton. At least the mail packets were still sailing. After he read the letters, he rose from the desk and strode from his study to the breezeway, and then outside. He stepped off the porch, closed his eyes, and turned his head up to let the sun beat down on it. He felt younger, and more vital. The miasma of dread, regret and distress that had governed his thoughts and actions ever since he departed England months ago had suddenly evaporated, and blood seemed to run more quickly through his veins. He stood and watched his tenants reassemble the repaired conduit in the distance. He was sensible to nothing then but the glory of being alive.

He heard hooves pounding to his left, and turned to see Obedience Robbins, Jack Frake's business agent, riding towards the great house from the town. Robbins saw him and reined his mount around in Hugh's direction. Then the man stopped, but did not dismount. Hugh did not like the look of urgency in the man's face.

"Good morning, Mr. Robbins," said Hugh. "Is there a problem?" He paused. "Have you heard from Mr. Frake?"

"Sir," said the business agent, "Mr. Frake has been back a day or so! He is in Sheriff Tippet's jail!"

"What?"

"He was arrested this morning, by Sheriff Tippet and Mr. Roane. He is to be charged with treason!"

"By whom?"

"The new committee of safety, sir!"

Hugh pointed a finger at Robbins. "Accompany me, sir, while I find a mount."

\*     \*     \*

As Hugh saddled a horse in the stable and as they rode from Meum Hall to Caxton, Robbins related to Hugh what had happened. "He has been back a day, sir. The Company came down from West Point on a schooner, and were put ashore at the old Otway place. Then they marched to Morland, where Mr. Frake dismissed the men, who returned by the Hove Stream Road to their homes. Mr. Frake was more tired than I had ever seen him, but the first thing he did was read his mail. There was a letter from Mrs. Frake, you see, that he knew would be there. I asked him about Boston, and he said it was a terrible affair. And Jude Kenny, and several men, were lost in it. And as they marched back here from Massachusetts, they were harassed by loyalist bands, too. He asked me about some plantation business, then he retired to his quarters. This morning Sheriff Tippet and Mr. Roane arrived with a warrant from the court. Some armed men from Mr. Vishonn's militia were with them. It was all by order of the committee. Sheriff Tippet put cuffs on Mr. Frake, took him away on a mount from his stable."

"Why did you not come to me sooner with this news?" Hugh demanded.

"Mr. Hurry and I have been endeavoring to persuade Sheriff Tippet to release Mr. Frake on bail or bond. I have just come from the jail. But the committee, Sheriff Tippet says, will not grant either. He has been instructed to hold Mr. Frake indefinitely, until a special court can sit." Robbins paused. "We think Reverend Acland is behind it, sir. He is on the committee. You know what the Reverend thinks of Mr. Frake."

"Too well, Mr. Robbins. Did Mr. Frake send you for me?"

"No, sir. Mr. Hurry and I just thought you might be able to do something."

The Caxton jail was a separate brick structure on the side of Sheriff Tippet's house. It contained three contiguous cells, each six feet wide and deep. A high-walled yard enclosed the cell doors. Each door had a trap at the bottom, through which Muriel Tippet, the Sheriff's wife, fed prisoners, usually leftovers from the Tippets' own meals. The doors also had barred openings at head height. Each cell contained a plank bed and a chair. The floors were dirt covered with straw.

When they arrived, they saw Sheriff Tippet standing with William Hurry, Morland's steward, and George Roane, the under-sheriff, at the gate to the jail yard. Hugh dismounted, tethered his mount to a post, and walked furiously up to Tippet, forgetting that Robbins was with him.

Tippet saw the murderous look in Hugh's face and braced himself as though he expected to be struck. Before Hugh could say anything, the sheriff said, "It wasn't my doing, Mr. Kenrick! The committee voted on it, and I against it, but Mr. Cullis signed a court warrant, and there's the gun that used to stand here that's missing, too; it's county property, and I cannot —"

"I wish to see Mr. Frake, Mr. Tippet," was all that Hugh said.

"Of course, sir," said Tippet, hurriedly taking a ring of keys from his belt. He turned nervously to unlock the yard gate, then led Hugh inside to one of the cell doors. The other men followed them.

Tippet stopped before the door. Hugh glanced at him. "Open it, please."

Tippet sighed and unlocked the cell door.

Hugh saw Jack Frake sitting on the plank bed. One of his ankles was manacled with a chain to the cell wall. The chain was long enough to allow him to move around, even outside to the yard. He wore a frock coat — the very one Hugh had seen him wear the morning he departed for Boston on the *Sparrowhawk* — and his hat sat on the bed beside him.

Jack Frake looked at the men who stood at the door. He saw Hugh Kenrick and smiled. It was not the smile of a man who was glad to see a friend. The gray eyes were fixed on the master of Meum Hall, somber, critical, and wondering.

Hugh Kenrick sensed that something was terribly wrong other than that Jack Frake was sitting in jail. He stepped inside the cell. "Leave us alone, please."

The other men moved back into the yard. Tippet closed the door, leaving it ajar.

"Jack," said Hugh as he stood in front of the prisoner, "I'm getting you out of here. I'll pledge my property as bail or bond, if necessary. And if they won't accept that, I'll demolish these walls to free you, even if it means killing Tippet or anyone else who stands in my way! Cullis, Vishonn, anyone!"

Jack Frake looked up at his friend with sadness and nodded.

Hugh came and sat on the bed beside him. He remembered the time when Jack Frake had once called on him, the evening of the day in Williamsburg he had lied to save Patrick Henry's resolves.

Hugh studied Jack's demeanor. "It must have been terrible, Jack. Charlestown, I mean."

"It was terrible," answered Jack Frake. "But necessary. We fought well. The Sons of Liberty gave a good account of themselves." He permitted himself a chuckle. "We're not all pen and paper," he mused, recalling Colonel Stark's compliment. "We were the only Virginians there."

"Jude Kenny," said Hugh. "He was killed?"

Jack Frake nodded. He pronounced the names of seven other men in the Company who had died. "Two on the way back, in Maryland. We were ambushed by loyalists. Drove them off. The war is in full tilt, Hugh. There's no going back. The Congress might try to, so I hear...." He shook his head and let the sentence trail off.

"Mr. Proudlocks," asked Hugh. "He is all right? And Jock Fraser?"

"They came through without a scratch. They're home. Cletus and Travis, too. A ball grazed Will Kenny's violin arm. We found a surgeon at Cambridge who patched it up. He had hoped to be buried beside his brother, when the time came. But we had to leave Jude behind on the field." Jack Frake paused, then rose and paced once in front of his friend. The chain of the manacle dragged noisily through the straw. "Hugh, you may not want to post bail for me, or kill anyone, except me, when you hear what I have to tell you."

Hugh frowned. It was not like his friend to give warning about what he was about to say. He would simply say what was on his mind, and let his listeners wrestle with the words.

"What?" asked Hugh.

"Your friend Roger Tallmadge is dead, as well. I killed him, during the third assault, as we were retreating up the hill."

Hugh sat still. He asked softly, "I don't understand, Jack."

"He was there, Hugh." Jack Frake refused to say more, refused to justify himself, or explain the circumstances. He stood looking down on his friend, his gray eyes cruel and waiting.

Hugh sat and tried to absorb the news. He remembered Roger's last letter. He tried to speak, but his tongue and lips seemed frozen. After a moment, he managed to whisper hoarsely, "How?"

"He was leading a charge to drive us up the hill. I aimed at his heart and shot him."

"Did you know... it was him?"

"Not until it was too late."

After another long moment, Hugh asked, "Did he know...it was you?"

"I think so." Jack Frake seemed to relent. "He faced it bravely, if that is any consolation to you. I know that much. And that he died instantly."

"He was waiting to go home," said Hugh, more to himself than to Jack Frake. "He was detained there because he chose to defend your home from the Customsmen, Jack. He could have been court-martialed for that. He did not want to be there...."

"He was there, Hugh. He paid the price for aiding the Crown in our conquest. He could have resigned his commission. He couldn't both sympathize with our cause, and help to crush it, too." Jack Frake added, after a pause, "He was the enemy."

"He was my...brother."

"Am I still yours?"

Hugh did not answer.

"Think what you wish, Hugh," said Jack Frake with a sigh of finality. "I don't regret having killed him. Only that he was your friend."

Hugh rose abruptly, brushed blindly past Jack Frake, and left the cell. He did not stop to speak with the men waiting in the yard. He mounted his horse and rode off at a gallop. Citizens on Queen Anne Street who saw the horseman speeding toward them stepped lively out of his way.

# Chapter 11: The Counselors

He sat in the sand near the Meum Hall pier, leaning against a boulder on the beach beneath the bluff. He had ridden here from Caxton because he could not bear to see anyone else. On one hand, he was ashamed of himself for having fled the jail; on the other, he was frankly angry with Jack Frake. He did not then trust himself in the man's presence. He was more than angry, he admitted to himself; a peculiar kind of rage had welled up in him when the fact of Roger Tallmadge's death found a place in his mind. He had wanted to strike Jack Frake. But the violence of that action was stayed by a violent revulsion for committing it on such a man.

The rage still gripped him, a rage as hot and glowing as an iron bar from Henry Zouch's forge. And in the seething turmoil of his emotions he found time and energy to shed some tears for Roger Tallmadge. He was torn between grieving for his friend, and smashing everything in his path.

But now, Jack Frake's words kept resounding in his thoughts: *He was the enemy....He was there....I killed him...I aimed at his heart and shot him....He was the enemy....He was the enemy....*

He knew he should adopt a greater vision of the matter. But the pain was as shattering as what he felt when his friends the Pippins all perished, and Glorious Swain, and Dogmael Jones. And when he knew he had lost Reverdy, once and for all. The pain of loss, and the cruelty of the circumstances of Roger's death, would not let him think clearly. He knew he must. He sat forward and covered his face with his hands. His world was unraveling. Could he forgive Jack Frake? Could he forgive his own friendship with Roger? Could he forgive Reverdy, or himself for his marriage to her? The sounds of insects, and birds, and the river breezes gradually faded from his consciousness as Hugh Kenrick reached down to the depths of his soul in a desperate effort to quench the heat of the rage.

After a timeless moment, he felt a presence near him. Startled, he glanced up and saw that John Proudlocks had appeared and was sitting beside him, resting back against the boulder. Hugh did not know how long he had been there. His friend held the stem of a licorice plant in one hand and was casually chewing on it. His mount was tethered to a post of the pier, together with his own mount. Proudlocks tossed the licorice stem aside and smiled at Hugh with an oddly lighthearted solemnity.

"I recognized your friend before Jack did, on that hill in Charlestown," said Proudlocks without greeting or preamble. "I was certain something like this would happen, once we returned. I have known it for many years." He paused. "Mr. Hurry came to tell me about Jack, after you left the jail. I have spoken with Jack."

When Hugh looked away and did not respond, Proudlocks said, "The gorget you gave him in Yorktown that morning saved his life, for I am sure the ball that struck it would have found his heart, instead, just as Jack's shot found your friend's. You ought to ask him to show the thing to you. I know him well enough that he will not offer to show it himself. You know he is not a boastful man. A British ball struck the hilt of his scabbard, too, smashing the catch and trapping his sword. Not that he ever had a chance to use it, that awful day. There is also a ball hole in the left cuff of the coat he wore then. He did not notice it until I pointed it out to him."

Hugh remained silent. Proudlocks continued. "I am fond of you and Jack both, my friend, but I am fonder of him, for he gave me life. I will tell you about that someday. I do not ask you to find it in your heart to forgive him. I ask you to find it in your mind, for I have observed this in both of you and in others, and even in myself: that which resides in the heart, must first be sired in the mind." He paused, and smiled in reflection. "He is a unique man, Mr. Kenrick. So many others carelessly shipwreck themselves on the rock of his soul. Others see the danger, and come about to flee before their own fragile souls are ruptured on its unyielding strength. I am not sure this is the right word for what he is, or what he possesses — a *soul*. Perhaps it is his spirit, or character."

For some reason, Proudlocks's presence was reassuring and tempering. Hugh had always envied the man's infectious tranquility. "A spirit, or a soul, or a character," he mused out loud, speaking slowly, choosing his words, and he spoke more to himself than for his companion's benefit, "is a man's cargo of virtues, uniquely and singularly framed." He was staring at the patch of water near the pier, where Reverdy had stood and waited for him to come to her, a long time ago. He was thinking of her words, and why she had rejected him, twice.

Proudlocks laughed. "Ah! You must settle on a genus among so many examples, but there is a definition not to be found in Mr. Johnson's *Dictionary*! My compliments, my friend!" He paused. "Do not flee him, Mr. Kenrick. It was important to Jack that he told you about Captain Tallmadge."

Hugh glanced at Proudlocks, and thought, "He needn't have." And just as he thought it, he glanced away swiftly in self-rebuke. He knew that Jack Frake was incapable of deceit or cowardice.

But Proudlocks seemed to read the thought, and shook his head. "You slander his character with the thought, my friend. And belittle yourself. Jack is no false cambist. He wishes you to remain his friend, on honest and frank terms, as you have always been. He credits you with so much, Mr. Kenrick. As do I. Please credit him with...what is that wonderful word I encountered lately in Mr. Burke's *The Sublime and Beautiful?*... yes, credit him with the rectitude."

"Roger represented my youth, Mr. Proudlocks." Hugh was thinking out loud, and back to all the people who had abruptly vanished from his life. Hulton. Reverdy. Dogmael Jones. And now Roger. "We were brothers."

Proudlocks sighed. "Many things will perish in the days ahead of us — brothers, friends, and friendships. It is an entailing risk. These are terrible but needful times." He frowned. "I know that you considered Captain Tallmadge your brother, Mr. Kenrick, and that you shared with him a fruitful childhood. Just as I consider Jack my brother, for the same reason. But, between Jack and Captain Tallmadge, which man would you choose as a greater sibling in spirit to you? You must decide that."

After a while, Hugh asked, "Did *he* ask you to see me?"

"No," answered Proudlocks. "He merely related the substance of your last meeting."

"They want to try him for treason, Mr. Proudlocks. That means a hanging."

Proudlocks laughed in dismissal of the idea. "He will not be available long enough for them to read him the charge."

"Does it not trouble you to see him chained to a wall, as though he were a common horse thief?"

Proudlocks shrugged. "It troubled me, at first, when I saw him like that, but not overly so." He smiled again. His smile was disarming. Hugh could never resist it. "He will be free again."

He did not elaborate. He seemed to reach a decision about Hugh, and rose. "Well, I must go to visit a friend." He slapped Hugh on a shoulder once. "Yes, Mr. Kenrick. Your gorget saved his life. You would do well to think of its inscription. It will save yours, too." And without further word he walked away to mount his horse. Then he rode back up the rolling road of Meum Hall and disappeared behind the trees.

Hugh turned around and stared into the distance. He asked himself: Did the pain and rage come from the loss of a friend, or because a friend had caused that loss?

And Proudlocks was right. In the end, which would be the greater loss? He knew he was not meant to shipwreck himself on the soul of Jack Frake.

He remembered the inscription on the gorget: *Sapere aude. Have the courage to use your own reason.* "Have the will to think," he mused, would be a better construction. Hugh Kenrick smiled. His tutors would have given him an argument about that translation, had he proposed it to one of them. He was remembering a day long ago and the words he had spoken then to Reverdy: *A mind can accrue honor, too, and carry its own colors, and be proud of its traditions and history...I am an ensign in our country's most important standing army — for how secure can a country be without its thinkers?* I am a thinker, and this is a new country.

Hugh Kenrick sobbed, then cried — in relief, because he had come so close to betraying that idea, but had not betrayed it, because he knew he could not; in joy, because he had betrayed neither himself, nor his past, nor all the wonderful things in it; in pride, because he was still the owner of his life and of all its glory.

*   *   *

Jared Hunt was suddenly and quite astonished with the scope of his power to plan and command, once he was given leave to act. He did not think he could return to his old role of being his patron the Earl of Danvers's secretary and factotum. Here before him, trying with only some success to repress their fear and dislike of him, were several men who were wealthier and formerly more powerful than he, sitting in guilty deference to his words and wishes.

"I shall seize Morland Hall in lieu of Mr. Frake's armed rebellion and treason," he announced to them. "In addition, there is the likelihood that he profited from the false documents produced by the *Sparrowhawk*'s captain. According to Mr. Geary, the former captain of that vessel was a John Ramshaw, now retired. I shall not pursue him, for that is not my object." He stopped to grin. "My object lesson is to impart, in no uncertain terms, to all who may be tempted to emulate him, or sympathize with him, that such behavior as Mr. Frake's will earn severe and final punishment for deceiving and defrauding the Crown and raising one's hand against it. I am not for deferring to judges and writs and such in the administration of justice in such matters, when the crime is so obvious."

Around a table inn a private room of the Swan Tavern in Yorktown, sat Jared Hunt, Edgar Cullis, Reverend Albert Acland, Reece Vishonn, Carver Gramatan, and Sheriff Cabal Tippet. It was two days after Jack Frake's arrest and incarceration. An exchange of notes by courier between Hunt in Hampton and Cullis in Caxton had caused the parties to agree to meet in the establishment, at Hunt's tactfully strenuous suggestion. He wished to apprise the committee of safety of his appreciation and plans.

"I tell you this so that you will not be troubled when the Customs sails up the York and our men appear in your town. When do you think you can dispose of Mr. Frake?"

"We are scheduling a special trial to take place in two days, Mr. Hunt," said Edgar Cullis.

Reece Vishonn volunteered, "He raised a militia company in defiance of my authority, Mr. Hunt. I am colonel of this county's lawful militia. Mr. Frake's independent company is no better than a vigilance band, organized around another illegal assembly, the Sons of Liberty. They absconded with county militia arms, powder, and equipment."

"Much of it was expended on that band's expedition to Boston," remarked Carver Gramatan.

Sheriff Tippet was tempted to interject, "And they fought with all those other rebel bands in Charlestown, a month ago." But he said nothing. Until Crown authority was restored in Williamsburg, he owed his position to Reece Vishonn and the authority of the county court.

"The hubris of him!" exclaimed Hunt. "He is deserving of the severest penalty! I shall see to it that his estate reimburses your county for the damages and costs. Excellent, gentlemen," said Hunt.

Reverend Acland spoke up. "Sir, when you seize Morland Hall, there is an important matter of my compensation."

Hunt nearly laughed at the idea. "Compensation? For what, dear sir?"

"You see, Mr. Hunt, for some time, years, in fact, Mr. Frake has been lax in paying our parish tithes. Neither the vestry nor the county court pressed him on the matter." Acland threw a reproving glance at Reece Vishonn, who was both a vestryman and a magistrate, and had recommended that Morland Hall not be dunned for the taxes. Vishonn glanced away and said nothing. "That negligence apparently was on the advice of another magis-

trate, the late Thomas Reisdale. Then there is the matter of Mr. Kenrick and
Meum Hall. Lord Kenrick is guilty of his own passel of offences. Through
some infernal legalistic trick he freed his slaves, removing them from our
right to lay tithes on them. He was explicitly exempted from tithes, also by
the vestry and court, and also on the advice of Mr. Reisdale."

Hunt frowned. "How could he free his slaves, Reverend? The law in
this colony is quite clear that he cannot."

"He accomplished it through some ruse with Quakers and the Earl of
Danvers. It was the Earl of Danvers who nominally owned them, and then
freed them, or sold them to a Quaker, who freed them. Perhaps it was the
other way round. The event caused a sensation here, but was never investigated." Acland paused. "Mr. Kenrick is a nephew of the Earl, so I understand. He is a baron."

For the first time in a long while, Hunt was speechless. He sat and
stared at the minister for a moment, then glanced around the table to the
others in silent question. All the men nodded in confirmation of the truth
of the minister's statement. Hunt remarked, "A baron, you say? Well, that
is not the same thing as an earl." He grunted once in amazement, and
looked at Cullis. "Well, sir, there is a bit of twaddle my informants neglected
to pass on to me."

For a moment, Jared Hunt forgot his company. What news this was! he
thought. He would write the Earl about it! Imagine what a frothy delirium
it would cause in the old bastard! Hunt wondered if the Earl's brother,
Garnet Kenrick, had had a hand in the ruse. Doubtless, he had. He wished
he could witness the bout between the brothers over that matter! What
entertainment that would be!

Cullis replied, "There is that matter of Reverend Acland's, sir, in addition to all the treasonous statements Mr. Kenrick has made in the House
about the Crown, and His Majesty." He paused. "If His Excellency the Governor could pronounce Patrick Henry an outlaw, I fail to see why Mr. Kenrick cannot likewise be so called. He has contributed mightily to the disaffection so evident in this colony. He has not merely spoken against the
Crown, but written seditious pamphlets, as well."

Hunt grinned. "I have read the literature, sir. I have plans for Mr. Kenrick. He has been known to me for years."

Cullis frowned in confusion. "How, sir?" He knew that the man had
appeared only recently in their lives.

"My secret," replied Hunt.

Cullis merely blinked in astonishment.

Carver Gramatan spoke up. "There are also Mr. Frake's cronies to consider, Mr. Hunt. Jock Fraser, who is a middling planter here. And that damned Indian, John Proudlocks. He inherited the late Mr. Reisdale's estate, in contravention of Virginia law. Both men accompanied Mr. Frake to Boston. It would be quite galling to allow them the freedom to stir up more disaffection."

"Will your committee deal with them?" asked Hunt.

"After we have dealt with Mr. Frake," said Cullis. "They will be similarly charged. When do you plan to seize Morland Hall, sir?"

"Soon after you have dealt with the man," answered Hunt. "We must be orderly about this, don't you think?"

"Of course," said Reece Vishonn. "Order, peace, and loyalty are our paramount concerns."

"Amen," said Reverend Acland.

"One last matter before we adjourn, gentlemen," said Hunt. "Mr. Vishonn — can your lawful militia be counted on to preserve that order, peace and loyalty?"

"Yes, sir. They are likewise content with Crown authority, and worry lest turmoil upset their lives and livelihoods. Many of them have confided that unless order is restored here, they will remove themselves to England, or Canada, or some other law-abiding venue."

"And welcome they would be there, if they must resort to that extremity!" chuckled Hunt. "However, we must all work to ensure that they needn't so trouble themselves. I think we share that determination, and I shall write His Excellency about — "

A man opened the door to the room and rushed in. It was George Roane, the under-sheriff. He removed his hat and worried the brim with nervous hands. "Excuse me, sirs, but I have…news."

"What?" demanded Hunt, displeased with the interruption.

Roane gulped and addressed Hunt. "I was guarding the jail, and Mrs. Tippet and Clemsy our servant was preparing a meal for Mr. Frake — "

"What *news*?" insisted Sheriff Tippet, alarmed by Roane's presence.

"Mr. Fraser, and Mr. Proudlocks, and several men came with arms and freed Mr. Frake! They took the keys from me and bound me and Clemsy and Mrs. Tippet up in the house! Not two hours ago! Then they rode off!" He glanced apologetically at his superior, Sheriff Tippet, and looked at the floor. "We shouted for help, but no one heard, sir. It took me an hour to loosen my ropes, and then I released Mrs. Tippet and Clemsy, and then I rode here straight away, where you said you'd be. They're in such a state! I am sorry, sir. But we was taken by surprise!"

"The scoundrels!" exclaimed Carver Gramatan.

"What evil audacity!" sputtered Reverend Acland.

Sheriff Tippet rose and confronted his subordinate. "Was Muriel harmed?" he asked about his wife.

"No, sir! Just affrighted. They took care to tie her up gentle like. Clemsy, too. With me, they weren't so gentle. Got rope burns on my wrists."

Edgar Cullis rose and asked, "Was Mr. Kenrick among those men, Mr. Roane?"

"No, sir," answered Roane, surprised that anyone should include the master of Meum Hall in the crime.

Jared Hunt clucked his tongue. He rose and looked sternly at his company. "Sirs, this is not good. I say that you see to your duties this very moment, while I see to mine."

"What duties, Mr. Hunt?" asked Reece Vishonn, startled by the news, but more perplexed by the meaning of Hunt's command.

Hunt took one last gulp from the tankard of ale in front of him, then picked up his hat and put it on. "Why, the duties of a committee of safety! Behave like one! Assert your authority! Recapture Mr. Frake, and find his friends, and lock them all up, and post a militia guard on them! If you can manage that, I will stay for the trial and hangings."

"And you, sir?" asked Cullis. "What will you do?"

"I am back to Hampton. And then I shall sail up to Caxton, to see that justice is done. If you people can't manage it, I certainly intend to." With that, the Inspector Extraordinary of the Customs turned and stalked out of the room.

# Chapter 12: The Words

On the day of Jack Frake's arrest and imprisonment, John Proudlocks rode from Meum Hall, first back to Caxton to call briefly on Lydia Heathcoate, the seamstress, to assure her that he was well, and then on to Jock Fraser's place, to organize with that man the rescue of Jack Frake. Until Proudlocks appeared on his plantation and roused him from a sound sleep, Fraser had been ignorant of his superior's arrest.

After Fraser finished cursing individually each member of the committee of safety, he calmed down enough to listen to Proudlocks's plan.

"It's a good plan, sir. And I know a farmer up at West Point who would take Jack in until things are cleared up."

"Good," said Proudlocks.

"And any man in the Company will help us in the work."

"This is true," answered Proudlocks. He sat in a rattan chair on the porch of Fraser's modest house, watching his host pace back and forth on the floorboards. He seemed to be waiting.

Then Fraser stopped and frowned in realization. "But, good God, man! If we do this, they'll lay the charge on us, as well! Have you thought of that?"

Proudlocks nodded. "It has occurred to me."

"We couldn't come home again! They'd come after us!"

Proudlocks cocked his head in concession. "They might," he said. "But, they might not, if the Company opposed them. I do not think Mr. Vishonn's new militia is either as numerous as our Company, or as eager or ready to fight." He raised a finger to make a point. "The two most powerful men on the committee are Mr. Cullis and Reverend Acland. They have an unsavory dislike of Mr. Frake, and wish to see him dead, or at least severely punished. Sheriff Tippet and Mayor Corbin are merely perpetuating their positions. I do not think their hearts are in the matter. Mr. Vishonn?" He shrugged in disgust. "He has fantasies of reclaiming his patents over the mountains, and reopening his mine, and reliving the ease of the past, all by grace of the Crown."

Fraser stood for a while to consider these observations. He asked, "Does Mr. Kenrick know? About Mr. Frake, that is?"

"Yes. And I believe he will approve of our action. But we must not implicate him in it. He must remain free." Proudlocks did not mention the contention between Hugh Kenrick and Jack Frake.

"Why?"

"To advise us of the enemy's doings. That enemy now, besides Governor Dunmore, is some of our own countrymen."

"But once the deed is done, sir, how can we stop the committee from harming us, or our property?"

"I shall compose a letter to be left on Mr. Cullis's and Mr. Vishonn's doorsteps, warning them that any action taken against us, or any further action taken against Mr. Frake, will invite…reciprocation. In it I shall assert that the sole legal power in this colony, given Governor Dunmore's abdication, now resides in the Virginia Convention, presently meeting in Richmond town, and that Mr. Vishonn's committee of safety is extralegal and will be held accountable for its actions, when order is restored here."

Fraser shook his head and sighed. "Sounds like anarchy, sir. No good can come from it, I'm afraid."

"I am afraid we are in a political…what is that word?…a political purgatory, until the Convention can assert its authority. We must defend ourselves the best we can until then."

Fraser hummed in concession of this point. "Have you informed Mr. Frake of this plan?"

Proudlocks shook his head. "No. I merely assured him that he will be free again. Sheriff Tippet was standing outside the door. Mr. Robbins and Mr. Hurry had been there, but Jack sent them home to await events and go about their business. It was Henry Buckle who told me what had happened. He had gone to town to purchase some wares. And it is Henry I shall send round with my letter." He paused. "I do not recommend that you go to town to see Jack. You might be arrested, as well."

"Why weren't you?"

Proudlocks laughed. "I am now Sheriff Tippet's attorney. And Mayor Corbin's. I inherited their affairs from Mr. Reisdale's practice. At least, they have regarded me as their attorney."

*   *   *

As the committee of safety rode back to Caxton, Reverend Acland, riding a mount loaned to him by Carver Gramatan from his inn stables — and who was surprised that the minister could ride at all — lectured the others on Hugh Kenrick. "You must concede that his offenses are as many and craven as Mr. Frake's. I have not seen a penny in tithe from him, either. He freed his slaves, in defiance of the law. He has frequently spoken treason in the Assembly, as Mr. Cullis can attest. He has written treasonous tracts. He has obstructed officers in the commission of their duties, thrice to my recollection. He attended that illegal assembly in New York some years ago, representing himself as a delegate from this colony, if I am not mistaken. He has never attended services in my church, in defiance of the law. He married a disreputable woman. And, I am certain that his prosperity flouts the legal precepts of fairness and equity. That has been his career in these parts. If the information provided me by my correspondents in England is to be credited, his career there can be described as no less than that of a renegade."

"We shall see justice done to him, as well, Reverend," said Edgar Cullis. "Have no fear. But, one renegade at a time, sir. We have limited means at our disposal, and it is a delicate situation."

Vishonn volunteered, "True enough! If it were not for Mr. Hunt's assurances and encouragement, we should not be able to act at all. We shall govern only on the sufferance of our county's citizens. We should do nothing that will provoke any resentment against us. We must be cautious."

"Once justice has been served on Mr. Frake," said Carver Gramatan, "there will be no question of the legitimacy of our authority. Prosecuting Mr. Frake may seem an outlandish and risky thing to do, but it will serve to establish our authority in the strongest terms. And, as you have just now pointed out, Mr. Vishonn, we will have the support of Mr. Hunt and his authority. I see few difficulties ahead of us."

"It must be impressed on both of them that there is a higher authority than their own reason and vaunted liberty," insisted the minister, who was still contemplating the fates of his two nemeses. "And on others, too. That authority is God, His Majesty, and Parliament, in that order."

Cullis frowned. The minister was beginning to annoy him. He said, "Dear sir, the committee must announce its authority and intentions. I propose that we leave it to you to compose that decree."

"It would be my pleasure, Mr. Cullis," replied Acland brightly. He smiled in anticipation of the task. Mayor Corbin, who was riding beside him, blinked in astonishment; no one in Caxton had ever seen the minister smile before.

The other men readily agreed to this proposal.

Cullis himself smiled. He recalled the note that Hugh Kenrick had sent him two days ago, a note that was pedantic and insulting in its implications. He turned to address the men riding behind him. "We are the sun, sirs, and shall decide when it is day and when it is night."

Reece Vishonn, who had read some books, suddenly and worriedly frowned as he remembered the story of Canute, the eleventh-century Danish king of England who, in a failed demonstration of his omnipotence, ordered the tides to cease. But he said nothing. He hoped most earnestly that the committee of safety would be exempted from such an embarrassing phenomenon. And, in lieu of the setback of Jack Frake's rescue from jail, he could only wonder at the attorney's levity.

Some hours later, the committee rode boldly into Caxton and visited the jail. Mrs. Tippet, who was left alone by George Roane and had armed herself with her husband's musket, immediately came out of her house and handed her husband a letter delivered by Henry Buckle not an hour before. Buckle, they knew, was John Proudlocks's cooper, and was not a member of the Company that went to Boston. When Sheriff Tippet opened and read the letter, he gasped and passed it on to Edgar Cullis, who in turn passed it around to his colleagues.

They immediately repaired to the Gramatan Inn for another meeting on what to do. After much loud and frustrating debate, they decided, in order to assert their authority, and on Carver Gramatan's suggestion, to close Steven Safford's tavern, noting that it harbored rebels and encouraged unlawful assemblies against the Crown. Safford's Arms was a less formidable foe than were Jack Frake and the Company. Sheriff Tippet volunteered that Safford had been late in paying the most recent tax assessments, as well.

"What about Fern's?" asked Gramatan, referring to a disreputable tavern close to the bluff that overlooked the riverfront.

"It is patronized by hands from the ships and the river trade and other low fellows," said Vishonn. "It is better to leave them some place to go, for otherwise your fine establishment here will be crowded with them, and we should be reluctant to favor you with our custom."

"Excellent point, sir," agreed Gramatan, liking not only the idea, but the way in which it was put.

And when Edgar Cullis and Reece Vishonn returned to their homes, they found letters waiting for them, as well, identical in wording to the one received by Tippet. All the letters had been signed by Jock Fraser and John Proudlocks, and challenged the authority of the Queen Anne County committee of safety.

\*     \*     \*

Hugh Kenrick refrained from returning to the Caxton jail, for John Proudlocks had alluded to some action he planned to set his friend free. When that would happen, and how, Hugh did not know. Presumably Jock Fraser would be a partner in that action, and men from the Queen Anne County Volunteer Company would probably join them.

He refrained also because Proudlocks had not invited him into the conspiracy. He could not fault the man for that. He wanted to see Jack again, and apologize to him. And he wanted to see Proudlocks again, to thank him.

It occurred to Hugh that whatever action Proudlocks took would put many county citizens in open conflict with each other over the committee of safety's precipitous assumption of authority, which was a dubious authority in the least. After all, he reflected, during his political career here, the county freeholders had almost always evenly divided themselves during the elections in their choice of burgesses between Edgar Cullis, the epitome of "moderation," and himself, the epitome of "radicalism."

For the moment, he contented himself with finishing a letter of condolence to his sister, Alice, about Roger's death. He had delayed writing it for two days, for he kept imagining the effect it would have on her. Not to mention on his and Alice's parents. He could not be certain that any fellow officer of Roger's in Boston had devoted time to the sorrowful duty.

He finished the letter, signed it, and added it to a pile of letters for Mr. Beecroft to enter into the letter book, then take to Safford's Tavern to await a mail courier. The others were to Otis Talbot and Novus Easley in Philadelphia, and another to a bookseller in New York, inquiring about some books he had ordered before he left for London half a year ago but which had not yet arrived.

For a moment, he sat at his desk, toying with his brass top. He wondered if Jack Frake had been freed from the Caxton jail yet. Then he rose, found the two letters from Roger, and put them inside a leather portmanteau. Then he searched for another sheet of paper, and smiled to himself for the first time in days. He put that in the portmanteau, as well. He left the study and strode outside to the stables.

Jack Frake was indeed home. Several armed men from the Company stood in a group near the porch of the great house. Their mounts were tethered together at one of the railings. The men doffed their hats in greeting to Hugh as he rode up. He returned the greeting, and added his mount to theirs.

Ruth Dakin, a servant, answered his knock. He asked to see her employer. She left him in the hallway and went to the study to announce his visit, and came back a moment later and escorted him into the study.

Jack Frake sat at his desk. Jock Fraser and John Proudlocks stood before it. All three turned to him when Hugh entered the room. They exchanged silent nods of greeting.

Proudlocks said to Jack Frake, "Jock will ask two men to stay here as guards. The others can go home. We must leave, as well, to see to our own business."

"Fine," said Jack Frake.

Proudlocks and Fraser left the room and the house. As the men passed by Hugh, Hugh said to Proudlocks, "Thank you for your thoughts this morning, sir." Proudlocks nodded in acknowledgement.

Through the study window Jack Frake and Hugh Kenrick watched the men collect their mounts and ride off.

When they were gone, Hugh turned to his friend and said, "I apologize for leaving you the way I did in the jail." He paused. "John found me later and reminded me of who I am."

Jack Frake smiled. "You would have remembered, in time, if he hadn't found you."

Hugh brought forward his portmanteau. "I wish you to read something. Letters from Roger. His last to me, from Boston. Please understand that I do not intend them to be an excuse for me, or a rebuke to you. I merely think you should read them." He paused. "And then I have something marvelous for you to see. Would you read his letters?"

Jack Frake nodded.

Hugh took the letters from the portmanteau and handed them to Jack over the desk. Then he sat down in a chair in front of the desk to wait.

Jack finished reading the letters, and looked up at Hugh. "I see. I suppose he was a good man, Hugh. Loyal, diligent, and not a shirker. But, he was at Charlestown." He put the letters aside. "I think that the war that is coming will claim many of his caliber." He handed the letters back over the desk to Hugh.

Jack Frake this time did not end with a note of regret. As he reclaimed the letters, it was then that Hugh fully appreciated Proudlocks's allusion to the man's rock-solid soul, and why so many had shipwrecked themselves on it, and hated him for it. It was then that Hugh fully grasped that Jack Frake was the best friend he could ever have — and ever had. All his past and dearest friends were from the old world. Jack Frake was of Hyperborea — of the new world. Of a new country. A country they had both sought and found.

Still, he thought, there was a lineage of thinking that could be traced back to those other friends, the lineage of a quest for the words that would identify what had moved Jack Frake and him all the years of their lives. Hugh was certain that he had found the words. He had written them down. He took from his portmanteau the paper that contained them, and handed it over the desk to Jack Frake. "I have found the words we have been looking for," he said, not knowing that Augustus Skelly had bequeathed the same task to Jack Frake, but assuming that Jack Frake was in search of the words, as well. "There they are. I wrote them down after I left you in the Caxton jail."

Jack Frake took the paper and read the elegant handwriting on it:

*All the great arguments for liberty, for life, for freedom, rest on one great necessary and ineluctable condition: that one must source oneself, for everything else to have any meaning. God has nothing to do with it. The Corpus Mysticum of royal sovereignty has nothing to do with it. Nor the power of Parliament. Nor even of the Congress in Philadelphia. This is the truth which that body must recognize when it someday convenes to establish a just and lasting polity among us. One owns one's own life; it is a thing that was never theirs to grant or give, covet, own, or expend; it is a thing never to be granted or surrendered to others, regardless of their number or purpose. That truth is the source of all the great things possible in life.*

Jack Frake thought: I have always known it, without thinking it. It was so simple a truth. He had never before encountered that particular formulation of what drove him all his life. Yet, if it was not sensed, and then thought, it could not be expressed. It could be found and expressed only by those who sought it. He remembered all the times when he would sit alone, during moments of peace and contentment and self-possession — before the fire in the Sea Siren tavern in Gwynnford, on a cold, windy beach on the Cornwall coast, waiting for contraband, or on quiet nights on his own

porch here at Morland, and all the other times of untroubled solitude —
and the words would hover on the edge of his mind, and seem to dare him
to pursue them, but as he turned his consciousness to them, fly away in a
playful taunt that nevertheless assured him that, sooner or later, he would
find them.

And he remembered the last time the words had not hovered just
beyond his reach, but gripped him with a kind of solemn fury, and how
knowledge of those unseen words had burned fiercely inside his mind as he
retreated up Breed's Hill in Charlestown, the words drawn there by the
imminence of death, as reward for having risked his life in order to preserve it and all the great things possible to it, past, present, and future.

He glanced up at Hugh with a smile of gratitude. "Yes," he said with a
simple nod of his head. "You have found them." After a moment of quiet
elation, he wondered how he could reciprocate the paper in his hand. He
looked around at the clutter on his desk. His sight fell on the steel gorget.
He picked it up and placed it on the desk in front of Hugh. "You saved my
life, too, Hugh." What else Hugh had done for him, did not now need to be
named.

Hugh smiled. Proudlocks had said that Jack Frake would never offer to
show him the gorget. But he knew that Jack Frake was making an exception now, not in a vain gesture of boasting, but in grateful tribute. He
picked up the gorget and examined the whorl that nearly obliterated *Aude*.
How pointlessly ironic, he thought. As ironic as Roger's death. No, he
thought. Roger was there. He said to Jack Frake, "I almost wish I had been
there, too, with your Company." He nodded once in acknowledgement to
his friend, then gently replaced the gorget. He pointed to the paper still in
Jack Frake's hand. "That is your copy, Jack. I made one for myself."

Then they talked of other things, including the letter from Etáin Jack
had found waiting for him when he returned from Charlestown. Jack said,
"She writes that all they talk about in Edinburgh is war, and how the
colonies must be punished. She keeps her own counsel, however, and helps
her mother in her shop. Mr. McRae found her a harp, and she practices on
it often."

Their talk turned to the prospects for tobacco and other crops this
summer. They went outside and strolled through Morland's fields together.
Jack stopped to inspect the newly planted tobacco transferred from the
seedbeds, and the sprouting corn stalks. Then they turned to look at the
great house in the distance.

"This is the end," said Jack Frake. "There is no going back to what it was. What was, cannot be perpetuated, cannot be regained. Should not be regained, or perpetuated, even if it were possible to go back to it." He paused and looked at Hugh. "You know this."

Hugh nodded. He was thinking of Meum Hall.

Jack swept a hand over the vista of Morland Hall. "I've known it for years. I've braced myself for the possibility of losing all this."

"I, too," said Hugh.

"When it is over — and there will be an end to it — perhaps I can return here, with Etáin." He paused. "Somehow, I wish it would not happen. A man likes to live in peace, with his own ambition to move him. But, I've had my ambition, and my years of peace. For the time being, they are no longer in my future. We must remove Damocles' sword from over our heads, once and for all."

Hugh chuckled. "Actually, it was the tyrant Dionysius the Elder's sword that dangled over Damocles' head." Then he asked, "What will you do now?"

"Perhaps stay long enough to see Governor Dunmore defeated. John and I want to go back north with as much of the Company as will join us and enlist in General Washington's army. Mr. Robbins and Mr. Hurry can see after Morland — if this place survives the war." Jack Frake studied Hugh. "And you?" he asked.

"I must stay here," Hugh answered, "and deal with my uncle's emissary, the malign Mr. Hunt. Mr. Proudlocks recognized him from his time in London. I am certain that his presence here is neither coincidence nor happenstance." He paused. "My uncle is my mortal enemy, and Mr. Hunt is his proxy. It is a matter I must settle — once and for all."

"And after that?"

Hugh shrugged. "Perhaps join you and Mr. Proudlocks, whether or not Meum Hall survives."

# Chapter 13: The Soldiers

As British rule increased its grip and became more and more arrogant in a manner that could not be mistaken for the actions of a benevolent despotism, those who denied that the mother country was not capable of any despotism, together with those who applauded it for the sake of a perishing status quo, faded into the background of obscurity and irrelevance. Many prominent and not-so-prominent citizens of Virginia placed announcements in the two Virginia *Gazettes* stating their imminent departures for England. John Randolph, the Attorney-General, and Richard Corbin, the Receiver-General, bid farewell in the fall of 1775. Peyton Randolph, the former Attorney-General and now the Speaker of the House of Burgesses, completed his chores as a delegate to the second Continental Congress in time to return home and die in October of an apoplectic seizure.

He and Richard Bland, who was now almost completely blind, had charged themselves with the duty of containing the "hot heads" of revolution among their countrymen and leaving open the chance of reconciliation with the mother country. Bland would die a year later. The "old guard" in all the colonies found themselves without a means to enforce their loyalties and without any convincing arguments that would counter the growing conviction that it was not only best to separate from the mother country, but absolutely necessary, if liberty were to be preserved and advanced.

They and their fellow "moderates" and loyalists seemed to be swept away by the hurricane that came over Hampton Roads in early September of that year. It was an apt punctuation mark for the end of an era of accommodation and moderation, and for the beginning of the war.

Other loyalists, embittered and shaken by the spectacle of what they perceived as rampant anarchy and treason, decided to remain and take up arms in the name of a status quo they presumed could be reinstated on the intemperate and reckless among them.

\*   \*   \*

"My orders were to take the next available vessel from Barbados and proceed with my battalion to Hampton, where further orders would await me. Well, I am in Hampton, there are no further orders, and I am now in the damnable position of awaiting them, instead."

"A delicate situation, to be sure, Major Ragsdale," agreed Jared Hunt. "From whom were you to expect further orders, may I ask?"

"From Admiral Graves in Boston, I suppose. At least, my last communication from him was dated mid-June, two weeks after the captain of the *Hare* notified him of our incapacitation. My further orders will come from Graves, or from the Admiralty itself."

It was an early August afternoon. Jared Hunt sat with Major Eyre Ragsdale in one of Hampton's better taverns, sipping ale and dining on cold cuts, and taking refuge from the suffocating heat outside. Ragsdale commanded the 6th Battalion of Marines, which totaled eighty men. The battalion would have arrived earlier, but the frigate *Carlisle*, on its first stop from Barbados, had also transported an army regiment to East Florida to replace two companies of the 14th Regiment, which were sent on to Portsmouth to aid Governor Dunmore. The *Carlisle*, Ragsdale, and his battalion had had to wait in Florida until Governor Tonyn approved release of the regiment to the homeless vice-regent of Virginia.

Ragsdale's own assigned warship, the *Hare*, had been careened in Barbados to repair its hull, which was dangerously riddled with worm and so smothered by barnacles that the vessel could barely move through the water even in the most favorable winds, rendering it virtually useless as a warship. Ragsdale had jestingly referred to it as the *Tortoise*. The captain of the *Carlisle* had stayed in Portsmouth only long enough to disembark the army regiment. Having heard of Governor Dunmore's temper and acquisitive habits, he immediately weighed anchor again for Hampton, out of harm's way. After staying a single night there to restock ship supplies, the *Carlisle* set sail for England the following morning, per the captain's own orders.

"A disturbing predicament, indeed," said Hunt. "Undoubtedly, there has been a fouled exchange of signals between Admiral Graves and the Admiralty. It is not good for so fine a unit as your own to lie in idleness, sir, and I am certain that neither of them intends that." Hunt had watched the marines disembark from the *Carlisle* — one company of regulars and one company of grenadiers. He observed that they did not seem particularly robust. He supposed the Caribbean heat must have sapped much of their vigor. But it never hurt to compliment a commanding officer on the condition of his men, even if they seemed listless and careworn. The battalion in the meantime had been billeted in an empty warehouse in Hampton.

Ragsdale shrugged. "Their intentions are irrelevant. I am blamelessly idle." After a pause, he mused, not happily, "I suppose I should report to Governor Dunmore and offer my services for the time being. He is sure to have heard of our presence."

Jared Hunt blinked once and shook his head. "Not necessarily, Major," he suggested.

Ragsdale frowned in surprise. "I should think his ear would be alert for the presence of a convent of nuns, if he thought they could help him reestablish order here, sir. Governor Tonyn sent him only sixty men from the regiment down there." The major scoffed. "They could hardly help him secure Portsmouth, never mind the rest of Virginia."

Hunt leaned forward and in a low voice said, "I protest the highest regard for His Excellency, however, I do not believe you would want to place your battalion in his hands. Besides, I am certain he is not even aware of your presence."

"Why would I not wish to serve the Governor, sir?"

"Because he will probably ask you and your men to help coddle all the runaway Negroes who are drawn to his benevolent rule. He is toying with the idea of emancipating them, you see, at least those belonging to rebels, and forming a regiment of Negroes to serve under His Majesty's colors." Hunt saw confusion in Ragsdale's eyes, and leaned back to speak in a more casual, deprecating tone. "*Someone* must train them in the arts of war. I honestly cannot imagine your battalion encamped next to them, for months on end, listening to their blather and exposed to their contagions and ailments, as well. But, what better way to employ an idle force than to train another? I am acquainted with the Governor's goals, and that will certainly be the bend of his thinking. You must own that you could not relish the prospect of becoming a nursemaid to scamps and slothful fools, when there is fighting to be done."

Ragsdale sighed. "No, I would not relish the prospect."

When Ragsdale said nothing else, Hunt shook his head and smiled. "However, I have a better idea. You and your battalion are at liberty, so to speak, and my proposition may be amenable. You see, His Excellency has given me leave to act as a kind of vice-admiral in these parts. I have at my disposal the *Basilisk*, a sloop of eight guns, and the *Sparrowhawk*, a merchantman of twenty guns. Nominally, they are in the service of the Customs, but they can perform the same role of authority as the *Otter*, the

*Kingfisher*, and the *William* now under the Governor's command. It is understood between His Excellency and me that he will secure the James, and I the York." He smiled. "The *Sparrowhawk* is more than commodious enough to accommodate your battalion, Major. I am planning an expedition up the York soon to aid some patriots in the establishment of Crown authority. The presence of your battalion could not help but ensure the success of that project."

The major raised an eyebrow. "Patriots?"

"Subjects loyal to His Majesty, of course."

"Of course." Ragsdale sipped his ale in thought. After a moment, he said, "Well, it is an idea. I don't like keeping my men idle. And, there is a rebellion to be put down, and my duty in that regard. My officers and I have speculated about our ultimate destination. We were thinking we might be ordered to Boston. We read reports that the marines with the fleet there were terribly mauled taking that rebel redoubt." After another moment, he added, "Well, as you say, until I receive further orders, my battalion is at liberty, and I cannot be faulted for taking some initiative when circumstances avail themselves and for employing my fellows to the best advantage. I accept your proposition, Mr. Hunt. When may we embark on this punitive expedition?"

"Soon," answered Hunt. He had received a message the day before from Edgar Cullis expressing both his outrage over the freeing of Jack Frake from the Caxton jail and the fear of the committee of safety that if they attempted to re-arrest the man, the committee's own militia — and the only legitimate one in that county — might be obliged to face the independent company "with undesirable results." It was imperative that the committee establish its authority in the county, but its members did not think that could be accomplished without some support from the Crown.

"Otherwise," Cullis had written, "we should simply throw up our hands and allow the only remaining loyal county on the York to fall under the influence of renegades and lawless bandits. Mr. Frake's wretched company of impenitent malefactors refuse to acknowledge our committee's authority, accuse us of the grossest intentions, and threaten retaliation if we exercise our legal prerogative. For the time being, however, the committee have decided on a less conspicuous action as a more modest step in establishing authority, viz., the closing of the tavern in which the renegades have met and plotted their crimes and treason. But we will not act until we have an assurance from your office that we will be sanctioned and supported."

Hunt had sent a courier to Cullis's home with the reply that the *Sparrowhawk* and *Basilisk* would sail in a few days to support the proposed action, and advised the committee of safety not to act until the vessels had tied up at the Caxton piers. "Acting together in unison will doubtless impress upon the citizens of your fair town the permanence and power of Crown authority, and of the many advantages of submitting to it. We should then be able to better deal with those miscreants among the populace who thumb their noses at His Majesty, His Excellency the Governor, and Parliament. I remain your most sympathetic and dutiful servant, J. Hunt."

\*   \*   \*

Two mornings later, when John Proudlocks visited Morland Hall, the first thing Jack Frake said to his friend was, "Should you ever open a law practice, John, you won't collect many fees for patching up things between disputants."

"On the contrary, Jack," said Proudlocks, "I could charge disputants for having kept them out of court. I should point out to them that arbitration would be a much less costly pursuit of satisfaction and equity."

They did not need to mention the role that Proudlocks had played in resolving the conflict between Jack Frake and Hugh Kenrick. Jack Frake merely grinned at his friend's reticence and persistent imagination.

Jack Frake, as captain of the Queen Anne Volunteer Company, had the day before sent a servant to Proudlocks's Sachem Hall and to Jock Fraser's place with orders to assemble the Company this morning at the camp and drilling field that had been established at the far end of Morland's fields. He wished to advise the men that they needn't feel obliged to stay in the Company, that they could return to their homes and trades, or join one of the neighboring county militias, or journey back north to enlist in General Washington's new Continental Army. He would tell them that those who wished to remain in the Company, he would lead, whenever circumstances demanded action.

He and Proudlocks stood together now in the cellar of the great house. Jack Frake held a lantern. Before them was a freshly mortared brick wall that had been removed years ago to add a chamber to hold powder and arms. The plank door to the chamber had been taken off, and the original bricks carefully restored. Aymer Crompton, Morland's brickmaker, had also managed to color the new mortar so that it was the same gray hue as the brick mortar on either side of the restored wall. Evidence of the chamber was nearly obliterated. The great house could be destroyed, and its debris collapse into the cellar, but the chamber would remain intact and untouched.

"When was this done?" asked Proudlocks.

"Mr. Crompton finished it this morning," Jack Frake answered.

Sealed inside the chamber now were not powder and arms — they had been removed to the ruins of the Otway plantation months ago for safe-keeping against Crown discovery and confiscation — but objects and records that Jack Frake wanted to preserve and reclaim when he was free to live in peace again: legal documents, deeds, correspondence, some books — his copy of *Hyperborea* among them — pencil and ink portraits of Etáin, Skelly, and Redmagne drawn by Hugh Kenrick, Etáin's harp and dulcimer, and all of her music paperwork, and some other objects. And his copy of Hugh's "words."

The chamber also held a few iron boxes containing gold, silver, and copper coins, specie that he had culled over nearly two decades of planta-tion business. He wanted to save all those things from seizure or destruc-tion. The specie would help him start over again, once the war ended. And if he lived to see its end.

Jack Frake told Proudlocks what was inside the chamber, then said, "If anything happens to me, you know of the existence of this trove. Help your-self to it, allowing for Etáin's share, of course."

Proudlocks nodded. They did not dwell, either, on such an uncertain and perilous future as the end of a war in which they would fight. Proud-locks asked, "What of Mr. Settle, and Mr. Robbins, and the other men here? If something happens to Morland, what will they do?"

"I've discussed the possibility with them. If Morland survives, they may come back here, if they've not left, and if there is still a Morland Hall to return to. Otherwise, they have all said they will join Mr. Washington's army, as well." Jack Frake glanced at his friend. "What of Sachem Hall?"

Proudlocks sighed. "I have buried some money on the grounds. But there are so many books. It would be futile to bury them. They would rot." He shrugged. "Sachem Hall will need to take its chances, as well. Mr. Corsin will oversee the place while I'm gone." Enolls Corsin was Proud-locks's business agent and steward. He had worked in that capacity when

Thomas Reisdale owned the plantation, known then as simply "Freehold."

The two men threaded their way back through the cellar and climbed the stairs to the first floor. "I wonder how Mr. Kenrick will fare," remarked Proudlocks as they emerged into the breezeway.

"He said he may join Mr. Washington's army, as well," answered Jack Frake. "But first he must deal with the devil his uncle sent over here."

"Mr. Hunt," said Proudlocks. "Yes, of course. A veritable devil."

"Mr. Hurry returned from errands in town earlier. At Safford's he heard that the Governor has been made a gift of two companies of other devils. Sixty or so men from the Prince of Wales's own regiment, from Florida. And a battalion of marines from the Indies has landed in Hampton."

"Who told him that?"

"Mr. Safford. The postboy riding from Yorktown brought the news when he stopped at the tavern to pick up and leave mail." Jack Frake stopped in his study to don his gorget and buckle on his sword. "Well," he said to Proudlocks, "let's not keep Jock and the men waiting."

*   *   *

"*Hulton?*"

At Meum Hall that same morning, Hugh Kenrick was in his study, about to decide on what to pass an hour reading before he resumed his plantation chores: Thomas Gray's *The Progress of Poesy*, or Gray's *The Bard*, or the first volume of Smollet's translation of Alain-René Lesage's *Gil Blas de Santillane*. Those books and others had arrived from Philadelphia just before he journeyed to England the year before, as a partially filled order from his favorite bookshop in that city. Otis Talbot had recommended Lesage's novel for its satiric humor, he remembered. He decided that he needed some humor as an antidote to his recent glumness, and was reaching for the first volume when Mandy, Mrs. Vere's black housekeeping assistant, came in and announced a visitor.

"Who is it, Mandy?"

"He would not say, sir. He looks troubled and hungry and beggarish-like, but says he knows you."

Hugh smiled in wonder. He was intrigued. "Well, please show him in."

The servant returned with a man Hugh did not recognize for almost a full moment: Thomas Hulton, his valet and companion from his London and Windridge Court years. Twenty years ago the man had been dismissed by Hugh's uncle on a trumped-up charge of theft. Out of desperation, because he knew no other trade but that of valet, Hulton had enlisted in the army, and vanished into the maw of military administration. Hulton had written him one letter from an Isle of Wight marshalling camp, and then all contact with him had ceased.

"*Hulton??*" he repeated. He frowned and took a step closer to the man. Mandy gave the visitor a dubious look of suspicion, then curtsied and left the room.

Hulton, of course, had aged. White hair, unbarbered for some time, fell in a tangled, uncombed mass from his head to cover his ears, and white bristles on a lean face unshaven for days gave him the look of feral destitution. He wore a black frock coat two sizes too big for him, tattered hose, dirty buff breeches, and thin shoes a week away from disintegration. His cotton shirt needed either repeated laundering or discarding. A sword and a canteen hung from cross belts across his chest. He wore a knapsack around which was wound a rolled gray blanket. He stood at the door, battered tricorn in hand, slightly stooped, with the suggestion of a smile on quivering lips and a pleased but tired look in his eyes.

He nodded, and said, "Sergeant Thomas Hulton, milord, late of the Irregulars and Boston." Then his eyes dropped to stare at the floor. "And a deserter."

He looked up at Hugh, blinked once, then closed his eyes and fainted. Hugh caught him before he hit the floor.

An hour later, Hugh was bent over his former valet. Hulton lay in a bed in the guest room. Beecroft and Spears had helped Hugh carry him upstairs and undress him. His head rested on a pillow, and he was covered with a sheet. Hugh had pulled up a chair and sponged the man's face with a cloth dampened in a washbowl. Hulton finally opened his eyes and saw his former master staring down at him worriedly. "Forgive me the bother, milord," he said.

Hugh shook his head. "Hulton, when did you last eat?"

Hulton gave the question some thought. "I had an ear of corn in some field near a town called Port Tobacco across the river out there a few days ago. Before an overseer chased me out. I think."

"You shall sup today, but in easy stages, for otherwise you will get sick. You will begin with a broth. My cook recommends it. She is preparing you a meal now." Hugh paused. "Hulton, are you strong enough to talk? How did you come here? And why? And how?"

Hulton smiled. "You are looking very prosperous, milord. Prosperous but not purse-proud. You look exactly how I always imagined you'd look, when you passed your majority."

Hugh grinned. "I hope that's a compliment, Hulton. And you look…as though you've seen the world. A world far beyond Windridge Court."

"I have, milord. I became a man, and I commanded men. As private, corporal, and sergeant." Hulton sighed. "I commanded men. And saw them die, and helped to bury them. And wrote their kin." He smiled again. "And saw some victories. I was at Quebec, you know, when Wolfe bollixed the French."

Hugh shook his head again. "I wouldn't know, Hulton. Why did you not write, after that last letter?"

Hulton shrugged his shoulders. "I thought that if I was to become a man, I had to learn how to become one on my own mettle, without advice or guidance." He frowned. "It's the only true way, you know. Although I must confess that I had you as a kind of model. You were a man when you were a boy, and I'll lay the man low who says you weren't!"

Hugh patted the hand that lay inert at Hulton's side in acknowledgement.

Hulton sighed. "Oh, milord! I have so much to tell you, and some sad news, too, and I don't know where to begin!"

"You'll begin when you've rested, and had some supper."

Hulton shook his head. "No, milord! I came all this way to see you, and to give you some things. Let me tell you now, because I am beginning not to want to. You see, it's your friend, Captain Tallmadge. I was in his Irregulars. 'Orphans,' he called us. But he died at Charlestown, and there was no one to see to his kit but me. He was a gentleman and a gentle soul, never mind his career, milord. He showed me many a kindness, and others in the company, too, though some of them didn't deserve it. I was not at Charlestown, you see, a few of our company were ordered to guard duty at the billet where Howe and Burgoyne and Clinton were put. But when we were relieved at dusk we were ferried over to Charlestown to help collect the dead and wounded. It was terrible, more terrible than anything I'd ever seen before. It was dark, and we kept tripping over the bodies, and sometimes they made a noise…."

Hugh patted Hulton's hand again. "I know about Roger, Hulton."

"He was unhappy, being there. He'd done some important work for the army, but wouldn't tell me what. And I'd only been in Boston six months, direct from Ireland, but the 81st lost many men at sea coming over, and then so many to sickness and desertion once we arrived, that the regiment was broken on orders from the Adjunct, and what was left of us was formed with other cast-offs into the Irregulars. Just me and another sergeant to partisan them. Then Captain Tallmadge came, and was ordered to straighten us out. Which he did. He taught artillery, you know, at Woolwich. And we got to talking, and it came out that we both knew you. I think I saw him once before, when he was no taller than your knee, there in Danvers, but not since, because I spent the rest of my service at Windridge Court."

Hugh ventured, "You must have been with your company at the Lexington and Concord affair."

"Yes, milord, I was. And a sad day it was, too. You see, it troubled me to be fighting the people here, which I'd not done before. And it troubled Captain Tallmadge, too. After the last war, Colonel Beckwith's 71st was broken, and I was transferred to another regiment in Ireland, and then I saw service at Gibraltar, and was finally taken in by the 81st. It's been quite an adventure, milord."

"Why have you deserted, Hulton?"

"Because after the Lexington and Concord affair, I couldn't bring myself to fight the people here. Their grievances are good, you know. Captain Tallmadge had a way of putting it, and it made sense to me, that the lords and ministers there in London wanted to turn the colonies into a great Fleet prison, and appoint the most scurrilous caitiffs to run it, just so the lords and ministers could be assured their chocolate pots every morning and His Majesty his allowance from Parliament. His very words." Hulton turned from staring into the distance to face Hugh. "And the day the Irregulars were to be rowed over to Charlestown, he came to me and gave me leave to see to his things, if anything happened to him. Officers usually ask other officers to do that, you know, before an action, but he asked me to. He described to me where you were to be found. And here I am." The sergeant's eyes roamed the room. "Where is my pack, milord?"

"In the corner there," Hugh answered, nodding to the knapsack.

"His things are in it. And something of yours, milord."

"Of mine?" asked Hugh, surprised. "What?"

"The book you loaned me, milord, the night we went to that tavern in London, where you met your special friends. Mr. Shakespeare's *Histories.*

I've read it many times, and always meant to return it."

It was too much for Hugh. With a deep sigh he rose abruptly to pace back and forth for a moment, his hands behind his back, eyes closed. The memory seemed to transport him back to that time, and to what he was then, to how he felt and how he proposed to spend the rest of his life. Then he stopped pacing, for he realized that he hadn't changed, not in any fundamental sense. He wondered if it were possible to retain one's youth, after a lifetime. But he stopped wondering, because he knew it was.

"Have I offended you, milord?" Hulton asked.

Hugh turned to him with a smile. "No, Hulton. You have not. You merely reminded me of one of the bright spots in my life. When you are up and about again, I shall relate to you my own adventures. There have been many, since we last spoke."

There was a knock on the door. Hugh turned to open it. It was Fiona Chance, the cook, holding a tray with a carafe of port, some glasses and a bowl of steaming broth.

*     *     *

Hulton narrated to Hugh over dinner that afternoon — a light one for him, as a precaution, he would have a full supper in the evening — how he deserted, leaving his billet at night, making his way past British and American pickets outside of Dorchester Heights, and walking south for a month. As he went, he discarded as much of his uniform as he could, trading his red tunic especially for a homespun frock coat. What little money he had was spent on food in taverns and ordinaries; when the money was gone, he raided crops, or stopped at parsonages and relied on the good will of a minister for food. Except for going days without food, it was an uneventful journey.

Hugh ordered most of the clothes Hulton was wearing when he arrived at Meum Hall burned; they were filthy, crawling with lice, and decrepit. He asked Rupert Beecroft to loan the man a new suit of clothes, hose, and a new pair of shoes; the two men were about the same size. He gave Beecroft money and asked him to go into town to the tailor's and purchase Hulton his own garb and shoes. He took Hulton down to the river and made him bathe before donning the clothes. Radulphus Spears trimmed Hulton's hair and shaved him.

By suppertime, Hulton looked refreshed and presentable. "Are relations between your father and the Earl still bad, milord?" he asked.

"They are worse."

"Captain Tallmadge married your sister."

"Yes. I attended their wedding." Hugh paused. "I have written Alice about Roger."

"I would have, but was not sure of her address."

From the knapsack before supper, Hulton produced the volume of Shakespeare's *Histories*, which Hugh told him to keep. Hulton also gave Hugh what things of Roger Tallmadge's the sergeant had been able to stuff into the knapsack: a bundle of letters to Roger from Alice, her parents, and his own parents; a copy of the report to General Gage; writing materials and paper; shaving implements; miscellaneous items; and the tin gorget Hugh had given Roger, inscribed "A Paladin for Liberty."

Hulton saw Hugh holding it in his hand. "Captain Tallmadge showed me that once, milord, and said it was a gift from you. It was what got him into a bad way with the army, wasn't it?"

"No," sighed Hugh. "It was a gesture of friendship that did that. An act of brotherhood. This was my token of gratitude." He put the gorget down. "I will keep it, but send all the rest of his things on to Alice." He glanced at Hulton again. "When you were sent over to collect the dead and wounded, Hulton, you didn't perchance come upon him, did you?"

Hulton shook his head. "No, milord. All our fellows were buried in bunches in great holes there near Charlestown. One of our fellows who was with him and the Fusiliers saw him shot, near a rail fence. But I was sent to look after the south slope of that redoubt, where the marines fell by the dozen, and I never had the chance to look for him or go see where he died." The former sergeant paused. "We worked all night and into the morning, before the sun came up again."

"I see." Hugh decided not to enquire further about Roger.

Over supper later, he said, "Hulton, you will not be able to return to England."

"I know, milord." The former sergeant looked resigned. "There was nothing to return to, except your good family." Then he smiled. "I remember that you and your father wished to establish me in a tobacconist's shop."

"It is still possible — I'm certain my father would advance the funds — but you would need to move to a large town or city here. And now that there will be a war, we should wait until it is finished. The tobacco trade is sure to be interrupted. All trade, in fact."

"Is there news of Mr. Runcorn?" asked Hulton. "We were friends."

"Mr. Runcorn married Bridgette, and Mr. Runcorn is now employed as the warden of Danvers. I have not met the family's new major domo." Hugh laughed. "And Mr. Curle continues to bow and scrape at Windridge Court. He is a perfect servant for my uncle."

"He's a snake, that one," remarked Hulton. Then he rushed to correct himself. "Mr. Curle, I meant, milord!"

Hugh laughed again, and paraphrased something he had said to Hulton long ago, when they went to the Fruit Wench, and Hulton, having read *Richard the Third*, asked if it was permitted to call a late king a bastard. "Hulton, it is right to call my uncle anything — or nothing at all!" He took a sip of his wine, then said, "And you must call me 'Mr. Kenrick.' I have dispensed with the balderdash of 'milord' and other such terms. I have forbidden the appellation. This is not England."

Hulton blinked once. "Yes...sir."

"And we must decide what to do with you."

"I could act as your valet...sir."

Hugh shook his head. "I have a valet. Mr. Spears. No, you must learn another trade. Mr. Zouch, my brickmaker, could use some assistance at the kiln. You will be paid. That is, if you wish to remain here." When Hulton said nothing, he continued. "You are a free man, in a manner of speaking. It is for you to decide."

After a long moment, Hulton replied, "Yes, sir. I accept. I am...unsettled, you see, and don't know what else to do now. It has been a trying time."

"Of course. But first, you shall rest, and regain the strength of mind and body." Hugh studied his former valet for a moment. "It is good to see you again, Hulton. Never doubt that you are welcome here. My parents will be happy to learn of your resurrection, as well!"

"Thank you...sir." Hulton glanced around the supper room, and for the first time noticed the Westcott portrait of Hugh's parents on the wall across from him. "How did you come by this place...Mr. Kenrick? Captain Tallmadge once described it to me, but I could not quite believe it."

Hugh smiled. "Now it is time to relate my own adventures, Hulton."

# Chapter 14: The Augury

That same day, Under-Sheriff George Roane rode about the county with a black servant from Sheriff Tippet's household, to post a broadsheet delivered that morning from Williamsburg, where it had been printed on the press of one of the *Gazettes*. Composed by Reverend Acland, it read:

*"Recent contentions and troubles coursing among the denizens of our fair colony have made it imperative that loyal and respected citizens of Queen Anne County move to fulfill their spiritual and civic obligations to their fellow citizens to establish a COMMITTEE OF SAFETY in defense of Christian civility, justice and temporal security. The COMMITTEE have assumed the burden of ensuring the serenity of this County in these unsettling times until the power and office of His Excellency John Murray, Earl of Dunmore, our lawful Governor and Protector, have been reinstated in their proper legal and appointive venue in the capital. The COMMITTEE OF SAFETY, composed of the undersigned persons, will henceforth direct and oversee the function of our court in both civil and capital matters, and also to enforce standing regulations, statutes and taxes, and overall be responsible for the orderly conduct of our lives. All ye who reside in or enter Queen Anne County are bound to submit to the COMMITTEE's authority. God save the king. Decreed on this 30th day of August 1775, by order of:*

*Reece Vishonn, Enderly*
*Edgar Cullis, Cullis Hall*
*Carver Gramatan*
*Moses Corbin, Mayor of Caxton*
*Cabal Tippet, Sheriff of the County*
*The Reverend Albert Acland, pastor of Stepney Parish"*

Roane put the broadsheets up on the doors of the courthouse, various shops, the church, the tobacco inspector's office on the riverfront, on the posts of the Hove Stream Bridge, and in other places where they would be noticed. Edgar Cullis and Vishonn at first questioned the wisdom of ending the decree with "God save the king," but they had read that delegates to the Virginia Convention and the Congress in Philadelphia continued to assert their loyalty to the sovereign even in their most outrageous addresses to

Parliament, so it was decided to leave it in.

Roane also rode to the properties of the leading planters and farmers and delivered copies of the broadsheet to their proprietors. Jock Fraser happened to meet Roane as he rode up, and promptly tore up the broadsheet and flung its pieces into the under-sheriff's face. Jack Frake, riding out of Morland Hall to call on John Proudlocks, met Roane on the connecting road, was handed a copy, and said to Roane, "You may tell your committee that I do not recognize their authority." He calmly tore the paper into neat pieces and handed them back with a smile to the wary officer.

"There will be trouble, sir, if you don't," warned Roane.

"There will be trouble, regardless."

Roane also nailed broadsheets to the doors of Caxton's three taverns: the Gramatan Inn, Fern's, and Safford's Arms. Steven Safford heard the hammering above the hubbub of his patrons, and went out to see Roane and the servant riding away. He tore off the broadsheet, read it, and took it back inside. He flung the broadsheet into the cooking fireplace.

Hugh Kenrick learned about the broadsheet from Spears, his valet, who found it folded and inserted inside the jam of the front door of the great house. He took it to the supper room where his employer was having dinner with Hulton. "I did not see who left it, sir," he said. Hugh glanced at it, then asked Spears to put it on his study desk. He was too distracted with Hulton to pay it closer attention. It was only in the evening, after Hulton had retired in the guest room, that he read the broadsheet and pondered the implications of its contents. He left the study, walked to the stable with the broadsheet, and rode to Morland Hall.

He reached it just as the last light of dusk was ebbing to darkness. He found Jack Frake sitting on the porch, seegar in hand, a crystal decanter of Madeira on a side table with glasses. His friend waved him to a chair on the other side of the table and offered him a glass of the wine.

Hugh nodded to the decanter as Jack Frake poured the liquid into both glasses. "French?"

"Italian, I think," answered Jack Frake. "The set was a wedding gift from Etáin's parents. We used it only on special occasions. On our anniversary, mostly."

Hugh considered this answer for a moment. "Is this…a special occasion?" He asked, accepting a glass from Jack Frake, and for some reason, dreading the answer.

"Yes." Jack Frake nodded to the broadsheet in Hugh's other hand.

Hugh could not mistake the look of sadness in his friend's glance. He gestured with the sheet once, then lay it on the table. "Did you not receive one?"

"In person, earlier today. I told Mr. Roane I did not recognize the committee's authority, and gave it back to him in half as many pieces as there are words in that decree."

Hugh let a moment pass before he said, "They will not brook defiance or disobedience, Jack."

"So I was told by Mr. Roane." Jack Frake paused. "And I will not brook tyranny."

Hugh could not help but feel a sense of resignation in his friend's demeanor, that Jack Frake was enjoying his property perhaps for the last time. The dread welled up in him again. He smiled tentatively, and as they sipped their Madeira, told Jack Frake about Hulton, including his service under Roger Tallmadge in Boston, and why he had returned.

Jack Frake smiled. "There's a man who seems to have a grip on himself. I'm happy for you that he found you again." He paused. "We shall see much desertion in the years ahead, from both sides."

Hugh nodded agreement. "You shall meet him, tomorrow, I hope."

They were silent for a while. The darkness enveloped the fields beyond. Only a few lights from the tenants' cottages in the distance suggested the substance of those fields, together with the sounds of crickets, owls and tree frogs. Jack Frake and Hugh Kenrick sat quietly, staring into the darkness, alone with their own thoughts.

Jack Frake said, "I refused to be sold into slavery. That was the beginning of my life."

"I would not bow or apologize to the Duke of Cumberland," Hugh answered. "That was the beginning of mine." Then he shook his head. "No, we are both wrong about that, Jack. Our lives began when we chose to think, long before either of us acted."

Jack Frake looked at his friend and smiled. "Correction noted, and accepted." Then his expression altered. He looked grim and merciless. He said, "The *Sparrowhawk* must be destroyed, Hugh, when she reappears. And she will come for us. Then we will be free. Both of us."

Hugh Kenrick held his friend's glance, and nodded silent agreement.

*　*　*

Early the next morning, the *Sparrowhawk* appeared on the York River, followed by the sloop *Basilisk*. Both vessels flew the Customs Jack over their sterns, and Customs pendants from their main topgallants, and took in sail to stop at Caxton. The sight startled the early risers of the town, among them Sheriff Tippet, who witnessed the arrival from the office window of his house, which sat on the bluff that overlooked the riverfront. He sent a servant to inform Mayor Corbin of the vessels' arrival, and to instruct George Roane, who lived in a cottage a short distance from Tippet's house, to ride to Enderly with the news and the suggestion to Mr. Vishonn that the loyal militia should be assembled and ready to march to the town, and to Cullis Hall, to alert the committee of safety's most important member.

The *Sparrowhawk* dropped her anchors in the river some distance away from the piers. The *Basilisk* tied up to Caxton's main pier, and six men descended the gangboard, among them Jared Hunt. One of the men, wearing the uniform of an officer of marines, walked beside Hunt. The party passed the tobacco inspector's house and climbed the road to Queen Anne Street. Tippet searched for his long-glass and trained it on the *Sparrowhawk*. On its deck he saw several other men in red mingled with the crew, who were busy preparing longboats to lower over the sides. So, he thought, the hearsay was true: Mr. Hunt had got himself some marines, and Governor Dunmore himself a portion of an army regiment. Tippet put down the long-glass and left the room to instruct his wife to have some refreshments prepared for visitors. "Oh, Cabal, is there going to be trouble?" she asked worriedly.

"I don't know, Muriel," answered the sheriff. "I hope for all our sakes there isn't."

"Does Mr. Safford know what's to happen?"

Sheriff Tippet shook his head. He returned to his office, found a pistol, and loaded it with powder and ball for the first time in years. He had used it only twice since then, to shoot a raccoon that had mauled one of his dogs, and then later on the dog itself, which had gone mad and fought with the others in his kennel. He had had to dispose of all of them.

Some minutes later there was a knock on his front door.

Two hours passed in the Tippet residence, filled with many draughts of tea, a plate of sweetmeats, and convivial conversation. Jared Hunt was in a jaunty mood, enquiring about the business at hand only to determine if the "true" county militia was to be expected soon.

Sheriff Tippet assured him that it was. "The committee, too, sir," he added. "Mr. Vishonn and Mr. Cullis agreed that it was imperative that all parties be present today."

"Imperative it is, my good man," replied Hunt. Then he began to regale his hosts and companions with several anecdotes of his adventurous life in London and Hampton, omitting, of course, to mention his relationship with the Earl of Danvers and his true mission on these shores.

Major Ragsdale said little. The other Customsmen deferred to Mr. Hunt in setting and dominating the subject of conversation. They were joined shortly by Reverend Acland, who had been working in his garden and noticed the vessels. He had quickly discarded his apron, donned his frock coat, and rushed to the Tippet house. He knew what was to happen today, and did not want to miss anything. Mayor Corbin, roused from sleep, followed him shortly thereafter.

Carver Gramatan was alerted to the vessels' presence by Mary Griffin, his serving girl, who had also seen the vessels arrive. He quickly walked down Queen Anne. After being introduced to the party and apprised by Tippet and Hunt of the situation, Gramatan engaged the major in a separate conversation about the nobility of the English countryside. It was revealed that Major Ragsdale was a distant relation of the tenth Earl of Pembroke of Wiltshire, while Gramatan claimed that his family was "closely related" to two Wiltshire families that had intermarried with the Pembrokes. "For all we know, sir," said Gramatan, "we may be cousins." The major rolled his eyes away from this rustic. He took some snuff and wished the man would go away. There is a hierarchy even among would-be bloods.

Then they all heard a drum. The militia was marching into town. The gentlemen all rose and left the house to walk up Queen Anne Street to meet the militia in front of Safford's Arms Tavern. Sheriff Tippet, his pistol fixed firmly in his belt, asked Jared Hunt, "What role will Major Ragsdale's marines play in this affair, sir?"

"None, Mr. Tippet," answered Hunt. "Not unless a shot is fired." He turned and pointed to the *Sparrowhawk* in the river. "The good major's officers watch us." As they walked, Hunt said, "I have suggested to Major Ragsdale that if his fellows are needed here, they may billet in the tavern."

Sheriff Tippet shrugged. "If it is closed, I cannot think of a better purpose it could be put to, sir." He glanced back once at Hunt's colleagues from the Customs. "What is the purpose of your fellows here, sir?"

"Doubtless a man of Mr. Safford's character will have contraband to find and seize."

As they approached Safford's tavern, they saw that Vishonn's militia had already formed into two lines across Queen Anne Street from the tavern, muskets shouldered but at ease. Reece Vishonn sat on horseback at the end of the lines, looking very much like a colonel. The "true" county militia numbered twenty men, some of whom were veterans of the last war, and one or two had marched with General Lewis's forces last fall during Governor Dunmore's campaign in the west.

Jared Hunt, Sheriff Tippet and the major strode up to Vishonn. Hunt introduced the major, then asked, "May we proceed, Mr. Vishonn?"

"We should wait for Mr. Cullis, sir," answered Vishonn. In a lower voice, he added, because townsfolk were beginning to collect in curiosity around them, "He has the warrant, and the committee concur that all on it should be present, in order to make a proper impression."

"Fine idea, sir," Hunt said. "Let us be *proper*."

Major Ragsdale stood a little apart from the group and militia.

As if on cue, Edgar Cullis was seen in the distance to come onto the street with George Roane. A minute later, they rode up to join the tableau. Cullis doffed his hat, and introductions were made. The lawyer then beckoned to Sheriff Tippet, who approached. Cullis handed down a folded paper. "There is your warrant for Mr. Safford's arrest, which also orders his establishment closed." He saw the sheriff gulp once. Cullis added with a mocking grin, "The committee will present it together. No need to fret."

Tippet unfolded the warrant and read it. He nodded, and turned to face the tavern. Several boat hands had come out onto the tavern porch. Edgar Cullis dismounted and handed the reins of his mount to Vishonn. Tippet gestured to Roane to join him. Roane dismounted and tied his mount to a hitching post in front of Lucas Rittles's store. The five committeemen and Hunt crossed the street and mounted the steps of the tavern porch, followed by the four Customsmen. The boat hands moved out of the way.

The intruders all breathed easier when they saw only Steven Safford, a serving boy, and two patrons in the room. Sheriff Tippet stepped forward, cleared his throat, and announced, "By order of the lawful committee of safety of this county, I am empowered to order the immediate closing of this establishment, and the arrest of its proprietor, Mr. Steven Safford, for having permitted said establishment to be used to harbor conspirators and conspiracies against His Majesty's authority over the dominion of Virginia." The patrons glanced at each other, then rose immediately from their table and left.

Before another word could be said by anyone, Jared Hunt turned to his Customsmen and pointed to the door of the Olympus Room. "That is the room where the crimes were committed. Search it." This command surprised Cullis and the other committeemen, except for Gramatan, who had supplied Hunt with the information about the room.

The Customsmen left the group and entered the room. Safford came out of the bar and walked up to meet the intruders, his face livid. "I don't recognize your authority! You may leave now, and take those cussed rummagers with you!" He pointed wildly at the Olympus Room.

Tippet proffered the warrant, but with a smack of his hand Safford brushed it and the sheriff's hand away. "Get away from me, traitor! You are no longer welcome here!"

"I regret to inform you that it is you who will be leaving, sir," said Edgar Cullis. "You are under arrest, and will be charged with treason. And if these gentlemen find any illegal goods on the premises, you will be charged with that offense, as well."

The Customsmen returned to the main room. "There was nothing and no one there, Mr. Hunt. All we found was this," said one of them. The man held the ensign of the Queen Anne County Volunteers on its oaken staff. Jock Fraser had returned it a few days after the Company returned from Boston, so that it stood in its "place of honor."

Jared Hunt glanced at it, then stepped forward and lifted a corner of the flag.

"The rebel militia carried it to Boston, Mr. Hunt," volunteered Cullis. "It is the banner of the vigilance club here, the Sons of Liberty."

"You don't say," mused Hunt. He chuckled and nodded to the bullet holes among the red and white stripes. "It would seem that some of our brave fellows at Boston took grave exception to the idea, as well." He grunted once in disapproval when he read the words in the cobalt canton: *Live Free, or Die.* He abruptly dropped the corner and ordered, "Take it outside, sir."

The Customsman obeyed. Hunt went to the cooking fireplace, found a piece of firewood in the stack next to it, lit it in the fire, then walked outside. He took the staff of the ensign from the Customsman and planted it in the dirt at the bottom of the tavern steps, then set fire to the cloth at its lowest drooping point.

All the men, including Safford, stood at the door and watched the flames quickly consume the cloth. Charred brown and black flakes flew out and rose to waft in the air. A breeze blew them and the smoke over the heads of the growing crowd of townsfolk. When the cloth was completely obliterated, Hunt lifted the smoldering staff and tossed it with disdain to the ground. He glanced up at Cullis. "And that, sir, is how one treats treasonous rebels."

A murmur rose among the townsfolk. Reverend Acland stepped to the edge of the porch and addressed the crowd in his most righteous voice, "It was the device of Satan! It is appropriate that it was consigned to flames!" He pointed at Safford. "Let him flaunt it in Hell!"

Safford, a tall, lean man in his sixties, and a veteran of two wars past, glared at the minister, and stepped up to address him. "*You* are Satan's spawn, you foul, miserable boot-lick!"

Acland, his knees suddenly shaking and his eyes wide with fright, winced, gulped, and retreated a step before this attack. He had time to imagine that the fury he saw in Safford's face was the very visage of Satan himself before Safford raised a fist and struck him on the jaw. Acland did not fall back from the blow; his knees failed, and he collapsed on the porch of the tavern at Safford's feet.

"Wait a moment! You can't strike a man of God!" Edgar Cullis moved and put a hand on Safford's shoulder, but Safford turned and struck the attorney, as well, with another well-connected punch on the jaw. Cullis, though surprised, kept his balance and stepped back to avoid another blow.

Before anyone could say anything else or stop him, Safford turned and raced down the steps and jumped on Jared Hunt, knocking him flat on his back in the dust. Safford straddled him and pummeled him mercilessly, shouting, "You cowardly, useless caitiff! Placeman! Parasite!...."

The blast of a pistol shot was heard then. Safford jerked up and looked around. He and everyone else but Hunt saw Sheriff Tippet on the porch, smoking pistol in one hand and the rejected warrant in the other, and a look of anguished surprise on the sheriff's face. Safford's eyelids blinked several times in rapid succession. Then his taut frame went limp. He leaned to one side and fell to the ground, dead, a ball in his back.

With his elbows and legs, Jared Hunt, wearing an expression of horror — no one present knew of his fear of violence, especially violence he himself had caused in his career — scurried away crab-like from Safford's still body, not wanting to touch it.

The pistol and warrant dropped from Tippet's hands. "Oh, God, what have I done??" he wailed, raising his hands to cover his face.

Cullis stopped rubbing his jaw long enough to stare angrily at the sheriff. "Control yourself, man!" he ordered with nervous bitterness. "You did your duty! He was a traitor, and we are saved the pain of prosecuting him!" Then he noticed Mayor Corbin struggling to help Acland to his feet, and stepped past Tippet to help.

Jared Hunt picked himself up from the ground. Blood flowed from his nose and bruises began to form on his jaw, cheeks, and forehead. He stood and looked down with amazement at Safford's body. He took a handkerchief from inside his coat and began dabbing his face with it, his sight transfixed on the object at his feet. "Hellion!" he muttered.

Major Ragsdale walked over leisurely and stopped to glance once at the body. "My captains will have heard the report, sirs," he said to Hunt and the group on the porch. "They will come shortly. There will be no more of this silliness." He glanced with mute amusement at the usually voluble Hunt, stooped to retrieve the man's tricorn and offered it to him, then turned and walked unconcernedly away, hands behind his back.

And then they all heard the sound of another drum, coming from the direction of the Hove Stream Bridge half a mile away at the end of Queen Anne Street.

# Chapter 15: The Skirmish

Israel Beck, Jack Frake's bookkeeper and secretary, ventured by dogcart into town early that morning to purchase paper and ledger books from Lucas Rittles, who had taken over the miscellaneous stock of the departed Arthur Stannard. He saw the *Sparrowhawk* in the river drop her anchors, and the *Basilisk* being secured to Caxton's main pier. His eyesight, complemented by a pair of bifocals, was sharp enough to espy the redcoats on the deck of the former merchantman. After purchasing his supplies, he rode the dogcart as quickly as he could back to Morland, and found his employer at breakfast.

He stammered the news to Jack Frake. "And they are sporting the Customs Jack, sir! What has happened?" Beck had known both captains of the *Sparrowhawk*, Ramshaw and Geary, and it seemed inconceivable that the vessel was now in the hands of the Customsmen.

"The inevitable, Mr. Beck," Jack Frake answered. "Have my horse saddled, then find Mouse and send him to alert Mr. Proudlocks and Mr. Fraser about this, with orders to assemble the Company on the south end of the Hove Stream Bridge."

"Immediately, Mr. Frake!" The bookkeeper rushed from the supper room.

Jack Frake finished his breakfast. Jock Fraser would have Cletus, who with Travis Barret was employed on Fraser's plantation, beat the assembly, which could be heard by most of the Company's members. They all had needed to pass the bridge to reach the encampment at the far end of Morland's fields, but they would not be assembling there now.

He had only heard a rumor that the *Sparrowhawk* was seized by the Customs; this news confirmed it. Its seizure and impressment into the Customs service was what he at first thought was inevitable. It brought me here, long ago, he thought, and perhaps now it has come to reclaim me. There was some logic in the matter, he reflected. Not so much irony, as justice. He thought he must write Ramshaw about it.

He glanced around the room, and wondered if this would be his last breakfast here. He looked up at a watercolor portrait of Etáin, given to him by Hugh Kenrick years ago, on one of the walls, and smiled. He had not put it with the other things in the sealed chamber in the cellar, for he wished

to have her present in some form. He rose and went to his study to don the
sword, steel gorget, and red sash of his rank. He did not look at the bare
spots on the walls that had once been occupied by portraits of Augustus
Skelly and Redmagne. By the front door of the house he had readied his
musket, a pistol, knapsack, and cartridge pouches. He collected these and
left the house, making for the smaller house that was home to William
Hurry and Obedience Robbins. He told them what Israel Beck had seen,
and where he was going and why.

"Marines, you say?" Robbins said.

"A battalion, I've heard," said Jack Frake. "Cullis and his committee are
working hand in glove with this Customsman, Hunt. He's certain to come
here on a raid. Or to Meum Hall."

"Do you think it wise to oppose them, sir?" asked Hurry.

"They must be opposed sometime, somewhere, Mr. Hurry. I don't
know if a show of force will change their minds. I doubt it. Cullis and the
committee will want me rearrested, and Hunt will want to retaliate for last
summer, when you and Mrs. Frake and the others forced him to retreat."
Jack Frake paused. He had advised all his staff and tenants to prepare to
stay or flee if the Crown attempted to invade and seize the county. "The
war has begun, sirs, and those who helped to bring it about will be the first
to be punished." Jack Frake doffed his hat, turned, and left the house for
the stable.

He rode up the length of Morland Hall's fields to the Hove Stream
Bridge, casting only one lingering look back at the great house and the life
he had lived there. He rode past the little plot where his first wife, Jane, was
buried, along with his infant son, Augustus. He passed John Proudlocks's
old shack, now occupied by Mouse, Henry Dakin's apprentice cooper. He
passed the brickworks, and the carpentry shed, and the tobacco barn,
doffing his hat to the men working in them without stopping to explain. All
his tenants saw the sword, and sash, and gorget, and knew where he was
going. And if they did not know, they would soon enough.

*   *   *

"Who is this?" asked Major Ragsdale.

All eyes — those of the Customsmen, of Vishonn's militia, of the committee of safety, of the townsfolk — were turned watching the approaching
rival militia as it marched down Queen Anne Street in perfect step, its

steady cadence punctuated by a flawless drumbeat, muskets shouldered. Ahead of them, on horseback, rode Jack Frake. As they watched, they saw other armed men racing to catch up with the militia, and others appear from the sides to join the rear rank.

"These are the rebels, Major," said Edgar Cullis, stepping down from the porch to join. "The riding man is their chief, Jack Frake. He took those villains to Boston. They were at Charlestown."

"I see," sighed the major. "Well, if they wish to cause a commotion, I'm certain my marines can chastise them. They look so...*pathetic*."

Cullis felt that the major had slighted him as well as the approaching militia. A little rush of resentment welled up in him, enough to cause him to reply, "I hear they fought well at Charlestown, Major. They were the only Virginians there. I would not dismiss them as harmless."

The major merely pursed his lips at this unexpected rebuke.

Cullis glanced at Reece Vishonn, the only other person on horseback. The planter turned colonel looked nervous, and fiddled with the reins of his mount. His "loyal" militia was outnumbered two to one. Every man in it appeared apprehensive.

The townsfolk who had gathered on that side of the tableau moved out of the way of the Queen Anne Volunteer Company to stand on the sides. When the Company was about ten yards from Vishonn's men, Jack Frake held up a hand. Jock Fraser ordered the Company to halt. The drumbeat stopped, and so did the Company.

Jack Frake sat in the saddle for a moment to take in the situation. His sight roamed critically over everything and everyone. It stopped on the body of Steven Safford lying near the foot of the tavern steps. He glanced back at Jock Fraser. "First rank, charge muskets, Mr. Fraser," he said.

Jock Fraser, after a moment's pause, relayed the order. The eight men in the first rank silently swung down their muskets and held them at the ready.

Jack Frake dismounted. John Proudlocks, musket in hand, rushed from the second rank and held the reins of the horse.

Jack Frake, carrying his own musket, walked forward to see whose body lay on the ground. Jared Hunt and his Customsmen moved away. When he saw who it was, Jack Frake asked, "Who did this?"

"Sheriff Tippet," answered Cullis, "in conformance with his duty, when Mr. Safford went berserk and attacked not only Mr. Hunt, but also Reverend Acland and me. We are here to close his place and arrest him for contributing to your own treason."

Jack Frake turned and saw the sheriff on the porch. Tippet averted his glance and stared at the porch floorboards. Jack Frake said, "You were arresting him and closing his tavern. Of course, he would go berserk."

"You, sir," said Ragsdale, "will order your men to ground their arms and disperse."

Jack Frake addressed the officer. "With what consequence, if I do not, sir?"

Major Ragsdale shrugged and nodded at Vishonn. "Then your countryman there may ask his men to persuade you of the consequence."

Jack Frake smiled. "I am happy that you express doubt about the consequence." He turned and strode up to Vishonn. "Are your men ready to fire on mine, Mr. Vishonn?"

Reece Vishonn would not look down at his fellow planter. He stared into the distance and stiffened with as much dignity as his back would allow. "I may ask you the same question, sir."

"We are," answered Jack Frake. "And if your men are not ready, then you should disperse and disband them. They serve no purpose here."

"That remains to be seen, Mr. Frake."

Then they all heard another drum. Two drums.

"Ah," said Major Ragsdale, "here comes *my* consequence."

Edgar Cullis, Reverend Acland, and the other committeemen wished it were possible to rearrest Jack Frake. But they would not move for as long as eight muskets were ready to protect him. They were certain that all the other muskets in the Company were primed, as well. And all the members of the "loyal" committee of safety now began to rue their actions here. They sensed that the major was spoiling for a fight, and that the matter might now go beyond what they had planned. They began to wonder whose authority was being imposed.

Jack Frake strolled with apparent unconcern back to his horse, but did not mount it. And with John Proudlocks, Jock Fraser, and the others in the Company, he witnessed the spectacle they had seen at Charlestown.

The grenadiers appeared first over the top of the bluff, muskets shouldered, bayonets fixed. As they made the rise, they quickly formed into a line as broad as Queen Anne Street, ten men across. Behind them followed the regulars. Jack Frake estimated there were about eighty men in the force, exclusive of its officers. They had about a quarter mile to cover before the marines passed the courthouse and came within a few yards of Safford's tavern. Jack Frake casually paced back and forth, not taking his eyes off the marines. Major Ragsdale strolled in the direction of his approaching battalion.

Few of the townsfolk had ever seen such a display of military force. Some watched the marines with fascination, others with trepidation. Lucas Rittles and a few other tradesmen stepped back into their shops and quietly locked their doors and closed their shutters. Lydia Heathcoate moved from the door of her millinery, made her way through the crowd of onlookers, and walked boldly up to Proudlocks. "John," she said, "they burned your ensign. I saw them do it. That brute over there put the match to it," she said, pointing to Jared Hunt.

Proudlocks nodded and replied, "You'll sew us another, Lydia. Now, go back into your shop."

The woman touched a sleeve of Proudlocks's coat, and obeyed.

Jared Hunt also paced back and forth. At one point, he stopped to survey the faces of the men of the Company. He grunted once, then braved a question. "Mr. Frake, I do not see Mr. Kenrick in your ranks there. I did not know you had a coward for a friend."

Jack Frake studied Hunt with contempt. "He is a soldier of another kind, and certainly not a coward. Say no more about him."

"I'll say what I please," muttered Hunt to himself as he turned away.

A pair of barking dogs paced the marines. One nipped at the heel of an officer, who took a swipe at it with his drawn sword, cutting its back. The dog ran off, howling.

Major Ragsdale stopped, and nodded to the leading officer. The officer, a captain, shouted a command to halt, relayed by a lieutenant and a sergeant. The formation came to a halt.

"Front rank, charge bayonets, Mr. Crofts," said Ragsdale.

The captain gave the command. The front rank of grenadiers brought down their muskets with a "Huzzah!" "Front rank, kneel, Mr. Crofts," said Ragsdale, "second rank, charge bayonets."

The orders were repeated. The front rank dropped to one knee, while the one behind it repeated the first action. Ragsdale then turned to face Jack Frake and the Company. He saw, much to his surprise, that the militia had silently copied the same actions. He drew his sword. "Now, sir," he said in a raised voice, "will you order your men to ground their arms and disperse, or shall we have it out here?"

"Leave our country, and we will disperse at leisure, Major," Jack Frake answered. He turned to face the Company, and raised an arm as though to give a signal. Jared Hunt and his Customsmen, suddenly realizing that they were in a possible crossfire, rushed to join the men on the porch.

But Reverend Acland dashed by them from the tavern porch in the opposite direction and across the street, snatched a musket from one of Vishonn's men, cocked the hammer, and aimed it at Jack Frake. "The Lord has commanded that I cut you from the flock of the righteous! Begone, Satan's emissary!" he shouted. He raised the weapon and took a few steps closer to Jack Frake to ensure that he did not miss.

Jack Frake, surprised, turned to face his assailant. John Proudlocks let go of the reins of the horse he was leading away, quickly raised his musket, and fired at Acland.

The ball struck Acland in the neck. The minister's head whipped to one side as though he had been slapped. His musket discharged, its ball striking a pillar of Safford's porch. Acland gasped, then gurgled, and fell to the ground.

Everyone but Jack Frake and his men looked dumbly at the body of Acland kicking in its death throes. Proudlocks slapped the rump of the horse, which cantered away, then quickly reloaded.

Even Major Ragsdale looked stunned. Then he frowned, stepped swiftly to one side, raised his sword, and commanded, "Front rank, present firelocks and prepare to fire!"

The grenadiers cocked their hammers and raised their muskets to their shoulders.

"Fire on those rebels!" shouted the major.

In the meantime, Jack Frake and Proudlocks had taken their places. Jack Frake gave the command to the two front ranks of the Company to fire.

A deafening roar came first, then tongues of flame leapt from the two opposing lines. Screams and gasps and expressions of horror followed almost simultaneously. Six of the Company's men were hit, and four grenadiers. The spectators scattered to find cover.

Most of Vishonn's militia had crouched to the ground to avoid being hit by the grenadiers' volley. Reece Vishonn struggled to calm his panicked horse.

Ragsdale quickly ordered the second rank of grenadiers to fire. But because he had not yet informed his officers who were the rebels and who were the loyalists, that rank's lieutenant ordered his men to train their muskets on the kneeling loyalist militia he could see through the smoke. He assumed they were preparing to deliver a volley. Ragsdale noticed the error too late to correct it. The lieutenant gave the command to fire. Again the air thundered. Glass shattered and shouts were heard.

Half of the loyalist militia never rose again, but rolled over where they had crouched, dead or wounded. The survivors jumped up and ran, many tossing their weapons to the ground. Not one of them stopped long enough to notice that their colonel had toppled from his horse, dead. Vishonn's horse, a fine thoroughbred the planter had purchased in Fairfax, fled with the loyalists, balls in its haunch and neck.

The grenadiers reloaded. When the lingering smoke had cleared enough for him to see through it, Ragsdale grimaced when he saw the carnage dealt on the loyalists. He also saw that the opposing militia were gone. "Mr. Crofts, Mr. Selwyn!" he shouted to his captains, "flanking parties on both sides! Now! They think they're going to pull a Concord road on us!"

Half a company of grenadiers and half a company of regulars instantly broke ranks and swept to both sides of the street. Already Jack Frake's men were firing from behind the houses and shops that lined it. They were immediately engaged in running firefights with the flankers who dived into their task to rout the militiamen.

Ragsdale ordered the remaining marines to rise and advance with bayonets leveled. He beckoned to a corporal and ordered him to return to the *Sparrowhawk* to summon the surgeon. The corporal took off in a trot.

As they came upon the fallen loyalists, the major pointed to them with his sword. "Never mind these fellows," he said, "they were here to oppose the rebels. But any rebel ahead of us who shows life, finish him and show no mercy! They show us none!" Three of the Company who were wounded and unable to move were subsequently bayoneted by the grenadiers. Ragsdale came upon the body of Reece Vishonn, shook his head in disgust, and glanced at the men on the porch, who were all on their stomachs. All except Sheriff Tippet, who sat on the steps, bawling. Edgar Cullis got to his feet, looking appalled. Carver Gramatan and Mayor Corbin also rose. Jared Hunt and his Customsmen remained on their stomachs, waiting until they were absolutely certain they would not be mistaken for rebels.

As the marines marched past the tavern, Cullis stepped down from the porch in a daze of disbelief, walking awkwardly like an infant, unsure of his steps, and unsure if he wanted to take them. He looked down at the bodies of all the men he had known, known for years. Some had voted for him in past elections. One had been a client who had recently hired him over a surveying dispute with a neighbor. He stood for a moment over Reverend Acland, then over Reece Vishonn.

Oblivious to the musketry around the town, he glanced up and noticed the broken glass of Lydia Heathcoate's millinery. He swallowed once, and crept inside the shop. The woman lay dead on the floor. A grenadier's ball had struck her in the breast. Her eyes were still open, and seemed to stare back up at him in accusation. He left the shop and sat on the edge of the brick sidewalk that Hugh Kenrick had donated to the town years ago. Ten of Vishonn's men lay before him, dead or wounded. Cullis sat there, unable to cry or feel anything. All he could do was blink in incomprehension.

When they saw townsfolk venturing out again, and that the marines had gone far up the street, Jared Hunt finally rose with his Customsmen. He sniffed once as his sight roamed over the carnage. He glanced down with disdain at Sheriff Tippet, and scoffed in mockery at the sight of Cullis immobilized in front of the millinery. Then he turned and said to one of his men. "So, this is how they want it! Return to the *Sparrowhawk!* Tell Mr. Tragle to prepare to go up river. We will be by presently, after I have apprised Major Ragsdale of my plan." He smiled. "I will destroy Morland Hall!"

# Chapter 16: The Retribution

Jared Hunt searched for Jack Frake among the dead and wounded strewn on Queen Anne Street. He was not to be found. It meant that the man was still free to harass and snipe at the Crown. He was also disappointed that Hugh Kenrick had not been present.

In time, the musket fire around the town lessened, then ceased altogether. Hunt and his men wandered around the outskirts in search of Jack Frake. They found a few more bodies of the rebels, but not that of Jack Frake. They returned to Queen Anne Street. Major Ragsdale reappeared at the head of a platoon of marines, while the remaining marines drifted back to the street in groups and reformed under the direction of their sergeants and officers. Some redcoats were collecting the dropped arms of the dead, wounded, and deserters alike. Hunt intercepted Ragsdale and told him what he planned to do next. The major was indifferent to the Customs man's purposes, but he would cooperate in any venture to enforce Crown law and authority.

They stood in the street outside Safford's tavern. Hunt nodded to what remained of the county committee of safety. Mayor Corbin and Carver Gramatan were helping Edgar Cullis to his feet. Sheriff Tippet was not to be seen. "Not much authority left here to assert, Major," remarked Hunt, "excepting our own." With a chuckle, he nodded to Cullis. "That man is in need of some smelling salts. I suppose he thought authority would come as a plate of bloodless mutton." He gestured to the scene at large. "Well, the tavern is closed, as they wanted, and its proprietor arrested for all eternity!"

The major sheathed his sword. "Where do you think the rebels fled to, Mr. Hunt?"

"Possibly into neighboring counties, Major. I don't believe any of them would be foolhardy to return to their homes."

The major cast a speculative glance at the body of Albert Acland. "I was quite astounded when one of those villains potted Reverend Acland," he volunteered unexpectedly. "Not that the reverend was a wholesome fellow to know. I saw the signs. He reminded me of my father, who was a minister, as well, and quite intolerably righteous. There is a certain kind of righteousness that means no good, not to anyone. Still, I knew at that moment that I must do my duty, and bring force to bear."

Jared Hunt was, for once, amazed. "But, Major, the good man was about to pot Mr. Frake."

"Well, Mr. Frake must have done some unforgivably wicked thing in the past to so aggravate the fellow. He did call him Satan, as nearly as offensive an utterance as taking the Lord's name in vain."

One of his rare pensive moods gripped Hunt, and he considered the problem. Then he shook his head. "No, Major," he said. "I don't believe that Mr. Frake did anything to aggravate the reverend. I do believe it was simply a matter that Mr. Frake...was." He paused. "I understand from my informants here that the reverend's animosity for Mr. Frake was as old as their acquaintance. And, as it turned out, fatal." Hunt had sensed where his thinking was leading him, which was to a vaguely perilous knowledge that he shared that animosity. He snapped his mind away from the thought.

Then they heard a muffled shot from inside Safford's tavern. A lieutenant and some regulars on the porch rushed inside. Ragsdale, Hunt, and the Customsmen followed.

On the floor, near one of the tables, they saw the body of Sheriff Cabal Tippet, and a smoking pistol beside it, its trigger guard still holding the index finger that had pressed the trigger. In the back of the room, Safford's serving boy sat pressed against the wall, his eyes wide in trauma. They did not know if the boy's condition was a result of witnessing the battle, or the suicide.

Hunt said, without a trace of remorse, "I guess the good sheriff blamed himself for the affair. Never heard a man weep as much as he did."

The subject did not interest the major. He had no sympathy for crying men. He appraised the room they stood in. "This will make a suitable billet for my men. We can turn that room your fellows searched into a hospital of sorts for my wounded. The surgeon should be here soon." He sighed. "I expect we will be here for a while. I must find quarters for myself and my officers."

"Ah!" exclaimed Hunt. "Here comes your likely host!"

Carver Gramatan entered the room with George Roane. They saw Tippet's body. Roane stared open-mouthed at his superior, then ran from the room. With a great sigh of sorrow and tiredness, Gramatan moved away and sat down in one of the tavern chairs and worried his chin with a shaking hand. Then he looked at Hunt and asked, "What's to be done now,

Mr. Hunt?"

Hunt permitted himself a laugh. "You are a reduced committee, sir, but I don't see why you may not assert some authority here." He paused. "I suppose you can set up shop in the courthouse."

"Until you do," added Ragsdale, "consider this town under martial law. I shall endeavor to make our presence as painless as possible." He smiled. "My officers and I will need rooms. I hope you may accommodate us." He paused, and seemed to remember something. "Oh, yes. My gravest apologies for firing on your own militia, Mr. Gramatan. In the heat of battle, these kinds of things may happen. But, it seems that this Mr. Frake was right, at least about one thing. Your militia served no purpose here today, except as a luckless obstruction."

*   *   *

Hugh Kenrick said to Hulton, "When I purchased this place, it was in a state of advanced decrepitude, like a merchantman trapped in the Godwin Sands, subject to the indignities of pilferage and decay. Many planters hereabouts now consider it the mode of perfect business." They stood in the middle of Meum Hall's fields, next to the bamboo conduit. After breakfast, Hugh invited the former sergeant and valet to accompany him on a tour of the plantation.

Hulton was especially impressed with the conduit. "What an odd contrivance, sir," he remarked. "But I am sure its novelty is umbraged by its utility."

Hugh laughed. "What a superb choice of words, Hulton! You have much improved since we met last."

"I have been reading many books, sir," answered Hulton with pride.

It was at that moment that they heard the first volleys between the marines and the militia. Hugh Kenrick had only heard their like years ago, when watching George the Second review troops in London, and was uncertain of their cause. Hulton, however, knew the sound all too well.

"What the devil...?" exclaimed Hugh.

"It is a battle, sir," replied Hulton simply.

Tenants of Meum Hall had also heard the musketry. Many of them paused in their work to look in the direction of Caxton.

After a moment, Hugh said as he strode back to the great house, "Come, Hulton. I must investigate this. You will stay here. If Governor

Dunmore has raided the town with soldiers — and I have heard that half a
regiment has been loaned him from Florida — you would be at risk."

"This is true, sir," said Hulton, following. "If discovered, I would be
flogged, or hanged by my thumbs...or hanged."

When Hugh had saddled a horse in the stable and mounted it, the
former sergeant said, "Take care, sir."

Hugh had not gone far along the narrow road to Caxton when he
encountered men fleeing from the town. From them he learned what had
happened. "And Mr. Frake?" he asked.

"He is unhurt, sir," said one of the men. "We are to reassemble elsewhere, and continue the fight." The man paused long enough to say, "Mr.
Safford is dead, sir. He was shot by Sheriff Tippet, who was there to close
the tavern. And Reverend Acland took a musket from one of Mr. Vishonn's
men and tried to shoot Mr. Frake. Mr. Proudlocks shot him, instead. That
is what started it. And then the soldiers thought Mr. Vishonn's men were
with us, and fired on them, too." Then the volunteer turned and ran off in
the direction of Morland Hall.

Hugh Kenrick's heart sank as he rode into the town and saw the after-
math of the skirmish. Townsfolk were occupied collecting the bodies of the
fallen into one place, in an empty lot next to Lucas Rittles's shop. Some of
the wounded men from Vishonn's militia were being treated by the town's
barber, who had some surgical skills. The bodies of some dead marines
were collected on the other side of the street. He saw marine pickets posted
every twenty yards along Queen Anne Street. Marines swarmed in and out
of Safford's tavern. He saw Muriel Tippet rushing up the street from the
bluff with George Roane. They were stopped at the door of the tavern by a
guard, who told them that the sheriff's body had been taken across the
street to the empty lot.

He saw Edgar Cullis and Mayor Corbin wandering together in
apparent helplessness. Hugh rode over to them. Cullis looked up at him, at
first not recognizing his opponent. When he did, it was without his usual
hostility for the master of Meum Hall. "Mr. Vishonn is dead," he said.

Hugh did not reply immediately. He studied the man who had once
been his mentor in politics, but who had turned against him in incremental
degrees as resistance to Parliamentary authority grew. Hugh's mouth
twisted in merciless contempt. "You have reaped here what you have sown,
Mr. Cullis." Then he turned his mount around and walked it away.

Hugh stopped in front of Rittles's shop, dismounted, and tied his horse to the post there. He walked over to the empty lot to see if he could recognize any of the dead.

Muriel Tippet had found her husband's body. She sat in the high grass next to it, sobbing quietly. Hugh recognized many of the other faces, men he had known well or been acquainted with. Here was Will Kenny, brother of Jude, who had died at Charlestown. And young Travis Barret, still clutching his fife. Both had survived the ferocity of Breed's Hill, only to die here. Here was Steven Safford. Two bodies away from him lay Reverend Albert Acland. And, next to him, Reece Vishonn.

He moved on to another body, and with an involuntary exclamation suddenly knelt down next to it when he recognized the face of a man from Meum Hall, that of Champion, who had helped him fashion the pieces of the conduit years ago and had maintained it every since. The face was as black and well-chiseled as Glorious Swain's had been. The straps holding a powder horn and cartridge pouch crossed his broad chest; above where the straps crossed, his rough shirt had become matted to the blood of where he was struck by a musket ball. Champion had probably come here with his fowling piece, with which he had often gone hunting and brought back game for himself and for the table of the great house.

Hugh could not remember the man having expressed any political sentiments; he had not known that he had anything to do with Jack Frake's volunteer militia. But he knew that, even before news of Charlestown reached Caxton, there had been talk among his former slaves about which side to join, if war came: the British, because it was rumored that Governor Dunmore might emancipate Virginia slaves who left their masters to rally to the king's colors; or the patriots, because it was rumored that any slaves who joined them might be declared freedmen.

Champion's eyes were half open. Hugh reached over and closed them.

Some men entered the lot, carrying two more bodies from the outskirts of town. With them were two marines, carrying the dead men's muskets. Hugh rose. There was something oddly familiar about the bodies. Hugh held up a hand. The men stopped. He stood between the bodies and lifted the hats that had been placed over the faces. He gasped when he recognized Obedience Robbins and William Hurry, Jack Frake's business agent and steward. They had been bayoneted.

The marines moved on to add the confiscated weapons to a pile of them across the street. When they were out of earshot, one of the men, a farmer from across Hove Stream who knew Hugh, said, "It's a terrible sorrowful day here, sir. Will you tell Mr. Frake where his gentlemen can be found?"

Hugh could only nod. "How did these soldiers come here?" he asked.

"They're not soldiers, sir. They're marines," answered the man. "They came on the *Sparrowhawk*. It's gone upriver, to do more mischief, I suppose." Then he and his companion moved a few more steps and gently put down their burden.

"I see," Hugh said. He stood for a long moment, anguished and angry about what had happened here and what he had seen. Then he turned and walked back to mount his horse and ride back to Meum Hall. He could take no more of it.

As he passed Lucas Rittles's shop, he heard someone whistle. A narrow, grass-grown alley ran the length between Rittles's shop and the millinery. Hugh peered down it and saw a figure gesturing to him. It was John Proudlocks.

Hugh strode down the alley, and Proudlocks pulled him behind the shop.

"John!" exclaimed Hugh, holding the man's shoulders. "You're…safe! Where is Jack?"

Proudlocks glanced around the corner to make sure that Hugh had not been followed. "He is safe, Mr. Kenrick. He is rendezvousing with what is left of the Company at the Otway place. I left him to come here…to see Miss Heathcoate. But I would be recognized by any of those marines. I know she would be helping our wounded, but I have not seen her out on the street. I cannot risk going into her shop. Perhaps she is too frightened of those marines. Would you bring her to me? Here?"

"Of course, John." He wanted to ask his friend more about his interest in the woman, but guessed the reason before he could ask the question. Proudlocks could be as discreet as he could be talkative.

Hugh strode back down the alley to Lydia Heathcoate's millinery, opened the door, and entered. And saw the woman's body. It was too much. He groaned and sagged against the counter where he and Reverdy had many times chosen fabrics and discussed colors and fashions with the seamstress. He balled his hands into fists and pounded the counter top once. He looked up and saw the broken window glass, which a musket ball must have hit during the skirmish. Then, his expression grim, he lifted the woman's body, left the shop, and returned down the alley. Proudlocks saw him coming.

"I'm sorry…John." Hugh had never before seen grief in Proudlocks's eyes, and did not wish to see it again. Proudlocks leaned his musket against the wall and took the body from him. He gazed at the dead face, then pressed his lips on the woman's hair. He put her down in the grass, took out a knife, and gently cut a few tresses from her hair, then carefully removed a length of lace from the woman's cuff. He wrapped the tresses in the lace and put the memento inside his frock coat.

Hugh said, "I wish I could sketch her for you, John. Then you could have that to keep."

"I will not forget her face," answered Proudlocks, nodding in thanks but not looking up. He forced himself to rise. "Will you put her with the others, where they are putting the fallen?"

"Yes."

Proudlocks smiled sadly at Hugh Kenrick. He raised an arm and gripped one of his friend's shoulders. "You will join us. Meum Hall is doomed, as well. There are hard years ahead of us."

"Yes," answered Hugh. "Hard years."

Proudlocks glanced once again at Lydia Heathcoate, then turned and sprinted away.

Hugh stooped and lifted the body of the woman again, and walked slowly back to the empty lot. When at last he mounted his horse and rode out of Caxton, more people from the outlying parts of the county were streaming into town, to see what had happened, or to determine what had happened to relatives or friends. The last persons he noticed were Barbara Vishonn and a servant in a riding chair, arriving anxiously from Enderly.

\*   \*   \*

Major Ragsdale had inspected the room assigned to him on the second floor of the Gramatan Inn, and approved of it. His battalion was being billeted in Safford's tavern and in an empty shop across from it. He had sent for his and his officer's baggage before the *Sparrowhawk* departed upriver, and set a lieutenant to work writing a report in the battalion's daybook. He was coming back downstairs to the tavern below it when one of Jared Hunt's Customsmen saw him and approached. "Major, sir," said the man, "Mr. Hunt suggests that, if you have the time and when your men are rested, you might want to visit the plantations of two of the rebel leaders. He asked me to show you the way. They are not far."

"Whose plantations, sir?"

"One owned by Jock Fraser, who is a lieutenant in that militia. And Sachem Hall, owned by an Indian, John Proudlocks, who is a sergeant in the militia. They fired on your men."

"Oh?" said Ragsdale. "The chap who potted the reverend? That must be him. Well, sir, my officers and I will have something to eat here first, and then we will see to it. You will join us, of course, and inform us what we are to do once we call on these places." He smiled, looked convivial, and added with a wink, "And, you may also tell us a little about your Mr. Hunt. He is doubtless the most pushing man in service I have ever met, excepting myself."

*　　*　　*

Buell Tragle, master of the *Sparrowhawk*, ordered both anchors dropped when the vessel was positioned in the York directly opposite Morland Hall, as close to the riverbank as he could manage. There were ten guns on the port side, but only five had crews standing by. Jared Hunt waited patiently while other crewmen secured the sails above and until Tragle was satisfied that the merchantman would not drift from her position.

It was understood between Tragle and Hunt that Hunt was the nominal captain, because the vessel was now Customs property, and that he would command the crew in this aspect of the task at hand. One of the crewmen was a deserter from the navy, a former master gunner who was hired on with a group of unemployed seamen in Norfolk. He advised Hunt of the best way to assault a stationary shore target. Below decks was the ordnance that the vessel usually carried; to it had been added ordnance from a naval depot. Hunt did not need to worry about wasting shots.

One gun was consequently loaded with ball and fired to establish range. The violence of the report made Hunt start and nearly deafened him. Nearby waterfowl rose from the water and flew off, and birds in the trees near the great house swarmed away in confusion. Until now, Hunt had never heard a gun fired before, except in London from a distance, when troops were on parade. He watched closely from the quarterdeck to see where the ball landed. He observed a little puff of dust raised a few yards from the great house and a sapling whip back and forth as the ball came to rest against it. Some figures appeared in front of the house. With a spyglass he had appropriated from Captain Geary, he saw that they were two women and a man. Morland staff, he presumed.

Hunt shouted down to the gunners, "Fire another ball, and hit the house."

This was done. The ball struck a corner. Some bricks and masonry tumbled to the ground. The figures darted away and disappeared.

"We've fixed the right amount of powder to reach the house, sir," the master gunner shouted up to Hunt.

"Good. Now, gentlemen, try a carcass."

The carcass, or incendiary shot, took more time to prepare and load. Its components also had to be brought up by powder monkeys from below deck. In the meantime, the crews of the first two guns swabbed their weapons and prepared their own carcasses.

"Fire when you are ready," shouted Hunt. The third gun was fired. The projectile, a ball to which was attached by iron rings a "sabot" or sealed shoe containing the still glowing embers of wood and fragments of metal heated in the galley, hurtled at half the speed of sound over the water, bluff, and the great lawn. It struck the house below one of the second-story windows, exploding on impact and sending burning material in a short-lived star onto the lawn.

But luck was with Jared Hunt. He did not know it yet; one of the embers shot upward and fell onto the shingled roof of the great house. He could not yet see the fragment and its wind-swept column of white smoke. "Excellent," he said. "Let's see how quickly we can set the place ablaze. I won't leave here until nothing stands but the brick walls. And if we can manage it, not even those." He stepped down from the quarterdeck and addressed the master gunner. "In the meantime, two of your guns here can lob balls over the house to see if we can bring down some of the out buildings. I want this place rendered useless, fit only for the domicile of beggars."

"Yes, sir," said the master gunner. It did not matter to him what the Customsman's goals were. He volunteered, "These guns won't reach the fields beyond the house."

Hunt shrugged. "Major Ragsdale's fellows will visit the fields and burn them. We will leave the rebel nothing to salvage."

For the next two hours, the guns of the *Sparrowhawk* fired incessantly at the great house. Some of the carcasses fell short of their target to land in the lawn's manicured shrubbery, setting it ablaze. Hunt chuckled when he saw figures rushing madly around the lawn with pails of water, then give up and disappear. But most of the shells struck the house, a few smashing through the windows. Flames began to lick from them on both floors. With a grunt of satisfaction, Hunt saw a fire spread over the roof, and smoke rise from holes made by balls that had pierced the roof.

Hunt considered his task complete when the black rectangles of all the windows on both floors flared red with orange fire. The entire roof was on fire now, collapsing all of a sudden into the house. Hunt noticed some out buildings to the side of the inferno. The kitchen, he presumed. He was about to ask his gunners if they could perhaps land a few shells on them, when the east wall abruptly crumbled and fell onto the structures. He laughed and shouted down from the quarterdeck to the master gunner, "There's roasting for you, sir! Fine, absolutely fine work!"

The master gunner nodded in acknowledgement of the compliment, then raised his arm and pointed in a direction beyond the conflagration. "Look, Mr. Hunt. This isn't the only house burning."

Hunt turned and saw two pillars of smoke over some woods, separated by a few miles. "Ah! Major Ragsdale is roasting geese, as well!"

*     *     *

It was a hot, humid August evening. The heat seemed to emanate from the fires.

The remnants of the Queen Anne Volunteer Company — reduced by casualties to twenty men — stood in some woods on the Otway place and, across the wide fields abandoned to scrub and weeds, watched the destruction of Morland Hall. They, too, had observed the smoke rising in the direction of Sachem Hall and Jock Fraser's place.

Jack Frake stood alone, spyglass clutched in both hands behind his back. His men stood behind him at a distance, or rested on boulders or on trees felled by the hurricane that had ruined the Otway plantation years ago. Jock Fraser and John Proudlocks stood apart directly behind him.

Jack Frake's sight was fixed on what he could discern of the blackened walls and the dying red glow in the shell of the great house of Morland. If he detected movement, he would raise the spyglass to identify it. About an hour before, just as the *Sparrowhawk* hoisted its anchors and drifted back downriver, he noticed another kind of red moving around the plantation. He saw that it was a company of marines. Soon after their arrival, more fires broke out, in the tenants' quarters and in the fields.

Henry Buckle, Proudlocks's cooper, arrived on horseback just before dusk to inform his employer that Sachem Hall had been burned to the ground, the out buildings fired, and the crops destroyed. He added that he had seen a company of marines marching to Jock Fraser's place. "And Mr. Maxwell the tanner said he saw Mr. Hurry and Mr. Robbins amongst the dead in town," he said to Jack Frake.

This Jack Frake had guessed, or that they had been wounded or captured. His business agent and steward had rushed to join the Company as it marched into Caxton from the Hove Stream Bridge. He had felt a pride for them when he noticed them then.

"What of Mr. Corsin?" Proudlocks had asked of his business agent. "And the others?"

"Mr. Corsin left in the riding chair for Williamsburg, sir," said Buckle, "before the redcoats showed up. I saw him take his traveling bag. The rest of our people are making plans to see kin hereabouts, or go west away from such troubles."

At the moment, Jack Frake looked serene and untroubled. But many in the Company knew better. Proudlocks stepped forward and said to his friend, "That is the end of it."

Jack Frake at first said nothing. It was the most melancholy statement he had ever heard Proudlocks utter. His friend returned hours before, before Buckle appeared, and other than briefly describing what he had seen in town, remained quiet. Jack Frake knew the quality of the man's silence. Taking Proudlocks aside, he asked him what was wrong. Proudlocks told him about Lydia Heathcoate. "Mr. Kenrick brought her to me, from her shop. I think she died instantly, when the marines fired on Mr. Vishonn's men. Her last words to me were that they burned our ensign. And my last words to her were to go back inside the shop, where she would be safe, she would sew another."

Jack Frake could only say, "I'm sorry, John." It sounded hollow, but was not. Proudlocks knew the quality of his friend's courtesies.

Now he said, "Yes, that is the end of it." After a moment, Jack Frake asked, "Will you come with me to check on the staff and tenants? Just you and I. The rest of the Company will stay here with Jock."

Proudlocks nodded. "Of course."

After giving orders to Fraser, Jack Frake and Proudlocks crossed the darkened field and cautiously approached the worm fence that divided Morland from the Otway property. They saw figures milling around in the glow of the dying fire in the great house, and in front of the charred remains of the tenants' quarters, work sheds, and stable. The odors of burnt tobacco and corn hung in the air. There did not seem to be any marines about.

The somber welcome Jack Frake and Proudlocks received from the staff and tenants when they strode together into the open ensured them that they were not risking capture by the marines. Surrounded by the people they had known and worked with for years, all their faces lit sharply by flambeaux and fire, they told them about the fight in town, and learned what had happened at Morland.

There had been only one casualty, Henry Dakin, the cooper, who was in his shed when a ball smashed through the roof. Ruth Dakin, his wife and the housekeeping servant, asked Jack Frake for permission to bury him somewhere on the grounds. He assented. Mary Beck, the cook, and her husband Israel produced the portrait of Etáin, the crystal decanter and glasses, and some of their employer's clothes they had managed to save from the house. "It was horrible, Mr. Frake," said the cook. "There was no time to save anything else. Please forgive us."

Jack Frake assured them that it was all right. When they told him they planned to go to Richmond to stay with friends, he said, "Take the portrait and the other things with you. I'll fetch them another day." Most of the staff and tenants said they would be leaving the county for Williamsburg and other towns.

"Mr. Kenrick came by and said some of us could stay at his place until we were ready to go," said George Passmore, the overseer.

"What will you do now?" asked Susannah Giddens, the housekeeper.

"Fight on," Jack Frake answered.

A few of the men said they wished to join the Company, including Mouse and some of the other black tenants. "We've no home now, sir, and no kin to turn to," said Moses Topham, the carpenter. "We want to fight the Crown that did this."

"You're welcome to join us," said Jack Frake. "The Company has a cache of arms it can outfit you with. And I understand that the Virginia Convention is organizing the militia here. You might consider enlisting in one of the other county militias, too. The Congress has approved an army, as well."

"Where would we march to?" asked Aymer Crompton, the brickmaker.

"Nowhere, at the moment. The Company will stay here until we have accomplished one task."

Surprised by this statement, John Proudlocks turned to Jack Frake and asked, "Which is what?"

Jack Frake turned and looked at the scorched walls of the great house. He nodded once, and answered, "Destroy the *Sparrowhawk*."

"Why?" asked Proudlocks.

Jack Frake smiled. "To cut the last tie, John. To assert our independence."

# Chapter 17: The Last Pippin

When the world and all that is familiar in it to a man begin to crash around him, and he is helpless to combat the causes or consequences, he may retreat into moroseness, or seek refuge in drink or in a trivial distraction. He cannot remain indifferent to the fate of things he has long cared about, or depended upon. A cataclysm requires an action. A more fatal action, however, than lapsing into grim sullenness, inebriated forgetfulness, or reckless diversion, is the paralysis of hopelessness.

Hugh Kenrick had rarely felt it. When he had, he resented it, fought it, and silently cursed it. He did not wish to surrender to the inevitable. He did not believe in the inevitable. Hopelessness was an unwelcome intruder in his soul.

When that gloating harpy chanced to invade his soul to find a perch in it, Hugh's past had served as its purging antidote. This evening, he sought consolation in it, to draw strength from a time when his vision of the future did not include the things such as he had seen today in Caxton and at Morland Hall. His past had always birthed his future, and allowed him to act to reach it. "I have done this, and now I shall do that." There was nothing to stop him but himself. When he needed that reassurance, mere recollection was usually enough. But this evening he felt a need to put his hands on the physical evidence of his past.

He had just finished advising his staff and tenants of what had happened in Caxton, and warning them not to go into town while the marines were there, when the *Sparrowhawk* began its bombardment of Morland Hall. He remembered the words of the farmer, that the vessel had gone upriver to do more mischief. He instantly remounted his horse and galloped from Meum Hall and over the path that connected the plantations. When he arrived at Morland, all he could do was watch Jack Frake's home being turned into a funeral pyre.

The *Sparrowhawk* not only had set fire to the great house, but also was hurtling balls over it to fall onto many of the out buildings close to it. Many of the projectiles spat out dirt and stone as they fell and gouged out soil, and caused knots of the tenants and staff standing in the field to dart out of the way when the iron bounded a few yards more.

Hugh rode to some woods that bordered the great house and led to the bluff overlooking the river, the better to see the vessel. The smoke from the guns hung in the humid, unmoving August air alongside the *Sparrowhawk*, obscuring the deck and the figures on it before rising languidly to her masts. Every few minutes a flash would stab through the white haze, and a projectile strike the house or fly over it. He thought: That ship brought the both of us here, years apart, and now it has come to take us back. Jared Hunt was likely on that vessel. He thought: My uncle the Earl of Danvers sent that man to wreak a terrible vengeance on me. He is as determined to kill me as I am to live. Why does he wait?

Hugh wondered if he could ever resolve to destroy a man. Not just oppose him and defeat him, but eradicate him, so that he was no longer a threat or a concern to anyone. It would be necessary to extinguish that man, he thought, for he was an arm of malevolence, an envoy of hate.

Hugh shuddered at the prospect of removing Hunt from the realm of the living. He felt that it was too much like his uncle's resolve to destroy him.

Hugh rode back to the fields past the burning great house and addressed the first person he encountered, Israel Beck, Jack Frake's bookkeeper. He told this man, first, that Obedience Robbins and William Hurry were dead, and then that he would be happy to allow the staff to stay at Meum Hall or with his own tenants until they made further arrangements. "I cannot stay here and watch this," he concluded. "There is nothing I can do to stop it." Even as he spoke, a ball struck the roof of the house that Robbins, Hurry, and Beck and his wife lived in. Some fragments from the impact showered him and Beck, stinging their hands and faces.

Hugh rode back to Meum Hall along the connecting path. On his way, he encountered groups of his own tenants who had left their chores to walk to Morland to witness the spectacle or perhaps to offer assistance. He said nothing to them. They would see for themselves what might be the future of Meum Hall.

Back in his study, he paced back and forth, feeling restless but unable to find a task to occupy his mind. About an hour after his return, the sounds of the bombardment of Morland ceased. Hulton came in and discreetly enquired about his needs. Hugh could only smile. "There is nothing you can do for me," he answered. "Go to Morland and see if you can help anyone there."

"Why is that ship harming your friend's place?" asked the former sergeant and valet.

"Because my friend deserted the Crown, as well," Hugh replied.

Hulton nodded in tentative understanding, and withdrew from the study.

He was fond of Hulton, and glad to have him back. Some inexplicable connection caused him to glance at the shelf of juvenilia that he had put at the bottom of one of his bookcases. He saw copybooks from his tutoring days at Danvers and at Dr. Comyn's School in London. He felt a sudden urge to retreat into his past. He took a handful of them and took them to his desk.

He found the one in which he had written, on the day that he had neglected to bow to the Duke of Cumberland, "I would die inside, and nourish a wrong." *Hello*, he said in his mind to that boy. *I have been true to you.*

In another copybook from his later education in Dr. Comyn's School, he found an episode from one of his conflicts with an instructor there over a translation exercise from Alfred the Great's translation of Boethius's *De Consolatione Philosophiæ*, or *The Consolations of Philosophy*, into English from the Latin:

"True high birth is of the mind, not of the flesh; and every man that is given over to vices foresaketh his Creator, and his origin, and his birth, and loseth rank till he fall to low estate."

The surprise written assignment by the instructor was to translate in class the Latin into English, without having seen Alfred's translation or the contemporary translation of it from the Anglo-Saxon by a scholar from John Locke's time. The instructor then graded the students' translations according to how closely each matched Alfred's. Hugh had been awarded his class's only top mark by the instructor. This man, however, felt obliged to correct Hugh's parenthetical substitution in a lengthy digression of "nature" for "Creator," subjecting Hugh to a lecture that was more a disciplinary reprimand than instruction. Hugh conceded the fault, answering that since there were elements of Christian Platonism in the quotation, it all depended on one's definition of vice, as well. "Providing that an agreed definition of it may be arrived at, a man of reason, however, will eschew vice for vastly different reasons, reasons at odds with those which would move a devout man to eschew it."

He had written an impish comment in the margin of the copybook page on which he had narrated the episode, one that captured the instructor's rejection of his counter-arguments: "Certain clerisy will not tolerate heresy!" And, prompted and intrigued by the quotation in that assignment, Hugh subsequently read the translated *De Consolatione*, not caring for most of it, but finding in it little gems of insight and observation.

Hugh thought now: There were so many little truths admixed in so much wrong-headedness. Someday, a philosopher will take all those little truths and formulate a philosophy that cannot be refuted or opposed or contradicted. He smiled for the first time today. Glorious Swain thought I would be the one to accomplish that task. To fashion a golden orrery, that man had called it. To draw the map to Olympus. To conceive of a man-ennobling ethic that did not need the angel-water of any church to give it sanctity, as another Pippin had described it. Nor the leave of a sovereign.

No, he told himself. I am not the one for that task. I am more like King Alfred, the scholar, inventor, and unifier, and can only contribute notes and isolated truths and see the mere aura of a great possibility. If this new country is ever born, he thought, it will give a greater mind than my own the chance to fashion that orrery, to draw that map, to construe that ethic. It is the only instance of due deference I could ever grant, to a person I may never know.

Then his glance fell on the two volumes on his shelf of Romney Marsh's *Hyperborea: or, the Adventures of Drury Trantham, Shipwrecked Merchant, in the Unexplored Northern Regions.* Ah! There was another wonderful chapter from his youth, his discovery of that novel! He had not read it in years. He rose instantly and eagerly retrieved the books from the shelf, took them back to his desk, and was soon lost in rereading his favorite passages in the novel. He saw himself in that epic, just as he saw himself in the present one. He felt no difference in spirit between them.

Some hours later, after it had grown dark, he felt a mere twinge of irritation when Spears came in and announced the presence of Edgar Cullis. He closed a book and frowned. He had no reason to see the man ever again, just as he presumed that Cullis had no reason to see him. "I'll see him on the porch, Spears. Thank you." Hugh rose a minute later and left the study.

Edgar Cullis stood under the lit lantern that was suspended from the roof of the porch. He wore a suit of clothes different from those Hugh had seen him wearing in Caxton. He did not look dazed, or lost. His face seemed older somehow, and drawn. When Hugh came out, he turned and nodded.

"Yes, Mr. Cullis?" asked Hugh. He stood on the opposite side of the porch steps from the man.

"I came here to tell you that I am leaving Caxton, and the county. My father has…disowned me, and asked me to vacate his home at my earliest convenience. He holds me responsible for what happened today. I will leave tomorrow for Williamsburg, to stay with my cousin there, and arrange for my things to be sent there, as well. Then I shall make my way to Hampton, and, after I have settled some business and divested my clients, depart for England. I do not wish to be present when Virginia is subdued by the Crown." Cullis paused to take a deep breath, then added, "I tell you this now because you will learn of it soon enough."

Hugh cocked his head in indifference. "You could have sent me a note, sir, and saved yourself the trouble of coming here."

Cullis shook his head. "No, that would not have been to my pleasure. I want you to know that I hold *you* responsible for what happened here. You have always astounded me with the hubris of your convictions, with your immoderate pride in them, and with the betrayal of your natural station. I would say that the insufferable confidence that you put on the rightness of your ideas and actions has never failed to rankle me and many others. But it does not merely rankle. It offends. Perhaps it would profit you if you returned to England to rediscover your origins and your heritage. The colonies are not for you." He scoffed. "They are certainly no longer for me."

"I must agree with you, Mr. Cullis. You no longer belong here. This is a new country. However, I have not betrayed my natural station, which is here. As for the rest, I respectfully disagree, and offer no apology for having offended you or anyone else." But Hugh was puzzled by the man's presence. "Why did you come here to tell me this, sir? That you have, smacks of a certain feather of hubris itself."

"To prove to you that I have courage, as well."

Hugh shook his head. "Granted, that took courage. Would that you had found it when you pondered desertion of the Resolves ten years ago."

"You will never forgive me for that, will you?"

Hugh shook his head. "Never."

"Then I am finished here. Good night to you, sir." Edgar Cullis stepped off the porch onto the path and approached his horse tethered to the post in front.

When he had mounted it, Hugh asked Cullis before he could ride away, "Do you remember the day I first addressed the House, Mr. Cullis, over the wording of the memorial, and how excited you were over the row I raised?

We met outside the Capitol, in a chill evening."

Cullis scowled. What he was then, he did not care to contemplate. "I remember it. What of it?"

Hugh said, in the manner of a quotation, "Surely, sir, you know that as bees are lured by the pollen of flowers, bullies are drawn by the funk of the timid." He smiled. "The man to whom I offered that fillip of advice, is the man I wish to remember. Thank you for all your assistance, in those days."

Cullis looked wounded. He sniffed once, and remarked, "*Your* feather of hubris, sir, will be the death of you, some day." He muttered an inaudible imprecation beneath his breath, angrily yanked the reins of his mount around, and rode away at a canter.

*    *    *

Jared Hunt was sitting at a large round table in the Gramatan Inn with his Customsmen, and also with Major Ragsdale and his officers, when Edgar Cullis entered the establishment.

"Well, look who has arrived!" announced Hunt to his companions, nodding to the door. "Seems that someone administered him an ordinate dose of smelling salts!" Hunt had been drinking, more than any of his companions. He was about to stand and signal to the lawyer, but Cullis saw him first and came over. At Hunt's invitation, he found a chair and sat down at the table.

"I know where you can find Mr. Frake and his renegades, sir," he said without preamble. "They are at the Otway place. You might also find a veritable arsenal there, as well, if I am to believe my informant."

Hunt raised his eyebrows in pleased surprise. "Do you refer to that mess of ruins by the little inlet, farther up the York?"

Cullis nodded. "That is the place. It was a fine plantation, once. A hurricane swamped it."

Ragsdale laughed, and said to Hunt in mock accusation, "Then you destroyed the chap's place for naught, Mr. Hunt."

Hunt shook his head vigorously. "Oh, no, sir! Not for naught! I meant to destroy it in any event, as an object lesson!" Then he paused to study Cullis with some curiosity. "You say your informant told you about this place, sir. May I ask who?" He leaned closer to the lawyer. "You see, I have my own choir of them here, and they did not tell me about this sanctuary of Mr. Frake's."

"Perhaps it was because they had no knowledge of it. Since it will no longer matter to him, it was Sheriff Tippet, sir," said Cullis. "A six-pounder once stood in front of his place, and was used for years to celebrate His Majesty's birthday and such. Its theft one night a time ago inspired him to make some nocturnal observations. On two occasions he observed Mr. Frake and others journeying to the Otway place with cartloads of powder and arms. At least, that is what he thought they were. It was dark."

"So your fellow committeemen knew!" exclaimed Hunt.

Cullis twisted his mouth in disgust. "Only I, sir. Sheriff Tippet told me it in confidence. Now that he is...gone...there is no confidence to honor."

"Well, I did not know the man so well, Mr. Cullis, but from the beginning, I suspected Mr. Tippet of frail loyalty."

Cullis smiled. "*Frail* loyalty? My compliments, sir, on an apt description of his character."

Hunt waved over Mary Griffin, the serving wench, who happened to be one of his paid informants, and ordered another round of ale for his companions. "And bring Mr. Cullis here a double measure, dearie! He is an especial friend of mine!"

Cullis nodded thanks. "I don't know for how long I may remain your especial friend, sir," he said. "I will soon quit Virginia for England."

Hunt looked concerned. "Surely, not because of what happened here today?"

"No. Not entirely."

Hunt remembered then his knowledge of the conflict between Cullis and his father, Ralph Cullis, obtained by him through his tongue-wagging, gossiping informants in the past. "I see. Filial contentions, and parental preponderance! I know something about that, sir," remarked Hunt, thinking of his father, the Earl of Danvers. "Is there no chance of reconciliation?"

"Not a whit. My father can be quite...oxen."

"Well, you have my sympathies, and good wishes in England. Will you take up the law there?"

"That is my plan. I know some barristers there, and Mr. John Randolph, our former Attorney-General, has also departed for the mother country. I am certain I will not lack for occupation or place."

Hunt laughed and kept up his transparent *bonhomie*. "Well, they say there are too many lawyers, but I've always countered there are not enough, God bless them!"

It was transparent to Cullis. He did not mind. He was hoping the conversation would turn in a certain direction.

The talk continued in that light vein for a while. Major Ragsdale and his officers at length excused themselves and left to check on their battalion. Hunt leaned closer to Cullis. "There are two other large properties here, Mr. Cullis. Granby Hall, and Mr. Kenrick's place. The Granby people must keep to themselves overmuch. I have not been able to obtain much information on them. If you please, how might they fit into the situation here? I ask this so that I may avoid making errors of judgment."

Cullis replied, "Mr. Ira Granby died about three years ago. His wife, Damaris, is being courted by a gentleman from Williamsburg, whose eye covets Granby Hall more than the widow, to my mind. William Granby, the son, married my sister, Eleanor. They reside in Gloucester. Their daughter, Selina, married Mr. Vishonn's son, James. They have a place in Surry. I expect they will all soon congregate here for Mr. Vishonn's funeral, such as it might be, there no longer being a pastor."

Cullis sipped his ale, and shook his head. "They none of them fit much into the situation here, Mr. Hunt. They are decidedly without opinion." He smiled. "However, William Granby was once my fellow burgess. When he gave up the seat, it was filled by Mr. Kenrick, who has kept it ever since." He chuckled darkly. "I regret the day I ever pressed him to stand for the seat. For if there is a situation here, Mr. Hunt, he is the person most responsible for it." He smiled again, pointedly, for the conversation had turned in the right direction. "If it were not for him, and the treasonous Resolves he supported against my advice, perhaps there would be no... situation." He raised a hand and gestured vaguely to Queen Anne Street outside.

"I don't doubt that, sir. I have heard the most odious and blotting things about him," remarked Hunt. He knew, from his informants, that Cullis and Hugh Kenrick had once been friends. But Cullis was bitter, and he knew that embittered men had a reputation for being very cooperative in the matter of turning on friends and colleagues. It was a trait he appreciated and had often taken advantage of in service to his father. "Well, it may please you to know that I have an object lesson in mind for that chap, as well. I hope you may tarry long enough here to witness it."

"When, and how?" Cullis asked, not quite disguising his eagerness.

Hunt grinned, shook his head, and put a playful finger to his lips. "My secret, sir! My privilege!"

Cullis wrapped his hands around his tankard. "I do not know the character of your informants, sir, but they could hardly have told you odious and blotting things about Mr. Kenrick. Perhaps they confuse spite with sound appraisal, and misinformed you. He is without opprobrium or stain. That has been his danger, and the key to his influence, from the first moment I met him."

Cullis took a draught from his ale. "He and Mr. Frake are of the same stamp, mind you, and closer friends than I have ever observed. I rode to Morland this evening, to see the justice you meted out to the renegade. You may take it as a measure of the success of your justice that many townsmen here are shaking in their boots, and have put their resentments aside." Cullis looked across the room at the comely figure of Mary Griffin. "Should you decide to deal Mr. Kenrick the same justice, I believe the town and county will be yours, and His Majesty will be in your debt."

Hunt nearly blurted out the question, "He was a friend of yours, once?" but checked himself in time. Instead, he collapsed back in his chair, slightly stunned by both the confession and the callowness with which it was made. It rivaled his own hard-nosed manner. For the first time ever since he learned of his father's malice-driven obsession with Hugh Kenrick, and was despatched here to quench it, even now in his slightly inebriated state, he understood clearly the root of that obsession. Suddenly he was not comfortable with his purpose. It was too much like the matter of Dogmael Jones, whose demise he had arranged years ago. He had, much against his will, developed a grudging admiration for that man for the flagrant way he had defied the power of Parliament. An admiration that was a secret envy. He had consoled himself with the notion that the world was too corrupt for such admirable men, and good riddance to them, they ought to be grateful they can leave it.

He wished now that Cullis had not told him anything about Hugh Kenrick. He was no longer comfortable in the company of the man. There was an element of his father the Earl in the lawyer, except that this man was different. He had fallen from his own grace, whereas Hunt knew that neither he nor his father the Earl had ever attained any. He could deal with such "graceless" men as equals, and share their outlook on the world without guilt or reproach by them or himself. But some natural, ineluctable revulsion for Cullis welled up in Hunt. It was contempt. He was uncomfortable with that appraisal, as well. It was not practical.

Hunt took a last swallow of his ale, then put down the tankard and slapped his hands flat on the table. "Well, sir!" he said. "I must retire! Busy day ahead of me! And I am sure you have packing to do and such, settling business and ridding yourself of friends, if you are quitting Virginia." He rose and patted Cullis twice on the shoulder. "Good night to you, Mr. Cullis. And thank you for the information." He nodded to his Customs subordinates to follow suit, and turned and made his way through the tavern to the steps that led to the rooms upstairs.

Edgar Cullis abruptly found himself alone at the table, feeling again the angry humiliation of having been treated like a dependable and loyal dog. He stared into his ale, and wondered if he did not deserve it. But it was too late. He knew he could soften the feeling by drowning the regret in drink. He waved to Mary Griffin for another tankard.

*   *   *

Jared Hunt paced for a while in the tiny confines of his private room above the tavern, thinking furiously, and recovering from the unsavory emotions he had felt downstairs. Until Cullis had divulged where Jack Frake might be found, he had had no definite plan to deal with either him or Hugh Kenrick. But now an idea was germinating in his mind. He left his room and invited himself to Major Ragsdale's own private billet down the hallway to discuss the matter.

# Chapter 18: The Arrest

Only two walls of the Otway great house remained standing, and most of the other out buildings had been leveled into piles of rubble that were now sprouting chickweed, horsetails, and poplar saplings.

The smithy stood on slightly higher ground than did the other structures, far from the great house, and had not been inundated or weakened when the York was driven by winds to overrun its banks and flood the rest of the low-lying grounds. It had housed most of the ordnance and arms that Jack Frake had hidden. That very evening, the smithy was occupied by men, some who talked, and some who labored.

"How many of them can we make?"

"About a dozen."

"And our powder?"

"We have perhaps enough to fire six, if we leave enough to fire the other guns."

"Yes. Don't forget the swivel gun, and the long-gun. We'll need them all."

"The marines might attack us from the east and south, from across the Hove Stream."

"The pickets will warn us of their approach. And I'm certain the marines will come. Someone in Caxton is sure to remember this place."

"It is a whole battalion, sir, and we've barely half a company left."

"That major of theirs, he's quick and sharp. Took us by surprise in town."

"Some of their officers will learn from the mistakes of others."

"Why must we destroy the *Sparrowhawk*?"

"To deny the Crown her use as a warship, against us, against everyone. Remember, she was originally built as a warship, and if Hunt has kept only half her former crew, she would still be formidable."

"Could we not raid the *Basilisk*, sir? We could not sail it — none of us knows the first thing about it — but we could damage it or even sink it."

The captain shook his head. "There are more men in its crew than we have men here, Jock. Besides, marines guard the pier." He shook his head again. "No, the *Sparrowhawk* will come here. I am sure of it. We are Mr.

Hunt's unfinished business."

Jock Fraser looked disappointed. He did not like waiting for an enemy.

Jack Frake added, "If the marines had not done it first, Mr. Fraser, I would have put the torch to my own fields, to deny the Crown any value in it should they have decided to harvest the crops and send them to England."

Jack Frake, Jock Fraser, and John Proudlocks stood together in the smithy, their faces lit by flambeaux and by the fire in the stoked oven. Henry Buckle from Sachem Hall, and Aymer Crompton and Isaac Zimmerman from Morland were laboring over a bellows and forge, fashioning with hammers and tongs iron straps from metal debris found on the grounds. They were making the elements of carcasses.

Jack Frake was certain that either the *Basilisk*, or the *Sparrowhawk*, or both vessels, would come upriver to attack him and his men. He reasoned that the *Basilisk*, a sloop, would anchor in the shallow inlet west of the Otway place, and the *Sparrowhawk* on the river itself. His men were placing the swivel gun and the long-gun at the western edge of the property, close to the water, to counter the *Basilisk*. The wheeled cannon he and his men had taken from Sheriff Tippet's lawn months ago was being fixed to face the river and the *Sparrowhawk*. It was this gun that would attempt to disable the merchantman with the carcasses. Tied to bushes on the inlet were three boats that Jack Frake and some of his men had paddled upriver. They would allow the Company to escape, when the time came.

The men worked far into the night, preparing for the next day.

*   *   *

The next morning was bright and cloudless. It had not rained in weeks, and Hugh Kenrick wondered how long the drought would last. He was having breakfast when Spears appeared in the supper room. "Sir, there are men here to see you," he announced ominously.

"Who?"

"That Customsman, sir. He came with one of his own men. And there is an officer with some of those marines from town."

He waits no longer, thought Hugh. "Show Mr. Hunt only into the study, Spears." Hugh paused. "Is Hulton about?"

"He is preparing to have a bite in the kitchen, sir, and then he said he will assist Mr. Zouch in the brickworks."

"Fetch him first, Spears, and take him to the study. Tell him to hide beneath the desk. The space there is commodious enough for two men. Tell him that Mr. Hunt and I will have words, and I shall want a witness. Tell him to take pains not to let his presence known to me or to Mr. Hunt."

Spears looked puzzled. "Go on, Spears," said Hugh. "It will be all right. When Hulton is ready, then you may show Mr. Hunt in. I will not be far behind."

"Yes, sir." Spears turned and left the room to follow his employer's curious instructions.

Moments later, Hugh heard Spears admit Hunt and another man into the breezeway. He rose and went out. Hunt paused when Hugh emerged from the supper room. Hugh stopped and cordially indicated the open door of the study. Spears, standing behind the Customsmen, stared blankly at Hugh and gave an imperceptible nod. The men went inside. Spears closed the door behind them.

Hugh gestured to the chairs in front of his desk, and went to sit behind it. He pulled back his own chair, sat down, crossed his legs, and leaned back as though he were receiving a call from a good friend. "Well, Mr. Hunt. What is your business here?" The fingers of one hand rested on the desk, patiently toying with the brass top that was always there. He glanced out the window. Two more Customsmen stood beside their mounts. There were three other saddles. One, he supposed, for Mr. Hunt, one for the sour-faced man with him, and a third. A marine lieutenant and ten of his men lounged at the foot of the path leading to the porch.

"Beautiful morning, Mr. Kenrick," answered Hunt as he made himself comfortable. "I was almost tempted to walk the distance from town. But, Mr. Gramatan availed me of his fine stable. Oh, forgive me. This is Mr. Blassard, also of the Customs. He is a necessary appendage to my business."

The man called Blassard sat next to Hunt. He shifted his coat to reveal a pistol wedged into one of his pockets. Hunt then said to his companion, "Mr. Blassard, you will please wait just outside the door. I have confidential matters to discuss with our host. But be ready to enter at your own discretion, if need be."

The silent Blassard rose and left the room, shutting the door behind him.

Hunt grinned and slapped his hands on his knees. "First, a confession, Mr. Kenrick. We are cousins, of a sort," said Hunt. "I am the son of your father's brother, though I do not boast the same surname." He smiled. "To amend some Bible talk, I am a sin of a father visited upon the son of a brother! Very confusing matter, don't you think?" He was pleased to see the look of surprise on Hugh Kenrick's face. "Turley is my true surname. After my mother. A servant girl, expelled from Danvers."

After a moment, Hugh replied, "I remember the story. That explains much about you."

"Explains much? Explain *that*, if you please, sir."

Hugh shook his head. "What is your business here, Mr. Hunt?"

"My business? It is this: You and I shall leave these wretched shores for England, never to return. Lucre and other rewards await me there, by grace of your generous uncle. As for you, you will stand trial for treason. And perhaps be rewarded with the king's pardon or leniency, and enjoy the mercy of a man whose character you have so recklessly besmirched for so long. I do not know His Majesty, however, so I cannot guarantee such a felicitous end. But, I *know* your career, and all England shall know it, as well."

Hugh was unmoved. He said, "You murdered Dogmael Jones."

This time it was Hunt's turn to be surprised, and his glibness was temporarily stalled. He stared dumbly at the man, wondering how he could know such a thing. He had no knowledge of Hugh's father's suspicions, or of John Proudlocks's observations of him, both in London and at Meum Hall last summer. After a moment, he managed to reply gravely, "Sir, I do not know this person of whom you speak. Nor can I be expected to be appreciative of your accusation."

"I know *your* career, as well. You were my uncle's secretary, were you not? Do not deny it. I have reliable witnesses."

Hunt cocked his head in concession. "I admit the role of secretary, sir, but to nothing else. Your charge is hurting." He scrutinized Hugh Kenrick with new and worried interest. The man had idly taken up a pencil and was scribbling something on a sheet of paper. The man seemed bored.

Then Hunt recovered the momentum of his initiative, and said instead, "You are a prize, sir, and I shall take you back to England to stand trial for treason. Have I evidence to substantiate that charge? Ample and abundant!" He rose and paced back and forth before his quarry. "You speak of witnesses! Of course, there will be my testimony concerning the incident at Morland Hall, when you drew your sword against me, and discouraged my colleagues and me in the performance of our lawful duty. My father possesses pamphlets and other printed matter of which you are the author. There is a regaling account in one of the *Gazettes* here of your role in obstructing the law and Crown officers in their duty, when they tried to bring in legal stamps to the General Court some years ago. A ragged copy of the *Courier* contains a lengthy item about the Resolves of the same period, and extols them and your role in their passage in the late General Assembly."

Hunt paused and waited for a response from his host. None came. He glanced at Hugh. He had just dropped the pencil and was reading what he had written. There was a smile on the man's face. The Customsman continued. "It may please you to know that the newspapers were submitted to me by a fellow citizen of yours, Mr. Gramatan, and a former friend of yours, Mr. Cullis. I did not tell them how I planned to use the documents, and they have likely forgotten them, some time ago. In addition, I have collected many affidavits from leading citizens here concerning your character and actions." He permitted himself a smile. "All these things shall be laid before a magistrate and a jury."

Hugh glanced up. "What is the alternative if I choose not to accompany you?"

"The alternative? I will have you shot, if your resistance permits it, and I will be obliged to send a regretful report to my father. Otherwise, you shall be forcibly removed, injured or not." Hunt paused. "Did I mention that this is a kind of arrangement? You see, I know the whereabouts of Mr. Frake and his men. At the Otway place, just west of his own ruined kingdom. And here is my proposal: If you come peaceably, I will spare him, and sail away. However, with the *Sparrowhawk* and the *Basilisk*, together with Major Ragsdale's men, Mr. Frake can be surrounded and annihilated. You saw what the *Sparrowhawk* can do to a property, and how efficient Major Ragsdale's men can be. Once I signal that strategy to commence, there will be no stopping it. The choice is your own."

Then Hunt took a quick step forward and snatched up the paper that Hugh had written on. He clucked his tongue and wagged an admonishing finger at his host. He held the paper up to the light, and read it out loud: "I am Prince Alfred, and Mr. Hunt, Meleger, captain of the seven deadly sins. Actually, of only three: Envy, gluttony, and sloth. The remaining four — pride, lust, greed, and wrath — I would pare from that list — their sinfulness being open to Pippinish scrutiny — so that the number of deadly sins is not so daunting and magical. And, strangely, Mr. Hunt is neither ghostly nor gaunt, as Meleger is. I shall lift him from the earth, embrace the life from him, and he shall thereby vanish, and the world will be done with him."

"What educated folderol!" exclaimed Hunt with a laugh. He crushed the paper into a ball and tossed it into a corner. "I can see that you are capable of jollity!" Then he stood stiffly, and called out to Mr. Blassard. The man came in, holding the pistol. Hunt gestured with an open palm toward the door. "Shall we go, Mr. Kenrick? In the name of His Majesty, you are arrested."

Hugh Kenrick knew that if he resisted, he would be shot, or overpowered. If that happened, there was no predicting how the marines outside would react. He did not want to risk their accosting his staff or tenants. Both men looked strong and able and he did not doubt their strength or determination. He sighed, glanced once at pictures on the wall opposite, picked up his hat from a side of the desk, and stepped around to walk to the door. Then he paused. "Do you plan to sail the *Sparrowhawk* to England, Mr. Hunt?"

"Of course, sir," Hunt answered, startled by the question. "It is Revenue property now, and is a prize of another kind. And its new master is eager to return, as well. Why do you ask?"

"How long before you intend to sail?"

Hunt cleared his throat. "From Caxton? In a few days, once matters are cleared up here. We will stop long enough in Hampton for me to reclaim my kit, and then we shall go."

"I ask this because I am in need of my valet, Mr. Spears, the man who showed you in. Could he come aboard with me for the time being? He is blameless in all matters political. He would leave when you are prepared to leave Caxton."

Hunt grimaced in thought. "Well, I see no harm in it. Will he accompany us now?"

"No. Allow me to give him instructions to prepare my own modest baggage." Then Hugh stepped outside the study, and called for Spears. When the man appeared, Hugh said, "I am being invited aboard the *Sparrowhawk*, Mr. Spears. Prepare a bag for me for a few nights' stay. Then come to Caxton and the pier to deliver it. You will see to my needs once you are on board." After a pause, he added, "Be sure to pack a book or two for me to read. *Hyperborea*, for instance."

When Spears blinked in incredulity, Hugh said, "Go on, Spears. We'll talk when I see you again."

"Yes, sir." The valet turned woodenly and went upstairs.

Hugh Kenrick, Jared Hunt, and Mr. Blassard went out the door.

Thomas Hulton waited until he heard an officer shout a command, and the marching boots fade away, before he crept out from beneath the desk. He peered outside the window, and saw no one. Radulphus Spears came into the study, looking like he was about to cry. Hulton stared at his successor, then opened the sheet of paper that Hugh Kenrick had dropped onto his knees. It read:

*"Mr. Hunt means to murder me. My murder is necessary, for I accused him of a murder he knows he is guilty of committing. Take this note to Mr. Frake at the Otway place, and tell him to destroy the* Sparrowhawk, *regardless of my presence on it. Your most grateful friend, Hugh Kenrick."*

Hulton came around the desk and silently offered Spears the note. The valet read it and sobbed once. "Oh, Mr. Hulton! What shall we do?"

"Stop blubbering, man!" Hulton replied sharply. He was a sergeant again. "We'll think of something. First, you will tell me how to go to the Otway place."

# Chapter 19: The Answer

That was easy, thought Hugh Kenrick. And the hardest thing I have ever done. One note for Hulton, and one to Hunt to divert his attention. Prince Arthur versus Meleger, indeed! The hardest part was not rising to assault the man, for not only was Hunt guilty of complicity in Dogmael Jones's murder, but he was arranging another, my own. Of course, I meant everything I wrote in that "educated folderol," but nothing in it meant anything to Hunt. It was hard, because Hunt was there, open to whatever justice I could exact. But, Hulton had heard everything, and he had his instructions. The attentive Mr. Hunt was not as attentive as he presumed. He was too busy proposing his iniquities and gloating over their eventual triumph. The man's vanity had blinded him to a simple deception.

Destroy the *Sparrowhawk*, the last bond between him and England. The first bond between him and Jack Frake! Jack Frake had known it. Hugh had always known it, as well. How swiftly does justice act, when it is necessary! Hugh smiled, fondly remembering his last conversation with his friend on the porch of Jack Frake's place just a few nights ago. Hugh knew that Jack Frake was at the Otway place, waiting for the chance to accomplish that release. It was the only thing that kept him in these parts. And should he fail, he, Hugh Kenrick, might accomplish it. It was a risk. Jack Frake had taken so many risks. It was about time that he, Hugh Kenrick, took one himself.

No, he reproached himself. You are responsible for much that has happened. He had risked Reverdy, and lost her. And Roger Tallmadge. And now, Meum Hall.

The *Sparrowhawk* was now tied to the Caxton pier with the *Basilisk*. Hugh was not surprised when, after they boarded the *Sparrowhawk* and went below deck, Hunt and his colleague escorted him to the very same iron-gated berth that he had occupied many years ago — in another age! he thought — when this vessel first brought him across the ocean. Only this time, he was locked inside. Hunt gave the key to Mr. Blassard, then raised his eyebrows after the lock clicked shut and smiled a silly smile. "*You* are embraced, sir, and *you* shall vanish, and the world be done with *you*! Good day."

Hugh smiled back at the tormentor. There was no humor in his eyes. "Were those your last words to Dogmael Jones?"

Hunt's supercilious expression abruptly changed to rigid, hateful resentment. He did not reply, but turned and mounted the companionway stairs to the deck above. Mr. Blassard looked momentarily confused. Then he shrugged and followed.

There was no furniture in the berth. A rusty lantern chain dangled from the beam above, but no lantern. Hugh sat down in a corner. He was pleased again, in a way. This had been Reverdy's berth, when she left him to return to England in what seemed another age. The *Sparrowhawk* had brought her back to me, and took her away.

About an hour later, he heard footsteps on the stairs. Mr. Blassard appeared again. With him was Hulton, who carried a small traveling bag. Hugh almost gasped at the sight of his former valet. He got to his feet. Blassard took out the key and his pistol, and unlocked the gate. "All right, give 'im his things," he said gruffly. Hulton nodded and handed the bag into the compartment to Hugh. Hugh took it and set it down on the floor. "It contains your shaving kit, sir, and a change of shirt, and your special book," said Hulton. He cleared his throat. "Mr. Spears took ill. I volunteered to replace him."

"You want to join 'im in there and palaver?" asked Blassard. "I got things to do."

Hulton shook his head. Blassard shouldered him aside, closed the gate, and locked it. He disappeared up the steps again.

"What are you doing here, Hulton?" asked Hugh in a low voice. "You're a deserter!"

Hulton shrugged. "There are some marines aboard, sir, but they're not looking for me. Mr. Spears has taken your note to the Otway place. I claimed first right to come here as your valet. I am senior to him in that place, you know, even for the gap in service. He protested, but to no avail."

"You are in danger, Hulton. Leave now, while you can!" Hugh held the bars of the grate. "Hunt will think I told you as much as I know about him. He will murder you, as well."

Hulton shook his head. "I will not leave you to that man's mercies, sir. He's rotten." He smiled. "He is much like Richard the Third. A right bastard. Do you remember when I asked you about him, the night we left the Fruit Wench and those special friends of yours?"

"Yes, Hulton," Hugh answered. "I remember it well." He resigned himself to the man's presence. The man would not leave.

"Did this Mr. Hunt truly murder a man?"

"Or had him murdered. A very good friend," said Hugh. "On behalf of my uncle."

"Him again!" Hulton shut his eyes, then forced himself to exclaim, "Another right bastard!"

Hugh grinned. "That's the way, Hulton. We'll make an American of you yet!"

"Thank you, sir."

"Well, let's see what you've brought me." Hugh stooped and opened the bag. He found the things that Hulton said were in it: a shirt, a mug, some soap, a razor, and the books. He placed everything on the plank floor, including both volumes of *Hyperborea*. The last thing he took out was the tin gorget that was engraved, "A Paladin for Liberty." Hugh looked up at Hulton in question.

"For you to wear, sir," said Hulton. "You are a kind of knight. An officer of thought, kind of."

Hugh smiled in gratitude. He had said nearly the same thing to Reverdy in London. He took the hemp cord and slipped the gorget around his neck. Then he picked up one of the volumes. "Hulton, I don't suppose you ever had time to read this novel."

"No, sir." He nodded to the shaving kit. "Please hand me the razor, sir. It may be needed." He paused. "I was searched by Mr. Blassard when I came on board, and he looked into the kit there, as well. But it appears that he did not think a razor could be used for anything but shaving."

Hugh was momentarily stunned. The idea of gentle, deferential Hulton wielding a weapon was still not real to him.

Hulton sensed his friend's disbelief. He reminded him with amusement, "I was at Quebec, sir, and other venues, and had occasion to employ my halberd and sword on a number of Frenchmen and Indians."

"Of course." Hugh handed Hulton the razor, which was folded safely into the carved ivory handle. "Was this your idea, or Mr. Spears's?" he asked as Hulton slipped the razor inside his frock coat pocket.

Hulton said in self-irony, "I must credit Mr. Spears with the notion, sir. He was most emphatic about it."

Hugh chuckled. He leaned back against a wall and opened the volume of *Hyperborea*. There was enough light from a lantern on the side of the stairs that he could read the pages. "Sit comfortably, Hulton. I shall read you some marvelous literature."

Hulton obeyed, and sat cross-legged on the planks outside the gate.

Hugh read his favorite passages from the novel. Hulton listened, fascinated. They forgot time.

After a while, they heard shouts and a great clatter of feet above them on the deck. Then they felt the *Sparrowhawk* move. Hugh read on. The vessel jerked as it caught wind. Hugh eventually glanced up from the book. "Hulton, poke your head out of the hatch, and tell me what you see."

Hulton rose and obeyed. When he returned, he whispered, "We are going upriver, sir. We have just passed the windmill on the bluff. The sloop follows us."

"He lied," Hugh remarked with unconcern. "We are sailing up to the Otway place." He paused. "Be prepared, Hulton." He turned some pages of the book, and stopped near the end. "Here is a glorious conclusion, Hulton," he said. "Let us hope we can emulate it."

Hulton's brow furled as he listened to Hugh read the ending of *Hyperborea*. The former sergeant looked captivated; then Hugh closed the book and his eyes and sat quietly for a long moment.

Minutes later, they heard steps descending the companionway stairs.

*     *     *

The smithy was quiet this morning. The fire was out, and the tools laid aside. Two fires were burning elsewhere on the Otway place: a cooking fire near the ruins of the great house, and a fire by the wheeled gun that faced the York River, at water's edge, near the remnants of the Otway pier. The water was deep there; in the past merchantmen had tied up at the pier to load hogsheads of tobacco and corn. Four men of the Company were assigned to work the gun, and two kept the brick-protected fire there going, to heat the embers and metal that would go into iron bowls that would be quickly strapped and secured to cannon balls, then loaded down the muzzle of the gun, once it had been primed. John Ramshaw had taught Jack Frake about the projectiles years ago, and one had landed intact at Morland.

Jack Frake sat on a stool in the smithy, holding the note from Hugh Kenrick. Spears had arrived minutes before, brought in by one of the pickets who did not know him. The valet told him everything that had happened at Meum Hall. Spears stood before him now, waiting. Jack Frake looked up at the Company man who had escorted Spears across the weed-grown and scrub-dotted fields. "Ask Mr. Fraser and Mr. Proudlocks to come here. Then return to your post."

When Proudlocks and Fraser appeared, they nodded in surprise to Spears. Jack Frake showed them the note, then asked the valet to repeat for them what he had witnessed at Meum Hall. This Spears did, adding what Hulton had told him he overheard from beneath the desk. Jack Frake said, "All right, Mr. Spears. You should go back now. Can you find your way?"

Spears said he could. "Will you try to save him, sir? Staff are concerned, and the tenants."

"We'll try, Mr. Spears. That is all I can promise."

Spears wished them well, then hurriedly left the smithy.

"What can we do?" asked Proudlocks.

Jack Frake said, "Destroy or cripple the *Sparrowhawk*, if and when she appears. That man Hulton is with him. I haven't met him, but perhaps he is resourceful enough to help Hugh escape from it."

"And if he does not escape?"

Jack Frake said nothing.

Proudlocks said, "He is your friend, Jack. And mine."

Jack Frake simply held up the note, then folded it and slipped it inside his coat. "No more about it, John." It was a command. He rose and picked up his musket. "I'm going to the great house for coffee."

When he was out of hearing distance, Fraser remarked, "He can be a mean man, Mr. Proudlocks."

"But no less a friend," Proudlocks answered.

Jack Frake did not get far along the path that led to the ruins before a Company man ran up from the direction of the river and pointed to it. "Sir! They're coming!"

Jack Frake looked east. Against the clear morning sky, he saw the sails of the *Sparrowhawk* gliding up the York. Behind them were the smaller sails of the sloop *Basilisk*. "Find Cletus and tell him to beat the alarm." The man ran off.

Half an hour later, the vessels had anchored exactly as Jack Frake had predicted, the *Sparrowhawk* on the river, and the sloop on the inlet. Every one of his men was at his post — a few on the river side, fewer on the inlet side, most of them on the east and south sides of the immediate grounds, as concentrated as he could arrange them to meet an attack from the marines. The new volunteers from Morland were mixed with the veterans, bringing his Company strength up to twenty-nine. The ground leading from Morland and the Hove Stream sloped slightly to the river; the marines would have that advantage, as well as their numbers.

Jack Frake stood in the middle of the defenses with Proudlocks and Fraser. He used his spyglass to examine the *Sparrowhawk*. He saw men busy preparing the ten guns on the larboard side. He did not see Hugh Kenrick.

Another Company man ran up to him. "Sir, look!" He pointed east, in the direction of Morland. The three officers turned and saw a redcoated man advancing on horseback across the field, carrying a white flag on a stick. Jack Frake, Proudlocks, and Fraser began moving to intercept him.

Some minutes later, the officer reined in his mount, and Jack Frake and his companions stopped within a few yards of him. It was a captain from the marines. Without dismounting, the man doffed his hat and addressed Jack Frake. "Major Ragsdale sends his compliments, sir. I am Captain Crofts. The major wishes to know if you will surrender. He also wishes you to know that if you do not, *that* will happen." He pointed with the white flag to the *Sparrowhawk*.

Jack Frake turned to look again. He took out the spyglass and swept it over the length of the vessel. It was then that he saw Hugh Kenrick, standing on a chair or stool at the stern beneath a yardarm, a rope around his neck. He faced the Otway place. He was coatless, and his hands seemed to be tied behind his back. A man stood behind him. He examined the deck closely again, and saw Jared Hunt standing to the side. As his sight fixed on Hunt, that man raised his spyglass to fix it on him.

"The major has instructed me to inform you that should you fire on that vessel with the field gun I espy over there" — the officer gestured again with the white flag — "the gentleman will be immediately hanged. That vessel will then return fire, as well as the one in the inlet there. Furthermore, my battalion is ready to attack from numerous directions." The officer paused. "What is your pleasure, sir?"

Jack Frake did not answer immediately. He could not take the spyglass away from the sight of Hugh Kenrick. But he lowered it and said, "I will need some time to decide, Mr. Crofts."

The officer took out a pocket watch and consulted it. "I have been given leave to grant you half an hour, sir, should that be your answer. I will wait here. I will caution you that if any harm is done to me, or if Major Ragsdale or Mr. Hunt on that vessel suspects I am taken prisoner or hostage, they will proceed with an attack." After a pause, he added, "I should tell you that it is Major Ragsdale who has set these terms, excepting the one regarding the gentleman in question. Mr. Hunt wished to proceed with an attack without granting you the choice of surrender. But for the gentleman in question, Major Ragsdale prevailed."

Jack Frake glanced up at the officer. "Thank you for the information, Mr. Crofts." Without another word to anyone, he turned and walked away. Jock Fraser moved to follow him, but Proudlocks stopped him. He was the only man present who understood the decision that Jack Frake had to make, the only man present, other than the figure on the stern, who knew the story of Falmouth. They walked in another direction.

Jack Frake strode through the weeds and scrub, not taking his eyes from the *Sparrowhawk*. He stopped and rested his musket against a tree stump. He stared for a long time, still as a statue, at the figure on the stern, the spyglass clutched tightly in both hands behind his back. A paralysis seemed to turn him to stone, caused by a debilitating ague of doubt. There was no decision to make, but he did not want to do this again. In the figure on the stern, he saw Redmagne and Skelly. He owed Hugh Kenrick so much; he was faced with the prospect of repaying his friend with death, an agonizing, prolonged death, and he would be helpless to quicken it, as he had done for Redmagne and Skelly in Falmouth.

It did not matter that Hugh Kenrick wished him to destroy the *Sparrowhawk*, regardless of his presence on it. It did not matter that Hugh Kenrick and he agreed that the vessel's destruction was necessary. And it was irrelevant that Hugh Kenrick was willing to die that way. Jack Frake did not want to do it again. He knew that if he fired on the *Sparrowhawk*, it would be he kicking the stool from beneath Hugh Kenrick's feet.

That officer and Major Ragsdale were wrong, thought Jack Frake: It was Hunt who had prevailed; it was he who was setting the terms of life and death. Hugh Kenrick was as fated to die as had been Skelly and Redmagne. Hunt had marked Hugh Kenrick for death long before he met him or captured him.

Just as he had refused to allow the malignant motive of the Crown to govern his own life and the lives of Redmagne and Skelly, Jack Frake knew that he must refuse to allow it to govern the life of Hugh Kenrick. Just as he had always known the Crown's true motives for wanting to subjugate the colonies.

Still, even with that knowledge, Jack Frake did not want to condemn his friend to death.

Something glinted in the ascending sunlight. Jack Frake raised the spy-glass again, fixed it on Hugh Kenrick, and noticed a gorget suspended from around his friend's neck. Jack Frake sighed deeply. He did not know its his-tory, or what was engraved on it, but it seemed to belong on Hugh Ken-rick's person. Unbidden, at the same time that he recognized the object, memory shot to the forefront of his mind of a night long ago, when he had assured Hugh Kenrick that he had not betrayed himself or the Resolves, with these words: *If brave men survive their risks, that is all they can do. We honor their memory, if they perish, for we are heirs to their bravery....*He remembered a part of a poem that Etáin had written out for Hugh that night: *But bright thoughts, clear deeds, constancy, fidelity, bounty, and gen-erous honesty are the gems of noble minds....*

Jack Frake asked himself: What else had Hugh Kenrick been to him all these years, but all those things? He thought: I must grant you your last request, my friend.

He lowered the spyglass, picked up his musket, and walked back to the waiting officer. "Mr. Crofts, please inform Major Ragsdale that we will not surrender."

The officer studied Jack Frake for a moment. What recalcitrant crea-tures these colonials were! He wondered what accounted for the breed. "You will not survive an assault, sir," he said. "You are outnumbered, and out-gunned."

"So be it, Mr. Crofts," answered Jack Frake, "but that is not inevitable."

After another moment, the officer raised a hand in vague salute, reined his horse around, and rode away in the direction he had come from.

Jack Frake turned and glanced at Proudlocks and Fraser, who stood at a distance. He nodded once, and they left to take up their posts. In the woods to the east and west of the Otway place, Jack Frake saw the sun flash off of cap plates and bayonets. He knew that the marines would not attack until the *Sparrowhawk* and *Basilisk* had raked the position.

He strode down to the wheeled gun near the disintegrated pier. Aymer Crompton, Henry Buckle, and Isaac Zimmerman and another Company man were on its crew. Two other volunteers from Morland, Mouse and Moses Topham, were tending the fire. Cannon balls, bowls, and metal straps lay in a row near them. Their muskets were stacked a safe distance away. Near the gun were the rammer, sponge, ladle and wad hook. Without preamble, Jack Frake asked, "Is the gun primed, Mr. Crompton?"

"Yes, sir."

"Elevated to the best advantage?"

"Yes, sir."

"Assemble and load the first round. We must strike the masts, the biggest ones their topmen haven't furled. They all must be as dry as kindling. The fire will spread."

While the crew prepared the first shot, Jack Frake took the linstock, lighted the slow-match wound around it with a match he struck on a rock at his feet, and waited. He fixed his sight on the *Sparrowhawk* and the figure on the stern. When Buckle was finished ramming the carcass down the muzzle, Crompton stepped forward and addressed Jack Frake. "Allow me the first shot, sir." He held out a hand for the linstock.

Jack Frake shook his head. He stepped up to the right of the barrel, and said, "Brace yourself." The crew brought up their hands to cover their ears. But he had addressed Hugh Kenrick.

He lowered the linstock, and, a second before he rested the glowing end of the slow-match on the powder-packed touchhole of the barrel, turned and shouted as loudly as he could across the water, even though he knew that Hugh Kenrick could not hear him, "Long live Lady Liberty!"

The gun roared, bucking in response to the explosion that sent the carcass on its way. No one moved until they saw where the projectile fell. Jack Frake stepped to the side away from the gun's smoke in time to see the unfurled mizzen topsail shudder. Someone behind him cheered.

Jack Frake saw fragments of the carcass fall to the deck below, almost directly onto Hugh Kenrick. Dark lines were left behind on the rough linen, as though a cat had clawed it. "Reload!" he ordered. He heard the men prepare the gun for another round.

He raised his spyglass to examine the struck sail; he saw streaks smolder and grow up and down along its length. When he lowered the spyglass he saw the figure of Jared Hunt gesturing with his own spyglass at Hugh Kenrick. Then smoke from his own gun drifted into his line of sight and obscured the deck.

That was when the *Sparrowhawk* fired its first gun. The ball struck one of the standing walls of the Otway great house, bringing it down.

# Chapter 20: The Sparrowhawk

Jared Hunt, Blassard, and another Customsman came down the companionway steps. Before Hugh Kenrick or Hulton could rise, Blassard produced a short bludgeon and struck the valet hard on the head with it. Hulton fell backwards, unconscious. Blood oozed from his forehead.

"Finish him off?" Blassard queried.

"No," answered Hunt. "We will take him back to Hampton. The navy might impress him into service. He looks seaworthy." He turned to Hugh Kenrick. "Now, sir, if you please, I wish you to witness Crown justice. You will remove your coat, or my colleagues will remove it for you. We are going above. It is warmish. I wouldn't want to discomfit you. The gate, Mr. Blassard."

As Blassard found the key and unlocked the berth, Hugh said, "You are sailing to the Otway place."

"You are correct. You may thank your friend Mr. Cullis for the information. He has been most helpful all this while." Blassard opened the gate.

Hugh removed his frock coat and dropped it to the floor. Blassard and the other Customsman took out pistols and also stepped aside.

"What is that?" asked Hunt, nodding to the gorget. He leaned forward a little to read the engraving. He frowned in disapproval.

"My rank," Hugh answered. He said nothing more.

Blassard took a step and reached up to yank the gorget from Hugh's neck. Hunt stopped him. "No, Mr. Blassard. Leave him the emblem of his folly. It won't interfere." He smiled mysteriously. "Gentlemen, please secure Mr. Kenrick." He took a pistol from under his belt.

The Customsmen came inside, and while Blassard held a pistol, the other man turned Hugh around roughly, took a length of rope from his coat pocket, and bound Hugh's wrists behind him. When he was finished, he turned Hugh around to face Hunt.

Hunt said with a chuckle, "There! The 'Paladin for Liberty' has lost his liberty! Now, Mr. Kenrick, up the steps, please, or my colleagues will drag you up them."

Hugh stepped out of the berth, glanced once at Hulton, then carefully ascended the stairs. The three Customsmen followed. Hunt and his colleagues took Hugh along the deck, where crews stood at the ready at their guns, and up more steps to the stern.

When his sight recovered from the brightness, Hugh saw a noosed rope hanging from a yardarm, below it a stool, and beyond the noose the Customs Jack drooping limply from its staff.

When they stood before the stool, Hunt said to Hugh, "You know what to do, Mr. Kenrick."

"You are a yahoo, Hunt," said Hugh. He stepped onto the stool. Brassard found a coil of deck rope to stand on, and fitted the noose tightly around Hugh's neck.

"The term is foreign to me, sir," replied Hunt.

"A yahoo is forever ignorant of his own identity, and of his lineage," Hugh said.

Hunt stood on his toes and slapped Hugh across the face. "No more impudence, you damned *son and heir*! This bastard will triumph!"

Hugh almost lost his balance on the stool. As he struggled to regain his footing, Blassard reached up behind him and steadied him. "Not yet, son!" he laughed. "What's your hurry?" The other Customsman joined him with a guffaw. Jared Hunt did not smile.

Hunt paced officiously before Hugh. "Now, Mr. Kenrick, here is the plan. When we drop anchor across from the Otway plantation, the good major and his marines by then will have taken up positions to attack your friend, Mr. Frake. Eighty men, sir, against a couple dozen. Hardly a fair fight, wouldn't you agree? You will have noticed the guns being prepared on this vessel. They can complete the leveling of the plantation. My sloop-of-war will take a position elsewhere, and contribute to the affair. Mr. Frake will be given an opportunity to surrender. The good major insists on being sporting about the matter. That, I believe, is because he has some martial regard for your friend's warring prowess. It's nothing to me. If Mr. Frake does not surrender, and takes a hostile action towards the major or this vessel, you will be hanged forthwith. He will know this. The situation will be communicated to him in the clearest terms. Should he surrender, you will be spared to voyage with me to England and trial."

"And Mr. Frake and his men?"

Hunt shrugged. "They will be subject to the mercies of another kind of Crown justice. It is a military matter over which the good major has more authority than I have."

"Why should I believe you?"

"A rhetorical question, you must admit, Mr. Kenrick. You have no reason to believe me."

"It *was* rhetorical."

"Thank you for the concession. Mr. Blassard will remain here to hold your hand should you totter again." Hunt gestured to the other Customs man and started to walk away, but he paused to look up at Hugh and said, "I neglected to mention that, should the worst happen, I will return and remove the stool myself. It will give me the greatest pleasure. You may believe *that*."

Hugh smiled. "I have always believed in your vileness, Mr. Hunt," he said. "Your own, and my uncle's."

Hunt sniffed once, then turned and left the stern with his colleague.

*   *   *

Hugh watched the Otway plantation come into sight. As the crew of the *Sparrowhawk* prepared to drop anchor, and sailors mounted the rigging to take in sail, the *Basilisk* passed the merchantman and sailed farther upriver, then tacked its sails to maneuver cautiously into the inlet on the western end of the plantation. Jared Hunt seemed to be excited about the arrival. He came up to the stern and said to Hugh, waving his spyglass, "You know, Mr. Kenrick, I hope the worst happens. You will think it an odd thing to say, but after Morland, I have found a taste for the sound and smell of guns."

Hugh shook his head as much as the noose would allow. He looked off into the distance. "You overstep your station, Mr. Hunt. That is an appreciation acquired by true soldiers." Then he looked down on his tormentor. "You are a murderer."

Hunt frowned, and looked pensive. "If I take the sense of being a 'yahoo' correctly, then I am a yahoo from Lyme Regis, but I shall have victory over the stately Kenricks." He cocked his head once. "You are right, sir. I am vile, and a liar. But you harp on that other matter. So, I have changed my plan. I will not hang you, should they defy me. Your reward will be to watch the annihilation of your friends, if need be, then you will be hanged. If they surrender, you will wink out with the knowledge of it." He scoffed and shook his head. "You *cannot* win." Hunt imperiously turned his back on Hugh, and walked down the stern to the railing.

Hugh did not deign to reply. He looked away to the distance.

The remains of the great house and other out buildings stood in a cluster in a tiny corner of a broad rectangle of what were once productive fields, which were now taken over by weeds and other random growth. He saw men moving about the ruins, and a gun over the low embankment near the torn-up pier. He also noticed streaks of red, one in the woods south of the fields, another in the woods that separated Morland from the Otway property. To the west, the *Basilisk* had furled most of its sails, and stood ready.

A single patch of red detached itself from the streak in the Morland woods. It was a marine on horseback. A white flag fluttered lazily over his head. Some men moved out to meet him. Hugh supposed one of them was Jack Frake. Then they all stopped, and he supposed they were talking. After a minute, one of the figures moved away from the others and walked a distance. This figure raised an object, a spyglass.

Hugh smiled. It was indeed Jack Frake. It had to be. He was glad that he was using the Italian spyglass he had given him as a present long ago. It was only a figure; he could not make out any of the features. He could only wonder what Jack Frake was thinking. He thought to himself, in the manner of a prayer: *Please do not let me down.* Then he corrected himself: *I know you will not let me down. You know better, perhaps better than I do. Destroy me, if you must, but destroy the* Sparrowhawk. *If I have ever committed a sin, perhaps it was not having caught up with you soon enough, and this will be my atonement. You are Etáin's north, and were always mine, though I did not know it. But now we are both the north.*

Hugh stared hard back at the figure observing him from afar, hoping that Jack Frake could see his face, and know what he was thinking.

The figure turned and walked slowly back to the waiting marine. After a moment, the red patch and white flag turned and moved back across the field to the woods. The figure moved, too, faster now, heading for the river. It stopped at the gun emplacement. Moments passed. Other figures at the gun seemed to be preparing it to fire. Hugh Kenrick held his breath. He imagined that the gun was aimed at him. He did not even waste hope that Hunt would be the first to die. He had forgotten Hunt. The man did not belong in the cathedral of his soul.

When he saw a tongue of flame flash from the gun, he felt joy. He closed his eyes and waited for the inevitable. He heard the sharp slapping sound as the ball struck a sail somewhere above him, the report of the gun a moment later. The iron ball fell with some debris with a thud on the planks behind him, bounced once, and rolled heavily off the stern to the deck below. He could not see it, but one of the embers struck Blassard on a shoulder. The man yelled in panic, then cursed as he ran from the stern.

Hugh opened his eyes and saw Jared Hunt staring up worriedly at the sail above. Then Hunt, too, cursed and turned to shout down to the master gunner, "Fire when you please! Destroy that gun by the pier!" He strode up to Hugh. Shaking his spyglass at his captive, he said, "Does he think he's paying me back with fire, Mr. Kenrick? Watch as he is destroyed! Huh!!" he ended with a snap of his fingers. He returned to his place at the railing to watch the bombardment, oblivious to the little shower of sparks that began to rain down.

The guns of the *Sparrowhawk* began to fire, one after the other.

The ear-splitting crescendos reached the consciousness of a sleeping soldier and awoke him. Below deck, Thomas Hulton heard the sound of the guns. He opened his eyes, sat up, saw the empty berth, and jumped to his feet. He was about to run up the companionway stairs when Blassard came rushing down. The Customsman paused in surprise, but Hulton reached up, took a fistful of the man's shirt, and pulled him the rest of the way. He had seen from which pocket Blassard had taken the bludgeon before it was used on him. Pushing the confused man up against the door of the captain's cabin, he found the weapon and struck Blassard's skull with it. The man collapsed. Hulton dropped the bludgeon and removed the man's pistol from his belt, then turned and raced up the stairs.

No one noticed him or the side of his face that was covered in blood. The gun crews were too busy. He glanced around and espied Hugh Kenrick. He also saw things wafting in the air. Looking up, he saw that a sail had burst into flame. Further down the length of the vessel, a powder monkey had emerged from the hatch there, and a carcass landed and exploded a few feet away from him, strewing embers and hot metal. A crewman shouted and another found a bucket of water and poured it on the cartridge carried by the powder monkey.

But Hulton's attention quickly turned back to Hugh Kenrick. Now he saw Jared Hunt on the stern, as well. Hulton bolted along the deck, shoving crewmen aside, and shot up the steps. "No, you won't!" he yelled, and fired the pistol at Hunt. He did not see where he had hit the man, but Hunt barked once and fell to the planks. Without acknowledging the look of astonishment on his friend's face, Hulton found the same coil of rope that Blassard had used, pulled it over, stepped on it, and took out the razor. He dropped the pistol, opened the razor, and quickly sawed through the hemp. When he was down to the last few threads, he heard Hunt yell, "No, *you* won't, lackey!" He turned his head in time to see Hunt, still down, but leaning on an elbow, fire his own pistol.

The ball struck Hulton in the chest. His legs became weak and he fell against Hugh Kenrick. The last threads broke and they both collapsed to the planks. Hulton pulled himself away and sawed frantically through the ropes binding his friend's wrists. When he was done, he bent forward and gasped into Hugh's ear, "There, milord, you are free!" He rolled over and lay still on the planks next to Hugh, still grasping the razor.

Hugh rose to one knee and looked down on Hulton. Hunt's bullet had hit the former sergeant just below the heart. The man's eyes stared unseeing up at the burning sail. "Brave, true Hulton!" Hugh whispered. He reached over and closed his friend's eyes.

Hugh rose and glanced at Hunt. The man looked as though he were in agony. Hugh bent and took the razor from Hulton's hand, then ran to the railing. He saw quickly that the *Basilisk* was firing on the Otway place. The red streaks of the marines had moved from the woods to the edges of the field, but had stopped to wait until the bombardment ceased. He could hear Jack Frake's men firing back, and a babble of urgency near him.

He thought that was odd, until he realized that the *Sparrowhawk* had stopped firing. The babble was made by crewmen rushing to put out the fire that had burned half the mizzen topsail and was spreading to other sails near it. He saw men climbing the rigging with axes and cutlasses to try and sever the burning linen. Other men had formed a relay on another web of rigging to pass up buckets of water. Even as he watched, another carcass struck a studdingsail over the bow on the other end of the vessel.

Hugh stood over Hunt. The man looked up at him with a curious mixture of hatred and hope. Hugh said, "They shall not save the *Sparrowhawk*." He said it quietly, without emphasis, without care that the man believed him. Without waiting for a reply, he leapt over Hunt and ran to the stern steps and went down them against a stream of crewmen working to contain the fires set by Jack Frake's carcasses. Hugh knew the ship well. He knew how to get to the magazine deep in the bowels of the *Sparrowhawk*.

Jared Hunt yelled to one of the crewmen, "Damn your eyes, help me to my feet!" The crewman ignored him. "You there! Help me up!" he shouted to another.

*   *   *

Jack Frake raised his spyglass and trained it on the stern. With more relief than he had time to feel, he saw a rope dangling from a burning yardarm. It had been cut. Hugh Kenrick was nowhere in sight. Nor could he spot Jared Hunt. The mizzen topsail was completely aflame, the ends of furled sails on other arms were on fire, and fire was beginning to burn a hole through a sail over the bow. He lowered the spyglass to peer at the water around the *Sparrowhawk*. He saw no one in it.

Then he realized that the *Sparrowhawk* had stopped firing. As had the *Basilisk*. He heard distant drums now, the drums of the marines. The bombardment had claimed no casualties among his men. It had merely rearranged some of the ruins and debris, except that one ball had struck the smithy.

But the *Sparrowhawk* was at least crippled. Her crew would be fortunate to save a fraction of her sails. It was not a navy ship, with a navy crew, or a navy captain. She would be disabled for days. With luck, the fires would spread to the masts, and that would disable her for months. Perhaps forever.

"All right," he said to the men who had been firing the wheeled gun. "We're finished here. Fire once more. Then we must leave for the firing lines, and retreat to the boats."

"There's one shot left, sir," said Crompton.

"Quickly, Mr. Crompton. Fine work today."

When the gun was ready, Jack Frake took the linstock and put it to the touchhole.

The shot did not strike a sail, but exploded directly in the middle of the deck among the panicking crewmen. The clothing or hair of a few of them caught fire. These men began to mount the railing and dive into the river. Others followed them.

*   *   *

Hugh Kenrick descended into the holds of the *Sparrowhawk* through a series of ladders and gangways. There were few crewmen down here; most were topside fighting the blazes. What few he encountered did not know him, and did not stop him, even though the noose was still around his neck. He carried a lantern he had found in a niche; a powder monkey accosted him with the warning that he should not roam about with it. Hugh simply replied that the vessel was doomed, and that he should abandon it. "Swim ashore, son, and live to see a new country born!" The boy regarded Hugh with incomprehension, but ran to find the nearest ladder topside.

Hugh found the handling chamber first, where cartridges were assembled to pass on to the powder monkeys. Next came the filling room. Finally, the magazine itself. All three were divided by wet linen curtains that prevented sparks from traveling through the air. These compartments were also lit by lanterns that sat in recessed niches.

He stood in the dim, empty magazine, and regarded the shelves of waist-high powder kegs, and rows of leather sacks and wooden canisters that the powder monkeys would take topside to the gun crews, once they were filled with charges of powder. He suddenly remembered that Jack Frake knew these rooms, as well, when he was a powder monkey for John Ramshaw.

A powder keg had been rolled from a shelf and stood in the middle of the chamber. Its lid was ajar. He put down his lantern, removed the lid, and stood it against the keg. An empty sack lay next to the handle of a wooden scoop that protruded from the black grain. He smiled when he remembered his first day of work in Benjamin Worley's warehouse near Lion Key in London, when he was assigned to scoop snuff from a barrel into casks for sale to a city merchant.

The memory gave him an idea. With the scoop he could make a trail of powder that led back to the keg; he could overturn the keg and spill its contents over the magazine floor. He could light the powder at the bottom of a ladder with the lantern candle, then race topside and follow the advice he had given the powder monkey, and jump overboard. Yes, he thought: I, too, can live to see a new country born! I shall join Jack Frake in whatever fight he chooses!

"I thought so!"

Hugh turned to see Jared Hunt standing at the chamber door, leaning against the side, the curtain draped over one of his shoulders. Even in the dim light, he could see the man's sweating face. And the pistol in his hand.

"Your damned lackey got me in the side, Mr. Kenrick, but I'll live! Longer than you! Move away from that barrel!"

Instead, Hugh reached down for his lantern.

Hunt fired his pistol.

Hugh felt a punch in his chest. His knees weakened and with an involuntary gasp he fell to the floor.

The chamber was small enough that Hunt could reach down from where he stood for the rope end of the noose still around Hugh's neck and grip it. He began to pull Hugh away from the barrel. "Mr. Blassard was a navy man once, he knew his knots, didn't he now? Couldn't get it off, could you, you son and heir bastard! By God, I'll hang you below decks!"

Hugh had managed to grasp the lantern handle with his right hand. It caused him more pain than he had ever known, but he yanked himself loose from Hunt's hold, pivoted his body, and leaned against the chamber wall. Before the Customsman could make another move, he swung the lantern into the open keg. One of the glass lantern panes broke.

"*You* cannot win, Mr. Hunt. Long live Lady Liberty."

Hunt was stunned. How could this man have known? He rushed to the keg to remove the lantern, peering into it just in time to see the lit candle roll into the powder. There was a hiss, and then a flame, and the keg blew up in Jared Hunt's face.

Hugh Kenrick did not watch the inevitable. His eyes were closed; he was wandering through the cathedral of his soul.

*     *     *

Jack Frake helped row one of the three packed boats that were carrying the Company into the inlet away from the Otway place and certain defeat by the marines. The *Sparrowhawk*'s burning sails bought him and his men time to make an orderly retreat. The pincer movement executed by Major Ragsdale stalled halfway to the militia line when too many of his men paused to stare at the spectacle of the distressed merchantman. Ragsdale himself was momentarily distracted by it, then realized what his inattention was costing him, and angrily commanded his officers to keep the battalion moving. When they moved into the main militia position, it had been abandoned. They took as prisoner one swivel gun, one long-gun, and the wheeled gun. And about three dozen cannon balls that had been dropped on the rebels without measurable effect. His marines fired at the retreating boats; their bullets plopped harmlessly in the boats' wakes.

The *Basilisk*, which had taken a few hits from the militia's swivel and wall guns, had ceased firing when the *Sparrowhawk* fired no more. Its crew seemed more preoccupied with the *Sparrowhawk*'s worsening dilemma than with the boats making their way through the inlet right under the sloop's nose. Eventually the sloop's master decided to drop some sail and move closer to the *Sparrowhawk* to render some assistance to the men he saw jumping into the water.

Jack Frake's purpose was to get his men to the Gloucester side of the York, away from the marines. He glanced occasionally from his labor at the oar at the *Sparrowhawk*. Most of her sails were burning now. John Proudlocks sat behind him at an oar. "You did it, Jack."

"No, not completely. She can limp to Hampton or Norfolk or Gosport to be repaired."

"She won't sink," Proudlocks conceded. "We saw their gunners tossing their gun charges overboard when they saw how serious the fires were." He paused. "What do you think happened to Mr. Kenrick?"

"I don't know, John," said Jack Frake brusquely. "Perhaps he jumped overboard."

They were in the middle of the York, half a mile away from the *Sparrowhawk*, when they felt a concussion in the water, one that drove up through the keel and sides of the boat to throb in their feet and sting their hands on the oars. Every man stopped rowing to watch the merchantman.

The force of the explosion in the magazine, which was a few feet aft of center, first smashed the layer of iron pig ballast, and severed the teakwood keel of the *Sparrowhawk*, blowing a hole through her bottom. It then expanded to blow out the hull sides contiguous with the magazine, and fore and aft to obliterate neighboring holds. The force then burst upwards and erupted with flame through the deck, sending everything loose there — men and guns, as well — into the air.

As debris rained down on her, the *Sparrowhawk*, robbed of her keel, to which the rest of the hull was interlocked, began to pull herself apart from sheer weight. Deck and side planking shot out from the pressures of the twisting mass from every direction. The main mast, closest to the explosion and her footing instantly destroyed, toppled almost immediately, splitting at the deck and tumbling into the river, pendant and shredded sails flying. The burning fore and aft masts leaned crazily toward each other to form a fiery X as the bow and stern, no longer linked by the keel and amidships, ripped apart and began to sink separately.

The stern sank out of sight first; the last part of it that witnesses saw before it was swallowed completely in the river was a charred Customs Jack on its boom. The fore section sank with more dignity. The bowsprit was completely gone; connected by rigging to the fore mast, it had been ruptured by the mast's displacement and had followed it. The last thing to slip out of sight was the figurehead of the regal sparrowhawk, its yellow, baleful eyes staring at the sky. And then it was gone. A brownish cloud of smoke hovered over the scene, and slowly drifted away. The gray-green water was dotted with debris. Survivors could be seen splashing toward the riverbank.

"Oars, men," said Jack Frake, readying his hands on his oar. "There's nothing else to see."

John Proudlocks wanted to repeat, "You did it, Jack," but knew he should not. He suspected what his friend suspected, but could not prove: that Hugh Kenrick had destroyed the *Sparrowhawk*. He remained silent, and prepared to row again.

The Company camped that night on a sandy bank on the Gloucester side, directly across from the Otway place. The men were safe there. They made fires to cook what little food they brought with them, and drank what little liquor they had carried, talked about the fight at the Otway place, and speculated on the demise of the *Sparrowhawk*.

Jack Frake paced back and forth along the bank. Jock Fraser and John Proudlocks left him to his thoughts. They knew that he would know no peace until he knew for certain the fate of Hugh Kenrick.

Jack Frake was allowing himself the luxury of worrying about his friend. It was not something he did for other men. It was the first time he worried about someone other than Etáin.

The peace came an hour later. A picket came into the camp with a water-soaked boy, who was taken immediately to Jack Frake. "Says he was a powder monkey on the *Sparrowhawk*, sir," said the Company man. "Found him half-drowned, holding on for dear life to a plank. Tide washed him in."

"All right," said Jack Frake. "Leave him here. Return to your post."

The militiaman obeyed.

Jack Frake pointed to a log by his fire. The boy sat. "Hungry, son?"

"Yes, sir," answered the boy. He scrutinized Jack Frake warily. "Are you one of the rebels we was shootin' at?"

"I'm their leader," Jack Frake answered. "What's your name?"

"Tom Doherty, sir."

Jack Frake reached for a biscuit in a pan at his feet. "Here."

The boy took the biscuit and inspected it. He was surprised to see no maggots or worms. He bit into it, then coughed. Jack Frake handed him his mug of coffee. The boy washed down the piece of biscuit that had caught in his throat. "Good mess, sir. Thanks."

Jack Frake nodded and asked, "You were on the *Sparrowhawk*?"

"Yes, sir. Was on her for three years. Hired on in London. It was that, or Bridewell...or worse."

"How old are you?"

"Twelve, I think, sir."

"How did you get here? To where my man found you, I mean."

"I jumped ship, sir, from the wrong side. The starboard. Didn't want anyone to see me on the larboard. Someone might've shot at me. Mr. Geary might not have, but Mr. Tragle, he was no good."

"Why did you jump ship, Tom?"

Tom Doherty took another swallow of coffee. "Well, after they calls off the guns, because of the sails bein' on fire, most of us were ordered topside to help. I was the last. The gent they was goin' to hang, I run into him in the hold, still wearin' the noose. Says I, you can't bring a loose lantern down here close to the powder. Says he, the ship is doomed, and I should swim for it, to see a new country born. I thought he was crackers, and went on my way. Then I was goin' up the ladder, and Mr. Hunt, who owned the ship now, comes down it and shoves me out of the way. He was carryin' a pistol, and that weren't allowed down there, either. Then when I get topside, I see how bad it was, and I thought, maybe the gent is right, the ship is doomed. So I jumped." The boy stared into the fire. "I been wantin' to."

Tom Doherty sighed. "Then the ship blows up, powerful like. Thought it'd break my ears. Guns and rope and men and parts of them dropped all about me. I saw how far the shore was, and grabbed a plank. Knew I couldn't make it that far on me own arms. Paddled the rest of the day, and all night, fightin' the tide, goin' in circles, I think, until I came up where your man found me. I just wanted to find dry land and sleep." The boy stared into the fire for a moment, then asked, "Who was that gent, sir?"

"A friend, Tom. A very good friend."

Tom Doherty could not be sure if it was a trick of the light of the flickering flames, or if they were real tears in the man's eyes. He did not think he should see them, and glanced away to stare at the shadows of other men in the camp.

But Jack Frake smiled, reached over and squeezed the boy's shoulder. "I am in your debt, sir. Don't forget that."

The boy nodded. After a moment, he turned to look into the void at the opposite bank, which was in complete darkness. Not a single light shown.

He said, "I lost some friends out there, too."

Jack Frake studied the boy for a moment. "Would you like to see a new country born, Tom? Stay with us, and you'll see how it's done."

The boy looked doubtful. "A new country? The king won't let you. He'll hang you for tryin'."

"We'll see about that."

"What'll you call it? Virginia?"

Jack Frake shook his head. "No, Tom. We might call it Hyperborea."

# Epilogue

A day after the sinking of the *Sparrowhawk*, on September 2, a hurricane swept over Chesapeake Bay, destroying or beaching many vessels throughout the Roads and causing property losses on all the peninsulas. Jack Frake and his Company experienced little of the storm. By then, they were on their way north to enlist in the new Continental Army. Tom Doherty accompanied them.

Major Ragsdale, his battalion of marines, and survivors from the *Sparrowhawk* were marching back to Caxton from the Otway place when the hurricane struck. Over the objections of Rupert Beecroft and William Settle, Ragsdale took refuge at Meum Hall, herding most of his men into the great house and tenants' quarters to wait out the wind and rain. Making himself at home, the major found many interesting books in Hugh Kenrick's library. When the battalion left, some of them were included in his baggage.

Quite unintentionally, he left a lit seegar in a plate at Hugh's desk. It rolled off the plate and into some papers. The great house burned to the ground. By then, Ragsdale and his battalion were boarding the *Basilisk* in Caxton to be transported back to Hampton, and were not aware of the disaster. In Hampton, the major found waiting for him orders to proceed to Boston.

The staff and tenants of Meum Hall tried to preserve the plantation. But without Hugh Kenrick's guidance and energy, they failed. His death was a cruelty that seemed to disable them. The plantation was abandoned, and its staff and most of its tenants dispersed to other quarters of Virginia in search of employment and livelihood.

Caxton suffered the same fate as Londontown in Maryland: it vanished, nearly overnight. The windmill, the courthouse, and Stepney Parish church were severely damaged by the hurricane, as were all the dwellings and shops on the riverfront, many of which were swept away by the York. It was a catastrophe from which it never recovered.

Months after the demise of the *Sparrowhawk*, the town was raided by one of Governor Dunmore's navy vessels and the army for supplies and to destroy reported caches of rebel arms. The army found plentiful supplies, but no arms. Some of the county crops were burned, as well as many dwellings of farmers and planters, because the county was known to be a haven for rebels, and the officers in charge of the raid did not trust the veracity or loyalty of the owners who claimed fealty to the Crown.

The town was eventually deserted by its residents, who also dispersed to other localities for employment and livelihood. The town no longer had a means or a reason to exist. Empty houses and shops fell into disrepair and collapsed from neglect, scavenging, and vandalism. It took nature a generation to reclaim Caxton, replacing it with new trees, weeds, and other growth.

Late in October 1775, Basil Kenrick, Earl of Danvers, was being dressed by his valet, Claybourne, in preparation to leave his residence at Windridge Court in London to attend Parliament, when he was given by Alden Curle, his major domo, a letter of condolence from a senior Customs official. It reported the death of Jared Hunt, "your esteemed protégé, of whose amicable acquaintance I had the privilege of making when he was nominated by you for appointment, in the course of fulfilling his service to His Majesty in crushing the rebellion in Virginia. I regret to inform his lordship that Mr. Hunt's remains could not be found or recovered by the Customs officers, or the circumstances of his brave but tragic death investigated much by them there, before those gentlemen were obliged to remove themselves from the hostile attentions of local rebels and other law-breakers...."

Curle, of course, did not know the contents of the letter — it was given to him by a messenger only a few minutes before — and had retired from the Earl's bedroom to attend to other duties.

Basil Kenrick abruptly exploded in a rage. "No! No! No!" he shouted. "*What* did he do about my nephew?? Did he *punish* him?? I demand to *know*!" This outburst caused Claybourne to slip into a closet and close its door. The Earl glanced around, looking for him. "Traitorous worm!" Then he repeatedly and insistently yanked the bell cord by his bed for Curle, until that man appeared. The Earl proceeded to blast him with accusations of disloyalty, and traduced his long service. "You insignificant worm! You put this man up to this just to spite me, didn't you?" he said, almost sobbing, waving the letter from the official in the air. "You and my brother! That's it! It's a conspiracy between you and my brother and this damned placeman!"

Curle stood speechless and quavering before this onslaught of insanity. He was older now, and slightly bent. And he was worried. His employer had been growing madder by the month for years; it was a subject of grave but discreet jollity in the servants' kitchen. But the violence of this outburst was a new level.

"God damn you, Curle! I am not amused by this prank! You will pay, and this placeman, and my brother! But, you shall pay first!" Still holding the letter, the Earl stepped up to the major domo and slapped him over and over, first with his palm, then with his backhand. "Don't you know he is my *son*? *My son*! And you have the temerity to say he is dead! I am not *finished* with him! But you are finished here! Get out of my sight!"

"Your lordship, I do not know — if you will only let me — "

"Be quiet!" Basil Kenrick raised a fist and struck Curle in the mouth.

Curle fell backward, close to the fireplace. The Earl stooped over him, kicked him in both legs once, then bent and waved the letter in the major domo's face. "Lies are thy sustenance, worm, so consume this!" He reached down and tried to force the letter into Curle's bleeding mouth. Curle gagged. He was terrified. Struggling desperately to find leverage to rise and flee, one hand fell onto the fireplace poker. Without thinking, he clutched it, and swung it up at the Earl's head.

The pointed claw near the tip drove into his head, just above his left ear, into his temple. He gurgled once and collapsed immediately onto Curle. Claybourne emerged from the closet and saw what had happened. He stood gaping at his superior and the Earl. Curle dropped the poker, pushed the body away, and stood up to face the valet. "We must flee! We will be hanged, surely!" Claybourne nodded agreement, and they did flee, but not before Curle stopped to snatch the letter from the Earl's hand. They discreetly packed their belongings, and some other things not their own, and without informing the rest of the household, slunk undetected from Windridge Court, never to return. A maid found the body of the Earl hours later, and raised the hue and cry.

A day later, Garnet Kenrick, the Earl's brother, received a letter at his residence at Cricklegate, Chelsea, that contained the Customs official's letter, and a note from Curle, announcing and explaining the Earl's death. "He said this Mr. Hunt was his son. I do not know if this is true, but I always suspected some relation." The Baron did not bother to press the authorities to search for Curle and Claybourne. They had vanished into the anonymity of London. He thought: Good riddance to all three. He and his wife, Effney, and their daughter Alice, now a widow, quietly rejoiced. Garnet Kenrick and his family elected not to wear mourning blacks; the

Baron forbade his staff to don them, either.

Thus did Garnet Kenrick become the sixteenth Earl of Danvers. He interred his brother without ceremony and under a plain tombstone in an anonymous London cemetery. Keeping a vow he had made many years ago, he had the casket of Dogmael Jones moved from St. Giles in the Fields to the family vault in Danvers. The marble tablet that marked the barrister's tomb read: "Here Lies Sir Dogmael Jones, Barrister and Member for Swansditch. 1719-1766. Friend of Liberty. Fiat Lux."

He half believed Curle's assertion that Jared Hunt was his brother's son. He summoned Crispin Hillier, member for Onyxcombe and his brother's political crony, and queried him about it. Hillier confirmed the fact with profuse apologies and explanations. He dared not lie to the new Earl. Garnet Kenrick told his wife, Effney. "Then justice has been done, if it is true," she remarked. "He sent his son to murder our son, just as he sent him to murder Mr. Jones."

But they had not heard from Hugh in months. They would not receive news of his death for a year, until they received a letter from Jack Frake, followed by another from Rupert Beecroft, the former business agent of Meum Hall. It was then that they donned mourning blacks.

Reverdy Brune-Kenrick was preparing to accompany her brother and sister-in-law to a gay evening at Ranelagh Gardens when Garnet Kenrick came to Berkeley Square with the news of Hugh's death. The servant who came to her bedroom with his card on a silver salver said nothing about the black silk armband that Garnet Kenrick wore. When Reverdy descended the stairs to the foyer and saw the armband, and then the grave, sad look in her father-in-law's eyes, she knew the nature of his call. From across the space, she asked in a whisper, "Is it about Hugh?"

Garnet Kenrick nodded. "He died a hero, my dear. In September, a year ago. I'm sorry." There was an unspoken question in his eyes: *Are you?*

She was suddenly struck with the incontrovertible knowledge of a world without Hugh, her life without Hugh. She felt tears form in her eyes, and she rushed to Garnet Kenrick and pounded his chest with her fists. "Damn you for bringing that man into the world!" she shouted at him. "Damn you! I *knew* she would take him from me, forever! That damned mistress of his! *Why* must the best always perish first? *Why*??" Then she dropped her head on his chest and sobbed without control or care.

Garnet Kenrick encircled her with comforting arms. "Come home to us, my dear, and we will try to answer that question."

John Murray, Earl of Dunmore, after nearly a year of raiding and plundering Chesapeake Bay and making more enemies than friends on both sides of the conflict, quit it on August 1, 1776, a month after the Declaration of Independence, and made his way back to England. It was also a month after publication in England of Adam Smith's *An Inquiry into the Nature and Causes of the Wealth of Nations*. In Book Four of it Smith proclaimed that America "will be one of the foremost nations of the world," tempering that prophecy with a judicious sop to the North ministry and critics by advocating colonial representation in Parliament, a project he privately considered impractical.

William Pitt, Earl of Chatham, in April 1778 attended a debate in Lords on whether or not to continue the war against the American colonies. Earlier in the debate, he rose to reply to a proposal by the Duke of Richmond to include in an address to the king an acknowledgement of American independence and a recommendation to withdraw British troops from the colonies. Pitt protested the "dismemberment of this ancient and most noble monarchy," and scoffed at fears of a French invasion of Britain — the French recently having declared openly its support of the colonies. When he rose a second time to again answer the Duke of Richmond, he collapsed in a fit. He died in his son's arms on May 11, 1778.

A pundit wrote in a London newspaper on the occasion of Pitt's death: "Throughout much of his truculent but admittedly glorious career, Lord Chatham, one must opine, was painfully afflicted with a number of familiar ailments, including an insupportable and incurable contradiction concerning the mutualism of power and liberty. One must consequently speculate whether or not he succumbed also to the deleterious effects of said malady, and not exclusively to a combination of merely physical ones."

In Williamsburg, Virginia, the marble statue of Baron Botetourt in the open corridor of the Capitol was subjected to some patriotic stone-throwing. One missile gouged out a part of its pug nose. Although the Virginia Convention in Richmond had assumed the reins of government, and had recessed in late August, thirty-seven burgesses dutifully arrived at the Capitol in mid-October 1775, believing that the General Assembly under the royal government was still the legitimate institution, regardless of the Convention's presumptions and actions. They were not enough to form a quorum. They went home, tut-tutting the delinquency of other burgesses and the desecration of the statue.

In March of the following year, thirty-two burgesses arrived. Adherents to lawful procedure, and hoping against hope, they rescheduled the General Assembly for May 6. And on that date, oblivious to the fact that Patrick Henry that very day, before the fifth revolutionary Convention in Richmond, called for Congress to make a Declaration of Independence, and was also elected by the Convention as the first governor of Virginia, a member plaintively entered in the House journal, that only "several members met, but did neither proceed to business, nor adjourn, as the House of Burgesses. FINIS."

*    *    *

Jack Frake and most of his Company reached Charlestown and enlisted in the Continental Army. It was not from indifference to the fate of Virginia that he persuaded his men to follow his example. "Virginia is too big and too populous for the Crown to attempt its conquest. The Crown will first try to subdue the smaller colonies, or the weaker ones. If the war continues for many years, eventually we will return to Virginia."

He was proven right. He rose to the rank of major of a regiment in General Anthony Wayne's Pennsylvania Line. Follow that general's military career, and you will follow Jack Frake's. He served with distinguished intelligence and heroism. He traded his rough fighting garb for Continental blue. And he always wore the gorget that Hugh Kenrick had given him, the one engraved *Sapere aude*.

In 1781, he returned to Virginia with the Pennsylvania Line. He commanded his men at the battle of Green Spring near the James River, and took part in the siege at Yorktown. He stood with Lieutenant John Proudlocks and Lieutenant Jock Fraser in the front rank of Americans receiving the surrender of Lord Cornwallis's army.

Even though a war existed between their nations, mail packets continued to carry correspondence between Americans and Britons. Jack Frake wrote dozens of letters to Etáin in Edinburgh, and to John Ramshaw in Norfolk, England. He forbade Etáin to return until the war was over. "Morland is gone," he wrote in one. "Caxton is in ruins. Meum Hall is gone. And our dear, precious friend, Hugh. Most everyone we knew is dead or gone. When you return, we shall begin over, on our own terms. Mr. Ramshaw writes that after the war, commerce will resume again between Britain and America, and I am thinking of engaging in it. I have saved some money, and memories, and will retrieve them from the ashes of Morland when I am free to. Lieutenants Proudlocks and Fraser send you their salutes and warmest regards...."

The most difficult letter he wrote in this period was to Hugh's father, Garnet Kenrick. In it, he confessed without guilt his role in Roger Tallmadge's death at Charlestown — an action that had made Alice, Hugh's beloved sister, a widow — and explained in detail why Hugh had died on the *Sparrowhawk*. "We agreed that the *Sparrowhawk* must be destroyed. We completed halves of that task, but Hugh paid the higher price." He sent the letter on, expecting neither a reply nor ever to be welcome in the Kenrick household.

It was a reasonable assumption. It was one of the very few things about which he was wrong.